ON A DARKLING PLAIN

A Fighter Pilot's Journey from War to Peace

L. D. Bruce

On a Darkling Plain: A Fighter Pilot's Journey from War to Peace
Copyright @ L.D. Bruce 2021

All rights reserved. No part of this publication may be reproduced, stored in a retrieval system, or transmitted in any form or by any means – for example, electronic, photocopies, recording – without the prior written permission of the author or publisher. The exception is brief quotations in printed reviews.

Printed in the United States of America.

Cover art by Rolando Ugolini.
Cover design by Rolando Ugolini.
Developmental editing by Sarah De Mey.
Copy-editing and formatting by Désirée Schroeder.
Jungle photo by Ren Ran on Unsplash.

Notice: Some names and locations have been changed to protect the privacy of persons involved. Any resemblance to people you know by these names is entirely coincidental. Footnotes are given whenever possible from material researched from books, news media, and/or Internet searches.

All rights reserved.

ISBN: 9798591016319

Imprint: Independently published.

In astonishment, to

יְהוָה

Ἐγώ εἰμι ὁ ὤν, ὁ παντοκράτωρ

Dover Beach
By Matthew Arnold
(1851)

… The Sea of Faith
Was once, too, at the full, and round earth's shore
Lay like the folds of a bright girdle furled.
But now I only hear
Its melancholy, long, withdrawing roar,
Retreating, to the breath
Of the night-wind, down the vast edges drear
And naked shingles of the world.

Ah, love, let us be true
To one another! for the world, which seems
To lie before us like a land of dreams,
So various, so beautiful, so new,
Hath really neither joy, nor love, nor light,
Nor certitude, nor peace, nor help for pain;
And we are here as on a darkling plain
Swept with confused alarms of struggle and flight,
Where ignorant armies clash by night.

Contents

PART I: THE BATTLE AT PREY TOTUENG, DAY ONE
Chapter 1: Scramble Blade One 1
Chapter 2: Ground Fire 17

PART II: THE CAVE
Chapter 3: The Book and the House of Evil 29
Chapter 4: The Mark Twain National Forest 37
Chapter 5: The Spring 47
Chapter 6: The Cavern Measureless to Man 53
Chapter 7: Down to a Sunless Sea 57
Chapter 8: The Living and the Dead 65

PART III: LIVING ON BARNES STREET
Chapter 9: Cry of the Loon 73
Chapter 10: Love and the Hornet 79
Chapter 11: The Death of God 89
Chapter 12: A Bend in the Road 97

PART IV: THE PHILOSOPHER
Chapter 13: University of Kansas 103
Chapter 14: Terror in the Tunnel 109
Chapter 15: Divine Madness 115
Chapter 16: The Limit of Reason 125

PART V: INTO THE BURNING BLUE
Chapter 17: Heartless Discipline 135
Chapter 18: The Young Tigers 145
Chapter 19: The Delta Dagger and the Dream 149

PART VI: THE COLD WAR
Chapter 20: The Worst Weather in the World 167

Chapter 21: Kidnapped 173
Chapter 22: Close to Death 185
Chapter 23: The Hula Girl 191
Chapter 24: A Dangerous Watershed 199
Chapter 25: Death Wish..209

PART VII: SURVIVAL
Chapter 26: Pipeline to War 219
Chapter 27: The Discipline of Survival..225
Chapter 28: Snake School 239

PART VIII: ON THE DARKLING PLAIN
Chapter 29: To War 247
Chapter 30: A Message from Charlie 253
Chapter 31: Unclean 259
Chapter 32: Engine Fire Light..263
Chapter 33: The Doppelgänger..265
Chapter 34: The Day the Music Died 271
Chapter 35: Dangerous Rejoin 279
Chapter 36: Phnom Penh..287
Chapter 37: Into Cambodia, Again..297
Chapter 38: How the Mighty Has Fallen....................................301
Chapter 39: The Smell of Alienation...305
Chapter 40: Firebase Six..311
Chapter 41: Annihilation..319
Chapter 42: A Desperate Act 327
Chapter 43: A Band of Brothers 333
Epilogue 341
Acknowledgements 347
About the Author..349

PART I:

THE BATTLE AT PREY TOTUENG

Day One

CHAPTER 1

Scramble Blade One

Phan Rang AB, Vietnam
December 10, 1970
1400 hours

Captain John Malik stood on the edge of the Phan Rang Air Base flight line staring across acres of fighter aircraft, row after row, bled colorless in shimmering waves of heat. They stretched for nearly a mile along the tarmac, sinister in their rattlesnake paint schemes. The mere sight of these machines once thrilled Malik's soul. Fighters like these had taken him to the high frontier of the atmosphere, far above the surly bonds of earth. Hovering there supersonic Malik once briefly thought he had experienced the ineffable presence of God; at that moment he believed there was a purpose for his life, that it mattered that he had lived, that he could be forgiven. But the impression passed and never returned.

Cynical and battle-hardened, Malik now saw these machines for what they were, cruel weapons that he operated with dispassion in his workaday world of killing human beings and destroying their works. This war had been his last chance to live or die for a cause greater than himself. But this was no righteous war. He had been a fool to believe it was. This war was a meat grinder with no strategic objective but the amassing of body count. And he was no champion; he was cannon fodder.

He turned to watch a flight of two F-100s roll into takeoff position on Runway 04. Their engines ran up with a roar. The leader released brakes, and the hard-lighting J-57 afterburner ignited with a boom. Six seconds later, his wingman released brakes and lit his burner. Boom. Like all departing fighters, they were at max gross weight, bristling with bombs.

Malik watched them streak past him at mid-field. Their rudders were deflected to the left to counter a stiff crosswind off the South China Sea. He stopped breathing as the leader approached the "coffin corner," the segment of the takeoff roll where the pilot could neither reject and stop on the runway, nor survive an ejection. As the leader approached the arresting barrier, he staggered airborne, followed by his wingman. The blare of their afterburners receded as they crossed the shimmering fields and rice paddies to the north and disappeared into the haze.

Seconds later, Malik closed his eyes, grimaced, and turned his head away as the hot sea breeze swept their coils of burning jet fuel past him. The air temperature spiked twenty degrees and subsided. He took a deep breath, lifted his forearm, and wiped the sweat from his forehead with the sleeve of his prickly Nomex flight suit, a fire-resistant material that basted him like a turkey in his own sweat. He now reeked of atomized kerosene that settled from the swirling thermals.

Malik's wingman, Second Lieutenant Ron Sauer, stood beside him, noticeably weaving a bit as he watched the approaching crew van. They boarded.

"Alert Complex," Malik directed the driver.

Malik hefted his parachute and helmet bag onto a vacant seat and sat on the left side of the aisle. He turned to stare out the windows to the west, drawn to the jungle ridge known as Charlie's Mountain lying several miles west of the base. For a month, he had been sitting in the evenings at the picnic table outside the squadron barracks contemplating this mountain.

In a persistent vision, he saw his own undiscovered remains lying on the jungle floor, hidden from the sky beneath the jungle's triple canopy. His dead body was alive with ants and maggots and other creatures harvesting his bulging eyes and gas-bloated corpse. In time-lapsed frames, his putrefied remains morphed to bone, then to tattered cloth, until finally only a corroded pair of dog tags protruded from the humus. The military would declare him MIA—missing in action—and eventually KIA—killed in action—the last record of a pointless and unremarkable life.

As Malik followed the mountain with his eyes, Ron Sauer passed through his line of sight. Unshaven and unkempt, his hair tousled, Sauer smelled of alcohol, sweat, and puke. His strained expression showed pain and remorse. He looked toward Malik and started to say something. Malik interrupted him.

"Are you really fit to fly?"

"Yes, sir." Sauer looked everywhere but at the captain. "May I say again how sorry I am for my behavior last night. I don't drink, but they kept forcing it on me." His hands were spread, palms up. "And what I said about my wife ... I'm so ashamed of that. Please forgive me, sir."

"Forget it." Malik waved him off and turned to look out the front window of the van toward the Alert Complex, a quarter mile away. Slobbering drunk or not, a man was responsible for his words. Malik had wanted to believe Ron Sauer was a righteous man, but he wasn't. There were no righteous men.

It was the coarseness of Sauer's words that disappointed Malik. Sauer said his wife was the ugliest woman he had ever seen. He was ashamed of her and intended to divorce her. Why had he revealed this moral torment to John Malik? Malik didn't care about anybody's issues. He was no counselor. And no one cared about him, except maybe Christine.

He absently unzipped the top of his webbed survival vest festooned with radios, survival gear, and a pistol, and stuck his fingers underneath it to feel the contours of her picture in the left breast pocket of his flight suit.

Ron Sauer's resemblance to Malik's brother, now twelve years dead, was uncanny. Malik had been unnerved by the resemblance from the moment he laid eyes on Sauer a month ago. A vague sense of dread had distilled into the certainty that the day of reckoning for his crime was imminent.

Before Sauer's arrival, Malik had reached a terminal state of bleak cynicism. He remained high functioning though spiritually dead and mentally compartmentalized. But now the memory loop played day and night: he could see his brother in the inaccessible reaches of the cave. He could see himself, turning away, leaving his brother entombed alive in utter darkness.

What Malik had done was unknown to anyone. Unconfessed, unforgiven, the deed had cost him his faith in God and his capacity to relate to other human beings. Thereafter he had survived in the twilight of human society. Now, in not many days, he would die a violent death. He had foreseen it.

The van stopped to pick up two pilots who had just landed. They chose to ride to the end of the line at the Alert Complex and then back to their squadron building, rather than stand on the blistering tarmac waiting for the crew van to return. Malik moved across the aisle and sat beside Sauer.

"One more briefing item," Malik said. "You do understand what it means that we're Blade One and Two?"

Sauer nodded. "Yes, sir. We carry the prime load for troops-in-contact. Wall-to-wall napalm. And we are the first to go."

Malik nodded. "That's right. And you're not ready for this. If we launch it will be a tactical emergency. Any target we get will be high threat. Guaranteed. So, what am I going to say now?"

"Sir, you will tell me again about 'curvilinear' attack geometry."

Malik closed his eyes. "And, again, what does that mean?"

"I'm supposed to 'vary heading, altitude, and flight path until just a few seconds before weapon release to disrupt enemy gun tracking.' I understand the idea, sir."

Malik turned to look Sauer square in the eye. "Then why can't I get you to do it?" His clenched teeth emphasized the final two words.

"I've been trying, sir. But if I can't hit the target because I'm jinking, what's the point of my being on the target?"

"Look, Sauer, staying alive is more important than hitting the target. How would getting yourself killed help anybody? Your deliveries probably won't be a matter of life-or-death for the troops. But if you're wings-level for five seconds, the gunners *will* hit you. These are the best gunners in the world. And if you get shot down, it'll be on me." Malik shook his head, his gaze drifting to the window.

Looking at Charlie's Mountain he added, "I should not have certified you combat-ready. I don't know what more I can do if you won't listen to me." He shifted his eyes back to Sauer. "Don't kill yourself, Sauer. Do I have to tell you that?"

"No, sir."

The van stopped in front of the Alert Complex. Malik and Sauer climbed out with their gear and walked the short distance to the crew area in the middle of a line of ten concrete revetments that sheltered F-100Ds loaded with various kinds of munitions and cocked for immediate start. They entered the crew area and signed the roster. Malik picked up the landline to the wing command post and advised the controller that Blade One was down for crew-change. The crew being relieved followed Malik and Sauer to the two aircraft and retrieved their gear.

When Malik had cocked his airplane, he went into the next bay to check Sauer's aircraft. Malik walked around it, shaking the silver 750-pound cans of napalm to make sure they were secure on the pylons. He checked that the safeties were secure then duckwalked beneath the fuselage, looking for leaks and unsecured panels. Finally, he climbed the ladder and confirmed the cockpit setup was correct.

Walking back into the air-conditioned crew quarters, Malik picked up the landline and reported Blade One ready for launch. He followed Sauer over to the refrigerator and grabbed two bottles of water. Five pilots hovered nearby in animated conversation.

"What's going on?" Malik asked.

They stopped and looked at him, apparently surprised he had spoken, for he was known to be a man of few words.

"You don't know?" one of them asked.

"Know what?"

"Something big is developing to the west, maybe Cambodia. I'm talking big."

"Like what?" Malik shrugged.

"The command post has been keeping a lid on it for an hour. An ops guy went by there. He said everybody is running around like the place is on fire, including the wing and deputy commander. Whatever it is, it's about to cut loose. You're Blade One, right?"

Malik nodded and looked at Sauer, whose eyes widened.

Twenty minutes passed, and nothing happened. Malik unzipped the legs of his G suit and plopped down in a recliner. He leaned back, picked up the remote, and unmuted the volume on the TV just as the repeat of Walter Cronkite's Friday newscast came on. Sauer pulled up a chair and sat down beside him.

"Everything's a crisis with these guys," Malik muttered, glancing at Sauer.

It was Sunday. Duty days rotated between daily scheduled targets called frag missions, and five-minute alert duty requiring immediate launch for tactical emergencies and against ephemeral targets. Pilots had no days off. Every day was the same. But Malik knew when it was Sunday because, on Saturday night, the squadron pilots destroyed one squadron bar or another. They staggered off to bed, leaving the floor covered with sticky booze and broken glass.

This destruction was a self-inflicted wound of their sensibilities that would lie as a witness to their madness until Monday morning when the Vietnamese maids returned. These hapless women proceeded, with ill-disguised exasperation, to clean up the mess and restock the glassware.

Malik had picked his way through the reeking wreckage at noon Sunday, pronouncing a plague upon his colleagues. "Idiots," he repeated to himself.

He had eaten lunch at the Officer's Club before arriving at the 612th Tactical Fighter Squadron building on the flight line. Sauer had straggled in at the last minute and slumped down beside Malik at the briefing table. Glaring at him, Malik got up and moved to the end of the table.

They had received a weather and intel briefing, which included no inkling of significant developments to the west. Then they picked up their flight gear and proceeded to the Alert Complex.

Now they sat side-by-side engrossed in Walter Cronkite's war coverage. Cronkite's reporting was the primary source of information on the progress of the war for flight crews. What line combatants knew about developments in the war came from the nightly news or from short articles they read weekly in *Stars and Stripes*.

Malik and Sauer watched footage of a flight of fighters delivering napalm, one of the most popular depictions for journalists because of the roiling flames. Though he hated the stuff, Malik accepted that it was the best tactical weapon for friendly troops in close contact with the enemy.

It was jellied gasoline that pilots could deliver at close range to a friendly defensive perimeter, unlike high explosives that had a wide lethal radius of shrapnel and concussion. When ground troops in imminent danger of being overrun by the enemy declared a tactical emergency, they nearly always wanted napalm. In many cases, it was the only thing that could save them.

Napalm not only incinerated human flesh but consumed all the oxygen in its envelope, suffocating anyone near it. It was a flaming blanket of death that flowed into foxholes and bunkers and burned to ash anything in its path.

Cronkite shifted focus. He was narrating footage of the latest hippie riot when static crackled over the Alert Complex speaker. Malik slammed down the recliner's footrest, jumped to his feet, zipped up the legs of his G suit, and pulled on his gloves. Sauer did the same. They braced themselves, facing the steel blast door, hearts wildly beating from an adrenaline rush.

The controller at the command post had keyed the mic and was preparing to order a scramble. Malik touched beneath his survival vest to feel the edges of his picture of Christine.

After a dramatic pause of ten seconds, the command came with unusual emphasis, "Scramble Blade One. Tactical emergency. Troops in contact."

Malik and Sauer bolted out the door to their fighters in the adjacent bunkers as ground crews raced to the Blade One and Two airplanes from different directions. Malik sprinted up the ladder, strapped into his seat, pulled his helmet on and fastened his mask in place, then confirmed oxygen selected to 100%. Sauer quickly ran the same drill on Blade Two.

The ground crew pulled the ladder and gave Malik a thumbs-up. He hit the ignition. A canister of gunpowder began an explosive burn channeled to impinge on the turbine blades of the engine. The engine spun up as pungent smoke curled out the tailpipe. Malik moved the throttle out of cutoff, holding the ignition, and felt a mild bump through the aircraft at light-off. As the rpm reached idle, he signaled chocks-out and advanced the throttle.

Malik and Sauer raced their aircraft out of the bunkers toward the arming area 100 yards ahead. Both men braked to a halt and held up their hands in view of the arming crews. The armorers swarmed over the aircraft. They charged the four cannons in the nose and pulled the safety pins on the napalm cans and the pylons of the fuel drop tanks, then backed off holding the flagged pins. The chief gave thumbs-up and saluted. Malik returned his salute.

He and Sauer pulled down and locked their canopies and turned toward the runway. Cleared onto the runway by the tower, Malik stopped in the left center and clamped the brakes. He looked over his right shoulder at Sauer who nodded. Malik lifted his right index finger and spun a circle. They advanced throttles to 100%. The nose gear struts compressed as the aircraft hunkered down, straining for release. Malik's legs danced on the brakes as he scanned the instruments. All indications were normal.

He looked back at Sauer who nodded. Malik leaned his head back against the headrest and nodded forward as he released brakes and engaged the afterburner. There was a boom as the thrust pinned him against the seat. Six seconds behind him, Sauer released brakes. Just past the 7,000-foot marker, Malik reached rotate-speed. He eased back on the stick and lifted off.

*　*　*

The jungle-covered mountain three miles northwest of the base was rising under Malik's flight path. On the northwest departure from Runway 04, he would clear it by less than 1,000 feet.

For more than a 100 combat missions, he had leaned against the left side of the cockpit during the turn, craning his neck to look straight down into the dense jungle canopy. He always had the same queasy feeling in his stomach. F-100s crossing this terrain were low, slow, and heavy-laden with bombs and fuel. A single Viet Cong in the top of one of the 150-foot-high trees beneath the flight path could put a round through the engine or the fuel tanks of a passing fighter. Malik was certain this had happened twice in the last month. Two F-100s were destroyed, and the pilots were KIA. Both had just crossed this ridge when their engine fire lights came on. Malik brought his concern to the attention of wing intelligence, but no procedural changes were forthcoming.

Malik studied the passing green chaos. The trees, wet from a daily downpour, swirled with restless vapors that would marshal through the night to form a blanket of dripping fog. Near sunrise, the fog would flow off the mountain as though alive, gliding syrup-like down the slope toward the South China Sea, 12 miles east.

Every morning, this eerie phenomenon appeared in the distance as Malik jogged along the base perimeter road before sunrise. The thudding of his running shoes and the crowing of a rooster in a nearby village were the only sounds in this bucolic setting that seemed so far from war.

He pulled the throttle out of afterburner. The deceleration rocked him forward against his shoulder harness; reducing thrust further, he looked over his left shoulder to watch Sauer's aircraft rapidly converging on the inside of the turn, trailing rippling ribbons of condensation from the wingtips. Momentarily sheathed in a cloud of water vapor, Sauer's airplane stopped abruptly two ship-widths off Malik's left wing.

Sauer's airplane rocked and jerked with small movements as he maneuvered to hold exact position. Malik looked down his left wing at Sauer, whose camouflaged fighter contrasted against the jungle wheeling beneath them. Malik nudged the power up and smoothly rolled wings level, increasing pitch to hold climb speed.

Just beyond the high terrain, Malik surveyed undulating jungle stretching to the visible horizon. Miles ahead he saw a wall of black weather. Damn! He closed his eyes for a moment and breathed deeply.

On 100% oxygen, he toggled the emergency lever to pressure-breathe. This procedure effortlessly inflated his lungs to capacity with cool, calming oxygen. He released the lever to exhale. Again, and again, he charged his lungs to overcome his oxygen debt, hopped up on adrenaline.

Pellets of snow blasted out the air-conditioning vents and pelted his dark visor. Sweat that had streaked down his face to the margins of his mask dried. He tugged on the oxygen hose, unstuck, and reseated his mask.

"Blade One, contact Hillsboro," the departure controller said.

Hillsboro Control, an airborne command post, was orbiting at high altitude somewhere east of Pleiku. Malik checked in and received an immediate reply.

"Blade One, Hillsboro. Your vector is two-seven-zero degrees, two-hundred-thirty miles. Your Forward Air Controller is Nail One Nine, frequency two-two-eight decimal five." The controller then added, "Blade One. Message from Seventh: 'Maintain maximum forward speed, fuel permitting. The friendly situation is desperate.' FYI, I have multiple fighter and gunship assets coming up for this target. You are the head of the pack. The next flight is fifteen minutes behind you. This is a big one."

Malik acknowledged and nudged the power to 99%. He lowered the nose and increased climb speed to 430 knots, the maximum structural speed with fuel remaining in the external drop tanks. This was not an efficient climb speed, and the increased fuel burn would reduce loiter time over the target. But the urgency of the friendly situation was palpable.

There was no doubt. That distance west, 230 miles, was inside Cambodia. Were the friendlies Americans? As far as he knew, Sauer and he would be the first fighters to cross the border in close air support of ground troops. Certainly no one from the 35th Tactical Fighter Wing had ever been there.

What was American policy regarding air operations inside Cambodia? What responsibility might he bear for his actions? Walter Cronkite had said something on the evening news about a Cooper-Church Amendment. It forbade close air support for ground troops inside Cambodia.

The wall of black storms looming at 12 o'clock complicated a high-speed dash to the target. The F-100 had no radar, making weather penetration potentially dangerous.

Malik knew the answer before he asked, but he asked anyway.

"Hillsboro, I have heavy weather ahead. Any chance of a radar advisory?"

"Negative, Blade. We have no radar."

"Yeah, yeah, I know," Malik muttered to himself on the interphone. He was hoping Hillsboro might go to the trouble to contact the airborne air defense EC-121 monitoring transponder and primary radar returns of traffic in South Vietnam. They could paint the weather and give him a penetration heading, if they wanted to.

Without a radar advisory, Malik would have no choice but to drive blind straight into storms that might be violent. What lay ahead appeared to be a massive system.

The rising terrain of the Highlands forced an unbroken line of convective storms ever-upward. Malik looked over at Sauer, bobbing in fingertip formation off the left-wing. Sauer nodded. He saw it coming, and he inched closer to Malik. In 20 miles, they would slam into the black mass. Malik throttled back and leveled off, slowing to thunderstorm penetration speed, 275 knots. At higher speeds, the aircraft could incur G forces in violent thunderstorms beyond the aircraft structural limit, theoretically sufficient to break the wings off.

* * *

The flight was in and out of thin clouds, thudding through increasing turbulence. Beneath the overcast sky, the light faded by the mile. Sauer's right wing now overlapped with Malik's left. This produced an aerodynamic force that transmitted back to Malik's airplane, resulting in an annoying, slewing effect that made it harder for Malik to hold exact heading. But he would have to put up with it.

Malik turned his navigation lights to bright steady and turned off his rotating beacon and strobe. Strobing lights in weather would induce serious vertigo for a wingman. Malik stowed loose items, cinched his seat belt, and locked his shoulder harness reel. He turned on the cockpit thunderstorm lights and turned the rheostats for the instrument lighting to full bright. Finally, he lowered his seat to put his eyes directly in front of the attitude indicator and took his hand off the throttle. He would not touch the power until they were through the weather.

Sauer's cockpit rocked and pitched, now less than ten feet from Malik's wingtip. Glancing ahead, Malik leaned forward to survey the gigantic seething wall of energy racing toward him, seconds from collision. He held his breath and slammed into it.

Day turned to night. The G meter oscillated from peg to peg. Malik struggled to keep his boots against the rudder pedals and hold on to the stick. Out of the darkness, lightning flash-bulbed a torrent of rain roaring horizontally against the windscreen. The world spun, and vomit threatened to erupt into his mask. Unable to look away or blink, he fixated on a single instrument, the attitude indicator, trying to hold the wings level on the instrument and prevent the nose from pitching too far up or down. For a split second, he glanced to the left and saw Sauer, ghost-like, frozen in a flash of lightning.

Since Malik could not see Sauer's airplane, he knew Sauer could not see his. If Sauer was able to hold position, he could see only Malik's wingtip light. Based on personal experience Malik knew Sauer's equilibrium would be projecting violent maneuvers. His body was telling him he was inverted, diving for the jungle; it was sickening and terrifying, and his right biceps would be burning as he gripped the stick while jerking the throttle fore and aft with his left hand.

Malik was alternately hanging on the belts or being pummeled into the ejection seat while his legs flailed beneath the instrument panel, riding a whirlwind. The effect was amplified for Sauer. Surely, he could not hold on in this maelstrom. Seconds ticked into minutes as violent forces hammered body and mind.

They had endured ten minutes of relentless shocks when they rocketed out of the weather, sheeted with rain. Malik took a deep breath and collapsed within himself.

Ahead he saw high spires of towering cumulus defining canyons and corridors promising a visual way through to the west. He turned to look.

Sauer was still there.

Without being signaled to do so, Sauer moved away and dropped back, no doubt spent and drenched in sweat.

"Good show, Ron," Malik transmitted, his voice was hoarse from stress. No reply. A minute passed.

"Blade One, come up squadron common frequency." Sauer's voice was thready, barely audible.

Malik transmitted, "Hillsboro, Blade One will be off frequency for one minute."

"Roger, Blade One. Report back on."

Malik selected 234.5 on the UHF, looked over at Sauer, and saw him nod.

"Go ahead."

"Sir, I'm about to die." Sauer's voice was trembling with emotion.

"What? What are you saying?" Malik twisted his body sideways in the seat to look at Sauer.

"I just had a vision. It's my time, and there's nothing I can do about it .... I have done business with God. But one last thing I have to make right. You have to help me. I want you to tell my wife I loved her. I never once told her. I've always resented that I had to marry her. But it wasn't her fault she lost the baby."

He was sobbing, keying, and unkeying the mic.

"She's the best thing that ever happened to me, it turns out. I know that now ... now that it's too late. Tell her for me, John."

Malik stared incredulously at Sauer. He could see Ron's body shuddering while an otherwise expressionless, black-visored cyclops stared back, unblinking. Long seconds passed.

"I'll tell her. You have my word," Malik said.

"I hope to see you in the next life. I wanted to be just like you, Captain Malik," his voice almost a whisper.

Malik struggled to swallow. His expression was contorted in the mirrors mounted on the canopy bow. He watched his own tears stream down his cheeks, rolling along the margins of his mask. He blinked, looked forward, and transmitted, "Come up Hillsboro." Malik switched radio frequency and heard Sauer double click his transmitter, indicating he was on frequency.

"Hillsboro, Blade One back on," Malik reported.

"Roger, Blade One. Handoff in thirty miles."

Malik gently pitched the nose up and down, a signal to go into trail formation. He watched Sauer in his left mirror, dropping back.

Life slowed. He glanced at the jerking progress of the second hand of the clock on the instrument panel. Maybe this was the day he had foreseen, the day his own body, hurtled into the jungle, would begin its return to the elements in this far-away land.

He maneuvered aggressively to avoid entering the gigantic towers of cumulus burnished red on their western faces by the late afternoon sun. He pulled up and zoomed over the top of a cloud formation; topping it, he rolled inverted and nudged the stick forward to drift in zero-G over the backside. Floating against the belts, dreamlike, his consciousness was suspended momentarily in a euphoric weightless state. The Blade One flight maneuvered in trail like two porpoises, breaching the sea for joy.

The cumulus dissipated west of the Highlands. When the fuel light for his drop tanks blinked empty, Malik lowered the nose, pushed up the power, and accelerated to 500 knots, leveling over the top of an undercast cloud deck.

A memory arose, a scene from the movie *Dr. Strangelove*. In his mind's eye the cloud deck became the nape of the earth streaking just feet below him. He dreamed himself at the controls of a B-52 one hundred feet over the bleak Siberian tundra. Now well beyond the failsafe point, he was driving relentlessly toward a Russian ICBM complex to drop the thermonuclear weapon that would end civilization and life as everyone knew it. And he could hear the virile voices singing, "When Johnny comes marching home again hurrah, hurrah."

CHAPTER 2

Ground Fire

Blade One flight crossed the Cambodian border forty miles east of the target. Hillsboro directed the flight to contact Nail 19. Malik selected the frequency and looked left. Expressionless, Sauer nodded and clicked twice.

"Nail One Nine, Blade One, two F-100s with eight cans of napalm and sixteen-hundred rounds of twenty-millimeter. Forty miles east at eighteen thousand feet. Beacons on. Go ahead."

Nail 19's voice came on frequency, stressed and panicky. "Blade One, Nail One Nine. Below me here is a force of two-hundred-fifty Cambodian troops pinned down in a schoolyard in the center of a village called Prey ToTueng. The friendlies are surrounded by a large converging force of the North Vietnamese Army estimated at 5,000 men.

"This will be one hell of a fight. The good guys are hanging on by their fingernails. There's more ground fire coming up from here than anyone's ever seen outside of downtown Hanoi." Nail had to stop to take a breath. "Here's the deal, Blade. My earliest inbounds are fifteen minutes out. I can see the enemy massing for an overrun from the south. Assault could start any minute. If that happens, the friendlies are dead."

Nail held his UHF radio mic keyed as a second radio transmission came up in the background. There were screams on that radio. Nail went off frequency for several seconds.

"Blade, friendlies report fifty-plus dead or wounded. They can't lift their heads for the volume of fire they're taking. Their ammo is running low. The ground commander waves all restrictions. He wants ordnance on the wire. And here's the problem. I have Navy flights inbound from Dixie station, Huns coming from Phan Rang and Phu Cat, with F-4s and gunships inbound. All that firepower can't save these guys in the next few minutes. Only you can do that."

Silence. John looked over at Ron now off the right wing. Seconds passed. Then Ron nodded.

Staring at Ron, Malik transmitted, "Blade One will deliver singles followed by strafe."

That would mean a minimum of five or six attacks each. This decision was likely Ron Sauer's death sentence, if not his own. "It's my time, and there's nothing I can do about it." Ron's words echoed in Malik's head. But he could not think about that now.

Shielding his eyes with his hand, Malik could now see columns of smoke ahead through the glare of the late afternoon sun. He turned again to look at Sauer.

Nail came back on. "Thanks, Blade, that's what we need. There's one reason these guys are alive. You'll see a Spooky gunship in a minute. He got here about 15 minutes ago, working the northern perimeter of the friendlies. But he's in bad shape. Two aboard are dead from ground fire. The aircraft commander estimates a hundred rounds through his fuselage. He has sterilized three hundred meters on the north of the friendlies." Silence.

Nail resumed, "Okay, you'll do singles. I want you to deliver on the friendlies' south perimeter; it is an east-west street. You'll see it when I mark it. Your run-in is east-west or west-east only. The friendlies are in the schoolyard north of the street. You'll be dropping inside one hundred meters from them. Acknowledge."

"Blade copies, east-west, within one hundred meters." The flight continued inbound, descending. "Break, Blade Two, arm weapons. Set single deliveries, level release." A double click response.

Then Malik saw the Spooky gunship in the gathering gloom. Out of the side of an AC-47, tracers lashed the ground as multiple miniguns raked the northern perimeter of the friendlies. Some 18,000 rounds per minute were sparkling over the ground and buildings. Spooky pulled off with his guns dry just as Blade began a turn overhead.

* * *

Malik saw Nail's beacon followed by the streak of his marking rocket. In the same instant, Malik saw an arc of .51 caliber tracers climbing up like a flight of birds enveloping Nail's aircraft. Malik tightened his gut and inhaled sharply, positive that Nail had been hit. But he wasn't. Nail snapped his nose up and rolled away, transmitting expletives over the radio. Malik remembered to turn off his own beacon.

"Blade, lights off!" Malik transmitted to Sauer.

They were facing the most dangerous weapon a fighter could face in a low-altitude environment, a .51 caliber machine gun. It was firing from across the street from the friendly position, just south of the run-in line near the pullout point.

"Blade, do you see the three-story building fifty meters west of my mark?"

Malik's eyes searched the target area. "Got it," he said.

"That's your first target. Heavy weapons are pounding the friendlies from that building. Take it out. Then destroy every building on the street .... Oh, man!" Nail's voice cracked with urgency. "They're swarming like ants, forming up, massing. Hurry, Blade! They're about to begin an assault."

With weapons hot, the Blade aircraft in trail continued in a wide turn over the target, maneuvering for an attack with a westbound run-in. To survive the ground fire, Malik and Sauer would have to maneuver aggressively to disrupt tracking by enemy gunners. But they had to hit the target, which was challenging coming out high G turns an instant before weapon release.

Malik rolled into a descending 180-degree turn with power up and leveled westbound 200 feet above the terrain. He adjusted the throttle to achieve and hold 500 knots while turning and searching through smoke as structures passed beneath him in a blur. The ground was sparkling with ground fire aimed directly at him.

Along the run-in, he could again hear the snare drum and the strains of "When Johnny comes marching home again." The target appeared through the smoke. All parameters converged. Holding his breathing steady and even, he rolled wings level, unloaded backpressure, and pressed the bomb release on top of the stick the instant the crosshairs reached the base of the three-story building fronting the street across from the friendlies.

The can of napalm tumbled away toward the target. Malik pulled up hard, jinking left and right, and soared to 5,000 feet out of the .51 caliber envelope of tracers that showered him at the release point. He rolled over on his back and watched out the top of his canopy as the kinetic energy of the can of napalm swept the building off its foundations then erupted in fire. He held the nose up, climbing on his back, shifting his eyes to watch Sauer streaking toward the target.

Just at the release point Malik witnessed a tremendous explosion. Three thousand pounds of napalm, 800 rounds of 20-millimeter, two tons of fuel, wrapped around an engine spinning at 20,000 rpm, all detonated as a mother of all bombs in one blinding flash abeam the friendly position. From the fireball, a visible shock wave radiated outward, slamming through Malik's fighter with a jolt as fire and metal from Blade Two cascaded hundreds of yards along the street.

John's brain went numb. One instant, he was coherent, the next stupefied. "Breathe, keep it together," he muttered to himself over the interphone. "Many lives are in the balance." He continued his turn to downwind blinking away tears. But he maintained altitude past the roll-in point, continuing in a shallow turn over the target.

"My God, my God!" Nail wailed over the radio. "Oh, I'm so sorry, Blade!"

Nail's comments barely registered. Malik rolled in for his next delivery, driving grimly along the same line, snaking left-right, up-down, holding 500 knots. Tracers were coming up from everywhere.

He released his second can of napalm against a second building and snapped up, rolling, watching the heavy gunner reaching up for him.

On the next pass, he pulled off dry, unable to see through the smoke. Then for another delivery, defying all probabilities, he pulled off unscathed, and another building erupted in flames. Again, the gunner's tracers flashed over his canopy, in front of his nose, some falling away below him. The gunner had resolved his aiming lead for Malik's repeated attack geometry.

Malik rolled in to bring down the last building on the street with his remaining can of napalm. Fires raged along the street. And he heard it again as he drove inbound: the snare drum and the ironic voices singing his song, "When Johnny comes marching home again hurrah, hurrah. We'll give him a mighty welcome then hurrah, hurrah …." He heard his beautiful Christine in his memory saying, "Come home to me, Johnny. Please come home to me!" The song climaxed with the vision from the movie, the sudden silence, the thermonuclear weapon falling out of the bomb bay toward the Russian ICBM complex, the blinding flash, the end of the world—the end of Johnny Malik. Yet it wasn't.

At the release point, he held steady a second too long, and he knew it. He pressed the bomb release switch. There was a simultaneous detonation. In slow motion, he saw in his peripheral vision a line of green tracers stitching toward his left wing; it shaved beneath his fuselage and connected with the right inboard can of napalm the instant it separated from the pylon. A fireball bloomed around him, the aircraft slewed sideways, racked with a force that locked his shoulder harness. He heard a shriek on the radio, Nail's inadvertent transmission.

Malik blinked, and all was normal in front of him. He caged his sight, selected all four guns on the arming panel, engaged afterburner, and turned to watch the earth falling away beneath him. He searched for the gun site, a violent rage rising from his gut.

"Nail, can you mark the gun?"

"Here's your mark."

A white phosphorus "Willie Pete" rocket streaked out of nowhere and detonated. A narrow plume of white smoke rose from the impact. "He's within fifty meters of the mark," Nail said.

From above 10,000 feet, Malik pushed the left rudder against the stop and rotated the nose toward the ground, knowing this maneuver was near suicidal because of the steepness of the angle. The gunner began firing. Malik, screaming obscenities, pressed the trigger to the second detent. Like four jackhammers, his cannons launched 5,000 rounds per minute of 20 millimeter marked by red tracers that interlaced the gunner's greens that were engulfing him like rain on a windshield. Malik had only seconds to pull out. He pulled back hard. The G meter came against the stop and stuck at 9 Gs. Doubled over, he grunted against the forces, grayed out and went black for a second, certain the next thing he would see was the afterlife.

Inconceivably, the nose shuddered up to the horizon, rising. His vision cleared nearly at ground level. Fire, burning buildings, crumbling structures, corpses, men running in all directions, stopping to fire at him. With the nose above the horizon, Malik engaged the afterburner and struggled upward.

Topping 10,000 feet again, he displaced south one mile then rolled into a dive toward the target. He held the crosshairs on the gun position. Plummeting at 500 knots he delayed firing to 1500 feet, the range where the rounds of all four canons converged. He saw the gunner in an eye-blink; he squeezed the trigger and emptied his guns in one burst. For just an instant he saw the gunner before he vanished into red mist.

High above the target, Malik rolled onto his back, easing forward on the stick to join the Zero-G parabola, then rolled upright and checked his fuel. He was out of fuel with no chance of making it to Phan Rang. The closest airbase was Bien Hoa, and even that was iffy. He would probably lose the airplane and maybe his life.

Another set of fighters checked in with Nail. Malik's job was done, but he advised Nail he would make one more pass. He lowered the nose from ten miles west of the target, advanced power to 100%, and began a shallow dive toward the town. He leveled at 100 feet, holding 630 knots, almost supersonic, as he passed the edge of the village. Over the friendly position, he pulled the nose up to the vertical, lit the afterburner, and began a slow roll, his missing man salute to Ron Sauer. At 30,000 feet, he pulled onto his back, heading east and rolled upright, out of burner.

He transmitted, "Nail, remember Second Lieutenant Ronald Sauer, 612th Tac Fighter Squadron, in your after-action report. I want his wife to know he was a hero." With a catch in his voice, he added, "If you can work it into the report, mention that he wanted his wife to know that he loved her."

"I will do that, Blade. Your bomb damage assessment is four structures destroyed, one AAA site destroyed, and I'm making a wild guess here ... three hundred killed by air. That's got to be an all-time KBA record. Seriously, I can't count the charred bodies. They're strung out for three blocks. I state for the record, you saved the lives of the friendlies. I'll remember this the rest of my life." His tone softened. "I'm so sorry about your wingman, Blade .... Contact Hillsboro. Nail One Nine, out."

* * *

On the distant horizon, Malik could see the glimmer of the South China Sea and the expansive lights of Saigon just coming up as the day transitioned to twilight. At 30,000 feet, he stared at the radial and distance on his nav display showing 50 miles to the Bien Hoa TACAN. He stowed loose equipment, cinched his seat belt and shoulder harness, and searched again for loose items. He zipped his pockets closed and traced the edges of Christine's picture over his heart.

Hillsboro relayed his emergency status to Bien Hoa Approach Control and handed him off. Malik peeled his tongue off the roof of his mouth and checked in.

"Bien Hoa Approach, Blade One, forty-five miles off Channel eighty-two with a fuel emergency."

"Roger, Blade One, Bien Hoa Approach Control. Copy your mayday status. Advise ready for descent."

"Bien Hoa, I'm going to flame out. But if I can make the runway, I'll try to deadstick it. Otherwise, I'll bail out. Requesting Nine Right."

"Roger, Blade, that's approved. Say fuel now."

"Zero. Tanks show empty. But it's still running. Starting descent."

Malik had calculated the mileage for an idle descent from 30,000 feet to arrive at 8,000 feet over the end of the runway. If he could achieve this, it was theoretically possible to deadstick the airplane. He had practiced this a dozen times in the F-102, but never in the F-100.

Sudden silence. Passing 20,000 feet his engine flamed out. From this point he had to get it exactly right. On profile, he began rehearsing the sequence of actions in his head. *Drop the tail hook ... check airspeed below 150 knots before drag chute deployment ... blow the drop tanks and pylons off before barrier engagement ... release brakes just before crossing the barrier cable ... don't blow the tires! You've only got three brake applications before the pressure fails.* He unhooked the zero-delay lanyard for chute deployment then reached up and turned off the anti-skid; he rehearsed the sequence again.

He locked his shoulder harness and prepared for ejection. If he had to do it, he would roll the airplane away from a populated area, likely on a southwest heading. To ensure the aircraft hit an unpopulated area he would delay ejection to no later than 2,000 feet.

He was descending through 8,000 feet as he came over the approach end of Runway 09R heading 180 degrees. He began a high sink-rate 270-degree turn toward the runway, finessing distance versus altitude in the turn. He lowered the gear and flaps with hydraulic pressure from the ram air turbine, deployed the tail hook, and rolled out aligned, aiming one-third of the way down the runway. A steady green light appeared in the tower: cleared to land. Emergency vehicles with flashing lights lined the taxiways.

The engine was windmilling as he crossed the overrun, providing diminishing but enough hydraulic pressure to power primary flight controls. He spiked the aircraft onto the runway at 200 knots, held the nose up for three seconds, then lowered it and gently applied the brakes, increasing pedal pressure. He deployed the drag chute at 150 knots and braced himself for barrier engagement coming up fast. No way could he stop. What was he supposed to do? He reached up and pressed the emergency jettison button and blew the drop tanks and pylons off the wings so they would not deflect the barrier, and he released the brakes just before crossing the cable at 100 knots. Past the cable, he stood on the brakes. The aircraft rapidly decelerated in the overrun and rocked to a halt.

The hook had engaged the barrier as advertised, drawing him to a smooth stop 900 feet into the overrun with 100 feet of hard surface remaining. Assisting his arrestment was the fact that his wheels had bogged to the axles in soft asphalt.

Malik released his drag chute, shut off the electrical switches, and unfastened the connector on the left side of his oxygen mask, letting it dangle. He stared through the windscreen at the lights glowing brighter in the northeast Saigon suburbs; he entered a time warp, mesmerized by the lights. His adrenaline rush was gone, replaced with vacant wandering thought.

When would his day of reckoning come? He had lived in dread of God's judgment for years. Twelve years, to be exact. Today Ron Sauer had died instead of him. Perhaps in his place? *Why Ron and not me?* Against the odds, John Malik had survived another brush with death. How many times could he pass through the fire and not be burned alive?

From somewhere came an insistent and unbidden question he hadn't considered in twelve years: how had his brother's body come out of the spring? *Why had Ian died instead of me?*

Someone was pounding on the left side of his canopy. This jerked him out of his trance. He turned and looked into the alarmed face of a man on a ladder outside his cockpit. The man yelled, "Sir, unlock the canopy, or I'll have to blow it!"

PART II:

THE CAVE

CHAPTER 3

The Book and the House of Evil

Springfield, Missouri
Early June 1958

Sixteen-year-old John Malik squeezed the trigger on a grease gun, watching for it to ooze out around the right front ball joint on a '51 Mercury sitting on the grease rack above him. He released the trigger and looked toward the gas pumps. A horn blared. On the outer pumps, a '48 Ford pickup had just pulled up. The guys John worked with were all making a beeline toward the office.

Lowering his head, taking a deep breath, John replaced the grease gun in its holder, wiped his hands on a red rag he retrieved from his back pocket, and walked out from under the rack toward Mr. Norbert Hixson. Why couldn't somebody else wait on him? The elderly farmer who lived east of town was cheap, and he always had a long, bizarre story John was obligated to endure.

Mr. Hixson climbed out of his truck as John approached. "The usual," he said. He leaned back against the bed of his truck carefully watching John insert the nozzle into the gas tank receptacle and begin pumping gas slowly. If he didn't do it just right gas would blow back on him, irritating Mr. Hixson.

A few moments of silence were too much for Mr. Hixson. "You know about the haunted house just east of here?" he asked.

"Here it comes," John muttered to himself. "No, sir. Don't believe I do," John said, staring at the digits on the pump as they passed four dollars. If he went over by two cents, he would have to pay the overage out of his own pocket.

As John eased the pump passing $4.88, Mr. Hixson turned and began kicking the knobby rear tire of his pickup with first one boot then the other. Clots of dried cow manure fell to the pavement. John would have to sweep that up.

John stopped the pump at exactly $5.00 and replaced the fuel nozzle. He then cleaned Mr. Hixson's windshield inside and out, and the side and rear windows. Mr. Hixson would insist on this. John moved on to tweaking the air pressure in all tires, including the spare, all the time listening to the story of the haunted house.

Mr. Hixson followed John around the truck as he swept the manure out of the cab and checked all the fluids under the hood. On and on, Mr. Hixson droned about the haunted house on East Farm Road 132, a mile from the Hixson farm.

John tried to figure out the manure routine. He decided Mr. Hixson stepped both boots into a fresh cow patty just before coming to town for gas. He evidently took some perverse pleasure in doing this to annoy John.

Mr. Hixson was describing how the original inhabitants of the haunted farmhouse left in the middle of the night, leaving furniture, clothes, and everything they owned. That was 20 years ago. He remembered those people, and he didn't like them. Lawyers and others came looking for contact information, but Mr. Hixson knew nothing.

Others had moved into the house briefly over the years. But they fled within a few days, terrified by something in the house. One theory was that it was built on an Indian graveyard. But Mr. Hixson believed the house was cursed because the original family was a bunch of criminals that invited the devil to live in the place.

"I tell everybody, that's Satan's lair. Don't touch or take anything out of that house." He clucked his tongue to let the cursed pronouncement hang in the air.

John stood sweating for five minutes after he had finished his chores on the truck as Mr. Hixson completed his story. When he was finished, Mr. Hixson counted out $5.00 in change, dropping some of it on the concrete, which John retrieved from under the truck. John thanked Mr. Hixson for his patronage and walked into the office where the other guys and the manager were grinning at him.

At first, John dismissed Mr. Hixson's story like all the others. But the more he thought about it, the more the idea of exploring a haunted house seemed like a great adventure. He would get Ian to go with him. Ian was afraid of everything.

* * *

It took a few days, but John convinced Ian that he actually wanted to go into a haunted house in the dark. According to what John could find out, the house actually existed. The chief hard evidence of the haunting was that mechanical timepieces inside the house stopped every night within a few minutes of midnight. There was also a palpable sense of terror in the house, most evident on moonless nights, according to Mr. Hixson.

The two boys decided they would explore this haunted house one Friday night, though Ian had grave reservations. The folks gave John the keys to Uncle Sean's '46 Ford so he and Ian could go to the drive-in movie. They collected six watches and a half-dozen windup clocks from home and from friends and went to the Sunset Drive-In.

At 11 p.m., they left the drive-in. Half an hour later, they were sitting in the car looking at the dark shape of the partly collapsed clapboard farmhouse. Their flashlights revealed the front door hanging askew and all the windows broken out.

John whispered, "Okay, we leave your Timex on the dash and take all the other timepieces into the house. We go in at 11:40." He jerked his head left and right, craning his neck.

Ian scooted against John, looking around for the imminent peril John seemed to sense.

"We can either stay inside the house or come back to the car until 12:45 a.m.," John whispered.

"But if the timepieces all stop, we won't know what time it is."

"Okay, we come back to the car and wait."

Ian nodded emphatically.

At 11:40, they eased out of the car, switched on their flashlights, and moved as silently as possible toward the house. The closest neighbor was a half-mile away so no one would hear them, but sneaking quietly seemed the thing to do in case ghosts, or worse, inhabited the house. They waded into dew-soaked weeds, through the broken-down picket fence, stepped onto the porch, and peered into the entry with their lights. The exposed wall studs resembled the bones of a long-dead creature, and the air reeked of decay, mold, and the strong stench of animal urine and feces. John hesitated, trying to get his breath. Ian gripped John's belt from behind.

They shuffled inside in lockstep. The interior was cluttered with debris and broken-down furniture. Shadows flitted around the room as they jerked their lights first one direction then another. They moved like a four-legged creature into the bedrooms and the kitchen, mouth-breathing to avoid the suffocating smell.

As his light passed over the fireplace mantle, John saw a book with a green cover lying beneath layers of cobwebs and dust. He removed the watches and clocks from the paper bag and placed them on the mantle, then picked up the book, shaking loose the cobwebs. He paused, remembering for an instant Mr. Hixson's warning not to take anything from this house. He took it anyway. They ran out of the house and through the gate of the picket fence to the car.

They slammed the car doors closed, rolled up the windows, and locked the doors. John's heart was racing, and his hands were sweaty.

"You watch the house. Watch for movement," John stuttered. He opened the green book, examining it with his flashlight, glancing up toward the house. Somehow, he sensed this book was important. He looked up, "You're watching, right?"

Ian nodded, wide-eyed, and hunkered down against John, jerking his head in all directions.

The pages of the book were yellowed and weathered. Some pages fell out where the binding-glue had dried to powder. The silver lettering on the cover read *The Wild Caves of Missouri*.

Inside the cover was a handwritten name: Frederick Evans. The book opened naturally to an article titled "Lost Man's Cave," in the Carter County chapter, where a folded topographical map had been inserted. Unfolding the fragile document, John saw an "X" inked along dense contour lines defining a ridge. Above the X, someone had scrawled "Lost Man's Cave." An hour passed as John read to Ian from the book. Sensing the time, he reached back and laid the book on the back seat.

Ian held up his Timex. It read 12:45 a.m. They looked at each other wide-eyed. Were they really going to go back into the house? John had never felt such foreboding. But they had no choice. If they didn't come home with all of the timepieces, Mom and Dad would discover them missing sooner or later, and John would be in big trouble for bringing Ian here.

They got out slowly and again, as silently as possible, followed their trampled path through the weeds to the front door. After deep breaths they entered, mouth breathing, and crept to the fireplace mantle. Ian raked the timepieces into the paper bag along with dust and cobwebs. They turned and bolted through the door to the car. As John got in, he found the green book on his seat. He pitched it into the back, started the engine, and spun out in the gravel, laying rubber in their getaway.

A mile away, John pulled off the road and stopped. "Did you put the book on my seat?"

Ian was shivering, his teeth were chattering, and he seemed hardly aware of the question. He shrugged. "I don't know what you're talking about."

"Okay, if you say so .... Now to find out if there's anything to this."

He turned on the interior lights and dumped the timepieces and dust from the paper bag onto the seat between them. All eleven timepieces had stopped within a few minutes of midnight. Ian's Timex, the one left in the car, had kept on ticking.

The shivery mystery of the stopped clocks was beyond rational explanation. More compelling was what seemed a sinister message from the green book. It alluded to a dead man long forgotten in darkness.

* * *

The author of the green book had inventoried hundreds of wild caves in Missouri, having interviewed explorers of known caves, county by county. The author had explored many of the caves personally. But of all the caves mentioned in the book, only Lost Man's Cave had never been entered, according to the author.

It seemed almost certain to John that no one could have found it, given the remoteness of the area and the almost-impossible-to-discover entry. Current maps of the area of Carter County showed sparse population and no roads into the wilderness area of the cave.

In the article on Lost Man's Cave, the author described the entry as exceedingly dangerous. He had come upon it accidently in the summer of 1933 when he was a crew chief working for the Civilian Conservation Corps. His crew was tasked with building logging trails into the remote forest southeast of Van Buren, Missouri.

One day, one of his workmen disappeared. There was food missing from the camp stores and several of the author's crewmen claimed the man, whom they believed was a thief, had headed through the woods for Van Buren, maybe to catch a Greyhound bus home. But the author believed the man had fallen into Lost Man's Cave, as the author himself had nearly done.

The author had found the opening on a hike along a ridgeline the very day he was told by the CCC to pull his team out and abandon the project. He provided this detail: "The project lost its funding when somebody realized these blackjack oaks were useless for commercial timber." He added, "I expect the forest will soon erase any evidence of our presence. And I do not expect that anyone will ever see what only I have seen and have named 'Lost Man's Cave.' I believe it is the last resting place of Wilbur Evans."

In the book's epilogue, the author stated that the following year after he left the CCC he resumed his studies at the prestigious Rolla School of Mines.

* * *

Six weeks later, John and Ian Malik climbed into Uncle Sean's '46 Ford to begin an unsanctioned trip into the night that would change both of their lives forever.

CHAPTER 4
The Mark Twain National Forest

Just before sunset, John and Ian departed their home in Springfield, Missouri, driving east hour after hour into the night on Highway 60. They stayed on 60 at Willow Springs, leaving the main route that ran south through West Plains, Mammoth Springs, and on to distant Memphis.

John glanced from time to time at Ian who stared out the windshield into the darkness, pensive, expressionless, scared. Ian clearly didn't really want to do this, but he idolized John. A week ago, his mother told John yet again, "You are your brother's keeper."

Near midnight, 150 miles from home, they coasted through Van Buren, still on Highway 60. Ten minutes beyond Van Buren, the road turned from southeast to east. At that bend in the road, they pulled over onto the shoulder to check the map again using a flashlight. They saw to their right, as expected, a little-used and rutted dirt road leading south. This was their first landmark, an unimproved road that appeared on modern maps. But it led nowhere, apparently ending some miles south. Their 30-year-old map showed this road, too. It also showed their next landmark, a logging trail two miles south along this dirt road. But this trail did not appear on any current map.

John turned right onto the dirt road, ignoring the weathered sign filled with bullet holes that announced a dead end six miles ahead. Ian noted the odometer reading and the time. Ten minutes later, they stopped. When the trailing dust cloud cleared, they panned the powerful beam of a six-volt dry cell light across a 15-foot gap in the otherwise solid forest. Though there were no mature trees in the gap, the underbrush had grown up to waist height.

"Is that it?" John twisted his neck to look down onto the map. Ian panned his light from the gap in the trees to the map.

"If that's it, we'll need a tank to make it through there." Ian shook his head.

"Ah, we can make it," John said. But he wasn't sure he believed his own words. In the next moment, his mouth was opening, and venomous words poured out. "If you ever tell the folks, or *anybody*, that we came here, I promise you'll regret it. You got that?" He leaned toward Ian with bitter malice in his voice and demeanor—to John's own surprise.

Ian withdrew against the car door and whimpered. "I'm not going to tell anybody, John. Did you think I would? I'm just glad you wanted me along."

"Yeah, birthday boy!" John chewed on words he had been mulling over for a hundred miles. But he didn't say more. Dad had just bought Ian a brand-new Vespa motor scooter for his fourteenth birthday to replace the new bike he bought him last year. In fact, he bought Ian a new bike every year, but he had never bought John a bike. Dad always traded in the old bike.

John had to walk wherever he went. He walked two miles each way to work after school, five days a week. He worked until closing. And on Saturdays, he worked twelve hours. Six days a week he walked four miles to work and back home. More grating than the long walks was the requirement that he give his mother half of everything he made for room and board.

His parents loved Ian with unnatural intensity. Their attitude toward John was growing in inverse proportion to their cloying affection for Ian. For years they had made it clear that Ian was their preferred son, but now they seemed barely able to restrain their contempt for John. There had been a change in the family dynamics that had begun within the last six months. John could mark the day.

Some distant relatives of John's mother from Niangua, Missouri visited one evening. As John withdrew to his room, he heard the woman commenting on how handsome John was becoming. She thought he resembled Tyrone Power or Errol Flynn, or maybe some British lord.

As soon as the company left, John's parents got into a heated argument that lasted late into the night. They were saying awful things to each other in their bedroom. Judging by the number of times they invoked his name John could tell they were talking about him.

John realized he was staring coldly at his brother who was wide-eyed and braced against the car door. No, this wasn't Ian's fault. He was as kind as anyone could be and must have regretted the obvious favoritism.

John looked away as an owl called in the deep forest that stretched as a wall of darkness for a hundred miles. He shook his head as though awaking from a dream and blinked his eyes. "Oh, I'm sorry, Ian. What did I say?" He knew his apology was empty but continued with it anyway. "I didn't mean to talk to you that way."

Ian looked down at the floorboard and said nothing.

John shifted into gear and advanced at idle toward the brush, holding his breath. "Pray this beast holds together, little brother. You forgive me?" He looked at Ian.

"Sure, John." But Ian was still leaning hard against the door.

They had seen no cars nor lights of farms since leaving Van Buren. And there was no moon. The only light was the yellow glow of the headlights.

Revving the engine in first gear he plowed into the brush, laying down a swath beneath the bumper. The stars vanished, and the forest swallowed the car. The brush passed scraping and screeching beneath the frame and along the sides of the car. In some places they bogged down, backed up, cleared brush, and again moved slowly forward. It had turned cold under the trees, and the heater wasn't keeping up.

At points Ian had to get out of the car and direct the way ahead with a flashlight. Several times both got out and chopped brush with machetes, dragged limbs out of the way, and pushed fallen trees aside with the front bumper. The terrain rose toward the ridges that defined the Current River valley.

Thirty minutes passed. John shifted to neutral, came to a stop, and revved the engine, trying to get more out if the heater. He spread out the map on the seat between them and switched on his light. "I've been thinking. See this?" He pointed with a pencil. "This is Big Spring feeding into the Current River. It's about a mile north of Lost Man's Cave. The geologists say it's an outlet from one of the largest cavern systems anywhere. But no one has ever been in it because it's full of water. What if our cave is part of that system?"

Ian shrugged. "What would that mean?"

"It means that if it is, we'd be the first ever to enter it. Can you image? Being the first?"

Ian seemed unimpressed.

"Don't you want to see what no human has ever seen before? I do." John's voice trailed off, along with some of his enthusiasm.

John almost hated his brother for not being more excited about this adventure. He was suffering an acute episode of resentment, and right then he didn't like Ian very much. The resentment led to guilt, as it always did. He had lied to his parents about where they were going; he was ungrateful for the things his folks did do for him; and he suffered torment for the unseemly visions of girls that obsessed his waking thoughts. As moral conflicts increased his faith in God languished.

* * *

Three grueling miles had finally clicked by on the odometer since they had entered the trail. It had taken three hours of plowing through the brush at a glacial pace to reach a promising indicator, an unmistakable gap in the trees leading north. With the engine idling and the brake set, John pointed out the right window. "Is that it?" he asked.

Ian rolled down his window and leaned out. His breath drifted as a stream of fog toward the trees. He held a dry-cell light in his right hand, sweeping the beam across the gap between trees that seemed to frame a narrow passage leading north.

Dewdrops sparkled in the light. They clung like pearls to spiderwebs strung between saplings and brush within the opening. This gap in the trees appeared to correspond to a dotted line on the old topographical map. The legend showed it to be an exploratory trail.

John was distracted by the misfiring of the V8 flathead engine convulsing on its mounts. The fenders rattled, and the tailpipe knocked against the frame. Cursing under his breath, he revved the engine savagely to clear the fouled plugs before he turned toward his little brother.

"Well, is that it or not?"

"How am I supposed to know?" Ian snapped. The two lapsed into silence for several seconds. "Sorry," Ian said, and turned his light back onto the map. "The mileage is right. That has to be it, don't you think, John?"

Ian's teeth started chattering. He switched off his light, cranked up the window, and hugged his thin frame with his arms. John watched Ian shuddering for several seconds then switched off the headlights and turned off the ignition.

John stared through the windshield, trying to swallow but he had no spit. This was surely the way to the cave. Why weren't they excited? He seemed powerless to turn away from what had become an obsession. He was going to find and explore this cave, no matter what.

The dim forms of the blackjack oaks seemed vaguely disturbing. This vast forest stretched for a great distance in all directions across the flinty hills in south-central Missouri in the heart of the Mark Twain National Forest. By John's reckoning, they were 15 miles southeast as the crow flies from Van Buren, the nearest town, and likely the closest human presence.

With the engine off, cold quickly invaded the interior of the car. John cranked the engine again. They huddled before the heater vents, staring into the gap. He was convinced. This was the remnant of a long-abandoned exploratory probe leading off the logging trail at right angles into deeper darkness.

John was gripping the steering wheel, twisting his hands in opposite directions. He forced himself to relax and glanced over at his brother, who was shaking. "Let's press on. We're equipped and trained, aren't we? One step at a time."

Ian, looking even younger than his 14 years, jerked his head toward John and nodded. "Okay," he said, his teeth clicking like castanets.

John remembered again what his mother had said: "John, you're your brother's keeper, his hero, and guardian. Be careful about how you influence Ian. He's not strong like you."

John turned on his dry cell light and directed it into the back seat. He rummaged among the gear and found a denim jacket. "Here." He tossed it to Ian. The engine was misfiring again.

The car had a lot of problems. The mixture was too rich. John would have to adjust the carburetor jets again. The exhaust was smoky and pungent, smelling of fuel and oil. The rods knocked, and it took two quarts of oil for every tank of gas. Most of it was passing the piston rings into the combustion chamber and out the tailpipe.

John knew he was a fool to have conceived this adventure in this car. No one knew where they were. No one would ever find them if they broke down.

"You warming up?" John asked.

"I'm okay. I'm ready. We've got to get to the campsite, if we can find it. I'm so sleepy, John."

"Well, here we go. Take a deep breath and pray." John turned the steering wheel toward the side of the trail, gunned the engine, and plowed over a shoulder of gravel, dragging the muffler and sending a shower of rocks from beneath the bald rear tires. The car lurched over the shoulder and rocked to a halt among the trees. John shifted to neutral.

As far as the lights could show through the dust, a path of low undergrowth extended straight ahead under overhanging branches. This was a manmade trail.

John shifted back into first and proceeded slowly ahead. Saplings screeched along the sides of the car and raked under the bumper. Fallen limbs crunched beneath the wheels, and rocks skittered from under the tires and rebounded off the frame. Gnarled oaks lumbered through the periphery of the headlights, reaching down with their jagged limbs like monsters.

"This isn't as bad as the logging road. But it's a lot narrower," Ian said. He looked so small and frail, huddled against the door, shaking uncontrollably.

"It's the trees. They block the sunlight so everything's stunted underneath them." John leaned forward to look up into the overhanging limbs.

They didn't talk much. John could feel the strain on the tires and undercarriage of the car. What would they do if they got a flat tire or if a limb skewered the oil pan?

* * *

Just short of a mile of rocks, dead limbs, and saplings had passed beneath their wheels when John eased to a stop and pulled up the handbrake with a clunk. The headlights now shone into the tops of trees. A partial view of the night sky appeared above them.

"This is it. You agree?"

Ian trained his light again onto the map and leaned over to check the odometer. "We're at one mile. Here's the ridgeline and the trail." Ian pointed to the map as John leaned over to confirm. "Downslope ahead. That means the cave is … out there." He spoke the last phrase at a lower octave as he aimed his light out the right window into the dark.

The topographical map showed them at the summit of the ridge in which they would find the cave. John turned off the lights and the ignition to experience the night and to contemplate events ahead that might change their lives. It was pitch black among the trees. The pings of metal cooling in the engine compartment and the sounds of insects buzzing around them played against a background of otherwise extraordinary, ear-ringing silence. Several minutes later crickets resumed their chorus, and an owl called.

As his night vision took effect, John could make out an immense number of stars stretching across a gash of the tree-lined sky. Meteors streaked across the opening.

"Isn't this great!" Ian said, his teeth chattering again.

John inhaled the pristine smells of decaying trees, limbs, leaves, and rock weathering to soil. The distinct aroma of sycamore trees, damp earth, and cold spring water wafted up the slope in front of them.

The cold crept back into the car. Ian could not get warm. "John, are we supposed to be here? Did God bring us here?" he stammered.

"God's in charge of everything. And if we're called to His purpose, everything is supposed to work out. That's what the Bible says."

"But why is Dad so against us exploring caves? He said we weren't ever to go into caves. We're supposed to obey our parents. That's what God says. So how do you figure it's okay for us to be here?"

John folded his arms, closed his eyes, and took a deep breath. "Sure, Ian, we're supposed to do what Mom and Dad say. But there's more to it. Dad and a friend of his got lost in a cave once. Mom said

Dad went berserk before someone found them. That was just before I was born. She said he was different after that. Anyway, just because he had a bad experience is no reason to keep us from exploring caves."

"Yeah, how are we ever supposed to learn stuff if Mom and Dad keep us from doing the things they did? When you look at it that way, I guess it's okay. We can always say we're sorry and they'll forgive us, right?"

John turned toward Ian and pointed his index finger in his face. "Let me makes this clear. Do not tell anybody what we're doing. Not even God. You understand? Dad had a talk with me and laid down the law. If I let anything happen to you, I'm as good as dead. *You can never* tell anybody we did this. You got that?"

"No one will ever hear it from me. See, I'm zipping my lips shut."

"See that they stay zipped if you don't want my blood on your hands …. Did you bring your harmonica?"

Ian nodded.

"Okay, let's get the camp set up, and you can play us some tunes. We're about to have the time of our lives. We'll *never* forget this."

John cranked the engine, released the brake, and allowed the car to roll down the trail that now continued downhill. He was not sure the car could climb back up the slope. But he would worry about that tomorrow.

The map had been right so far. They rocked down the trail and rolled out into a glade. John stopped short of a creek of deep, fast-moving water. Across the creek was an unbroken stand of giant water oaks and sycamores. A cold layer of air blanketed the glade, and the gurgle of rushing water came from somewhere in the darkness.

They set up the tent and gathered firewood. The light of a crackling campfire drove the night's chill and loneliness beyond the circle of the dancing flame. John sat on a log staring into the fire while Ian played an extraordinary repertoire of songs on his harmonica. The selections were moving, even heart-rending and haunting. He had composed numerous songs. He was the music and the joy of the Malik family.

The boys crawled into the tent and burrowed into their sleeping bags. They continued to watch the dying fire through the opening. Their parents believed they were camping out on the James River, ten miles from home. They promised to bring home a mess of fish. But that was a lie.

When the last ember flared and expired, utter darkness prevailed. John closed his eyes. Lines of Coleridge's "Kublai Khan" welled up in his memory. In Xanadu, Kublai Khan had built a stately pleasure-dome beside Alph, the sacred river. The river ran for five miles, meandering with a mazy motion through wood and dale until it reached the caverns measureless to man and sank in tumult to a lifeless ocean. Somewhere beneath them, John believed, there lay a lifeless ocean and a river that ran heedless of the affairs of man. The sound of the river in his mind mingled with the gurgling stream near their tent, lulling John into a fitful sleep.

CHAPTER 5
The Spring

John glanced around the inside the moldering frame house, windows painted black. Exposed studs and timbers, the ribs of the interior of the structure, were weathered and twisted from the ravages of hot summers and cold winters. Warped and weary beams seemed unable to support the roof any longer, yet the structure stood.

A single candle radiated a dim yellow glow through a cobwebbed room cluttered like the burrow of a packrat. Dusty broken-down furniture, faded pictures, cardboard boxes bursting with mildewed books, piles of disintegrating clothes, and a myriad of other domestic artifacts—as much as a half-century old, challenged the mind to discover any order or focus in the cramped space.

A foul smell of rotten teeth, bile, and the pasty body odor of the unwashed aged drew John Malik's terrified eyes up to the face of an unshaven old man who loomed over him, holding him by his shirt with strong bony hands. From the man's transparent bluish skin, flakes of epidermis spalled off. His ravaged eyes were red-rimmed and veined with broken vessels. The corneas were eaten away by enlarged pupils clouded with milky cataracts. The wattles below the man's eroded jawline undulated as he squeaked in a falsetto voice.

"You are the damned!" he hissed. "Chains in everlasting darkness and a lake of fire, that is your portion. And here," he pointed behind himself, "I have called your master." With a grotesque grin, he shuffled back into the shadows.

Attempting to stand and run, John found his forearms were tied to the arms of a chair. He sat rigid with fear, unable to utter a sound. The man summoned something in one of the unlit rooms. John's eyes went wide, hearing claws clicking, moving toward him, on the curled-up linoleum floor. A ponderous tread sent tremors through the floor. John struggled against his bonds. "Help me!" he screamed in his mind. His throat was paralyzed.

The ghastly experience and his pounding pulse faded into the recesses of his subconscious as John sensed himself awakening. He was aware of his breathing and the aroma of brewing coffee. After several minutes, he opened his eyes and strained to recapture a glimpse of the vision. Had he dreamed this before? He could only get a sense of his passing terror, his dry mouth, his triphammer heartbeat, the metallic taste in his mouth. The vision was gone before he could map the details into his consciousness.

Snuggled in the warm sleeping bag, he shook off any remnants of the nightmare, and savored not only the delicious smell of the coffee but the sharpness of the early morning air. The cheerful song of meadowlarks greeting the sunrise brought John a sense that all was well. He was safe.

He rolled over and pushed open the dew-soaked tent flap. Ian was squatting by a fire, tending a skillet popping with eggs and grease. "Hey," John called as he crawled out of the tent and arched his stiff back, focused on the skillet of eggs and the smell of coffee.

"Hey. You have a bad dream?"

John didn't answer. As he surveyed their location, he was struck with wonder by the face of a bluff looming a hundred yards away in the woods. The fast-moving stream that flowed beside their campsite appeared to be emerging from the bluff. "Look at that, Ian!" He quickly pulled on his jeans and boots then ran toward the bluff.

Ian moved the skillet off the fire and followed. "It's a spring. You can't get in it."

At the base of the overhanging bluff, they stood peering into a pool of gin-clear water 20-feet across and 30-feet deep. A great volume of water issuing from a black hole in its depths mounded the surface.

"I've been staring into this for an hour." Ian shivered and hugged himself, but it wasn't because he was cold. "Is it coming out of Lost Man's Cave?"

John studied Ian for a moment. "Probably," John said. "Same ridge."

He, too, felt something threatening and hypnotic when he looked into the spring. For many minutes he stared transfixed. "No one will ever know what's down there. You may as well be on the far side of the moon, as be down there in that eternal darkness."

Sunrise filtered through the trees and glinted off the stream flowing from the spring. A low layer of cold fog hovered upon the surface of the creek that trailed away through the woods to the Current River, a mile away. Along the banks of the creek, mighty sycamores and giant water oaks stood rigid like sentinels. In their branches, birds were singing, and squirrels were rattling through the leaves. It was a picture of exquisite beauty and peace. The crisp air smelled of new beginnings, of joy coming in the morning.

John found no peg upon which to hang the morbid residue of his dream and shrugged off the ominous portent he had seen in the depths of the spring. The future seemed hopeful in that moment, and his heart was pulsing with anticipation.

They returned to the fire. Ian served up eggs, bacon, and buttered bread on paper plates. He poured John a cup of black coffee.

"You'll make somebody a good wife," John said.

Ian sneered at the comment; he had always seemed a little sensitive about his masculinity when compared with John. As they finished breakfast, Ian collected the trash and burned it in the fire. He took the utensils to the stream, scrubbed them with sand, and rinsed them clean. When he had done that, he retrieved the book and the map from the car and returned to the fire. John was leaning against a log, his face irradiated by the morning sun, luxuriating in its warmth.

He sat up. "All right. Let's decide what we're going to do."

Ian spread out the map onto the tarp they were sitting on.

"Here we are." John pointed at their location on the map with a stick. "Here's the ridge. And the cave is somewhere north of the trail." He traced a line. "But we don't know how far. There's this X. But we don't know if that's the cave entry. The ridge is two miles long. The opening could be anywhere."

Though the narrative in the book offered no clue how far the cave might be along the ridge, there was the mysterious "X" on the map at a point about a half-mile east of the trail.

"What do you think this X means?" John asked.

"It was Frederick's book, right? His name's in it. I think he drove to Rolla, found the author, and got him to mark the cave site." Ian shrugged. "But, how accurate could the mark be? Years could have passed since the author saw the opening. Anyway, Frederick Evans probably never found the cave. I'm thinking he left the map and the book so we, or somebody, could find his relative, his brother probably. He's the lost man. I have the feeling we're supposed to find Wilbur."

Ian as much as said he believed there was some moral purpose at work that overrode the explicit prohibitions of their parents. This was to John's advantage in motivating Ian to undertake this adventure.

John nodded. "That's the best explanation. And I hope you're right. It's going be hard enough to find it, even if it's at the X. But if it's not, we may never find it. The author said he was within a few feet of the opening before he came across it, and it almost cost him his life."

John looked up the side of the hill into the trees, chewing his lip. "All right," he said, "we'll find brother Wilbur. Here's the plan. We pack up the camp like we're going home. Leave no sign we were here. Burn all the trash. Scatter and cover the ashes and evidence of the fire. Pack everything out. We start the search from the top of the ridge. We follow it east. I'm not sure we ought to pack everything with us. Let's find the opening before we take everything. But we should carry all the rope, our lights, and some stuff for the backpacks so we can go in for a quick look before getting everything to the bottom. Does that sound good to you?"

Ian nodded. "You want me to reread the account; see if we missed anything?"

"Sure. One more time."

Ian opened the book to the passage.

John leaned against a log, his eyes closed, and he waited. But Ian was silent. "Well, are you going to read?"

"I've been feeling so strange, John. Sometimes I feel like I'm dreaming. I'm in darkness. It makes no difference if my eyes are open or closed. I put out my hand and touch something scary." His voice was small.

"What do you think that means?"

Ian shook his head. "I don't know, but I'm afraid, John."

"I've had a bad dream too. Let's not make too much out of it." John studied his brother's face. "Mom says we're 'old souls.' Two professors don't raise normal kids, do they?" John gently elbowed his brother in the ribs.

"What am I seeing, John? What's going to happen?" Ian wouldn't be distracted.

John shrugged. "Hamlet says, 'There are more things in heaven and earth, Horatio, than are dreamt of in your philosophy.' I know the book answer. You know where you're going when you die, don't you? There's no need to be afraid. You believe that, don't you?"

Ian nodded. "I do. It wasn't chance that we found the book and the map, was it? We were supposed to find them, right? And if that's so, then God brought us here. Is that right?"

John looked away to the dying ashes in the fire and shrugged. "I don't know, Ian." John could quote Scripture, but he no longer believed it as he once had. He had lost the ability to pray about what they were doing, to feel any assurance that what he was doing was prudent, let alone safe and moral. He was sensing the outer current of a whirlpool, still resistible. But without immediate and decisive action, he believed it would suck him into the vortex. Something was driving him forward in defiance of an inner witness and his better judgment.

CHAPTER 6

The Cavern Measureless to Man

John sat beside the embers of the fire, looking up the tree-covered hillside. Did the car have enough power to climb the grade, and with bald tires? They had packed the car and turned it around; they were ready to go. But they continued to sit on a log looking up the slope and at the bluff.

"Read it one more time," John said.

Ian opened the book and read:

I felt obligated to find Evans. Hiking along the ridge, I saw some food wrappers that convinced me he had gone this way, no doubt thinking it would be a short-cut to the highway. The damp earthy smell of a cave was strong as I came upon the entry. If I had not caught hold of a tree, I would have fallen in. The evidence was clear. Someone had recently fallen into the opening. I am certain this is the tomb of Wilbur Evans. (I advised his next of kin.) Entry into this cavern at this point would require sophisticated equipment. I estimate its depth at 100 feet, based on the time it took heavy rocks to hit the floor. It is probably deeper since the opening is a ceiling collapse that always produces a cone of debris. I do not believe there is a natural opening anywhere.

Ian closed the book. "And that's all we know."

"Okay, we've got a job to do." John got up, brushed grass and dirt from his jeans. "Let's go find Wilbur Evans."

Two hours later, on the ridgeline, the fragrance of sycamore trees was heavy in the stagnant morning air. John and Ian clawed chigger bites, rubbed scratches from blackberry brambles, and wiped stinging sweat from their eyes. Under his breath John cursed the author of *The Wild Caves of Missouri* for sending them on a wild goose chase.

They tramped parallel, fifty feet apart. On their backs, they carried heavy packs, and over their shoulders were long coils of rope. Hooked to their belts were six-volt dry-cell lights.

"Do you smell that?" Ian called to John. He had gotten a powerful whiff of a damp earthen odor like wet limestone.

"Stand still!" John's heartbeat quickened. "Don't move. Wait until I get to you."

With Ian holding on to John's pack strap, they moved forward step-by-step through the brush until they were within a foot of a vertical fissure. There was no evidence of its presence in the surrounding woods. They backed away and unburdened themselves. They clung to trees on the edge of the precipice, straining to peer down into the black opening.

"Okay, I'm ready to go home now." Ian was wringing his hands, licking his lips, and moaning.

John threw rocks into the opening. The stones vanished silently into the dark. He turned to Ian. "We can do this."

"Do you think so, John? You know this isn't smart."

"We can do it. How many times did we practice the descent and ascent in the trees behind the house? Fifty times? A hundred?"

"Yes, in daylight. I could see, and we were safe. I have to go into the dark first."

"That's because I can pull you out if I have to, but you can't pull me out, can you? It's the only way."

They had practiced rappelling in the 80-foot-high water oak in the backyard. Their mother used to watch them with wonder, skeptical of their explanation for what they were doing. And the precocious blond-haired girl next door didn't believe their explanations at all. Her name was Christine Charis and, according to her, she was going to marry John Malik. Every day that they were in the trees she watched them closely. Her presence and piercing insight was a distraction to John.

John thought of Christine just now as he prepared himself to undertake a deliberate and dangerous act of defiance of his parents and perhaps even God. There was a point of no return, and he was about to pass beyond it.

"We came here to do this. Let's do it." John took Ian by the shoulders and looked him straight in the eyes. "You want to see what nobody else has ever seen, don't you?"

Ian looked away from John. He stopped shuddering for the moment and nodded. "If you say so. My life is in your hands."

John stared at Ian for long seconds. Strapped to Ian's belt was a 6-volt dry cell light. He wore jeans, hiking boots, and a red flannel shirt. In the face of such a tremendous feat, he looked so small, so young.

"Like we practiced," John said, holding Ian again by the shoulders. "I lower you to the floor of the cave. You do a brief survey and return to the rope. Tie yourself to the rope and shake it. I pull you out." He gestured to the tree. "I pull, take up the slack, and I bring you up. It's easy. Questions?"

Ian shook his head, no. He furrowed his brow; sweat streamed down his face.

"Put your gloves on. Get your harness and pack on." John wrapped the rope around a tree and tied the end around Ian's waist. He checked his watch, 11 a.m. "Ready?"

Ian nodded. His eyes were wide. John had one last chance to keep this from happening. But he didn't take it.

Ian gripped the rope and took a deep breath. He turned his back to the opening, stiffened his legs, and nodded to John. Ian picked his way back into the steep fissure as John paid out the rope, urging it to release from the bark of the tree. Ian leaned back against the rope and placed one foot below the other. John could see his legs bouncing.

Ian descended into the mouth of the crevice on a 60-degree slope. The walls were slick with seeps of water that nurtured velvety moss and ferns. He fended himself off the rock and placed his entire weight on the rope, dangling in a beam of sunlight, moaning. John stopped his descent and held him still. He watched him, a black and white contrast in a shaft of sunlight, twisting on the rope.

Ian reared his head back on every rotation of the rope as he came face-to-face with the crevice wall that was alive with daddy longlegs and other insects working in the piles of soggy decay. He was afraid of copperheads lying in such places and said as much in a falsetto voice.

John wrapped another line around himself and leaned out above Ian, who was 30 feet down, approaching the dark void.

"Stop," Ian called. He pulled up the light dangling from his belt, turned it on, and aimed it into the dark. "I can't see anything, John. We may need the extra rope. You won't be able to hear me once I get below the ceiling."

"I'll figure something out. I won't lower you into water."

John resumed paying out the line and watched Ian disappear. Pebbles and other debris, dislodged by the rope, rained down into the opening. Slowly, chafing around the bark of the tree, the rope paid out. It disappeared in the darkness, rigid, vibrating. Then it went slack. Ian had touched down. John rappelled thirty feet into the fissure and spread-eagled over the opening.

He heard Ian scream from below. "What are you doing? If you fall in, we're both dead!" His words were volleys of echoes.

"I won't fall. Are you okay?" John hollered.

"I'm alive. I ... am ... not ... okay!"

"This is more fun than mowing yards, isn't it?" He watched Ian's light beam pan across a boulder-strewn landscape as he worked his way down the shoulder of a high cone of ceiling-collapse.

"I wish I was mowing yards right now. I'm going to look at something over there," He pointed with his light. "I ... will ... be ... right ... back."

CHAPTER 7

Down to a Sunless Sea

But Ian didn't come back. The sun had moved well past the zenith and was now low in the west. John held his brother's lifeline, waiting to feel a tug that he now feared would not come. He was sick to his stomach. No one knew where they were. His head spun when he thought of this. Several times he had to lie down on an incline with his head below his feet to combat symptoms of shock.

When the shadows of the afternoon sun were long, and the cloudless sky had turned indigo, John began lowering himself into the cave, more afraid than he had ever been in his life.

He reached the floor and looked up, astonished by the great height of the opening. He listened to the drips of water that fell silent from the great height hitting the rock with a splat. The air smelled of rock and earth imparting an overpowering sense of loneliness, sensing the void's indifference to his presence. The opening above was a portal to an unreachable world.

As he looked up, he thought of the parable Jesus taught of the rich man and the beggar Lazarus. When Lazarus died, the rich man looked up to heaven from his torment in Hades and cried out in anguish. Fixed between himself and Lazarus was a chasm impossible to cross.

John's plan for climbing out had been utterly unrealistic. He realized they could not get out this way. And the author of the cursed book believed there was no other way out.

John turned away from his study of the ceiling and began his search for Ian. The void was huge, but where was the river that had made this vast passage? He plodded over treacherous rockfall from one side-passage to another, calling and listening. He explored a short way in each of several channels, only to turn back to the entry room to reorient himself. He could not gauge the passing of time. The sound of his voice was a screech of terror, mocked by inhuman echoes rebounding from the walls. Shuddering from cold and fear and exhaustion, he repeatedly found his way back into the entry room.

Again, he looked up to the opening, now a faint glow in the faraway ceiling through which he had come. He followed the trajectory that falling things would have followed to the mound of rock that was once part of the ceiling. Upon the slope he saw a tuft of red flannel in his light beam. Climbing up onto the mound, he found the lost man, surely the remains of Wilbur Evans. His body parts had cascaded over yards in a trail of shattered bones and a battered skull; the flesh was long gone.

And now there were three lost men.

He climbed back down. Setting his light at his feet, he took hold of the two lines of rope that passed around the trunk of the tree far above. Lost in a morbid reverie, he cursed himself for his stupidity. He jerked on the two parallel lines that extended out of sight through the ceiling. He pulled the lines up and down mindlessly, as though milking a cow. Then one line slipped from his grip as he gave a jerk to the other.

To his horror, the short end shot up just out of his reach. It hovered, wiggled, and moved upward faster and faster toward the ceiling. Within twenty seconds, the rope had slithered around the tree above, and the entire 300 feet of it had come tumbling down into a pile beside him.

He screamed again and again until no sound came from his throat. The volleys of his words became a ghoulish inhuman mockery that resounded through a madhouse.

He could not tell how long he sat upon a boulder, staring in the dark at where he had last seen the pile of rope. Time had little measure in the dark, and his mind was blank, inert. But his awareness did return. He stood, switched on his light, and began trudging through yet another succession of torturous passageways, stumbling and falling on the slick rockfall.

Fine sticky clay coated everything with a shiny glaze. It bonded to his boots in ever-enlarging clumps. He bruised his knees and hands in several falls, and his ankles were aching from being twisted. Then he fell again and crushed his watch against his wrist, freezing time at 9:22 p.m. As he extricated his mangled hand from among the jagged stones, he realized that if he smashed the light, all hope would fail. He had to protect the light at all costs.

The time dragged on, and the specter of death began to dog his steps. When the light failed, he would die. He would wither away, groping insane and blind in a vast tomb. What would his mind do to him?

A long indifferent expanse of time had passed before the forces of the earth had carved this void. There would have been no perceptible change for eons until the ceiling collapsed in a matter of seconds, and the cave opened its eyes to the world.

It was clear that a vast river once flowed through these corridors of stone. It had carved the walls and then receded from this level. Perhaps there were channels below where John stood, a level where the river still flowed and gave rise to the spring beside which they had camped with such expectation in another life.

The sun had set long ago, and the dark fissure in the ceiling revealed neither moon nor stars. He pondered their destiny. John and Ian Malik had disappeared. The car was never found. Their parents would search for them for years, their grief unresolved until they gave up and consigned them to memory.

John dug a sandwich from his knapsack, ate it, and washed it down with water from a canteen. His head cleared a little. Rummaging in the pack again, he hung his head when he discovered that he had left his spare battery in the car. In despair he raised his arms and screamed at God, pleading for deliverance or peace.

But there was no resonance. John Malik had defied God. He had silenced his own inner witness and willfully disobeyed his parents. He was jealous of his brother and bitter toward his parents. And now God had turned His back to him. Wasn't it better to believe God did not exist … that oblivion awaited him and not hell?

* * *

John once again panned his light across the walls in the main chamber. Where could Ian have gone? Then the beam vanished into an opening he had not seen before. Picking his way over the treacherous floor, he leaned down to inspect a passage as smooth as a lava tunnel, the conduit of an ancient torrent of water. He waddled into the opening and aimed his light down the steeply inclined passage. The beam had no return.

Before John could turn around, his feet went out from under him, he fell onto his backside, and he began a downward slide, scrambling for a handhold. His light banged against the narrow walls as he struggled to get onto his feet to stop his uncontrolled screaming descent.

Then he was in mid-air, falling head-over-heels in a breathtaking plunge. He hit the surface of a deep body of water and sent up a plume into a space that enclosed an underground sea.

He sank into the frigid cold, slashing his light through the depths. His downward plunge slowed, and he rose. He struggled against the weight of mud-caked boots and clothes until he clawed to the surface, the light still in his hand. Ahead was a ledge. He reached for it and felt himself being dragged onto it.

John lay on the shelf of stone, gasping and coughing. When he was able, he lifted his head. Ian tottered before him, blinking in the light.

"Well, where in the hell have you been?" Ian demanded, looking equally as if he wanted to punch John and hug him.

Then, just as quickly, a wave of hysteria overcame them. They laughed until their stomach muscles cramped. Finally, exhausted, they listened to the echoes of their insane howls dying away in the hiss of a distant waterfall.

* * *

The brothers sat shoulder-to-shoulder, blinking in the darkness. Ian was shuddering so hard John had to hold him tightly to still the convulsions. Ian's body heat was ebbing away.

"Are you hurt?" John asked.

"I don't think so .... But I died, John. I was watching my body. When you fell into the lake, I was alive again."

"You were hallucinating."

"No, I saw what's going to happen. I'm as good as dead."

"Don't talk like that. Stop it!" John screamed and shook him. "Stop it!" He hugged Ian. Tears rolled down both boys' cheeks. John breathed onto Ian's neck and face, trying to warm him up. "You will not die. We will find a way out."

John switched on the light. "There. See? That's the way out." He pointed the beam along the wall, tracing a stone shelf along the margin of the lake. It appeared to continue along the river that flowed from the lake at the very limit of the light beam. "The water is flowing that way. Get on your feet; get the blood flowing."

"If you say so, John. But you can't save me. This is where I will die."

"Don't give up, brother. I love you, Ian. I'm so sorry I got you into this."

"No hard feelings, John. I would have followed you anywhere. I'm proud to have been your brother."

John turned away. Minutes passed as he composed himself. "All right, on your feet."

Ian staggered to his feet. "I'm so cold, John."

They inched their way along the slippery shelf of stone, one step at a time. They had gone a hundred precarious yards when they looked around a bend. A winding river channel continued with a shelf along the edge as far as the light revealed.

They made slow and painful progress, testing every step on the ledge, bracing themselves against a fall into the deep moving water, fearful of seeing the first flicker of a failing light beam. Only their breathing and the scuffing of their feet now disturbed the utter silence of the confined space. A hemisphere of eerie illumination lit the walls of the narrowing channel.

Around an upcoming bend, the river would dive beneath the rock. Or the ledge would end. They could not get back to the lake before the light failed. And why would they go back?

The light was fading. John banged it every few minutes to restore its intensity. He wanted hypothermia to take them both before they went mad. Better to die with Ian than to die alone.

John stopped. Ian stopped behind him and braced himself against the wall. "What time is it?"

Ian opened his eyes, tilted his watch to catch the light. "Midnight." He was swaying, his speech labored. "Look," he yawned and pointed. "The wall."

Ian slumped down onto the three-foot-wide stone shelf and huddled against the wall. John forced him to take off his shirt. John took off his own shirt and pulled Ian against him. Ian's shuddering subsided, but his body was cold, very cold. He was evidently in the final stages of hypothermia.

John held Ian, rocking him gently as they sat on the cold hard stone that was draining their body heat. He was staring at the far wall of the channel in the feeble yellow glow of the light when it finally went out. Now in the utter darkness he could feel his slowing heartbeat and his body growing colder. He smelled the glistening limestone. He could sense the flow of deep water moving silently at his feet. And by some gift of grace, he accepted his imminent death.

* * *

Hours passed as he grew colder. He finally opened his eyes to see a glow from the river illuminating the channel. He grabbed Ian's wrist and read the time on his watch, evidently 6 a.m.

Ian opened his eyes blinking. "What's that?"

John struggled to his feet. "That's the way out, Ian!"

At the bottom of the river, light was coming through a hole thirty feet down.

CHAPTER 8
The Living and the Dead

John squatted down beside Ian and placed his hands against Ian's face. He was as cold as a corpse. "Listen to me, Ian. There is only one way out. It's down there." John nodded toward the hole at the bottom of the river. "You have to get up and do this. You cannot stay here."

Ian's head was drooped, his chin resting on his chest. He struggled to speak in a whisper, "John, I can't even stand … you go … I'll be alright … so sleepy. I just want to go to sleep …. I told you I was dead already. And I don't want to be here anymore …. Please accept that."

John turned away, lowered his head, and pressed his knuckles against his teeth. "Even if I live through this, God will never forgive me for what I have done," John whispered. He turned to Ian. "How can you forgive me for what I have done to you?"

"Not your fault …. Don't believe it." His words slurred, barely audible.

"Ian, you just can't stay here. You have to try. Even if I could get out and find help, there's no way to get back in here. And you don't have much time. You have to follow me …. Please, Ian! Don't die in here. Please, God, don't leave him in here!"

But Ian could not move. His head lolled to the side, staring blankly into the water. His breath was coming in shallow puffs. He was as good as dead.

John got to his feet, clenching and unclenching his fists. He pulled off his boots, tied the laces together, and draped them around his neck. He began heaving deep breaths and blowing them out. Light-headed, his face streaked with tears, and contorted with agony, John arched his back for a maximum lung-full of air and dove into the shock of the frigid river.

* * *

John was observing himself stroking down, pinching his nose to equalize the pressure. Then he was reaching out for the rock as he approached the opening, deeper than he had ever dived. His chest heaving for air, John looked up for an instant then turned and entered the opening. The current swept him away leaving Ian to die alone in the dark.

John's belly scraped along the rock, and his head knocked against the walls as he tried to fend himself off the confines of the narrow passageway against the force of the current. His eyes were bulging. Panic welled up in his chest. As he was about to open his mouth and draw a fatal breath the channel made a sharp turn, and an opening appeared. John clawed through it. Sunlight and trees mirrored on the surface above him.

He stroked with all his strength and broke through the surface, shrieking for air. For long seconds he heaved for air before stroking for the edge of the pool, where he dragged himself up onto a large flat rock beside the spring and collapsed. Five minutes passed before he recovered his breath and struggled to his knees and began to pray, begging God to bring his brother through.

Minutes became an hour. The bright morning sunlight that warmed him was incongruous with his vision of Ian languishing, fading away, dying in the cold where no one would ever find him.

John continued to stare at the hole at the bottom of the spring, pleading with God. The sun had moved an hour through the limbs of the sycamores when he blinked to confirm what he was seeing. A dark form appeared in the opening, drifting up slowly on the current, hair floating—his little brother.

Lifeless.

John leaped into the water, pulled Ian to the surface, turned him on his back and dragged him out onto the rock. Frantically he began alternately pumping Ian's chest and breathing into his mouth. For a long time, he compressed the lifeless form and inflated its lungs. But it was fruitless. Ian was long dead.

John cradled the cold body, staring at nothingness while the sun continued its ascent to the zenith and beyond. When a coherent thought passed through his consciousness, it was that God had not answered him. God had allowed Ian to die. John released his brother's body and stood up. Looking up into the blue sky he clenched his fists, and, with deliberation, he turned his back to God.

John pulled on and laced his boots then hefted his brother's body over his shoulder. He staggered along the creek then struggled up the slope to the car. When he reached the car, he laid Ian gently on the back seat, placed his hand against his brother's gray cheek, and smoothed his hair.

Then John started the car and made his way to Highway 60. From that point, he stared straight ahead 150 miles, conscious only of the story he would tell about what had happened. The hours passed, and it was evening.

With dread reaching a crescendo, he turned into the driveway at the house on Barnes Street. He turned off the ignition. Summoning all his courage and strength, he got out, dragged the body out of the back seat, and lifted it in his arms. Stumbling up the steps of the porch, he reached the screen door, got it open with his foot, and edged the body through the door. The screen door slammed behind him as he staggered in with Ian in his arms and lay him gently on the couch.

His mother, Claire, coming in from the back yard, recognized in an instant that Ian was dead and screamed. John turned away from the horror of her expression as she fell on her knees and embraced her son.

"Oh, my dear God!" she pleaded, blubbering through tears, "Don't let this be! Bring him back to me, Savior. Don't take my baby. I have no life without him." She looked up, pleading toward the ceiling, her hands outstretched. "Strike *me* dead, God. Not my baby boy."

Her shrieks subsided to unabated sobs as she cradled the cold body, talking to him in tender terms, kissing his cold, lifeless face. "What a joy you have been to me, my dear one. You were the light of my life, the tenderest part of my being, my hope."

An hour of exhausting grief ended in sullen silence and resignation. Claire got up off her knees, staggered into the kitchen, and sat down at the table opposite John.

"What happened that my son is dead, and you're alive?"

John swallowed, unable to look her in the eyes. "We were camped on the James River," he said, looking down at his folded hands. "Ian went down to the river to fish while I was building a fire. He must have slipped and fallen into a deep eddy. I saw where it must have happened and searched for hours along the bank until I found him against a log jam."

There was a long silence while Claire stared at John. "My husband will be home soon. We should wait to call the police and whoever else we're supposed to notify when someone dies. They'll probably want to know why you didn't call them to the river. But it doesn't matter, I guess."

"I'm so sorry, Mom. I wish it had been me. You wouldn't have felt so bad."

Her voice hissing, her words venomous, she leaned forward and said, "How many times did I tell you, boy? You were your brother's keeper. You were his guardian. And now our music is dead. Ian was the only bond that held this family together. You don't get that, do you? You don't know what this means, do you?"

John raised his eyes to look at her. "I'm so sorry, Mom. I didn't know."

She gritted her teeth so hard the veins in her neck pulsed. "Believe me when I say this—I hate you. I wish I'd flushed you down the toilet while I could. I wish I never had to speak your name again as long as I live."

John's eyes widened, pleading, his mind going faint. Her words were like repeated dagger blows; Caesar being assassinated by the one who loved him. "Mom, you can't mean that!" he screamed.

"Don't tell me what I mean, you bastard!"

There was a long pause as John held his head in his hands, weeping.

She tilted her head in a taunting expression. "You're a bastard. You didn't know that, did you? I had an affair with a man who was too good for me. He left me with you. And now you exist, my ever-living accuser before my husband. And this husband of mine is nothing beside the man I once had for a time, your father. Don't speak to me of logic or why it isn't your fault. You do not exist as a person for me. You are the embodiment of my sin, and I hate you with all of my soul."

The whirlpool had drawn him irretrievably in the spinning vortex. Claire got up from the table. She walked down the hall to her bedroom. He heard her slam the door and heard the door lock with a sense of finality.

Barely conscious, he opened his eyes, his gaze fixed at a point on the wall behind where his mother had been sitting. It was a red stain on the wallpaper where his "father" had thrown a plate of spaghetti against the wall. That stain was John's fault somehow. Now he understood why.

Who was John Malik? Why was he alive? Would he ever discover who his father was? Did his father know that he existed? Did his father love him? Did anyone love him?

PART III:

LIVING ON BARNES STREET

CHAPTER 9

Cry of the Loon

One Month Later

The house on Barnes Street sat two blocks behind the Kraft cheese factory and two miles from Consumer's Gas Station where John worked. He walked to work. He had no car, nor was he likely to get one. The math didn't work out. Paying half of what he made for room and board didn't leave enough to finance a car.

When he plodded down the last block on Barnes that evening and walked up the driveway, he found the manual push mower sitting on the front walk with the rake leaning against the handle. He set about mowing the yard and raking the clippings, adding another hour to his workday.

In former times, his mom would have welcomed him home with a plate of food and a pitcher of tea. But life was different now. He did not feel comfortable going inside the house. Plus, he smelled sweaty, and grease, oil, and grass clippings stained his pants.

When he finished with the yard, he sat down on the porch, his back against the clapboard wall, knees drawn up to his chest, his forehead resting on his knees. His six-month-old Jack Russell terrier, Socrates, lay beside him, paws extended, head lying on the wooden floor, eyes sad and forlorn.

John was exhausted. His 12-hour shift at Consumer's gas station had started at 6 a.m. It had been a long hot day, and he had eaten nothing.

He wished himself dead, pondering again the best way to take his life. How could he survive?

The cry of a loon drifted across a lake at twilight, a memory or vision as vivid as though John were standing beside the black lake waters in deepening shadows. He heard the cry and resonated with the unearthly voice so full of loneliness. The loon would have been his totem if he had been born an Indian. It was a forlorn solitary creature that seems to live only on the edge of night. That's where he now lived, on the edge of where other people lived, somewhere between light and darkness. He believed himself alienated from God and man; he would never again experience the warmth of human kindness and love. He deserved this fate.

The evening light was fading. He lifted his head to gaze at the twilight of the Indian summer day. Cicadas buzzed in the trees, shadows grew long, and fireflies blinked across the fragrant mown yard. He had happy memories of evenings like this when the family laughed and sang on the porch and ate watermelon and homemade ice cream. Ian would play his guitar and his harmonica.

One month had passed since John had returned from Lost Man's Cave with Ian's corpse. No one knew what John had done, except possibly Christine Charis. And she couldn't know for sure. Heartache piled upon heartache the day his mother sold the piano, packed up Ian's instruments, including his guitar, and got rid of them.

The window behind John on the porch was open. He heard his folks walking softly in the darkened house, speaking with forced civility in subdued tones, and only when necessary. The darkened house entombed a onetime love. Jealousy, wrath, sorrow, remorse, and unforgiveness had driven out love and joy.

In the fading light, John looked at the dense thicket across the street, wondering if there didn't used to be an old house over there, a ruin hidden behind the high grove of impenetrable thorns. Uneasy, he looked away, his eyes drawn to the house next door.

It sat forward of John's house; the front porch was a hundred feet closer to the street. He saw Christine Charis as she came out on her porch, jumped down, and walked toward the fence in a manner that could only be described as sultry.

She got down on her back and wiggled under the barbed wire fence, dusted herself off, and walked toward John. A paradox, a woman in a girl's body. Her shoulder-length blond hair, freed from its usual ponytail, shimmered like gold in the fading light.

For the first time, he recognized that she was physically precocious. Unease came over him, and a thrill pulsed through his body, catalyzed with guilt for seeing her in this way.

She gazed at him unblinking as she walked up on the porch. Yes, she was precocious.

"What are you doing?" she asked. She sat down on the swing.

"Watching the fireflies."

"Come here, Johnny." She patted the seat beside her.

"I smell bad." He wasn't exaggerating.

"I don't care."

John slowly got to his feet and sat down a respectful distance from her. The chains creaked as they coordinated their efforts and swung. They listened to the cicadas buzzing in the elms for a few minutes. John's heartbeat and breathing were rapid. She was radioactive. He took deep breaths. It didn't help. She was 14 years old, for crying out loud.

"Are you going to tell me what happened, Johnny?"

"I already told you I don't want to talk about it. It's not your business."

"It *is* my business. *You* are my business," she said. "When you hurt, I hurt."

"What? Since when?"

"Since the first time I saw you."

The words stunned him. Her words were like a cool drink of water to someone dying of thirst. He was famished for affection, for human touch, for a word of encouragement, for a single soul to care if he lived or died. He was wound up as tight as a cheap watch spring just before it snaps.

Beautiful, flawless, unaware of herself, that was Christine Charis. Her gaze was fixed on him. He inhaled her aromas from two feet away. In the three years, he had known her, he had never seen her as he saw her now, as she would become.

"You're fourteen now, is that right?" his voice unsteady.

"Going on fifteen. But don't let that fool you, Johnny. I'm mature for my age. When you turn twenty-one, I'll be nineteen. You have to wait for me because God has told me that you and I will be together." She furrowed her brow and put her hand on his leg. He flinched as though it had shocked him.

"You're claiming God told you this?"

"That's what I said. Am I not speaking plainly? It will happen. I know how you're hurting powerfully because I feel what you feel." She appeared to be looking deep into his soul. "I *love* you, Johnny, and always will. Please be well."

He returned her gaze. His lower lip quivered, then he lowered his head and convulsed into sobs. "How can you love me? I'm not worth loving. I'm worth nothing. I wish I had never been born."

Christine scooted over beside him, put her arm around him, and drew his head to her shoulder. "You are worth loving. I love you, Johnny. That makes you a person of worth. I can't help that I love you. I just do. And God can fix you, Johnny. He will."

John shuddered as he pulled back to look at her. Tears streamed down her face now. She leaned closer, her breath like peppermint, her hair like flowers, her wet eyes brilliant pools of light.

"God has left me," he sobbed. "He has turned His back on me."

"Don't believe that, Johnny. It's not true." As she leaned toward him, she whispered, "Kiss me, Johnny. Please kiss me and let me take your pain away."

In an instant, passion drenched him; he reeled with delirium. The pendulum swung in several heartbeats from mortal stress to passion. As their lips met in hard hungry contact, a thrill went through his body that empowered him to live. In that instant, he merged with another human, entwined, hungry, breathing each other's breath, their souls merged.

The screen door slammed open. John broke away from Christine and looked up in alarm. His dad strode toward him, nostrils flaring, face red, jaw clenched. He reached out and grabbed John by the hair of his head and shook him violently, then pulled him off the swing and dragged him by the hair into the house, calling over his shoulder, "Get home, girl! And don't come back! You better hope I don't tell your father what this boy has done."

Once in the living room, his dad shoved John down the hallway. "Get to your room and out of my sight, you pervert. And don't expect to eat at my table until further notice. You disgust me."

His mother sat on the couch, her legs crossed, her hands folded in her lap, watching.

* * *

John sat on the desk chair in his bedroom, staring in the darkness at nothing. He sat there for hours, wicking the serum and blood from his scalp into a handkerchief. The indignation of being shook and dragged by the hair in front of Christine had brought John so low. Did she still love him after seeing him dehumanized like that?

Something awakened him from his morbid reflection. He went to the window and looked toward Christine's bedroom window, remembering that she used to watch his window. He thought nothing of it until now. Now he craved her like an addiction. Christine had saved him. She was the only person who cared if he hanged himself. And that's what he had resolved to do until she kissed him.

She was sitting at her window, staring at him, her silhouette backlit by the bedside lamp. They communed, hungry for each other. She infused him with the will to live, to endure for her.

"Live. Wait for me," she seemed to say.

He waved to her and saw her shadow wave back. Then her light went out.

From that day, both households forbade contact between them. Rutger Malik, John's father, would tell Christine's father many terrible things about the perverted boy who lived in the Malik house.

CHAPTER 10
Love and the Hornet

Four months later, snow lay like a downy comforter on the roofs of the neighborhood houses. Pillows of snow rested on fence posts and in the boughs of the trees. Soft contours reflected dimly in the moonless evening. It was silent until John lifted his feet and crunched the snow beneath his boots. He trudged out into the yard, puffing fog in the cold air, looking up at the shimmering stars and admiring his '49 Hudson Hornet.

In the cold clear starlight, John ran his hand along the front fender, his eyes caressing the shape of the most beautiful car he had ever seen, sculpted from the mind of a genius. He started the engine and sat dreaming, smelling the interior, stroking the cherrywood steering wheel.

The night air smelled of wood burning in fireplaces in the neighborhood. He saw smoke drifting across the stars. But he imagined himself elsewhere on a spring morning. He was driving down the street in front of school with throngs of students all looking at him in his spectacular Hornet. He would be somebody now.

* * *

Two days before, an extraordinary thing had happened before the snowfall. On that cold Saturday afternoon, while John was working at the gas station, two cars drove up. The manager called John inside and introduced him to Rachel Hixson and Everett Scheid. Mrs. Hixson was in her Sunday best hat, white gloves, and blocky heels. And the unsmiling Mr. Scheid, a notary, wore a black suit.

"John," Mrs. Hixson said, "I buried my Norbert last week. He told me on his deathbed something he had told me before. He wanted to give you his car." She pointed through the window to a glistening black '49 Hudson Hornet. "That was Norbert's pride and joy; he kept it in the barn and waxed it every month since he bought it new. He wanted me to tell you that you are the boy he wished we'd had for a son."

John was not processing her words. He stood dumbfounded with his mouth open. The old farmer was dead? The pickup wasn't the only vehicle he owned? This beautiful car was John's?

"Here are the keys. Sign here," she said, laying a document down on the manager's desk and pointing to an X at the bottom of the form. Her eyes were tearing.

John stared at her, slack-jawed, incredulous.

"I'm serious, John. Sign this, and it's yours." She pointed again to the document and held out a pen. "It's paid off. It's full of gas. I have paid the transfer fees and taxes and the insurance policy for one year."

Taking the pen, John leaned down and signed his name, then backed up and broke down weeping. He turned away.

Mrs. Hixson, smelling of mothballs and baby powder, walked over to him, put her arms around him, and held him close. Then she cried with him. "Norbert loved you so much," she whispered through her own tears. "There is something so special about you. You will do great things. Think of him when you drive your new car. We would have done more if we had the resources." She kissed John's cheek and backed off, still holding him by the shoulders.

"Why would he do such a thing?" John sobbed.

"God does wonderful things in people. You touched my Norbert's heart. You were polite; you listened to his stories, which he spent all week thinking up. Visiting with you gave him such delight. The slightest kindness can sometimes change a person's life. My Norbert planned all week, every week, to come and see you."

Mr. Scheid notarized the transfer of title and registration. Then he and Mrs. Hixson left with much waving and well-wishing.

John turned, teary-eyed, to look at his manager, who was beaming. "John, I don't want you parking your car in front. Park in the back." The manager's eyes were misty. "And good for you, John."

When he got off work that evening, John drove his new car down to Shoney's. He ordered the southern fried steak dinner with three sides and an extra side salad, drank three glasses of tea, and had strawberry shortcake for dessert.

When he wasn't looking out the window at his new car, he was grinning at the waitress. She came by several times with an inviting smile, flattered that someone had noticed her. He left her a big tip.

* * *

The star-lit snowscape was a silent witness of the precision of the Hornet's engine. It purred; the muffler rendered the exhaust into a manly baritone. The heater warmed up the interior. On the radio, Billy Williams was singing about writing himself a letter and imagining it came from his love. John luxuriated in the aroma of his Hornet. The Green Hornet, on the radio, drove the same car.

He looked again at Christine's bedroom window. Her shades were down, and her light off. Where was she at this hour? He sighed. She was simply too young for him, and he needed to banish the images of her from his imagination.

His hunger for intimacy was restless, mindless, a ravenous beast within him. Now John was lovesick over Margo Lancaster. The onset of this plague of desire occurred the moment Margo sashayed into algebra class on the first day of the fall semester. When she passed him, the world shifted on its axis.

*　*　*

Margo was the brightest star in the heavens. He identified her voice in the cafeteria amid hundreds of others. When she came near him, he inhaled the scent of roses, and his brain shifted into a hypnotic state.

He sat in the back of the algebra classroom. Margo sat in the front to his left. From this vantage, he continuously stared at her, paying little attention to Mrs. Cunningham, the math teacher. One day Mrs. Cunningham had had enough. She called him out in front of the class.

"Mr. Malik. You're not interested in algebra, are you?" she said.

John sat up. "Ma'am?"

"I've been introducing quadratic equations. Are you aware that I've been talking about this?"

"Yes, Ma'am."

"Based on what I've said, can you define a quadratic equation, Mr. Malik?"

He nodded. "Yes, Ma'am. I apologize if I've offended you. You're doing a great job."

The class snickered. She was not amused. With a piece of paper in her hand, she returned to the blackboard where she wrote out two quadratic equations, one above the other. Dusting her hands, she turned to look at John.

"Now, Mr. Malik. We've not dealt with simultaneous quadratics before. But you know how to solve them. I gather that since you do not need to follow what I'm saying and prefer to study Miss Lancaster while you're in my class."

Margo spun around to look at him, flashing indignation in her eyes. He looked away, mortified.

Mrs. Cunningham said, "So Mr. Malik, will you please solve these equations simultaneously? Where do they intersect?" She reached over and picked up a piece of chalk and held it out. "Come up here and show us how it's done."

John's face flushed. He put his palm against his cheek to drain the heat away. Margo fixed him with a lethal stare. The class was giggling and looking at him and Margo.

"Well, Mr. Malik? I'm waiting."

John cleared his throat. "The equations intersect at two points, X equals 6, Y equals minus 5, and at X equals minus 10, Y equals 18."

Mrs. Cunningham looked down at the piece of paper, her mouth open. She looked up at him. There was a long pause. "Yes, that's correct. It took me almost an hour to solve this. Did you solve this in your head?"

He nodded.

"Let me give you another problem." She wrote out another second-order equation. "At what point is the slope of this curve zero?"

"Dy, Dx is zero at X equals 5, Y equals minus 11. It's a parabola opening upward."

"How did you do that?"

"Ma'am, it's an elementary solution in differential calculus."

Mrs. Cunningham dropped the piece of chalk back into the tray. "Please accept my apologies, Mr. Malik, for embarrassing you. I would like to talk to you after class, or anytime that's convenient for you."

John lowered his head and nodded with a feeble smile. "Yes, Ma'am. Again, I apologize for not paying attention."

Margo turned in her seat to face the blackboard with a smoldering expression. Utter silence prevailed in the room; astonishment registered on every face. John resisted staring at Margo and appeared to be paying close attention in class from that day.

***

Margo's long black hair shimmered like sunlight reflecting off a gentle sea. And when she walked, her body moved with aching grace—even more remarkable for the subtlety of the movement. She was slender, had bright eyes, a devastating smile, and the bloom of vigorous youth glowed in her skin. She knew the power she had, but she didn't seem too stuck-up. John only watched from a distance. She looked at him sometimes, but she probably didn't remember his name. He was a nobody.

One gray overcast afternoon late in leafless February, as he plodded across the school parking lot, John looked up to see Margo in a cranberry-colored sweater, standing beside his Hornet.

Suddenly conscious of his walk, his legs stiffened, certain he looked like the Frankenstein monster staggering toward her.

"Hello, Margo." He stared at the ground. He had never spoken to her before.

"Hello to you, John Malik. I want you to take me to the drive-in Saturday night. I'm tired of waiting for you to ask me. Here's my number. Pick me up at 6:30." She handed him a slip of paper and cocked her head, waiting for him to comprehend.

He looked up. Then, without waiting for a reply, she turned and walked off to join two other popular girls standing nearby. They were giggling.

***

John had driven by Margo's house a hundred times. He had spared no effort in his preparations, smelling of Old Spice and wearing a new plaid sweater. The Hornet glistened like onyx, and beside him, on the seat, lay a rose and a box of Whitman's Sampler chocolates.

Of the two drive-ins in town, John picked the Sunset, where, in his opinion, the two best pictures of the decade were both playing. Margo agreed over the phone that *The Mummy* and *The Day the Earth*

Stood Still were excellent choices. He felt his face flush when she said that.

He pulled to a stop in front of Margo's house and got out, rubbing his sweaty palms on his jeans all the way to the door. As luck would have it, an enormous man opened the door, Margo's father. Try as he might, John could not utter a sound. The man engulfed the doorknob in one massive fist. In the other hand, he gripped a rolled-up newspaper and appeared about to swat John with it.

"What do you want?"

"Uh, I, uh," John bobbed his head while attempting to speak, afraid Mr. Lancaster would brain him with the newspaper. Before he had to say anything, Margo bounded down the stairs in a green sweater and jeans.

"He's here for me, Daddy," she said in mild rebuke and stretched up to kiss his cheek.

The man grunted and glared at John as though he had read John's mind. "You be in early," he growled to his daughter without taking his eyes off John.

"Of course, Daddy," she said, smiling at John. John backed up, rubbing his hands on his jeans, and looking up at the man.

Margo skipped along the walk beside John. Her buoyant spirit lifted him to new heights of admiration. She slid into the car from the driver's side and settled beside John. He looked toward the front door of her house. Her father peered out through the side window with a ferocious scowl.

John fumbled with the ignition, and the engine whirred to life. As he ground the shift lever into first gear, his right elbow brushed against Margo's left breast. He almost swooned. This first-of-its-kind experience set off a buzzing in his brain that made him forget where to turn. She reminded him.

John parked on the second-to-the-back row at the Sunset, as Margo directed. The previews had just begun. She ate one of the Whitman Sampler chocolates and said she would wait until the intermission for popcorn.

John squirmed and perspired. Drunk with Margo's aroma, he worked his tongue against his lips. First, they were too dry, then too wet, then he was so aware of his lips he could focus on nothing else. They had to be just right.

When *The Mummy* began, he twisted around and tried to kiss her. But she pushed him away, slapped him, and slid away to the far side of the seat. She folded her arms and stared at the movie screen.

What did he know about women? Since Ian's death and the revelation of his illegitimacy, John had withdrawn from all his old friends and become sullen and reclusive. Everyone avoided him. But he had one confidant, an unlikely individual named Mikey. It was Mikey who told him that he should try to kiss a girl right away on a date so the girl wouldn't tell her friends he was a dud. Well, that didn't work with Margo.

"I'm so sorry," he said repeatedly.

"Will you please shut up? I'm trying to figure out what's going on in the movie."

After long agonizing minutes, she turned to him. "I'll take popcorn and a Coke now. And hurry, please."

He jogged to the refreshment stand and back. He handed her the cardboard tray and slid into the seat, compelled to apologize again. But as he settled in, Margo raised up, placed the tray on the back seat, and descended upon him, enfolding him with her arms. She pressed her lips onto his. He entered an altered state of consciousness.

* * *

When John got home from his job at Consumer's gas station on Saturday afternoons, he had to steer through the rapids of latent hostility that created continual turbulence in the household. While his folks weren't interested in what he did, he offered that he had a date that night. The conversation around the dinner table was at least civil, if icy.

His mother knew of his obsession with Margo. While indifferent to his issues, she pointed out that he was setting himself up for heartache. He had exhausted multitudes of fads, including model airplanes, slingshots, pellet guns, stamp collecting, playing chess, cuneiform texts—and those were just the recent things before Ian's death. He still had the ant farm. But now he focused on philosophy.

John was an academic prodigy, like several recognized geniuses on his mother's side including John's second cousin, Leonidas Riley. But his mother observed that John did not understand people, and he'd better toughen up, for his own good. Her husband, the only father John had ever known, had nothing to say to him.

Margo raised him to heights of joy during their Saturday nights at the drive-in. But come Sunday afternoon, after church, she dropped him into the depths of despair. She didn't care if he came over or not. And Mr. Lancaster's presence terrorized him.

Sometimes she showered him with affection. At other times, she didn't want him to touch her. He worried he was losing her. Her circle of friends was so important to her, and they didn't relate to him. She refused to have anything to do with John's limited circle of friends. She was astonished that John acknowledged Mikey's existence.

His fear of losing her was a self-fulfilling prophecy. By early May, Margo was becoming more and more distant. John gave God another chance and tried praying. Every night he pleaded with God to make Margo love him.

On a Friday, the fourth of April, he rounded a crowded corridor at school and saw Margo holding her books across her chest, leaning back against her locker, eyes twinkling, while Erick Tandy, the popular junior quarterback, nuzzled her ear through her mass of perfume-scented hair.

John didn't have a chance against Erick and his circle of friends. Margo and John had several emotional conversations on the phone that afternoon. And that evening, while he was on his knees in his bedroom pleading with God, the phone rang.

"John, it's over," she said. "I want you to come by and pick up your records and your sweater. I'm leaving them on the porch. If you don't want that stuff, I'll throw it out. Don't call me anymore."

"Christine! Give me another chance," he said, then touched his mouth with his fingers.

"What did you call me? Who's Christine?"

He stuttered.

"Oh, who cares? I don't have time for this. You may be a genius, but you're *so* immature!" She hung up for the last time.

CHAPTER 11
The Death of God

Aweek later, John sat leaning against a tree in the backyard, staring at the horizon, soul sick. His puppy Socrates lay with his head on John's lap, grieving with him. His room was chaos. He had tacked a sign on the door, *Do Not Enter* above a radioactive symbol. The complex ant colony he had kept in a huge glass pickle jar had subterranean passages visible against the glass. He lost all interest in their industry. He no longer poured Pepsi into their bottlecap. They starved. Now dehydrated husks, they lay on their backs with their legs sticking up.

He had watched the giant ants that got irradiated from a nuclear blast in the movie *Them!* The heartless monsters ate cattle and people and made a wreck of Los Angeles. It was the gratuitous property damage that irked John most. He now despised ants. Vicious creatures.

John dumped his Israeli stamps into the trash along with his chessmen. Clothes were strewn everywhere. Dirty dishes with encrusted food and takeout wrappers littered the floor and nightstand. His mother had declared the room toxic; she had abandoned attempts to bring him to his senses—not that she really cared. He was unreachable, sick of everything. Life without Margo was cheerless and pointless. His life was over.

The crowning blow was the realization that Christine had lost interest in him too. She didn't watch for him from her window. Was she jealous of Margo?

And God had not answered John's prayers. God had caused—or at least did not prevent—this series of crushing disappointments including, above all, Ian's death. John's life was like a ship adrift over an abyss, unable to anchor.

John walked into the house, resolved to take a road he had never traveled. Though he had said it before, he meant it now: from this point, he would invest all his intellectual energy to prove that God did not exist. It was time to employ his will and his mental capacity to change his life. There was nothing but heartache in this place.

* * *

His new anti-theistic perspective offered immediate liberation from the guilt over his more frequent sexual fantasies. He stopped going to church. The rhetoric of "religious people" quickly became repellent. Their trite phrases, platitudes, and clichés seemed an insipid rote that had no clear meaning.

Reports in the newspaper or on the radio of a wayward preacher provided more evidence there was no God, that the whole religious enterprise was an elaborate hoax concocted by charlatans, shriveled-up prudes, and do-gooders. The moral system existed to keep people in line and to spoil everybody's fun. Nietzsche was right: the rules of religious people were constraining the *Übermensch*, the super-man. But the super-man would rise inevitably.

Two weeks after Margo dumped him, he petitioned to complete high school by exam. He had made a point of hiding his intellect before, but now the word was out. His math teacher had begun the disclosure of his genius. During his tests successive teachers were astounded by his intellectual capacity. In two hours, more or less, he could read a class textbook designed for a year-study. Closing the book, he could answer with perfect recall any question his teachers posed.

His teachers did not want him in their classes. He did not belong in high school. There was no place for him. And none of the students would even talk to him.

"It's not that they don't like you, John," Mikey said. "They just can't talk to you because they think you know everything. You make them feel stupid. Nobody likes to feel stupid."

Two psychologists from Duke University flew into Springfield to test him; his scores were off their charts. It was on their recommendation that the school board unanimously agreed that John should be graduated from high school in June, at the end of his sophomore year. He was excused from attending further classes effective the first week in May.

Prestigious universities soon heard of him and sent him applications for scholarships. The University of Virginia offered to send him an airline ticket to come for an interview, suggesting he consider entry in the fall.

* * *

It was a Friday evening, the 9th of May, when John broached news of his intentions. His mother, Rutger, and he sat at the table for another spaghetti dinner.

"Do you have something for me, John?" His mother, Claire, asked. She was ever and always cheerless.

John dug into his jeans and pulled out a wad of bills which he handed to her. He glanced at his black-ringed fingernails, drew his hand back, and closed his fingers into a fist. No amount of scrubbing could get them clean.

Claire evidently saw his fingernails. Her lip curled up, and disdain spread across her face. But she took the money and stuffed it into her apron pocket. "So, have you made up your mind?" She passed the garlic bread to Rutger. They looked at each other.

"I'm going to interview with the philosophy department at the University of Kansas. I have an appointment next week. I'll drive up Monday morning and stay overnight in the dorm." His sole academic aim in studying philosophy, which he would tell no one, was to prove that God did not exist. John Malik would make his findings known to any who would listen.

"Assuming they want you, when would you leave?" Rutger asked, as he shoveled a wad of spaghetti into his mouth, seemingly indifferent to a dribble of sauce that trickled down his chin.

John cleared his throat and looked down at his plate. "I may try for the summer session. I think it starts in late June."

Rutger looked at Claire and smiled grimly.

"Philosophy," she said. "You can't make much of living with that kind of degree. But you'll be on your own. Do what you want. You can always be a mechanic. You've got some experience with that." She focused on stabbing a piece of cucumber in her mixed salad.

How desperately John wanted his mother to be proud of him, to share his dreams and hopes. But she did not love him. Thinking about it now, he decided he didn't really care what his next step was as long as he left this house as soon as possible.

John had finished the dishes when Claire and Rutger went out the front door with their bags without a goodbye. They were headed to the lake for the weekend. He stood looking through the screen door as their car backed into the street and pulled away.

He then changed into his running gear, locked the door, and jogged down the driveway, checking Christine's dark bedroom window. She wasn't home. He turned north along Barnes Street as the streetlights came on, and the air turned noticeably cool. He increased his pace until he was flat out.

* * *

Three hours later John sat at his desk in his room, alone in the house, still high from a grueling fifteen-mile night run. He had always been a runner, but now, every day, he pressed to his limits and beyond, an exercise of the will. He had gained ten pounds of muscle in one month, and his body was hard—it obeyed him.

Since he no longer had to attend class, he spent his time working longer hours at Consumers and mastering Plato's body of work, the dialogues, the Republic, the Apology, and his letters. Plato was the most important philosopher who had ever lived in John's opinion. The experience of driving himself and his study of Plato had brought into high relief a dualism of mind and body that altered the way he saw things. He and his body were distinct entities. His true self was imprisoned within his body.

Behaviorism, the dominant school of psychology, said brain activity was the sum and substance of the self. Advocates of this theory claimed personhood consisted entirely of electrochemical activity in the brain. When the brain dies, the person ceases to exist. John wanted to believe this; he wanted to believe oblivion was his destiny, not hell.

And the evolutionary theory and its applications in the sciences and arts were in agreement with the view that brain death was the cessation of life. There was no need for a creator; there was no afterlife, no hell, no ultimate basis for moral restraint. He wanted to believe the philosophers could prove this. Within the writings of the great minds of human history, he believed he would find the proof he was looking for. But Plato presented a powerful alternative understanding of the nature of things.

While pondering these issues, he got up from his desk, opened the bedroom door, and looked down the dark hall. Curious. He had the impression someone was there. Open before him on his desk was Plato's dialogue *Timaeus*. He considered how he might challenge Plato's conclusion that a divine craftsman alone could have imposed order upon the chaos of the world. This was the issue of Plato's thought that he had to disprove.

The night had turned exceptionally dark. He looked out the window. A thick silent fog had crept down the street, reducing the streetlight in front of his house to a faint glow. He had never seen fog this dense. It had to be a temperature inversion layer.

He was alone with his pup Socrates. That's the way he liked it, just the two of them. Socrates had taken up his usual place on the rug under the desk with his head on John's foot.

John nudged him away as he got up and walked to the window hoping there was a light on in Christine's bedroom. But her room was dark. And he was uneasy.

He sat down and looked at the wall in front of his desk, studying the pattern in the wallpaper. How rude and indifferent he had become to people. Everything was about him now, *I, me, my*. What had possessed him to forsake his childhood friends and cease to care about people?

But then, most of them were deluded and ignorant do-gooders. Who needed them? He had been conditioned to bitterness in this loveless home. His parents tolerated his existence in the house because he paid his way, but they were counting the days until he left forever for college. The sooner, the better for all concerned. But what of Christine? If he left, he would not get to watch her grow up.

His eyes misted as he stared at the wallpaper, feeling sorry for himself. He felt as though a fog had drifted over his consciousness. He lay his head on the desk and closed his eyes. Though his eyes were closed, he still saw everything around him. How odd.

John saw the lamp on the desk. At his feet, he saw Socrates stir and raise his head. And the hair on John's arms stood up. Out the window, he saw the heavy blanket of dripping fog that silenced even the crickets.

Socrates got to his feet. The little terrier moved slowly, backing up, the nails of his tiny feet clicking on the hardwood. One step at a time, he inched backward across the room, staring at the doorway. When he reached the wall, his tail curled beneath his body, his lips peeled back from his teeth in the caricature of a smile, and his head twisted to the side as though being drawn into that position by paralyzing pain. And from beneath his belly, a stream of urine puddled onto the floor.

Infected with his pup's fear, John forced himself to turn to see what Socrates was seeing. He spun around toward the open doorway: only a dark passageway in a dark house.

The legs of the chair scraped on the floor as he pushed back from the desk. At the bedroom doorway, he peered around the jamb into the hall and saw nothing but darkness. His hands were trembling as he reached into the hallway and turned on the 25-watt overhead bulb. It barely illuminated the far end of the hall.

Something was there.

He stepped into the hallway, his back against the wall looking toward the darkness of the kitchen. He slid to the floor on rubbery legs. There was a clicking sound, something heavy, sending tremors through the floor joists. It lumbered one step at a time over the kitchen linoleum, coming toward the hall. John's breathing was fast and shallow, his heartbeat pounding in his temples.

Fragments of a dream. He struggled against ropes that bound him to the arms of a chair, looking toward a dark doorway in the light of a single candle. The old man backed away, leaving John Malik to his fate.

"Help me." A prayer. His throat closed over the words.

Evil was coming for him. He had been marked for destruction. His eyes bulged; he strained to seen into the darkness for his nemesis. And then it appeared.

An unholy creature stepped into the dim light. It filled the end of the hallway with flexing wings. Graven upon its monstrous features was unspeakable malice. For long moments its lidless, merciless eyes regarded him like a viper intent upon its prey.

John's vision dimmed, his head lolled onto his shoulder, his tongue hung out. His skin went clammy. The creature crouched, preparing to strike, to impale him. In resignation John rolled his eyeballs up to watch the horror of the mortal strike. But the creature suddenly turned its head toward the front door of the house, paused for moment, then backed into the kitchen and vanished in the darkness.

Someone was pounding at the front door. Then the door slammed open. "Johnny!" A frantic voice. In a moment, tender hands shook him. He opened his eyes. Christine was on her knees beside him in the hallway, holding his head to her bosom, sobbing, "Don't leave me, Johnny!" She sobbed hysterically as she rocked him back and forth. Seconds turned to minutes and Christine's sobs faded to slow, easy breathing. John's terror was displaced by a strange peace. He fell fast asleep in her embrace.

CHAPTER 12
A Bend in the Road

John drove to the University of Kansas campus the following Monday. The chair of the philosophy department and three other full professors interviewed him for several hours. This was the final step in the award of a four-year scholarship, with the possibility of a year's extension. Though grieved at the prospect of leaving Christine, John had to escape the house on Barnes Street and to cut ties with his family. He appealed for special permission to enroll for the upcoming summer session at KU. The school agreed. He would begin classes the last week in June.

The night of the demon had bound John and Christine together in some inexplicable way. Though they never spoke of it, she had become his protector. John now believed that her love for him was unconditional, something he had never experienced. The fact that a spectacular young lady like her could love him, gave him a peace he had never known. How could he leave her in just seven weeks?

Night after night they watched each other from their bedrooms. And there was yardwork.

Christine's chores in the yard began when John drove his Hornet into the drive on Saturday afternoon and got out to start the laborious job of mowing his yard with the push mower. Both concentrated their efforts in the front yard. Christine watered and weeded her lawn, with specific emphasis was on the south side of the house, the side along the fence that adjoined her house and John's.

In back-and-forth motions, John reduced the height of the grass while studying Christine out the corners of his eyes. She puttered in her yard in short-shorts and a tank top, making a show of pulling a few weeds from the lawn or flower beds. She held a weed for him as if to say, "See what a good girl I am." Her procedure for tending the lawn in small patches was Zen-like.

And the result of her efforts did not go unnoticed. People commented that the lawn and flowerbed on the south side of the Charis house were unusually verdant compared with the other sides. No one could explain it.

As they worked, Christine pantomimed an emotion or thought to John's amusement. But they did not speak, fearful someone might catch them. Christine left John notes on the top of a fence post. In these furtive messages, she expressed confidence that their time was coming. And she had plenty to say about that witch Margo.

Rutger, Claire, and Christine's father, Matthew, all ranked as full professors at the Southwest Missouri State College. They saw one another in the faculty lounge and visited at faculty conferences, but never socialized outside of school. Upon every encounter, Rutger had something negative to say about John. "He's a bad seed, a pervert," he told Matthew repeatedly. "Don't let your daughter anywhere near him."

Christine often overhead her dad talking to her mom about this. Christine got the impression that Rutger's agenda had worn thin, and his veracity had come into question by her parents. Yet Matthew continued to believe that Christine was gasoline, and John was a lighted match. They could not be alone together.

In her notes to John, Christine said she always stuck up for her Johnny. She told her father that Rutger Malik was a damned liar! For this outburst, she earned a serious reprimand. On another occasion, which she reported verbatim to John, her dad and mom were discussing Rutger's hostility toward John. Christine, standing behind them, intruded, "Don't you get it, Daddy? Rutger Malik is *not* John's father. And that has to be the problem."

Life in the Malik household was as bitter as ever, even though John's imminent departure was near. He had hoped for an easing of hostility, for some nostalgia. But it didn't happen. John likened his household to the fifth circle of Dante's *Inferno*. There, in the swampy reeking waters of the river Styx, those consumed with wrath writhed in the slime forever grappling one with another on the margin of the foul Stygian marsh. Those who were passively wrathful, lay sullen, gurgling beneath the waters, unable to express the rage that was forever drowning them. John was desperate to escape this living hell.

Their last Saturday together had come. John left Christine a note with his mailing address and his phone number at the men's dorm. He closed with hugs and kisses.

* * *

The day came, Friday, June 27th. He packed up the Hornet with his clothes and a few books. His mom stood at the screen door to watch him leave. With mixed feelings, he fired up the Hornet and backed up a short distance until he was abeam of Christine's bedroom window. He stopped and got out.

"Christine!" He yelled at the top of his lungs. He didn't care who heard him. "Come out here. And damn the consequences."

She scrambled out the front door, jumped off the porch, and ran to the fence. "Oh, Johnny." Tears streamed down her cheeks. "I'm so sad."

John grasped Christine by the waist and lifted her over the fence. They embraced long and hard, smothering each other with kisses.

"Take your hands off her, you son of a bitch!"

John turned to see Rutger standing on the porch beside Claire. John was bigger than his mother's husband now and much more powerfully built.

"With all due respect, sir, *go to hell.*" Suddenly relieved to have said what he always wanted to say, he laughed heartily as Rutger turned and stormed into the house. John felt as if he had vomited up something that had sickened him for 17 years.

John reached for Christine and hungrily pulled her closer. "Don't give up on me, Christine. The day is coming when I will never leave you. No one will ever keep us apart. You saved my life and gave me a reason to live. I can never repay you for that."

She held onto him tighter and sobbed into his chest.

After their emotions had calmed a bit, John let her go, got back in his Hornet, and backed down the drive. At the street, he stopped to look at Claire and the Charis family, now standing on their respective porches. Christine stood poised in his driveway, flexing her fists, ready to run to him if he called her.

They all stared at him. They may have held out little expectation for what the future held for one so little esteemed by his own family but so highly regarded by Christine. She was fifteen, going on twenty-three. What could she know of life at that age?

John backed out into the street and turned south toward East Sunshine Street. Rachel Hixson loved him. He had to see her before he left. What a difference she and Norbert Hixson had made in his life with the gift of the Hornet. After seeing her, he thought he might drive by Consumers and say goodbye to the guys again.

No, that would be unkind. Their lives and his were diverging. Their lives would probably be lived out in quiet desperation, as Thoreau said. Perhaps in John's new world, his life would achieve meaning. He might be able to forget the horror of the cave.

The way John read the Genesis account, Cain, who killed his brother, had been marked by God to preserve Cain's life at the hand of others. But the mark also identified Cain as a fugitive from society and a murderer. Divine judgment awaited Cain with no provision for redemption. In the same way, there could be no redemption for John Malik.

PART IV:

THE PHILOSOPHER

CHAPTER 13

University of Kansas

One Year Later

John sat on a picnic table behind the dorm, looking east at the lights of Lawrence twinkling in the dusk. He often sat here, alone, in the evening to review the events of the day and to mark his location on the chart of his journey. Was he any closer to understanding why he was alive?

It had been a year ago in June that he had turned north out of Springfield for the four-hour-drive to Lawrence, Kansas. He had called his mother once. She made it clear it was unnecessary to call again.

Christine had called him many times. He imagined her walking to Sunshine Street in the evening, exchanging dollars for a pocket full of quarters at the washeteria, checking her watch, and standing by the payphone until 6 p.m. She would place a call to the third floor of his dorm and ask for John Malik in room 306.

She never flagged in her passion and devotion to him; she was confident they would be together someday soon. Her letters comforted him and anchored his emotional life through the summer. But as the weeks passed, he adapted to life on his own; the differences in their worlds impressed themselves upon him. She was a kid, still in high school, still talking about God.

In contrast, he was surveying a new world with undreamed-of possibilities. But then she would pull him up short, keeping him from full commitment to this new world by sending him pictures of herself. Breathtaking, unsettling, innocent pictures.

The issues that had threatened his survival and sanity were receding in his rearview mirror. In class after class, he detected the gossamer structure of another world that was alluded to by every professor. It was a non-theistic, material view of reality that seemed to be the universal perspective of his teachers.

He concluded that no scholar of intellectual merit would speak of God, except in a dismissive vein. To speak of God as though He existed was academic suicide. Evolution and its myriad applications in human endeavors, that was the worldview that was being unveiled before him.

Maybe John's reservations about the evolutionary hypothesis in high school were premature. To him, in those days, its lack of substance seemed obvious, its logical incoherence evident. But in college he was discovering this view was the monolithic perspective in academia. It stressed two empirical deductions: Man had no detectable purpose or worth; and life did not extend beyond the cessation of brain activity.

Either the humanists and materialists were right, and there was actual evidence for their position, or it was founded on speculation motivated by belief and not fact. But, if there was no evidence for the theory, then its widespread adoption was being perpetuated by academic types who did not know the theory well enough to recognize its lack of merit. The only argument John had seen was an imagined tree of life based on morphology. He was going to find out. He would be objective. He wanted the theory of evolution to be true.

John burned through his core introductory courses and challenging electives in physics, chemistry, biological sciences, and math. He opted-out of a number of courses by exam; he carried an overload every semester.

The course work so far had not seriously challenged his capacity, allowing time to read in other fields. He observed a sociological phenomenon unfolding in the first days of his journey in academia. The fresh-scrubbed intellectual tyros in his classes were being immersed in the cold waters of iconoclasm. What these young scholars thought they knew, what they had always believed, what their parents had taught them, was wrong according to their professors. Reality was a brave new world, indifferent to man's desperate longings for worth, purpose, and an ultimate destiny.

John did not want God to exist, at least not the God he knew of from his youth. In that world, John Malik was damned. Already in his sophomore year, his coursework gravitated to the extensive offerings of his major department. He would soon discover what man could know and what his limitations were. The philosophers had the answers, if anyone did.

The lights of the town of Lawrence now lit the horizon to the east, glowing against the low-lying stratus clouds drifting fast to the northeast. An hour had passed as he sat at the picnic table reviewing and reassessing what he had learned in the first year of his journey. He considered this process a vital step in synthesizing his perspective and attempting to determine whether he had discovered any rock-solid truths. So far, he had not. Absolutes were phantoms that kept receding beyond the scope of every course he took.

Perhaps he should get back to the room. He got up from the picnic table. Maybe Christine had written to him. Oh yes, and he was getting a new roommate. He decided on dinner: an anchovies and pepperoni pizza from the local delivery.

* * *

Winston Symington III came through the door like a gust of wind. Turning the doorknob, he kicked the door open and dragged in his hang-up bag in one hand and a heavy suitcase in the other. He dumped everything onto John's bed.

John, engrossed in solving a math problem in celestial mechanics, spun around on his chair to confront this rude intruder. But he cooled when he realized this was his new roommate.

John looked at Symington's bags on his bed and pointed. "That's my bunk."

Symington busied himself, putting things into the closet. "First come doesn't mean first dibs." He stopped. "You're what, a freshman?"

"Sophomore. Be a junior next semester."

"Well, I'm a senior. I moved out of the frat house to get busy and salvage a *magna cum laude*. It's Wharton next year for me." He groaned and stepped over to the bed to pick up a tennis racket. He pressed down on the mattress several times. "I say, this bed works for me." He kicked the door closed and turned back to putting his clothes away, humming to himself.

"Okay, you can have the bed. But it's been mine for a year and two summer sessions." He added, "I peed on it once."

"Whatever." Symington got his underwear in the drawer, then turned, walked over to John, and stuck out his hand. "Winston Symington, the third."

"John Malik, the first."

Symington's personality and presumption would require John's accommodation in the interests of peace. But he would not be pushed around. At least Symington hadn't demanded John's desk.

John often daydreamed, looking out the window to the east. At the bottom of the hill sat the KU football stadium. It was in a horseshoe bowl formed by higher ground upon which the main campus spread for a mile to the south and southwest past the nuclear reactor. A sea of hardwood trees and green grass had become his world. He didn't have a home now, just this room overlooking an uncertain future.

He looked back at the math problem. The answer leaped off the page. He filled in the mathematical steps he had done in his head and sat back with a smile, shaking his head, marveling at the consistency of the natural laws encoded in mathematics. "Why does it work?" he said to no one but himself.

"I say, what's that?" Symington asked, rummaging in his suitcase. He looked up. "What's your major? My thing is French literature." And he rattled off some esoteric phrases in French with a supercilious pucker, looking down his nose at John.

"Philosophy and some serious science. Where are you from?"

"Boston. You'll note I have no accent. We're *nouveau riche*."

"Generous of you to admit it," John said over his shoulder, turning back to the math.

"Well, it is what it is, and I'm rich. I'm being groomed to take over the family business. French lit won't cut it. But for now, I'm living my dream, here with you, a benighted young idealist on a fool's errand."

With narrowed eyes, John turned around deliberately. Winston was busy placing his tee shirts in a drawer in the closet. This effrontery would not go unanswered. This clueless dolt would be grist for John Malik's evil genius. He would find a way to put him in his place.

Winston added, "Please take your sheets off my bed. I'll remake it with my sheets." He continued to be consumed in his activities, pumping his arms and shifting weight from leg to leg as he sang a sea chanty in French.

CHAPTER 14

Terror in the Tunnel

The fall semester began. John signed up for 24 semester hours, a heavy load even if the course content had been fluff. The hard nuts would be a cosmology course, the full-blown math version, and physical chemistry. When classes started, he had second thoughts about these courses.

On the first day in physical chemistry, John estimated a hundred students were sitting in tiered seats looking down on the stage. The professor walked in on time. He surveyed the multitude of students. Shaking his head side to side in apparent exasperation, he turned to the blackboard without a word. He picked up a piece of chalk and began writing line after line of partial differential equations. Five minutes later, he put down the chalk, dusted his hands, and asked, "Any questions?" There were none. He turned and walked out.

On the second day of class, twenty-five students showed up, including John Malik. The only reason he didn't drop the course was that he recognized the professor had demonstrated the first law of thermodynamics. If it didn't get any harder than that, he might pass the course.

* * *

John walked into his dorm room with a heavy rucksack on his shoulders, a pack he bought at the Army-Navy store. He dumped it beside his desk and extracted more than a dozen books, stacking them on the floor, since his shelves were full. He sat down at his desk, picked up one of the books and began to take notes on a yellow tablet, vaguely annoyed by his roommate's cavalier attitude toward academics.

Winston was lounging on his bed, holding a novel in French above him and chewing Ju Ju Bees. He picked them up one by one from a pile on his chest. There was a ceaseless procession of Ju Ju Bees moving from the collection on his chest into his mouth.

"I say, Malik, what's all this?" He turned his head. "Why do you insist on bringing all these books into my room, cluttering up my space? Why don't you just set yourself up in the library and live there?" He immediately lost interest in Malik, again engrossed in his novel, smiling, furrowing his brow, mouthing the words in French. He dumped another box of Ju Ju Bees onto his chest.

"Hey, Winston."

"You *sprechen* to *moi*?" he asked, returning to mouthing the words of his novel.

"You ever hear about the steam tunnels under the campus?"

"*Non.*"

"I understand it's possible to get into them in several places. I've heard you can get into every building on campus. The library, classroom buildings. And the girls' dorms."

Winston closed his novel, collected his Ju Ju Bees, and sat up. "Say what, Malik?"

"That's what I hear. My roommate last year had a map, and he went into the tunnels. He gave me his map." John held it up. "He said he'd spent hours looking through a wire grid into a girls' shower."

"You sure about this?"

"Would I lie to you?" John asked.

"Give me that." Winston got up and snatched the map away.

John shrugged and turned on his chair to face Winston. "I don't know if it's true. But you wouldn't catch me going down there."

"Why not?" Winston was studying the map.

"Well, you could do it only at night. Those tunnels go on for miles." John paused, his heart beating faster as he developed the scenario. "You might get lost down there." A long pause and these furtive words, "Or run into ..."

Winston looked up. "Run into what? What'd be down there at night?"

"Not what. Who." John leaned forward, speaking quietly. "The ax murderer."

"Who?"

"The ax murderer." John turned his head, looking left and right. "It's just a story, of course. And I don't put any credence in it. But somebody was killed in the tunnels during construction. It was a long time ago. Workers found lots of blood and body parts, like someone hacked limbs off with a hatchet. They never found the rest of the body. Then two years ago a utilities man had to go into the tunnels at night for an emergency repair. He saw something that turned his hair white. He claimed someone with an ax nearly killed him. He believed somebody lives down there.

"You wouldn't catch me down there." John shook his head side to side. "No, sir, I wouldn't go in there for anything."

Winston's mind was transparent to John. He could read his thoughts on his face. Winston was tracing a tunnel to the largest of the girls' dorms. He was imagining himself in the darkness settled in behind a steel grill watching girls frolicking naked like woodland nymphs in the showers.

* * *

"I don't like this at all, Winston," John said. He checked his watch. It was just past midnight on a chilly moonless autumn night. John shifted his rucksack and looked down at a steel manhole cover at his feet. "This just isn't right," he pleaded. "What about ... you know? And, hey, I doubt there'll be any girls taking a shower at this time of night. Do you think?"

"Look, Malik, you're with me. You'll be all right. You just stay behind me and be quiet. Have I ever let you down?"

"I guess not. Of course, I've only known you two months, so there's not much of a track record there."

"Trust me. Now, take the bar, insert it in the slot, and tilt the cover up. Then you hold it while I go down the ladder. And then you come down. You must hold the cover with one hand until you're on the ladder." He was speaking with body English, as though he were addressing an idiot. "You got it? Buck up, son." Winston slapped him on the back. "Let's get cracking."

John inserted the steel rod into a slot in the disk and pried it up. He held it as Winston ducked under the cover and placed his feet on the steel rungs of a ten-foot ladder leading down into the darkness. Step by step, he descended with his light playing on the concrete floor beneath him. He reached the bottom and surveyed left and right down the tunnel. He looked up at John.

"Okay. It's safe. You can come down."

John had the hard part. He had to hold the weight of the cover, get beneath it, and let it drop back into place once he was on the ladder. He managed it and reached the bottom.

Winston was studying the map and checking a compass. "Here we are," he said, showing John their location. "We go this way about three blocks, I'd guess." He pointed straight ahead. "Then we come to a cross-tunnel. We go right." He traced the route on the map. "This one leads to the dorm. Do you agree? Not that your opinion matters that much. I'm in charge, remember that."

John smiled at Winston.

"What are you smiling at?"

John shrugged and shook his head. "I'm just glad I'm with you, Winston. You make me feel safe."

Winston looked doubtful.

They tied a yellow strip of plastic tape onto the ladder to mark the way out and struck out to the southeast. "So, who's the little yellow-haired tart on your desk?" Winston asked. "That your kid sister?"

"No. That's my girlfriend. She wouldn't approve of me trying to watch naked girls."

"Well, you don't have to watch. But I want you as my backup." There was a long pause. "You know, you stick with me, Malik, and I might give you a job someday. Something menial that you could handle."

"That would be great," John enthused. "People tell me I'll have a hard time getting a job with my major."

They scanned the tunnel ahead. Overhead were steam pipes wrapped in asbestos. There were electrical cables and water lines strapped to the ceiling. But the floor of the tunnel was uncluttered and dry. It was about eight feet wide and eight feet high. The temperature was warmer than the night air above. They hurried forward block after block.

"I sure hope there's nothing down here," John said with anxiety mounting in his voice. "What would we do if we came across ... him?"

Winston stopped and turned around. "Now see here, Malik, find courage within you." He poked him in the chest. "Be a man. Frankly, you're getting on my nerves. I want you to stop this stuff about an ax murderer. Do you hear me?"

John tried to look rueful. They were approaching the loop. John had been here twice last year. A cross-tunnel was coming up. He would follow the loop and get one block ahead of Winston.

And there it was. John let Winston pass the opening about twenty feet, and then he stopped. "Winston, I've got to pee. Wait here for me. I'll go in that side tunnel."

"If you must," Winston said. He was manifesting evidence of a massive testosterone infusion. Naked woodland nymphs were surely dancing through his mind.

John carried his pack with him back to the cross tunnel. He rummaged in it for several items. He looked around the corner. Winston was squatting, looking ahead, fidgeting. John began jogging, making the turns, and re-approached the main tunnel a block ahead of where Winston was waiting. John stopped and put on a Halloween mask, a wart-nosed old witch. He donned a ball cap upside down and backward on his head; he turned his windbreaker inside out. With a hatchet in his right hand and a light in his left, he entered the tunnel ahead of Winston.

John moaned as he staggered in the main tunnel. He switched on his light, which he held at his waist, angled up onto the mask. He raised the ax and screamed as he started running toward Winston.

Winston disappeared in the distance, howling bloody murder.

An hour later, John strode into their dorm room. Winston was sitting on his bunk wringing his hands. He was wearing a different pair of pants.

"What happened?" John shouted. "I came out of the side tunnel, hearing all this screaming, and you're gone." John was waving his arms at Winston. "You left me in there by myself!"

Winston was chewing Ju Ju Bees feverishly. He looked up at John with a haunted expression in his eyes that morphed to an incredulous expression. "Didn't you see him?"

"See who? All I saw was your light disappear down the tunnel. And all that screaming. What was that all about? How could you leave me in there without a map? You didn't even wait for me." John's words spewed out like foam from his mouth. He was quite pleased with his performance.

"I can't believe you didn't see him!"

"I don't know what you're talking about."

Winston held his head down, massaging his forehead with the fingers of his right hand, eyes closed, slurping his Ju Ju Bees. "You wouldn't believe me if I told you."

"Gimme those." John grabbed the box of Ju Ju Bees out of Winston's hand and dumped the contents into his mouth. "You stink," he said.

CHAPTER 15
Divine Madness

Christine turned 17 just after the spring semester began. In the afternoon mail, John received a letter from her with several pictures. One showed her loving on Socrates. She had adopted him from John and coyly referred to him as their "love-puppy." He rifled through the images until he came to one that stopped the world.

Christine was wearing shorts and a T-shirt that exposed her midriff. It read "Sweet 17." The image set off a buzzing in John's head that neutralized all rational processes. He rummaged in his desk drawer for a roll of quarters. He slammed out of the room and quick-stepped down the hall to the payphone. He pulled a piece of paper from his wallet, held the phone against his ear with his shoulder, and fed quarters into the phone. It was ringing.

"Hello, who is this?" a woman said.

"Ma'am, this is John Malik calling for Miriam. Is she home?" His voice was breathy and urgent.

"All right, young man. Be patient. I'll get her. My, but you are in a state," she said as she laid the phone down. A minute passed.

"Hello, this is Miriam. Is this Christine's John?"

"Yes. I'm so sorry to ask this of you, but could you call Christine and tell her I have to talk to her right away?"

"Is this some kind of emergency?"

"I'd have to say yes."

"Okay. I'll call her. Have you been happy with the mail situation?" Miriam seemed eager to please.

"I am. Thanks for helping. You have a car now, don't you?"

"Oh, yes. It's a yellow 1953 Mercury convertible." John could hear the smile in her voice. "I'm so excited."

"Listen, Miriam." He took a deep breath. "Do you think you and Christine could go to the Sunset Drive-In Saturday night?"

"I don't see why not? I'll let her figure out why you're asking. I'll call her right now. You mean tomorrow night, right?

"Yes."

"I'm sure she'll call you as soon as possible." She cupped her hand around the mouthpiece and whispered. "To be honest, this whole affair between you two is the most exciting part of my life, you a big-time scholar and all. I've been hearing about you for years. And so handsome—"

"Thank you, Miriam." John didn't have time for her gushing tribute. "Could you please just call her now? I've got to hear from her."

"All right, John. Consider it done."

John heard the distinct click of the phone disconnecting. Then the dial tone. He checked his watch. He went back to his room where he paced back and forth, chewing Winston's last box of Ju Ju Bees. John was in a torment that had risen beyond his capacity to control it. He had to see Christine.

The phone was ringing down the hall. He burst through the door and raced for the phone, reaching it before anyone else. "Hello." Breathless.

"I'm calling for John Malik."

"Well, who do you think this is?"

"Oh, Johnny!" Christine sounded desperately in love. He could tell. Her words were like pouring jet fuel on a fire.

"Listen, I have to see you. I may not survive if I don't. I want you and Miriam to go the Sunset Drive-In tomorrow night. Park on the back row, right of the concession stand. I'm coming to see you. Will you do that?"

"Hold on. I've got a full schedule. Let's see. I may fit you in for that time slot. Are you going to bring me something nice?"

"I will. What do you want?"

"I want you. I'm so excited," she squealed. "But now, hold on, big boy. You don't think I'm going to give up the prize, do you? You're not expecting that are you, Johnny? We can't do that. That wouldn't be right."

He groaned. "Oh, I know. Just kissing and holding you might be enough, like an emergency transfusion. But if I don't see you, I'll collapse into a smoldering heap. My heart is pumping like a runaway train. This is your fault." He had to say what he didn't want to say. "Please stop with the provocative poses. You're killing me."

They talked until the operator cut in and requested more money. Christine had no more change, so they said goodbye.

John ran back to his room. He got out his best jeans and pressed them and then laid out his favorite shirt and socks, polished his shoes, and checked his toiletries bag to be sure he had toothpaste and floss. Before reaching the drive-in, he planned to stop and brush his teeth, floss, and use mouthwash. Then he would put just a dab of English Leather behind his ears and on his chest.

John believed his blood pressure must be in the critical range. It didn't help that Winston sauntered in, indifferent to John's condition, and complained that John had eaten his last box of Ju Ju Bees.

Thanks to Malik, Winston whined, he would have to get up, go down to the parking lot, drive his new Mercedes to the store, and buy more. He had planned to study tonight. Now those plans were ruined. "Frankly, Malik, you're among the rudest people I know. You're bereft of the slightest consideration for others."

Winston did not note the feverishness of John's actions, unable to recognize a man highly focused. John stood holding his chin, frenzied, yet pondering. What was he forgetting? Oh, he had to get the car gassed up, and he had to plan the exact departure time, allowing himself time to get down Glenstone to Sunshine, then to the theater at least thirty minutes early, allowing for delays. He would sleep late tomorrow morning because he would be up all night, driving back to KU.

He picked up his keys and started for the door. "I'm going to get gas and some supplies. I'll get you some Ju Ju Bees," John said.

"Capital. You're a good egg, Malik, if a little slow on the uptake. Don't eat my stuff unless I give you specific permission. You take unwarranted liberties."

John gassed up the Hornet and dropped by the grocery store where he bought some mouthwash and floss. He picked up five boxes of Ju Ju Bees and checked out. He stopped by the pizza place and waited while they made a large pepperoni with anchovies on one side and pineapple on the other.

Back in the room, he maneuvered the pizza box onto his desk and tossed the Ju Ju Bees onto Winston's bunk. Winston was at his desk studying, something he seldom did in John's experience. Winston got up.

"What's this? You know I don't like anchovies. And you've taken liberties in assuming I like this … whatever this is."

"It's pineapple, Winston. You like pineapple."

"All right, but you know I like banana peppers too." He collected paper towels from above the sink and scooped up half of the pizza, not offering to pay. As he turned away, he said, "Frankly, Malik, living with you has been a great burden to me."

"Well, frankly, Winston, the sentiment is mutual."

John looked at Winston. How could an idiot like Winston get accepted into Wharton? Could any company survive with him at the helm?

* * *

John pulled out of the dorm parking lot at 2 p.m. on Saturday. He had plotted the expected times at each major town. Based on his actual time, he could gauge his progress and speed up or slow down as necessary. Actual drive time was something over three hours for the 200-mile trip, but he allowed four hours. He chewed one box after another of Winston's Ju Ju Bees.

Christine's younger peers had just turned 16, and Miriam had gotten a car. This clandestine meeting could not have happened before now. The impossibility of seeing her alone had kept the genie in the bottle. But now the genie had burst the bottle.

Soon, road signs announced the turnoff to the eastbound loop around the north of Springfield. He was way too early. Turning south onto Glenstone, he found a gas station, filled up again, and bought a newspaper. With trembling hands, he turned to the movie section in the paper. The start time at the Sunset was 7:15 p.m.

He had two hours to kill. Maybe he should get something to eat, brush his teeth again, floss, and use mouthwash. That would take an hour. He drove by Consumer's gas station and saw two of the guys he used to work with still there. He drove out Division, past Mrs. Hixson's place. But he couldn't stop or let anyone know he was in town. It would get back to his mom and Rutger and then to Christine's dad. That couldn't happen.

At Shoney's he had the chicken fried steak, then spent some time in the restroom and came out smelling of English Leather and minty mouthwash. Back in his Hornet, he was hyperventilating as he started the engine, backed out, made the turns onto east Sunshine, checking his watch.

Passing the ticket booth at the Sunset entry, he drove along the east perimeter toward the back row, creeping along looking for a yellow Mercury. Still too early. He pulled the Hornet into a slot to the right of the concession stand and shut off the engine.

At twilight, he saw a yellow Mercury convertible with three figures in it coming along the perimeter toward the back row. It turned at the last row and pulled up beside him. From the passenger side, a magnificent creature beamed like sunshine. She got out of the car, strolled around John's car, and stuck her head into the passenger window.

"Hello, sailor. You lookin' for a good time?" she asked. Her long blonde hair shrouded half of her face as she leaned into the window in her Sweet 17 tee shirt. Then she slid into the car, slammed the door, grabbed John's shirt, and pulled him to her. She wrapped herself around him, moaning like a dove.

With the seat as far back as it would go, they slipped down the leather onto the floor of the passenger side of the car in a mad embrace and did not come up for air for almost two hours. By the force of her overpowering will, their virtue remained intact.

When the glaring lights of intermission came up, they struggled up onto the seat. Christine's hair looked like she was statically charged. She appeared drunk. John, bleary-eyed, finally hung the speaker on the stand, struggled out, and wobbled off for the refreshment stand. He returned with popcorn and Cokes for Miriam and her friend in the adjacent car. Handing it to them, he thanked them for being Christine's cover. They beamed at him, starstruck, unable to say anything coherent.

John and Christine planned to meet every other month under the same circumstances.

* * *

Two weeks later, John got a call from Christine. "Johnny, your father died this morning."

"How did it happen?"

"He died in the faculty lounge. My dad said Professor Malik was in a rage. He was going on about you. My dad didn't understand what he was talking about, but Professor Malik's face was red as a beet. Then a look of horror came across his face, as if he had seen the devil … and he just dropped dead."

There was a long pause. "I don't know what to say. I'll call my mother and see what the arrangements are. I doubt she'll want me to come to the funeral."

"Oh, Johnny, I wish I could hold you. You need so much love. My heart aches for you."

As predicted, John was not welcome at the funeral.

* * *

In the fall of John's third year, Christine got her own car. With a girlfriend, Christine met John in Bolivar, 30 miles north of Springfield. The trio ate at a diner, then drove back to Springfield to see a downtown movie. On another Saturday, they all met for a picnic in Ash Grove. Another time they explored two Civil War battlefield sites near Springfield for a paper Christine was doing. They drove to the river and waded and swam once. And they talked.

Christine had laid down the law about John's physical impulses. She scolded him like a wayward child, demanding that he control his urges. She had become the iron maiden, he the sheepish supplicant. Her reasoning was solid, she claimed. If God had declared intimacy verboten until marriage, then that's the way it would be. But, she added, she had every intention of making it worth waiting for.

He dreaded the day when he would have to talk about God. That discussion occurred in early March of John's fourth year. He had finished his BA and was well into the graduate program. Christine would graduate from high school in May.

John pulled beside her on the last row of the Sunset Drive-In at twilight on the third Saturday in March. How regal she was sitting in her black '57 Impala, the coolest girl in Springfield. He set the brake and turned to gaze at her. She smiled at him with that disconcerting expression that fit somewhere between the innocence of childhood and the allure of a siren. She beckoned for him to come to her.

She was delicious beyond words, full of grace. Five minutes of passionate license was all that she allowed. Then she stiff-armed him, pushing him away toward the passenger door.

"Why do you always get to be in charge?" John said, folding his arms.

"Because I hold the high ground, and you know it. It's time we got something straight."

John lifted his hands and turned away. "I don't want to talk."

"Johnny, I can't marry an atheist. Don't you understand that?"

"I understand it matters to you."

"I just cannot marry an unbeliever. Every time I've wanted to get this clear between us, you've avoided the subject. From the time I was four years old, when we were at Princeton, Daddy would sit me on his knee and tell me stories from the Bible. He would read to me. He believed the words would go deep into me and that it would be a light to my path. Every evening Mom and Daddy and I sit and read and talk about God and what He wants from us."

John stared blankly at her.

"I told Daddy I was coming to see you tonight."

"You what? Are you crazy?"

"My Daddy and Mom trust me. I haven't told them about our times together, but I will not deceive them anymore. Whatever happens, I love you with all my heart. Do you believe me?"

John nodded, waiting for the other shoe to drop.

"And I believe I'm supposed to be your wife. But that won't happen unless something radical happens in your life. Johnny, I've listened to that drivel you spout about the 'nature of things,' and Immanuel's Kant's categories, and all that other stuff that shines no light on where people live. The Bible alone explains your dilemma. You're either a prodigal son or you've never had a relationship with Christ. That has to be fixed. That's all that matters to me."

"Oh, boy," he smirked. "Here it is, we've come to the clichés and platitudes." John turned away. "You know what the Bible says. A person can't come to Christ unless God calls him. Isn't that what it says?" He turned toward her for emphasis. "Maybe I knew God once, before my brother died. But God did nothing to prevent him from dying. Everything changed after that. I have no family now. I don't have a home. If God exists, he did this to me." There was a bitter edge to his words that were ugly to himself, and surely to Christine. He looked away, on the verge of feeling sorry for himself.

"Look at me, Johnny." She reached over and turned his head toward her. "The fault is yours, not God's. You've done something that you've not confessed to God. I know it. Look at what happened to your dad, and what's happening to your mom. Do you think that has nothing to do with you?"

He turned away again. "You don't know what you're talking about."

"Something you don't understand about me, Johnny. God made me a light for you. He offers you a lifeline. I'm it. You'd better grab hold and listen to what I'm telling you."

He returned her withering gaze for long seconds; he had to turn away.

"I'm no fool, Johnny. You don't think I'm a fool, do you?"

"Clearly not." He was a scolded child, unable to face his accuser. He looked into the trees beyond the high corrugated fence surrounding the drive-in. He felt hope dying.

Christine turned toward the movie screen. She adjusted the volume knob on the speaker hanging on the window. "Maybe you should go now," she said, her voice trembling.

Dying inside, John searched for a response. He looked up at the screen just as Rhett Butler said to Scarlett, "Frankly, my dear, I don't give a damn."

But John did give a damn; but oh, how he wished he didn't. Christine was all he ever wanted, and now she was receding beyond his reach. He climbed out of her black Impala and drove back through the night to finish studies for which he had lost all interest.

CHAPTER 16
The Limit of Reason

John rapped his knuckles against the door frame of the office of Professor Hector Merkel, chairman of the philosophy department. The professor looked up from a stack of papers and books that cluttered his desk. He rose to his feet, walked around the huge desk, and greeted John warmly.

"So good of you come, Mr. Malik. Please, sit down and spend a few minutes with me." He gestured to a chair facing his desk.

John sat down, watching the distinguished white-haired scholar in a tweed jacket scurry back around his desk to sit down. Dr. Merkel pushed an ashtray with a smoldering pipe to one side, folded his hands with a kind expression, and focused on John.

"Have we told you how your academic achievements have encouraged all of us here?"

John raised his eyebrows and shrugged. "Thank you, sir."

The professor pulled some papers toward himself and glanced down. John tilted his head to see if it might concern him.

"Yes," Merkel said, looking up. "This is your transcript." He looked down at it and moved his finger along the list of courses Malik had taken. "Cosmology, cellular biology, genetics, even an intro to paleontology. All electives. I'm curious. Why did you study these subjects?"

"Background for the question of origins."

"You mean the universe and life?"

John nodded.

"Did you reach any conclusions?" The professor leaned back in his chair, picked up his pipe, and waited for John to answer.

"The evidence and logic indicate there has to be a creator."

Professor Merkel laid down his pipe again and leaned into the conversation. "Do any of your professors teach this?"

"Not that I can tell. Evidently they are uniformly anti-theistic." John was unsure where this conversation was heading, but he was not into it. He was burned out and couldn't care less if his views prevailed or not.

"Are they wrong?"

"Emphatically. The evolutionary theory is a logical shell game. It implies that genetic diversification accounts for speciation. There isn't a thread of evidence for that. And if the Big Bang theory is correct, how did "all that is" come from nothing? Order and intelligence cannot precipitate from time and chance. The concept swims upstream against entropy. But I guess evolution is easier to believe than the staggering alternative, that every species was uniquely formed and that the universe was created by an outside agent."

"So, you feel the logic and the evidence favors a theistic explanation?" Dr. Merkel seemed to express surprise.

John nodded without expression. "I do."

"Is this what you wanted to discover?"

John closed his eyes and shook his head. "No. I wanted to believe the evolutionary theory was demonstrable. Most people believe what they want to believe, and they find the rationale to support their convictions. That doesn't work for me."

"Is this issue important to you?" The professor seemed intensely interested, hearing this for the first time from the brightest of his students.

John squirmed in his chair. "Well, it's fundamental to everything. And there's the moral imperative." He looked out the window and took a deep breath. Trance-like he quoted, "'A man that doeth violence to the blood of *any* person, shall flee to the pit; let no man stay him.' So says Proverbs 28:17." He turned to look at Dr. Merkel.

Merkel furrowed his brow and leaned further forward, apparently trying to discern the meaning of this. He tugged at his collar with his index finger, easing the pressure of his tie against this throat and looked down at his desk plotter. "This is not my business, I'm sure. I have no idea what you're dealing with, but I'm good listener, if you need to talk."

Merkel looked up and stared at John for long seconds. John returned his stare and said nothing. Merkel cleared his throat. "So, you believe Plato's Good was based on the Hebrew God?"

John nodded but said nothing. That insight was water under the bridge. He would not elaborate or engage the professor on this nor any other academic issue. He had spent five years contending for and against ideas only to discover that Solomon had been correct, "In much wisdom is much grief: and he that increases knowledge increases sorrow." They continued to stare at each other.

"You've had enough, haven't you?" Merkel finally said.

John nodded and closed his eyes for emphasis.

Merkel leaned back. "Well, here we are, 'on a darkling plain, swept with confused alarms of struggle and flight where ignorant armies clash by night.' You quoted that in one of my seminars." The professor shuffled and stacked the papers on his desk, a segue to another topic.

"So, what do you want to do, John?" He held up his hand. "And before you answer, let me say several things. First, the faculty believes you've earned a master's degree, though you never officially entered the program. We're giving you an M.A. *summa cum laude.*"

"Thank you, sir." John again sat up straight but there was no light in his eyes.

"You've written enough seminar papers to qualify as a thesis ... your Plato-thing. And no need for exams." He scratched his forehead.

"Here's the second reason I asked you in. The department wants to offer you a full fellowship to complete the Ph.D." He raised his eyebrows.

John's expression did not change. He said nothing.

"The staff is concerned about you, John. I wanted a feel for your response before we officially extended the offer. Will you accept it?"

John turned to gaze out the window. Students scurried along the sidewalks heading for class. A few were motivated, eager to plumb the depths of human capability, hoping, expecting to find a foundation for their values and convictions, or to find new ones. But most cared less about the Socratic dictum regarding the unexamined life than what they would wear to the Red Dog Saloon Friday night. Which of them was the wiser? Vanity of vanities, all is vanity, said the ancient preacher. Was John Malik better off for having discovered the futility of all that man does under the sun?

He turned to Professor Merkel. "Sir, I believe I've explored all that the human mind can grasp about reality. It would be a waste of time for me to plow the ground any deeper. With thanks and respect, I decline the offer."

"I was afraid of that." Merkel sighed, picking up an unsharpened yellow pencil and flopping it end for end on his desk blotter. "So, what are you going to do? If you leave school, the draft will get you inside a month or two. You'll ship out for Vietnam and waste that great mind of yours. That's what will happen. You've already had dealings with the draft board."

"I've looked into the options. I'm going to join the Air Force and be a pilot."

"You're going to abandon the gift of a great mind to fly airplanes? That's not worthy of you. You really think there's nothing more for you to learn? Don't you need to nail down a solid worldview?"

"I discovered a fallback principle. It's intellectual hardtack, but I can survive on it."

"Well, I'd like to hear it."

"A character in a novel I read said, 'The meaning of life is to be found in the total involvement in meaningful activity.' The meaningful activity becomes one's purpose. That's the only takeaway I've found in my time here. And I got it from a novel."

Merkel looked away, scowled, and shook his head. "God help us all, Mr. Malik if that's the best we humans can come up with." The interview had come to a close. Merkel stood up. "You have to follow your own way, John, wherever it leads. I'm sorry to lose you."

John stood.

"Godspeed, John Malik. I hope you find what you're looking for."

* * *

Christine and John had not communicated since their last night at the Sunset Drive-In, the night a rerun of "Gone with the Wind" was playing. He would see her one more time.

John entered the back of the civic center auditorium. He took a seat against the back wall and searched the rows of graduates in their caps and gowns seated on the platform. There she was. Christine was scanning the audience, paying little attention to the speeches.

Her eyes locked onto him. She focused on him so intently the girl next to her had to nudge her to pay attention. They were about to call her name.

The presenter said nice things about Miss Charis. She had earned a 4.0 GPA. She had been awarded a full scholarship at Baylor University where she intended to study pre-med. Among other achievements, she was selected as Miss Springfield. The presenter was sure she would make her school, her town, her friends, and her parents proud.

Christine stood and walked with grace up to the podium to receive her diploma to a standing ovation. She nodded to the audience and then addressed them, speaking of new beginnings.

Mostly she looked at John. As she left the stage, she stared back at him. He nodded to her, lifted his hand in farewell, and left.

* * *

John finished the final week of his classes. He was now oriented to the south, to Lackland Air Force Base in San Antonio, Texas where he would begin officer training school, en route to pilot training and war. A new vision had dawned for him, a meaningful cause. He would defend his country against the global threat of communism.

The rising protests against the war infuriated him. Every evening Walter Cronkite documented the violent disruptions of American society by those drug-addled cowards who would not lift a finger to protect the heritage of America.

Though disengaged from people and uninvolved in the movements of his time, John grieved for his country's future. He saw it descending into anarchy. What part should he play in this drama? What difference could he make?

The day came when John loaded his few belongings into the Hornet before first light. He stood in the parking lot and looked up at the dorm. He looked east toward the football stadium as dawn was breaking across Lawrence.

He pulled out of the parking lot southbound and turned east along Jayhawk Boulevard for one last look at the classroom buildings and the libraries where he had spent almost a quarter of his life. He had perfect recall of the speculations of the greatest minds of human history. They had all failed to answer the fundamental questions of origins, purpose, and destiny.

His five years at KU had not been a total waste. Had he not walked this path, he would have continued to believe that it was possible for man to understand his nature and destiny, that there was a viable argument against the existence of God. He would have accepted that this was a scientific certainty, and he would have deferred to those conclusions. But they weren't true.

His journey had brought him to intellectual desolation. It was as though his brain had been bruised by blunt force. He didn't want to think anymore. Perhaps when death found him, the reaper would smile at him and excuse him for having done what he could with the light he had been given. Until the day he looked death in the eyes, he would pour himself into an activity that was meaningful, if mindless. He would fly airplanes.

* * *

Passing Wichita southbound, he glanced east toward Springfield. He imagined Christine packing for her first summer session at Baylor University. His route would take him through Waco, Texas, 450 miles ahead where she would begin the journey he had just completed.

Whenever he thought of her, it was like being punched in the chest. He could hardly breathe, so strong was his longing for her. How was it possible for him to move God to do the thing she had required? It was not within John's power to be consumed with her theological convictions, as much as he might want to share that with her.

Academia had failed him. And the devastating pronouncement from Christine that they were done had crushed his spirit. But just as the specter of utter despair could fully materialize, a ray of light penetrated his consciousness.

He was sitting alone in the common area of the dorm one night three months ago, watching TV. The midnight signoff feature came on. It was the dramatized poem "High Flight." An F-104 Starfighter was streaking over a cloud deck. The majestic words, set to music, became an ethereal dance of grace. The needle-nosed aircraft pulled up effortlessly, rolled, and descended to the top of the cloud deck. A close-up view showed the eyelids of the tailpipe open, a plume of fire blasted through the aperture as the afterburner engaged. A diaphanous shock wave appeared, wavering over the upper curvature of the wing; it moved back across the trailing edge of the wings and separated from the aircraft as the Starfighter went supersonic and disappeared into the sunset.

He would slip the surly bonds of earth and dance the skies on laughter-silvered wings. He would outrun the devil.

PART V:

INTO THE BURNING BLUE

CHAPTER 17
Heartless Discipline

Officer Trainee Major John Malik glared into the terrified face of a young officer trainee cadet whose eyes were focused through Malik on some distant point. The young man with a shaved head stood trembling at rigid attention. He was obviously struggling to come up with an answer to the question screamed at him by Major Malik. The question had been, "Are you eyeballing me, Cadet?"

"May it please the Major, sir, I did not intend to stare, sir!" he shouted.

OT Major Malik turned away, now facing down the long second-floor hall at 250 men under his command standing in a stiff brace beside the doors to their rooms. Malik charged down the hall like an enraged bull, glancing into rooms for evidence of disorder.

"You gentlemen have embarrassed me." His voice thundered down the barracks hallway. "I have been informed that today ... as you returned in your flights, jogging in formation from the exercise field, that some of you wanted to go faster. This created disharmony in the formations resulting in a ragged appearance. This squadron's formations, I'm told, resembled the opening shot at the Boston marathon. Does that seem right to you for a military formation?"

He paused for effect. "I say again, does that seem right to you?" The veins in his neck bulged with the energy of his words.

"No, sir!" came their reply in unison.

"Well, what to do? Here's an idea. From this day forward, you will jog in perfect formation and at the correct pace. You will be in perfect step. I hope for your sakes this never comes to my attention again." His volume modulated from a near scream to a conversational tone.

The squadron remained at rigid attention as Major Malik strode back down the hall and turned into his room. He undressed, folded his clothes, and crawled beneath the covers so as not to disrupt the stretched sheets.

His adjutant, standing at parade rest across the room, reminded him the men were still at attention. John looked at his watch. "I know that."

"Permission to speak, sir?"

"If you must."

"Sir, you are so hard on the men. They don't see any empathy in you."

John lifted his head and glared at his adjutant in utter astonishment. "What the hell do you think we're doing here? These men are on their way to war. Do you get it?"

His adjutant nodded.

"Dismiss the men."

* * *

Twenty percent of Malik's class washed out of Officer Training School in the first three weeks. But the rigor of the program did not approach John's physical or psychological limits, though the training challenged him. During waking hours John and his fellow OT cadets marched, ran, or sat in class or the chow hall, squaring off the movement of their eating utensils with feet planted in a V just in front of their chairs. Their bald heads and the constant screams in their faces by officers and instructors eroded their self-esteem and individuality. They were maggots. No, that wasn't right. Maggots had some purpose in God's order. They were unworthy of the title of a maggot.

For the first half of the training, John and his classmates were underclassmen. When John became an upperclassman, he was interviewed for a command position, marked by his training officer as one with leadership potential. The most powerful job was squadron commander with the officer trainee rank of major—the higher ranks had little direct contact with the men.

John sat at attention before a board comprising six officers. A major asked him, "Cadet, how are you enjoying your experience here with us?"

Malik replied, "Sir, many describe their experience here as the most miserable time of their lives. But, sir, I believe the correct answer is, 'I'm enjoying myself immensely,' sir."

The board dismissed him. He stood to attention, saluted, and thanked the board for their time and consideration. He squared off his steps and marched through the open door.

The board advised OT John Malik the next day that he would be the commander of Squadron Three, comprised of 250 men.

He was not a happy choice for the men he commanded. Malik's training officer, a commissioned first lieutenant, shook his head in dismay as he informed Malik that the cadets feared him more than they feared commissioned officers.

Underclassmen avoided passing him on the sidewalks. His roommate radiated hatred for him. Malik did not have a single friend throughout the training. He spoke to no one except in an official capacity. He aspired to be the perfect officer.

Malik looked forward to receiving his base assignment for undergraduate pilot training, hoping for Williams AFB near Phoenix, Arizona. But when the orders came down, he received assignment to Craig AFB in Selma, Alabama, his last choice.

***

Newly commissioned Second Lieutenant John Malik paced his room in the Squadron Three barracks in his crisp uniform, new gold bars on his collars. With three weeks of leave, he had nowhere to go. He looked out the window, leaning to get a view to the west, toward the parade ground, an expanse of shimmering asphalt upon which hundreds of men, in squads, flights, and squadrons drilled, toiling like insects over the black tarmac. Harsh voices echoed along the buildings.

He held a typed letter from Christine. It was her agreed-upon monthly update describing the events of her life since the last letter.

Yes, she had received his letter. She congratulated him on being a distinguished graduate and being offered a regular commission. She gave him news of his mother, still living on Barnes Street, and still teaching at the college. Her house remained dark at night. Christine reported on her parents and mentioned that Socrates wasn't happy since she left home. Rachel Hixson wanted a letter from John. He should write to her. And Christine mentioned a new friend, Justine, whose family owned an enormous ranch somewhere south of Waco. She spent a lot of time there, riding horses and studying on the weekends.

John's eyes scanned down again to where she wished him well. He read the typed word "love." She had signed it in her beautiful hand.

John walked over to the door and closed it. He returned to his desk in front of the window that looked across trees and fields to massive formations of cumulus clouds building in the distance. He sat down, held his head in his hands, and wept.

***

Lieutenant John Malik, in uniform, turned into the guard gate of Craig AFB and stopped. The guard saluted. John returned the salute and handed him his orders. The airman scanned the document. He pointed ahead and advised Lieutenant Malik to turn left at the first major intersection and proceed to the Visiting Officer's Quarters. Since he had arrived two weeks early, this would be his temporary quarters before the assignment of permanent quarters.

The adventure began. One year of intense training would include academics and non-stop flying. He would first fly the Cessna 172 at the local civilian airport with civilian instructors. This inexpensive training phase identified inept candidates or those who suffered chronic airsickness. A dozen washed out in this phase.

From that aircraft, his class transitioned to the T-37, a twin-engine jet. The T-37 military instructor was so irritated by Malik's gushing enthusiasm he sometimes chewed him out for no other reason than to dampen his spirits. But it didn't work.

With his instructor, Malik flew a 300-mile round-robin "oil burner" bombing route through sparsely inhabited parts of the state at 100 feet. He navigated by dead reckoning using a nav chart. Over each checkpoint, he adjusted the power to increase or slow his speed. When he came over the bomb release point and pulled up, he was two seconds early. However, the bomb impact would have occurred at the exact time he had calculated.

The T-37 was a challenging aircraft to fly, and the spins, sometimes inverted, unnerved him until he had done a dozen of them. The engines could deafen the pilot. The side-by-side seating and the instrumentation required so much focus that the expected state of poetic bliss described in the poem "High Flight" was an impossibility. Maybe he would find that state at the high frontier, in the T-38.

* * *

Second Lieutenant John Malik stood at attention along with two other second lieutenants before a small table in the squadron briefing room. Captain Christopher Taylor, their T-38 instructor, sat behind the table. He was lean and handsome, but there was no light in his eyes.

Taylor regarded the second lieutenants with a neutral expression and gestured to the chairs. The three sat down. Taylor yawned, and his half-closed eyes signaled that he was either tired or indifferent. Malik could not tell which, as yet.

"Let's understand each other from the start," Taylor said. "I don't want to be here. I have completed two combat tours in Vietnam, the first as a Forward Air Controller in OV-10s, the second in F-105s out of Takhli, Thailand. I shot down a MiG 17 and survived 120 missions over the north in the Thud. And the Air Force sends me here, instead of to a fighter wing.

"Many in my unit didn't make it to 100 missions. In fact, half of the guys in my squadron were killed. Now I'm training you hotshots to take their places." He looked at a far wall with paintings of all the century-series fighters depicted in various combat scenes. There was a long silence.

"Now that you understand something about me, don't take my attitude personally. Just do what I tell you and you'll get through the program. Questions?"

The students were silent.

Taylor turned to Malik. "I understand you're enjoying the program and on a fast track to fighters?"

"I hope so, sir."

"Okay, you get a combat assignment to Vietnam. You get your ass shot off and come home with an assignment to Air Training Command, a job like I've got here. You finally make it home and find your wife in bed with the neighbor. You make a scene. She leaves you. What now?" Taylor blinked; his focus drifted far away.

Malik and the other students exchanged furtive glances. Captain Taylor looked at the pictures on the wall. "You get where I'm coming from so don't gush all over me, Malik, because I won't share your rapture. You're up first, your 'dollar ride.' Let's get it over with. Oh yeah, you're able to quote all the boldface emergency procedures if I asked. Right?"

"Yes, sir."

"Without pressure breathing, what is the time of useful consciousness if we have an explosive decompression at 48,000 feet?"

"Three seconds, sir."

"Close enough. That's where we're going. I've filed a profile for a max climb to 48,000 feet then supersonic with a turn at Atlanta and RTB. That's 'return to base' in case you don't know the term."

Taylor got to his feet. "Get your gear. I'll meet you on the flight line bus."

Malik and his two colleagues snapped to attention. Taylor looked back at them. "You don't have to do that."

In the equipment room, Malik strapped on his G-suit, shouldered his parachute, and took his helmet off the rack. His hands were shaking; he checked the pockets of his G-suit for his checklists and other equipment.

The personal equipment sergeant watched him and smiled. He had surely seen hundreds of new students cycle through his shop on their first flight.

John sat in the crew van beside Captain Taylor who stared out the window without expression. The driver checked his list and stopped at the tail number for Taylor's scheduled aircraft. Taylor and Malik got out of the van.

John climbed the ladder to the cockpit and placed his parachute in the front seat and his helmet on the canopy rail; he checked and set up the cockpit before descending the ladder to follow Taylor for the exterior pre-flight.

Malik then climbed back into the front seat and strapped in, plugged in his G-suit, and set up the switches and controls for a start.

"You ready to start?" Taylor said in a monotone over the interphone.

Malik clicked the bayonet fastener into place, securing his mask. "Yes, sir."

"Let me see your hands."

Malik raised his gloved hands so that Captain Taylor in the back seat could see them.

"All right. Put them in your lap. From here on, you just watch. If you don't understand what I'm doing, ask me. But don't touch anything except the ejection seat hands if you hear me say 'Eject!' If you ask, 'What did you say?' You'll be talking to yourself. You understand?"

"Yes, sir."

Just below John's left and right shoulders within the narrow cockpit he could look almost straight down at the concrete of the parking ramp.

Taylor started the engines, accomplished the after-start checks, called ground control for taxi instructions, and gave the "chocks-out" signal to the crew chief. He pulled forward and taxied to the active runway without a word over the interphone. He held short of the runway for landing traffic.

When cleared into position, Taylor taxied onto the centerline of the runway and held the brakes. The tower issued departure instructions, including unrestricted climb clearance to flight level 480. Taylor read back the instructions and advanced the throttles.

Malik felt the nose tilt down as the nose gear strut compressed. He watched the tacs spool up to 100% on both engines. All indications were normal. The tower advised, "Talon Five, cleared for takeoff."

"Talon Five, cleared for takeoff," Taylor replied. "Punch your clock, Lieutenant," he said over the interphone.

John reached up and pressed the elapsed timer on the clock on his panel.

"Hold on," Taylor said through the interphone with a sadistic chuckle.

Taylor released the brakes and pushed the throttles over the detent into full afterburner. The acceleration pinned John to the back of the ejection seat and slammed his head against the headrest. The wheels whirred. He watched the 1,000-foot marker flash by. He glanced down to see the airspeed passing through 150 knots within several heartbeats. The aircraft broke ground at 1,500 feet down the runway, and the gear came up, all in a blur. He saw the end of the 10,000-foot runway rapidly approaching as Taylor held the aircraft 20 feet off the runway.

Just past the end of the runway, the airspeed reached 400 knots. The tower advised, "Cleared unrestricted climb. Contact Jacksonville Center passing 10,000 feet." Taylor acknowledged as he raised the nose of the aircraft to 30 degrees of pitch, holding his speed steady.

He contacted Jacksonville as John rolled his head to the side to see the earth falling away behind him as though they had blasted off a launch pad at Cape Canaveral. The altimeter wrapped around and around, through 20,000 feet, then 30,000 feet. At 40,000 feet, having transitioned from 400 knots to .90 Mach, Taylor rolled the aircraft inverted and began a smooth pull to bring the nose down to the horizon, rolling upright at 48,000 feet.

Jacksonville advised, "Cleared supersonic. Advise terminating." Taylor, who had come out of burner, re-advanced the throttles. The flight instruments fluctuated as the pressure wave passed over the static port, and the aircraft outran its shock wave. Malik was supersonic. Taylor continued in burner until the Machmeter read 1.3 and pulled the throttles back.

"Check your time."

John pressed the clock stopwatch function: four minutes from a standstill to Mach 1.3 at 48,000 feet.

With the throttles back, and slowing, Taylor reported subsonic. The Jacksonville high altitude sector controller would have logged the exact time and location of the supersonic flight segment. The FAA would be able to respond to any complaints of sonic booms.

But the aerodynamic profile of the T-38 was so slight that the pressure wave would dissipate long before it reached the ground.

Jacksonville handed the flight over to Atlanta Center. Taylor tuned the Atlanta TACAN station. The readout from the TACAN showed 70 miles west of Atlanta.

"How long to the turn Lieutenant?" Taylor asked over the interphone.

"Less than five minutes, sir."

They had just taken off from western Alabama.

"Okay, at what slant range should we start the turn north to remain with the airspace of the Jet Route?"

Malik calculated the slant range lead point for the turn. "Sir, we should begin a standard rate turn at seventeen miles on the DME."

"Okay, let's see if you're right," Taylor said.

The arc of the turn passed just short of the Atlanta TACAN as the DME counted down to a mileage slightly greater than their altitude, eight nautical miles. The turn kept Talon Five in the middle of the eight-mile-wide jet route outbound from the TACAN.

"Enjoy the ride, Malik. This is the last time you get to do nothing but watch," Captain Taylor said over the interphone. "Go ahead, hold out your hand and see if you can touch the face of God."

Taylor was being cynical. No jet pilot that flew to these heights and speeds was ignorant of the poem that spoke of this realm as ethereal. In truth, a half-inch of Plexiglas separated Malik from instant death.

He listened to his own breathing through the interphone and the distant whine of the engines against an otherwise silent background. Were it not for the instruments that showed they were crossing the ground at 10 miles per minute, one would assume they were motionless. Outside, the colors were stark and sterile, the sky was the deepest blue, and the temperature was 80 degrees below zero.

John put out his hand toward the windscreen.

CHAPTER 18

The Young Tigers

Malik's fear that he could never think fast enough to control the white rocket was unfounded. He was a natural in the T-38. He came across a life-changing book around this time titled *Psycho-Cybernetics* by Dr. Maxwell Maltz. The author had discovered that vividly imagined experiences could form neural engrams and motor skills without physically doing them. John applied this method throughout the T-38 program.

Night after night, he would sit on a kitchen chair in his BOQ room with a sawed-off broomstick in his hand, simulating the control stick, his eyes closed. In real-time, he imagined himself strapped in the cockpit.

Again, and again, he practiced the syllabus maneuvers. Advancing power, he began a four-G pull-up, easing back pressure as he approached inverted at 30,000 feet. On his back, he continued inverted until reaching 45 degrees of pitch nose down and then rolled upright, modulating the throttles to reach 500 knots at 20,000 feet. At the bottom, he pulled up with 4 Gs to complete the second half of a Cuban eight maneuver, ending up where he started.

On another imagined mission, flying completely on instruments beneath a hood in the back seat, he would follow vectors to final and complete a Ground Controlled Approach until reaching 100 feet above the runway, followed by landing and aerobraking as he held the nose high with the mains on the runway.

His classmates found his training regimen peculiar, but they couldn't argue with the results. His missions were near textbook perfect, and his check-rides were rated outstanding.

His social competence, outside the cockpit, was another matter. He had no close friends in the class. While he got along with most of his colleagues, one of his classmates made it public that he did not like Malik.

The only source of females was Judson College, a women's school about 30 miles northwest of Selma. Girls came down to the Officers' Club on Friday and Saturday nights. Malik had a few dates. He learned to dance, but he was uncomfortable doing it. It seemed so undignified.

His class, 68F, became one of the most infamous to pass through Craig AFB. The class voted for a patch for their flight suits and flight jackets that depicted the voluptuous cartoon character Little Annie Fannie, from Playboy fame. From her mouth came this single word, "FUMA." John was not a party to this, but the acronym stood for "Fly Up My A_ _." Malik was uncomfortable with the decision of his classmates, but he was not vocal.

Unlike his persona in Officer Training School, he was a non-entity in pilot training. He kept to himself and only rarely attended the near-nightly festivities in the stag bar at the O Club. Though usually invited, he seldom attended parties and was ill at ease when he did.

The class was unmatched in debauchery and hijinks. There was widespread wife-swapping occurring within the class among the married students. Drunkenness was prevalent.

Several forceful individuals insisted Malik attend the next Bacchanalia. It was a house party with about equal numbers of men and women, about 60 in all. After alcohol had been flowing freely for some time, everyone was herded into a large bedroom fitted with blackout curtains. The lights were turned off, leaving complete darkness. The instructions were to discover who had the sardine—whatever that meant.

The apparent aim was to grope members of the opposite sex with impunity and in complete anonymity. John found the door and left. What happened next came to the attention of the wing commander.

The class commander and his adjutant stood at rigid attention for an extended inquest before several officers chaired by the wing commander. It was during this grilling that the true meaning of Little Annie Fannie's assertion was to be determined. What did "FUMA" mean? The class representatives assured the wing commander that FUMA stood for, "Forming Useful Military Aviators." The commander was outraged, knowing this was a lie. He stood up and slammed his hand on his desk.

"You bunch of eight balls are on thin ice. I'm giving you a warning now. If I hear of one more infraction involving questionable moral turpitude from your class, you two will be eliminated from the program. You get your class in order, or I will. I'll eliminate the entire class if I have to."

The class commander, a captain, called a mandatory meeting of class 68F with instructions to bring their flight suits and jackets. They were to cut Little Annie Fannie off the shoulders and breasts of their flight gear. In her place, they were to affix a small unadorned patch depicting a black eight ball. The class commander relayed the warning of the wing commander. They would behave themselves or face elimination from flight school.

This social austerity did not cramp John's style since he did not run in the circles of those indulging in free love and alcoholism. But the eight ball identified all members of the class as pariahs. They wore the patch with a mixture of shame and pride, depending on one's perspective.

Fifty-five lieutenants and captains finished the course. At graduation, the Thunderbirds, operating F-100s, and Bob Hoover, flying a P-51, performed an airshow to commemorate the event.

Malik, first in the class, was offered a backseat ride in a Thunderbird F-100F solo aircraft. He was recognized at the graduation banquet and fawned over by the mothers of many of his classmates. Among his assignment choices were fighter-bombers to Thailand (bombing North Vietnam), fighters to Vietnam, and interceptors to Germany and Taiwan. There were no F-104s or F-106s, either of which would have been his first choice. Among the other assignments were bombers and transports and Training Command assignments.

Malik would have taken the F-105, the Thud, but the tour lasted only 100 missions, which could be completed in six months—if you lived that long. The loss rate was appalling. Three hundred Thuds had been shot down already. And if you completed 100 missions, you could not expect another fighter assignment, as Malik's T-38 flight instructor noted bitterly. Above all, Malik wanted to stay in fighters. It was in his blood. He had to live on the edge if he was to survive.

His choice was the F-102 interceptor with the base as yet undetermined. He was to report to Perrin AFB in Sherman, Texas, three weeks after graduation. Perrin was 150 miles north of Waco, where Christine was attending Baylor University.

CHAPTER 19
The Delta Dagger and the Dream

At first light on a spring morning, near the end of his training program in the F-102, First Lieutenant John Malik paced across the concrete floor of a small tin facility just off the end of Runway 17L at Perrin AFB, Texas. His pulse had been rapid for nearly an hour, expecting an imminent scramble. It could come any second.

Out the window he could see his aircraft, a magnificent new supersonic delta-winged machine 67-feet long. The pink light of dawn glinted off its camouflage paint scheme. Just looking at a fighter, any fighter, brought a smile to his face. There were more than a hundred of them just to the north, parked on Perrin's eastern ramp. And as much as he loved the planes and flying, only Christine held his imagination in such a tight grip at the moment.

He pulled her latest letter from the lower zippered pocket of his G-suit and read it for the third time. He could visualize her at Baylor in her dorm room. She was crawling out of bed, staggering to the sink; she washed her face, brushed her long blond hair, and then made her bed. The image of her was equally clear at Justine's ranch. Christine had described her friend's sprawling ranch so vividly he could close his eyes and be there with all his senses engaged.

He held the letter to his nose and inhaled a faint aroma of lavender. The very thought of her holding this paper brought a tremor to his hand. Deep breathing was the only effective way to still a rising passion. This periodic phenomenon had been unabated since it had first overtaken him at KU, the day he drove in feverish intoxication to see her at the Sunset Drive-In. That was six years ago. Now she was grown up.

She was a junior at Baylor and doing well in her biochem/pre-med major. Her family was well, Socrates was getting shaggy and slowing down a bit, John's mom was even more reclusive and morbid, and Rachel Hixson was doing well and wanted John to write her.

"What are your plans for your three-week leave, Johnny?"

John read this line, again and again, wanting it to say more. If only she had invited him to drive down to Waco to see her. Didn't she want to see him? He was going to Germany for a three-year permanent change of station.

Christine no longer gushed with terms of endearment—no words of encouragement. There were no further instructions on how he might reconcile with God and perhaps with his mother. What could Christine have known about that? She offered no more words of advice, no conditional words that might give him hope. Over the last year, her letters had become perfunctory, the kind one might write to a casual acquaintance.

Every time he tore open one of the type-written letters, he scanned it, fearful he would read that she had found someone and was engaged to be married. If only he didn't love her so.

As he stood looking at his fighter, he pictured her just then in the same dawn light he was seeing. He closed his eyes and was transported to the ranch. Christine, wearing a Stetson hat, sat astride an Appaloosa mare, looking out across a pasture knee-deep in morning fog. And he believed she was thinking of him. He carefully folded the letter back into the envelope and stuck it into his lower G-suit pocket and stared at his gleaming fighter.

Rosy dawn turned yellow, and the dew burned off the wings of his alert aircraft. It sat in front of the tin building 100 feet away on the ramp with the canopy up and the ladder in place. Gear pin flags fluttered in the breeze. At 0400, John had strapped his parachute into the ejection seat, pre-flighted the cockpit, and prepped it up for a rapid pneumatic start. He and his crew chief then retired to the "alert" building and waited.

This was one of his last training flights before he would be certified combat-ready with an assignment to Hahn AB, Germany. His mission today was a single-ship scramble against an unknown target or targets. The claxon could sound any second. Or he might sit here all day.

Nothing, except Christine, lit his fire like the prospects of air combat. Gut-wrenching Gs, sweat, and empowering fear. He now knew how to maneuver to defeat chaff, electronic jamming, and flares that attempted to divert his missiles. Most challenging were engagements against an enemy fighter in high-G combat with rockets as his only armament. The objective was to observe an X on the radar scope, electronic confirmation that the missiles or rockets would have destroyed the target. It wasn't personal. It was just academic.

Only this intense focus drew his mind from thoughts of Christine and his futile search for peace of mind. When hopped up on the adrenaline of combat, even if only simulated, he was fully alive.

He glanced up at the clock and checked it against his watch. The base was waking up. The flight line would soon buzz with activity. They'd probably scramble him soon, he figured. But no potential target aircraft had taken off that morning; he had been watching for this. If he was launched now, it would mean the target would be inbound from another base. His crew chief was lounging in front of the TV, eating a burrito. He had done this before. Lieutenant Malik had not.

As though Malik read the situation from over the shoulder of the air defense radar controller, he zipped up his G-suit, zipped his pockets closed and prepared himself for a scramble. "I think it's about to happen."

The crew chief set down his breakfast and got up. The claxon sounded.

They bolted through the door and raced to the aircraft. John sprinted up the ladder with his crew chief behind him. John nodded, and the chief crew slid down to the ground, took away the ladder, and spun his index finger.

Malik rotated the throttle outboard to engage the pneumatic starter and pressed the ignition button. The engine spun up. He brought the throttle over the fuel cut-off detent and the engine lit. The crew chief pulled the pins and waited for the chocks-out signal. He held his arms crossed in a hold-signal as Malik lowered and locked the canopy. The generator came online. John called ground control, "Perrin Tower, Tiger One, scramble."

"Tiger One, cleared into position Runway One Seven Left. Hold for departure instructions."

John signaled chocks out. The crew chief jerked the chocks out, gave a thumbs up, marshaled Malik forward, and saluted. Malik returned the salute and taxied a short distance onto the runway centerline, where he held the brakes awaiting clearance.

"Tiger One. Vector 300 degrees, altitude angels two. Gate. Contact controller airborne on channel one."

Malik acknowledged, advanced the throttle to 100%, checked the instruments, punched his clock, released brakes, and engaged afterburner. The acceleration slammed him back against the seat, the runway center stripe strobed beneath the nose, the wheels whirred, and the airspeed indicator wrapped up to 150 knots as Malik applied backpressure on the stick and broke ground. He immediately retracted the gear, pulled the nose up sharply by mid-field and turned northwest. He held a high-G turn passing just hundreds of feet over the trees west of the field in full burner, accelerating on a heading of

300 degrees as he leveled off. The airspeed indicator continued to wrap up to limiting speed with fuel in the external drop tanks. The command had been "gate," meaning maintain afterburner or maximum thrust to the target, which was apparently closing fast. His breathing, in contrast to the blistering action, was slow and measured.

The controller came on the frequency. "Tiger One, I have a fast-moving bogie at 150 miles on a direct heading for Perrin. Altitude is varying between 500 and 2,000 feet. Present speed 450 knots, head-on. Unable to position you for a stern attack. Target is too fast. State your intentions."

This was a Germany scenario. Fast-moving enemy fighters at treetop level carrying nukes would attempt to destroy allied bases. The enemy objective would be to take out the nuclear-armed F-4s before they could launch to their targets in East Germany and Russia. It was a life-or-death race. The only early defense was the interceptors.

A low altitude target was difficult to paint on the F-102 radar. Only a stern attack would allow the interceptor to get close enough below and behind the target to see it on radar using up-angle on the antenna.

At the airspeed redline for fuel in the drop tanks, Malik extended and retracted the speed brakes repeatedly to prevent over-speed on the tanks until they were empty. He was burning fuel at a prodigious rate.

"Range?"

"One hundred ten miles. Closure is sixteen miles per minute. Advise your intentions, Tiger One."

"Tiger One will maneuver for a stern attack. I'll do the math. I want a countdown starting at fifteen miles."

"Roger, Tiger One."

John descended to 500 feet holding 500 knots, his radar sweeping rhythmically with 10 degrees up-antenna, his breathing slow and steady.

"Fifty miles now. I say again, Tiger One, I don't see how you're going to do this. What can I do for you? Sorry, but I just can't get you behind the target."

"I will do the geometry. Just give range and bearing. Request continuous target information starting at fifteen miles."

Malik's drop tanks went dry. He retracted the speed brakes and increased speed.

"Forty miles, Tiger One. I track you now at 625 knots."

"Just so you will know, at eight miles I'm going vertical and reverse direction on the backside. I'll probably go supersonic to close for a stern attack if the tanks don't rip off. At eight miles I want continuous target bearing and relative speed. Confirm target altitude is angels two."

"That's affirmative, now holding 2,000 feet … thirty miles. Target bearing 300 degrees angels two, closure 17-decimal-5 miles per minute. Tiger One, target clearly resolves now to two aircraft. Holding steady for Perrin. Aircraft type unknown. I'm now seeing the wingman aft of the leader, a quarter-mile off Lead's right wing."

"Fifteen miles … ten miles … nine … eight miles."

John pulled up hard into the vertical, turning slightly right of a collision course to offset. If the bogies were painting him, they would only see him on one sweep of their antennas. There was a possibility they could see him climbing off to their left, but at this range, they probably would not spot him. Four Gs in the pull-up brought him onto his back at 10,000 feet.

"Tiger One, you have passed abeam of the targets, separation increasing. One mile bearing 130 degrees. Targets are holding course and formation. Come right to 150 degrees for convergence. Now three miles at 140 degrees."

Down the backside of the half-Cuban Eight, Malik rolled upright and dove in full afterburner, passing 670 knots. He pressed the first detent of the trigger to begin simulated missile prep. The three missiles in the forward missile bay went on internal battery power.

Their antennas slewed to the aircraft antenna and began transmitting their own radar signals while still enclosed within the bay.

Malik was streaking over the treetops with the throttle just back from the forward stop. He divided his attention between outside, to avoid hitting trees streaking below in a blur, and inside, staring into the radar scope glowing with ground clutter on a short-range selection. He tweaked the antenna up to find a clear area ahead of the ground clutter where the target would hopefully appear.

"Bearing to Bogie Two?"

"Bogie Two is now 12 o'clock, two miles, 2,000 feet, holding steady on 120 degrees, now 60 miles from Perrin."

And there he was, a bright blip just ahead of the ground clutter. Malik locked on. The missiles in the forward bay were now active. The firing sequence counted down as the steering circle collapsed to the fire signal. Malik pressed the trigger to the second detent. The missile bay doors slammed open in a fraction of a second, the rails lowered, and the simulated missiles were away at Mach two plus the aircraft speed. An X appeared on the scope. Malik turned left and called, "Splash Bogie Two."

Bogie Two, destroyed in the simulation, pulled away and climbed to the west.

"Bearing to Bogie One?" Malik was fully focused, breathing rhythmically, intent on destroying the second target. Never was he so engaged, never as alive as in this moment.

"Bogie One is one mile, bearing 110 degrees, descending, accelerating. He knows you're behind him!"

Just then, John saw a top view of an F-106 rising vertically. He attempted a radar lock but could not find him in time on the scope. This would be another kind of fight altogether, one in which the F-106 would win, all things being equal.

Malik pushed the throttle against the stop. In war, he would have blown his wing tanks as he pulled up sharply, leading the '106 with a two hundred knot advantage but without the raw power and the wing of the other aircraft. The '106 was going for altitude ... big mistake.

On the fire control panel Malik selected rockets without taking his eyes off the target that was rapidly filling his windscreen. He pressed the trigger to the first detent to open the missile bay doors packed with 24 rockets. His overtake and cutoff advantage closed the distance to 1500 feet in several eyeblinks. Within seconds of collision, Malik pressed the trigger to the second detent and fired a simulated volley of rockets that could not have missed.

"Splash Bogie One. RTB." Malik came out of burner and zoomed to 10,000 feet, with a minimum fuel light winking on the master caution panel.

"Roger, Tiger One. Standby for vectors to initial, Runway One Seven Right."

* * *

After landing, Malik was marshaled to the ramp and shut down. He unstrapped and climbed down the ladder as though he had just driven to the grocery store. He checked his armpits, no sweat stains, his hair was not plastered down with sweat. According to his instructors he was a genius with an airplane and as cool as ice

His flight commander, standing by the left wing, was just turning down the squelch on his hand-held radio, watching Malik step off the ladder onto the tarmac. Malik's flight instructor was also waiting for him, arms crossed. Malik, apparently, was in trouble.

The three of them walked around the aircraft looking for damage. The flight commander shook his head as they examined the right drop tank that was twisted on the pylon. "You're in big trouble, Lieutenant. The wing commander wants to see you right now."

Silent and grim-faced, they boarded the crew van and headed to base ops. They were ushered into the wing commander's office and stood at rigid attention before his desk. The wing commander leaned forward in his chair, propped his elbows on his desk, and stared at Malik.

"Lieutenant, this is a training environment, not all-out war. Review some regs with me, just to be sure I understand them. When can you make your first turn off the runway on takeoff?"

"Sir, that would be at the field perimeter and at least 400 feet, whichever comes last."

"Yes, that's what I thought. You turned before the gear was up. You almost took off the tops of trees at midfield. That's what the tower tells me. How about this? What is the closest you can come to property, structures, or persons in a rural environment?"

"Sir, that would be 500 feet."

"Yes, that's what I thought too. But the CGI controller plotted you at 200 feet over a small town where you should have been at least 1,000 feet. And what about airspeed? What's the fastest you are supposed to go below 10,000 feet?"

"Three hundred knots, sir, except in the training area."

"Right. Well, you were clocked supersonic, something above 680 knots at 500 feet. I didn't know the airplane would go that fast on the deck with drop tanks. I learn something every day. But, to get to the point, you've put me in a tough spot, Lieutenant."

He sat back and turned his chair to look out the window toward the runway where a formation of F-102s were just breaking ground. The wing commander seemed to be lost in thought. He scratched his forehead. No one said anything. His three subordinates continued to stand at rigid attention. Finally, he turned back and looked at Malik.

"You have anything to say?"

"Sir, I apologize."

"Do you mean, if you had it to do over, you would have done things differently?"

Malik did not answer.

"You didn't figure it out, did you? This mission had no solution. You weren't supposed to be able to stop the intruders. The scenario is the same that our F-4 nuke delivery force will execute crossing the East German fence if the balloon goes up. In theory, the East Germans can't intercept them."

Malik remained at attention, his eyes focused on the wall behind the wing commander, though he could see the commander's expressions.

The colonel continued, a strange expression on his face. Irony, perhaps? "I can take your wings for what you did. You know that, right?"

Malik nodded without expression

The commander continued, "I'm sure the F-106 drivers out of Richards-Gebauer had every intention of bragging at the stag bar tonight how they destroyed Perrin, and we couldn't stop them. It seems you have dampened their expectations. That's one for us. But you've damaged one of my airplanes and violated a half-dozen regs, any one of which could put you up for a review board. And beyond that, you've set the Air Force up for lawsuits from ranchers west of here. A shock wave off an F-102 at that altitude can shatter every piece of glass in a house, not to mention other damage .... So, tell me, hotshot, what were you thinking?"

Malik swallowed. "Sir, my mission, as I understood it, was to stop the enemy from destroying the base." He took a deep breath, expecting his career was over. But, growing resentful, he believed he had been entrapped. His voice was now emphatic. "This scenario was *not* impossible, as I just demonstrated. I practiced this geometry in my mind, did the calculations, and knew in advance exactly how I would deal with it. As far as I knew, sir, I did what YOU wanted me to do! Destroy the enemy. If, as you say sir, the scenario had no solution, what the *hell* was I supposed to learn? Sir! Let me say one more thing, if I may, sir. Had I not achieved those speeds Perrin Air Force Base would have been a smoking ruin .... Simulated, of course, sir."

The commander glared at him. His jaw was clenched, and his fists were balled. In Malik's peripheral vision, his flight commander and instructor stirred uneasily and glanced at each other out the corners of their eyes. They undoubtedly believed they were witnessing a career meltdown.

The commander stood up and seemed to cool down. "Lieutenant, I want you to write up a detailed account of how you splashed two F-106s from a head-on encounter at low altitude. And I want your calculations. Have it on my desk by tomorrow morning. You'd better pray we get no calls from irate ranchers and bills for damage." Then he began to chuckle, apparently impressed with Malik's cheek. "Alright, you're dismissed, Lieutenant. And I don't want to see you in here again, you got that?"

"Absolutely not, sir. Malik snapped a salute, turned, and marched out the door, leaving his instructor and flight commander to deal with the wing commander. Unless you were a general you never talked to a wing commander the way Malik had just done.

* * *

John rode a red gelding, and Christine was on an Appaloosa mare. They had been riding west at a slow pace for an hour with hardly a word between them. They were miles west of the main house on a vast tract of cattle land south of Waco, Texas, land owned by Justine's family.

From slightly behind Christine, he stared at her continuously. She persisted in a vacant gaze at the horizon, apparently lost in thought, almost as inscrutable in person as in her monthly letters.

Why had she invited him down to Justine's ranch? Only two ranch hands were on the property, living in their bunkhouse a half-mile from the main house. What could she be thinking? What did she expect from him?

Fenceless pasture stretched as far as they could see in all directions. Timbered hills rolled to the horizon, unbroken by any sign of human presence, except for galvanized stock tanks. Scattered white and reddish-brown Hereford cattle grazed in the open fields or rested beneath the trees chewing their cud.

Above the scene of solitude, colossal mountains of late summer cumulus clouds reached great heights in all quadrants of the sky.

They writhed with energy, heavy with impending rain. Powerful winds in the upper atmosphere blew the tops of the storms into the classic anvil shape of thunderstorms while John and Christine sweltered in the breathless afternoon heat.

John straightened his back and relieved the pressure on his rear end by bracing against the saddle horn with his hands. Did he dare look at her again? He couldn't help himself. She sat astride her horse ahead of him in the shade of trees, staring into the distance. Her fetching profile beneath her Stetson sent tremors through him.

What was it he felt when he looked at her? When he spoke her name, when he remembered her aroma, the beautiful slope of her nose, the gold dust in her eyes?

The leather saddles creaked, and one horse shifted its weight, lifted and dropped a rear hoof with a bored snort. Only these sounds broke the silence of the vast sky. The wondrous atmosphere was fragrant with horse sweat, leather, and the organic scent of trees and earth. The aromas cleansed and awakened John's sense of smell as he rested his hands on the saddle horn, holding the reins, enduring the disquiet of his pounding heart.

He cocked his head to locate a far-off rumble of thunder. Then the sky crackled with lightning and another rolling boom came over the treetops. He spun around in the saddle to see an angry black mass of curling cloud about to overtake them.

"It'll be a gully washer!" Christine's voice spiked with intensity. She turned to look at John, her eyes and face a mask of fear.

"Should we start back?"

"We'd never make it. I think there's a shed just over that hill. We'd better head for it as fast as we can."

They jabbed their heels into the horses' ribs and took off in a gallop down the knoll, across the pasture, and up the hill ahead, pursued by a cold draft of wind that smelled of torrential rain. Over their shoulders, a black wall bore down upon them. They urged their horses on, racing toward an open-sided pole barn with bales of hay piled high beneath the tin roof. They galloped under the structure and pulled up with a curtain of rain on their heels.

John looked over at Christine, her face lit with mischievous glee. "Let's get off and stay awhile." She had to yell over the rising fury of wind and rain that was just reaching the hay shed.

They dismounted and stood breathless, holding the bridles close, caressing the necks and muzzles of their spooked horses. They shivered in the wind that drove the slanting rain toward them. The tin roof began to clang with the hammering of rain and hailstones. Thunder crackled, and strobes of lightning illuminated the darkening scene of trees now hissing and steaming with rain.

The sky opened up, and water and darkness fell about them, obscuring the trees a hundred feet from the shed. The deafening deluge on the tin roof drowned out any attempts at conversation. Torrents gushed down the sides of the roof and streamed from the eaves in opaque sheets, leaving a view only out the ends of the shed. They laughed and squealed like children, and Christine's eyes danced with delight as she watched the rain. And that sparkle, he observed, remained when her eyes lingered on him. Her pupils were so large. She was looking into his soul, devouring him with her eyes. Her hair was blowing gloriously in the wind, the image of Aphrodite being born on the foaming sea.

With a barely restrained smile, she gazed at him for long seconds amid the maelstrom wreaking fury about them. Then she dropped her horse's reins and walked several yards to the end of the shed. She closed her eyes as the mist swirled beneath the tin roof. She leaned her head back and breathed deeply, lifting her chest, her arms wide.

John let go the reins of his horse and joined her. She turned to look at him again expressionless, inscrutable. She took his hand in hers and kissed it, as she had done so long ago on the swing on his front porch, the day she had kept him from committing suicide. Her eyes were tearing. She looked away toward the trees just as a bolt of lightning lit the scene with a white-hot light. The explosion rocked them backward and left their ears ringing. They quickly grabbed the reins of the horses that were about to bolt. They calmed them and tied the reins to a support beam in the lee end of the shed.

The torrent finally abated to a steady soaking downpour pattering on the tin. They climbed up on top of the bales of hay and lay down. They held hands, saying nothing, looking up at the dirt daubers' nests in the rafters. The intensity of John's passion mellowed; he regained control of his breathing. Slowly, deliberately, he inhaled the cool, wet, clover-scented air.

Christine snuggled against him. Her breath, smelling of peppermint, was shallow and rapid. He could feel her heart beating. Abruptly she sat up, shook her head, and took a deep breath. She looked into the trees whose limbs drooped under the weight of their drenched leaves. The rain had stopped, and tree frogs were peeping in the stillness of the first starlight.

"God is in all of this. I am as convinced as ever. From the time I first saw you, when I was ten years old, I knew it. And I told you then." She turned to look at him lying beside her. "You and I were born for each other. Nothing can change that." She turned away, "But, oh God, how can I endure the waiting?"

Silent for some minutes, her voice emotionally charged, she said softly, "Johnny, you have to return to God. *Promise* me you will. I want to sail away with you to some golden shore. All I want is to live my life with you."

She placed her hands over her face and broke into heavy sobs, racking cries of anguish that seemed to flood from the storehouse of a frustrated lifetime. "I've waited so long for you. I don't know how much longer I can wait."

When she was composed, she whispered, "Please, never forget me, Johnny. I wanted this time to say goodbye. For now." She gazed at him intently. "In some dark moment, when you need God with all your heart, you'll find Him. Then everything will change." She lay back down and clutched him tightly, sobbing.

For some time, she lay with her head on his chest, his arm around her. Then she nodded off, seemingly at peace. John watched

ON A DARKLING PLAIN

her eyes in rapid motion beneath her eyelids. He let her sleep, five minutes, twenty minutes—he lost track of time. His passion had abated, eclipsed by weightier issues that went far beyond the moment.

She woke with a start. "Oh, I'm sorry. Was I out long?"

"Just a few minutes." He disengaged from her embrace and sat up. "Look, I've been watching this spectacle. It's an epiphany." He pointed out the end of the shed to the now-inky sky spangled with countless stars strewn along the galactic plane. "I've been watching the long road of the river of stars."

"Is that a quotation?"

"It's a line from an eighth century Chinese poet named Li Po. Out there, time and space form a continuum. That river of light has arrived from vastly different ages, converging here in a single instant ... space-time, that's what Li Po understood a long time ago."

She pulled him down to her urgently. "Please, Johnny, come home to me when you're weary of the far country. You are a prodigal son. Please find your way home to me."

She rolled over and straddled him. She leaned down, hovering over his mouth, breathing his breath when he exhaled, as though she were trying to inhale his very life. Then she kissed him intensely.

* * *

John awoke with a start. He sat up, swung his legs over the edge of the bed, lowered his head. Another dream.

He dragged himself out of bed, got dressed, and walked to the O Club for an omelet. Back in his spartan room, he tuned in his favorite Saturday morning cartoons and then watched the Icky Twerp Saturday special.

For three weeks he watched TV, ate out, and went to movies. He repeatedly picked up the phone to check for a dial tone, to be sure it was working. With just days to go, he sold his Hornet. Using a government voucher, a shuttle service dropped him off at the

American Airlines ticket counter at the Dallas/Ft. Worth airport. He caught a flight to LaGuardia. After a long layover, he boarded a World Airways flight to Frankfurt.

PART VI:

THE COLD WAR

CHAPTER 20
The Worst Weather in the World

John Malik heaved to get enough air, verging on claustrophobia, sandwiched in a window seat between the aircraft sidewall and a 200-pound army corporal in the middle seat. The corporal was miserable. He had been thrashing in his narrow seat for five hours since departing Gander, Newfoundland. He had been unable to sustain civility and deference to Malik's rank. After an early scuffle for the use of the armrest, Malik conceded. But he used it when his seatmate wasn't paying attention; this led to another brief struggle in which Malik would again concede. The corporal needed it more than he did.

Malik leaned his head against the window, trying to control his breathing. Out the window, as the starlight was fading into dawn, he saw the wingtip light flickering through cloud tops. A monitor on the forward bulkhead showed the flight progress. They were at 35,000 feet approaching the coast of Belgium. Solid clouds at this altitude meant that an overcast seven miles deep blanketed all of Western Europe.

Fifteen minutes later, the airplane's captain began descent. In less than a minute, the wingtip light disappeared in dense cloud. Malik stared incredulously into the darkening weather with the realization that he would have to fly in this kind of soup, on the wing of another aircraft, and, God forbid, attack enemy aircraft. How could you fight an air war when you couldn't identify the target? For the first time in his Air Force career, he doubted his competence.

The slats and flaps extended, and the gear came down with a clunk as the aircraft rolled out on final approach. The runway approach lights appeared beneath as the DC-8 crossed the threshold of the rain-soaked runway and touched down. Cheers went up from 250 soldiers and dependents.

Out the window, Malik caught his first sight of Germany, gray and veiled in rain. He hated it. He had come here to fly the all-weather delta-wing F-102 interceptor as a combatant in the cold war, a war that could turn white-hot with little warning. Twenty minutes east a vast array of Soviet aircraft sat on runways and ramps and alert facilities awaiting an order to launch. Malik's job would be to absorb the first shock of World War III.

As he peered into the gloom, Malik saw a multitude of airliners moving along the taxiways. Continuous departures and arrivals were occurring on the parallel runways. As he looked back, he saw the landing lights of a Boeing 747 appear out of the fog. The aircraft passed over the approach lights and touched down in a spray. And he pondered another part of his job.

He might be scrambled to intercept any allied or commercial aircraft, especially airliners, that strayed into the buffer zone, a 25-mile-wide corridor paralleling the Air Defense Identification Zone. The ADIZ abutted the East German border. Inadvertent or not, the East German air defenses would shoot down any aircraft that passed through the ADIZ and crossed the political border. How could he intercept an airliner and turn it away from disaster in weather like this? Impossible.

The hard reality of air defense under these conditions far exceeded his worst expectations as he trained in the fair weather of north Texas. He once assumed all was well with the world. But it wasn't. Those who sat air defense alert knew better. Now he was to be a watcher on the wall.

At any given moment, the air defense shield of Western Europe relied on two alert aircraft each at six airbases that lay in a line stretching from the Netherlands to Munich, each guarding a sector along the Iron Curtain. Only a dozen interceptor pilots were capable of responding within five minutes to hostile westbound aircraft. And those inbound aircraft would be on the deck carrying nuclear weapons targeting Allied airbases and vital military facilities.

The DC-8 pulled into the gate. The seat belt sign extinguished. Malik and his seatmate worked their way into the aisle and collected their carry-ons from the overhead. They looked at each other, nodded, and smiled ironically, deferentially. Both faced a three-year assignment far from home. John's only light in this grim new world was the savor of Christine's last kiss, the earthy aroma of her breath and the taste of peppermint. That was only a dream, but it sustained him for now.

***

The blue USAF bus meandered along narrow roads en route to Hahn. Streetlights illuminated glistening rain-soaked village streets; the lights of businesses and homes lit the gloom as though night had persisted into mid-day. He checked his watch and reset it to local time, 11:45 a.m.

Two hours after departing Frankfurt, the bus turned in and stopped at the main gate to Hahn Air Base. The Security Police came aboard the bus to check everybody's credentials. Satisfied, they left the bus and waved it through the checkpoint. Malik had just entered a fortress on the frontier of the cold war.

He checked into the Bachelor Officers' Quarters. The German girl behind the counter gave him a manila envelope and a room key. He found his room on the second floor. Door levers? Why didn't they use knobs? Throwing his bags on the bed, he headed into the bathroom and was appalled to see a high commode tank and pull chain. After a shower in a tub with strange controls, he dressed in civilian clothes and sprinted through the mist to the O Club next door.

John frowned at the menu; they didn't even have hamburgers. Still hungry, he returned to his room, where he stared into the afternoon gloom, read his orientation materials, and mostly pined for Christine.

The next morning, he found transportation that took him to the squadron building, near the Alert Complex at the end of Runway 04. He knocked on the office door of Lieutenant Colonel Aaron Slavin, the squadron commander. Malik saluted. "Sir, Lieutenant John Malik, reporting for duty."

Slavin returned his salute, stood up to shake Malik's hand, and gestured to a chair. "So, you're John Malik. Your instructor at Perrin, Phil Murphy, joined us two weeks ago. He tells me you caused quite a stir there."

John sucked air through his teeth. "I hope I didn't get him in trouble, sir."

"Well, they had to rethink several training issues. Murphy got credit for training you, and that may have been a factor in his promotion to major below the zone; he just pinned on his leaves. A number of his students are in the squadron, but he tells me you were the best student he ever had."

Malik raised his eyebrows and smiled faintly.

"We're happy to have you and expect great things from you."

"I hope I won't disappoint you, sir."

Briefings lasted a week. Then Malik had his first flight in the two-seat TF-102 with an instructor. He saw the sun when they broke out of the weather at high altitude to conduct intercepts. The sunlight was like a tonic. He completed three intercepts and returned to base.

On his third night at Hahn, Malik wandered out the front gate in light snow into the local village. He had the *jägerschnitzel* at a quaint restaurant then walked down the street to a *bierstube*. As he stood at the bar, watching the clientele, he heard a song on the sound system that he believed must be German, despite the English lyrics. He had never heard this song before. The lyrics spoke of days the singers thought would never end, how they would sing and dance forever and a day. That melody stamped into his memory this time and place of gloom and snow and crystals of ice sparkling in streetlights at midday. He didn't like it here.

* * *

Lieutenant Malik learned what it meant to be at the bottom of the totem pole. He inherited the duties nobody wanted. These included buying plaques for the departing flight crews from the squadron slush fund, coordinating with the local German bootmaker for anyone needing flight boots, and ordering name and squadron patches. He had to maintain the movie projector and splice broken films in the Alert Complex. Any chore nobody else wanted to do became an additional duty for Malik.

One of the flight commanders discussed the squadron intelligence officer position with him. They might ask Malik to take that job. If so, he would be the custodian of the top-secret documents stored in a walk-in vault in the squadron building. Documents included war plans for both his unit and the 50th Tactical Fighter wing, the unit that owned the base.

Malik's new colleagues made it clear they expected him to show up at the Stag Bar in the O Club for camaraderie and beer drinking. The chief exponent of this activity appeared to be a senior captain named B. B. Regel, who had recently been passed over the second time for promotion to major.

Contrary to his disposition, John dutifully showed up a few times at the bar, noting single American women were there, schoolteachers and nurses. He watched one dusky-voiced beauty named Alice. But he didn't go to the bar often and didn't run into her anywhere else.

Weeks passed. Once acclimated to the aircraft, the airspace, the procedures, and the instrument approaches to Hahn, he began conducting intercepts on daily training missions in the single-seat aircraft and started the "No Guts No Glory" syllabus on air-to-air combat tactics, otherwise known as "dogfighting." Dogfighting defined what it meant to be a fighter pilot, the most grueling type of flying, one pilot against another. Any airborne fighter was subject to immediate attack. The contests involved high Gs, near-collisions, and heart-pounding fear. An hour of pulling Gs was like taking a beating.

F-4 and F-105 encounters with MiGs over North Vietnam made it clear that the doctrine of stand-off missile tactics would not work in jet fighter-to-fighter engagements. The Air Force had to revive the World War II and Korean War art of dogfighting.

Malik learned how to execute violent maneuvers to shake somebody off his six. He practiced the high G vector roll and high G barrel roll, the yo-yo, the vertical rolling scissors. Where possible, he learned to carry the fight to the top of the egg where gravity supplied an additional G to reduce turn radius to a minimum—if you were on your back, inverted, pulling positive Gs. He learned to feel the onset of the burble, the nibble of an approaching stall, where the maximum turn rate occurred. Victory often happened only along this narrow margin.

* * *

After a short stint living in the BOQ on base, Malik bought a sports car from a pilot shipping out and moved out into the country to a large rambling German home with multiple apartments and a remote cabin—where he lived at first. His landlord, Rudi, had been a German U-boat commander in World War II, recipient of the Iron Cross. However, in his broken English, he several times assured Malik he had not been a Nazi. No, he didn't like the Nazis, and he didn't like Herr Hitler.

The estate sat a mile from the steep slopes of the Mosel River Valley. And he hated it. The dark forest swallowed all light. Ice fog blanketed the trees. Everything seemed threatening and lonely. He had no TV and no radio. Silence and cold were his only companions.

CHAPTER 21
Kidnapped

Because he dreaded going home so much, and because he had limited tolerance for alcohol and little taste for it, thus avoiding the Stag Bar, Malik would sometimes hang out late into the night at the Alert Complex still in his flight suit. The Alert Complex was a reinforced concrete structure buried with earth on three sides. It had a central living area flanked with fighter bays housing four F-102s, cocked for immediate launch. On a scramble, the interceptors drove straight out of the bays along a high-speed taxiway onto the runway where they could accelerate for takeoff without stopping.

The four aircraft bays were enclosed by two-story steel doors on railroad rails that rumbled open when the scramble claxon sounded. In the center of this complex was a narrow three-story structure. The ground level housed the kitchen, dining area, and quarters for the crew chiefs. On the second floor, there was a theater/briefing room where the alert crews watched first-run double features every night. Forward of the theater was a lounge area with recliners, lamps, desks, and reading material. And in front of the lounge was the control center, manned by at least two non-commissioned officers who maintained communications with the radar sites monitoring the border. They managed the Alert Complex. From their position, they could look out through the bullet-proof glass at the runway and the base.

The sleeping quarters for the alert pilots were on the third level. Brass fire poles connected each level, allowing rapid descent to the fighter bays on the first level.

John often stayed in the complex to watch movies or to read while the squadron pilots were yelling at each other to be heard at the O Club Stag Bar. How was that fun? Their hands moved in concert, describing their latest dogfights. They watched the single women, and the single women watched them.

It was 2200 hours Saturday night. Senior Master Sergeant Franco Myers, the duty controller, glanced up when John walked into the command center to look out the thick glass into the winter night. Myers turned down the rheostat on the red lights that illuminated the consoles and joined him in looking at the vista. At the far end of the console was a young staff sergeant, also looking out the glass.

Snow swirled around the dark shapes of twenty-two jet interceptors parked on the ramp next to the Alert Complex. Pennants and flags, attached to landing gear safety pins and intake covers, whipped in the cold night wind, a wind that sent silvery sheets of crystals flying off the crowns of the high snowbanks that lined the edges of the ramp and taxiways.

"It's a bad night to fly," Myers muttered. "I hope we don't have a scramble tonight."

"Well, I'd rather fly than drive home in this stuff. Black ice scares me."

"You mean you have a home?"

John nodded. "Yeah, kinda."

"You know, Lieutenant, I don't get you." Myers turned toward Malik. "Why do you hang out up here? Nobody does that but you. You ought to find yourself a girlfriend or go to the Stag Bar. Or go home …. Are you hearing me, sir?" Myers tilted his head and raised his eyebrows.

"I don't want to go home. The heat doesn't work. When it does, I'm still cold. And I don't have a TV. It's like living in the Transylvania forest out there."

The Transylvania reference had special meaning tonight since the featured movie playing in the theater was *The Fearless Vampire Killers* with Sharon Tate. He had already seen it twice, as had the alert pilots who were watching parts of it for the third time just to see Sharon Tate. She was almost as winsome as Christine. Almost.

"Well, I'd like to give you a heads up, sir. How am I supposed to put it?" He scratched his forehead. "I don't think the other pilots understand why you're here, like you don't have a life. They have ways of conforming new guys to their ways. I hope you're hearing me."

John considered his words and shrugged. He turned to walk back into the complex but glanced back through the glass partition to see Myers turn up the rheostat on his reading light and pick up the phone. Myers turned to look at Malik as he spoke a few words then hung up.

Myers turned to look out into the night and raised his wrist and pressed his watch. That's what it looked like to Malik. What was that all about? He wondered. He settled into the recliner in the lounge, listening to periodic transmissions from NATO Air Defense Command squelching in the background. He opened his book, *The History of the Roman Empire in North Africa*.

* * *

From his console, Myers surveyed the approaches to the 496th Alert Complex, guarded by security forces. He peered out the window at the final checkpoint, wondering how this would play out. As he watched, two guards huddled over an electric heater in the tiny glass and plywood shack jumped to their feet and burst out of the shack with their weapons at the ready, aiming down the hill. Myers looked down the hill. A black Mercedes sedan jumped several curbs, plowed through a snowbank, crossed a median, and come barreling up an aircraft taxiway toward the Alert Complex.

The car streaked past the befuddled guards and came to a screeching stop in front of the Alert Complex. Three men in flight suits jumped out while the driver maneuvered, backing up to the entry door. The three disappeared inside while the guards raised their weapons and held their fire.

Myers headed toward the back stairs to confirm that the intruders were indeed the men he was expecting. They were. They brushed past him, ran through the movie theater and into the lounge toward Malik, who sat up in alarm.

Without saying a word, they grabbed Malik by the arms and legs. One of them threw his history book into a trashcan, and they raced for the stairs. Myers followed them as they carried the struggling Malik, bumping down the stairs to the ground floor and out the entry. They threw Malik into the open trunk of the sedan, slammed the lid, and sped away.

* * *

Malik was a loose missile in the trunk of the Mercedes. He flew from lid to floor and from side to side, choking in dust and debris. He fended himself off the loose spare tire, disoriented, unable to figure out what was happening. Why were they doing this to him? The final maneuver he sensed by the driver was a sudden stop, a crunch into reverse, and acceleration backward, followed by an abrupt halt that threw him and the spare tire against each other.

The trunk lid flew open, and he looked up into many intent faces peering down at him. Everyone was exhaling steam in the cold air and making comments to each other. There were nods and murmurs of approval. Malik's abductors, pilots of the 496th led by Captain B. B. Regel and others reached in, lifted him out of the trunk, and carried him on their shoulders.

He craned his neck, seeing the car's rear bumper just three feet from the entrance to the Stag Bar. He rode high on the shoulders of several people and glided on the arms of many supporters through the bar. A crowd of rowdy people parted as he came through their midst in the arms of his squadron mates who planted him on a bar stool, dusted him off, and straightened his flight suit. A stein of beer slid in front of Malik. Standing next to him Phil Murphy raised his beer and proposed a toast to the Roman Empire. Malik, with a pinched smile, raised his stein.

While everyone cheered and laughed at Malik's distress, B. B. Regel leaned against him and whispered in his ear, "You shape up, or I'll make your life hell in this squadron. You're supposed to be a fighter pilot. You give us a bad name. And frankly, I don't like you." Regel strutted away, leering at the young women who sat at a table. They weren't looking at Regel, they were staring at John Malik.

Another tall stein of beer sloshed in front of Malik, who was already feeling the effects of the first. He blinked, and Alice was standing beside him, saying something he couldn't hear for the noise. The party might go on all night. Almost everybody had tomorrow off. Where was his car? How was he going to get home?

What was Alice saying? He struggled to get the gist of her words as he plunged into the shrinking, spinning world of inebriation, being urged to chug his third complimentary beer. He heard this much: she had yelled in his ear, "B. B. Regel used to be Phil Murphy's best student at Perrin." He didn't understand why she was telling him that. He remembered nothing after that.

**

The 496th had to scramble in all weather conditions against impending air penetrations into their sector from the east. Fast-moving enemy aircraft sometimes dashed toward the border with a projected flight path that would cross the fence into West Germany. The enemy staged such incidents, perhaps to clock reaction times and to yank the Americans' chain. Or it might be that American F-104 crews had started this taunting by driving toward the East German border and pulling up at the fence.

When the alert pilots turned in for the night, they laid out their flight suits and boots in a line from their bunks to the fire pole where their flight jackets hung from a peg. They slept in their socks and long johns.

On a bitterly cold night, Malik awoke as though being electrocuted when the claxon sounded. He sprang out of his bunk and hit the floor running. Flight suit and boots zipped up, jacket slung on, he and his flight lead slid down two stories on the fire poles and slammed through the steel doors into the bays to their aircraft. Malik strapped on his G suit hanging on the ladder and bounded up the ladder to the cockpit.

In 20 seconds from the claxon, he had strapped in, his engine was spooling up, and the blast doors were moving ponderously on the rails, nearly open. Above the doors, a green light confirmed launch. Malik received a salute from his crew chief, pulled down and locked his canopy, and blasted out of the number three bay, pausing just outside to allow Lead to get ahead of him. They sped along the high-speed taxiway, angling onto the runway for a brief run-up.

All instrument indications were normal. Lead nodded forward and released brakes. Malik pressed the elapsed timer function on the panel clock. Six seconds later, he released brakes, glancing up at the dome of illumination in the fog of a 100-foot ceiling as he accelerated down the runway.

At rotate speed, he transferred his entire attention to the attitude indicator, the gyro instrument that depicted the roll and pitch of his aircraft relative to the horizon. He broke ground and raised the gear without taking his eyes from the attitude indicator. Immediately in the weather, he tweaked the radar antenna up on the short-range setting and saw Lead just beyond the ground clutter, one mile ahead. Lead had started a turn east.

In less than four minutes from a sound sleep, the flight was airborne, turning toward the target with Malik in radar trail behind Lead. They had no information on the target as yet. Their vector was straight to the fence, nine minutes ahead.

Ten miles from the border, the controller broke them off. The target had turned north. Malik and his leader pitched up and turned away, climbing westbound to 28,000 feet.

When launched without an eventful outcome, the alert aircraft, heavy on fuel, had to burn it off before landing. A hot scramble in the night reverted to a training flight in the dark on instruments. They butted heads, running intercepts on each other until they burned down enough fuel to return to Hahn.

It was more than just ironic that a helpful observation from the sleepy tower controllers reported the ceiling and visibility exactly at minimums. Any lower and the flight could not have begun the instrument approach. After landing they refueled, re-cocked their aircraft, and got back into their bunks.

This was the second time Malik had scrambled against this bogus target. A low altitude inversion layer had bounced the air defense radar beam to the surface, revealing a moving target that appeared to be airborne. This target was tracking for border penetration at 120 knots. It had appeared before at the same time, 0300, under the same meteorological conditions. It turned out to be a train on a track that ran west to a point one mile short of the border. At that point, the tracks turned north.

* * *

Malik was number four in a four-ship training flight led by Captain B. B. Regel. The training officer had instructed the intercept controller to provide the flight with only the target bearing information—altitude unknown. Regel had deployed the four-ship, line-abreast, side by side, at 25,000 feet. Below was a solid undercast.

In Malik's opinion, this was a dangerous formation. Each pilot had to divide his attention between outside, to avoid collision with the adjacent aircraft, and inside, searching the radar scope for the target. The flight should have been staggered in trail. But anyone under the rank of major did not argue with B. B. Regel.

The controller turned the flight head-on toward the target, 25 miles on the nose. The closure rate was higher than any Malik had experienced, over 22 miles a minute. The target had to be supersonic. What could it be? With this geometry the interceptors had just seconds to acquire and lock on to the target if the missiles were to have time to arm. Miles passed in seconds, and no one reported contact. If the narrow three-degree-wide radar beam was not aimed at the proper angle the target could pass them without appearing on the scope. Closure was growing critical in the seconds remaining. Where was the target?

Some intuition inspired Malik to press the trigger to the first detent, which began activation of the missiles (simulated) so they could transition to internal power, and the missile antennas could slew to the aircraft's antenna. He raised his antenna full up and engaged the afterburner, pulling ahead of the other aircraft. In one sweep of the antenna, he saw the target far above. He locked-on. The steering dot commanded an immediate pull up for a max effort climb.

Malik held the steering dot dead center in the radar scope as the firing circle collapsed, the missile bay doors slammed opened, the missiles rails extended, and the simulated launch of the missiles occurred as the firing X appeared on the radar scope.

With an extreme nose-up attitude he ran out airspeed and stalled an instant after firing. He rolled inverted and drifted at airspeed barely registering along the zero G parabola until he was in a near vertical dive. He plunged into the undercast on instruments.

In a perfectly calm voice he transmitted, "Tonto four, splash."

The other aircraft and the target returned to Hahn; he could hear their radio transmissions. They had landed when Malik made his approach and landed. The crew chief marshaled him in, crossed his arms while the chocks were installed then gave the cut signal. Malik shut down the engine and secured the cockpit.

As he stood up on the seat and turned to start down the ladder, he saw Major Frank Holscher looking up at him. Reaching the ground, he nodded to the major.

"Lieutenant, Captain Regel just told me you broke formation in what he considered a dangerous manner and did not advise him of your intentions. He says, in his opinion, you used poor judgment and more importantly, you lied about the splash."

John clenched his teeth but said nothing.

Holscher directed the crew chief to open the nose cowling to retrieve the radar tape. He took it from the crew chief. "You know, Lieutenant, if you lied about this …. Well, it won't go well with you."

Malik nodded but said nothing.

They walked into the maintenance shack where Holscher mounted the tape into the viewer drive, rewound it, and hit play. Appearing on screen was a recording of the radar scope from the moment Malik pressed the trigger to the first detent. The recording depicted the antenna angle going up to the maximum elevation, a bright dot appeared in one sweep at 9 miles, the range gate appeared, lock-on occurred, and the steering dot commanded a steep pull up. The target remained within the steering dot; the firing sequence collapsed to an X, missiles away. The display showed a roll inverted, a steep nose-down attitude, then the recording ended.

Five more times, Holscher watched the replay. Finally, shaking his head, he said, "I've never seen the like. A 25,000-foot snap-up! I was the target in case you didn't know. I was at 50,000 feet at Mach 1.3 when you reported contact. The point of this exercise was to show that it is impossible with our radar to acquire a target under these conditions in time to launch. But you've proven me wrong. You must be some kind of wizard."

"Will that be all, sir?" Malik glared at Major Holscher.

Holscher nodded. "I suggest you watch your six, Lieutenant. I don't think Captain Regel likes you very much."

Malik nodded without a word. He left the maintenance shack and caught the van to the squadron. Several days later he almost lost an airplane.

* * *

On a typical winter day with weather from the surface to above 20,000 feet, Malik was flying the two-seat TF-102. In the right seat was an excited young maintenance crew chief who was getting a dollar ride.

Malik and Lead had been running intercepts and rocket beam attacks and were preparing to return to base when Malik's cockpit went dead. Lights, instruments, and radios. Complete electrical failure. The cause could only have been a sheared accessory driveshaft.

Lead was some miles away. Malik began rocking his wings in an exaggerated motion. The controller advised Lead that Malik was not responding to radio transmissions and vectored him to Malik, who was flying in a triangular pattern. Lead joined on Malik's wing. Malik gave Lead hand signals for electrical and communications failure.

Lead nodded, patted his shoulder, the sign meaning to "land on my wing." Malik nodded and moved into tight formation on Lead's right wing. They descended into the weather; Malik assumed he would soon look up and see the runway straight ahead. Lead would point to the runway, Malik would nod, Lead would pull up into the weather, and Malik would land straight ahead. But it didn't happen that way.

When they broke out of the weather under a low ceiling, they were crossing the runway at right angles. Lead pointed down, Malik nodded, yes, he saw the runway below. But then Lead pulled up into the weather, leaving Malik on his own to maneuver to final approach under a low ceiling.

Malik started a turn to a downwind, watching the runway from the left quarter panel. Then he looked forward out the electrically heated windscreen and discovered it was opaque, iced over on the inside. If he entered the weather, he would have to eject since his instruments were electrically powered.

He was in big trouble, and his passenger, who seemed to be enjoying himself immensely, had no clue of their jeopardy. Malik pulled off his left glove, unstrapped, and leaned forward to reach the windscreen. Scratching at the ice with his fingernails, straining to avoid displacing the control column, he clawed a small spot about the size of his fist and held his hand against it to melt more, all the while maneuvering in a tight radius to keep the runway in sight out the side window.

Malik dropped the gear with the emergency release and S-turned toward the runway using the side window until, holding his breath and hoping he was over concrete, he leveled the wings, relaxed the back pressure, and planted the airplane on the runway. He deployed the drag chute and clamped on the brakes in a max effort stop. He opened the canopy, leaned his head over the canopy rail in the face of bitterly cold wind to taxi off the runway onto a taxiway and shut down the engine.

A ground crew towed Malik to the ramp and chocked the wheels. Malik climbed out to examine the aircraft. The leading edges of the wings were covered with ice that included foot-long cones of ice on the noses of the drop tanks.

Once in the Alert Complex, he got a call from the wing commander. He had been in the control tower, along with everybody else of rank, watching this potential disaster unfold. The commander ordered Malik to proceed directly to the Stag Bar where he and Malik's squadron commander would buy him a beer. They gave him the rest of the day off.

CHAPTER 22

Close to Death

Early morning sunlight glinted off the snowbanks that lined the country road. On the edge of a nameless farm village, John's MG idled in a cloud of steam as he waited for a farmer to drive his herd of milk cows across the road into a field where hay bales lay scattered across the snow.

John leaned forward to survey the margins of a sucker hole showing clear sky. On the margins of the hole were threatening clouds that would soon close off the sky, plunging the countryside back into the perpetual winter gloom that had defined his tour in Germany so far.

By the time he reached the base, he could not see the road without his headlights. He drove through the gate and turned north to the squadron building, arriving 30 minutes before the stand-up briefing. Stamping snow off his boots, he entered the briefing room and went straight to the scheduling board to check his name.

He stared at the entry for Friday: a cross-country to RAF Lakenheath, England, in the TF-102 with B. B. Regel. He focused so intently on the entry he did not notice when Major Phil Murphy walked up beside him. Murphy nudged John in the ribs with his elbow. John flinched then pointed to the entry. "Sir, what do you make of this?"

"Good morning to you too, John." The major's voice held just a hint of sarcasm. "It looks like a check-ride to me. Regel must have scheduled it."

"Can't someone else give me the ride, if I have to have one?" This would not end well, he knew it.

"I wouldn't advise you to make an issue of it. But let me give you some advice." Murphy turned to face Malik. "Spend time at Base Ops reviewing ICAO regs, procedures, and airspace rules for the countries you'll cross. The Base Ops people will help you identify jet routes and figure out a routing. They'll show you how to file an ICAO flight plan that will be approved. Regel will try to rattle you if he can; that's his personality." Murphy paused then added, "He has issues with you."

"As if I didn't know. What I don't know is why."

"My guess is, he's jealous of you. He's pretty transparent."

Malik shrugged. "What else do I need to do?"

"Get with maintenance. Learn how to repack a drag chute and to fuel and service the airplane. In a war, we might be scattered all over Europe. You can't assume every NATO base can service an F-102. You need to check that box."

* * *

Friday dawned beneath a dense overcast with snow flurries. Malik and Regel filed a flight plan at Base Ops at 0700 and proceeded to the flight line, where they pre-flighted the TF-102. John opened the missile bay and strapped his overnight bag on a missile rail, as did Regel. Malik closed the missile bay doors, climbed into the cockpit, and strapped in.

They spoke only when necessary. Malik called out the checklist items, Regel replied, and Malik started the engine then copied his clearance to Lakenheath. Hahn's visibility reading measured 3,000 feet visual range in snow flurries, ceiling 300 feet, with the same at Lakenheath. The forecast showed the weather barely legal for the hour-flight.

Malik took off. He climbed out on instruments and broke out of the weather above 30,000 feet. He crossed the Channel, descended, and executed a ground-controlled radar approach into RAF Lakenheath. Once inside Base Ops, he and Regel ordered ground transportation to the Visiting Officers' Quarters and checked into a shared double room with two queen-sized beds.

Malik didn't like this. It was bad enough sitting in the same cockpit with him. Malik quietly asked the desk clerk if he could get a separate room but discovered there were none.

They silently ate lunch at the O Club and headed back to the VOQ. Malik hoped to watch TV and turn in early. But when they got to their room, they discovered it was filled with squatters. Eight F-4 crew members had arrived in the afternoon from Hahn. Since there were no rooms for them, they had persuaded the staff that Regel and Malik wouldn't mind if they bunked with them. The room resembled a dormitory with rollaway beds. The F-4 crews had moved Malik's stuff off his bed and set up a narrow army cot for him in the middle of the room. They left him in the room and set off for the Stag Bar.

The plan was for all five aircraft to depart in formation for Hahn the next morning. But at dawn, Lakenheath and Hahn were both socked in, and the weather was forecast below minimums all day. They mulled over their options at Base Ops and finally decided to get drunk. They called for transport to the O Club. Malik had no choice but to go with them.

The darkened bar smelled of stale beer and overflowing ash trays. Malik's companions started banging on the counter, demanding someone come and open the bar. The British employees, ever indulgent of the rude American crews, found someone willing to open the bar. And hard drinking began at 8 a.m.

The pilots bought rounds so fast Malik could not keep up. Four untouched drinks still sat in front of him when he reached his limit. Regel forced the issue, claiming Malik had not bought his fair share.

Two hours after his first drink, Malik fell off the barstool, staggered to his feet, and set off, nearly blind, groping his way out of the club. Somehow, hatless, he fell, crawled, staggered, and stumbled through snow for three blocks into the correct VOQ building.

As he pushed open the glass door to the building, he saw a deranged and wild-eyed reflection in the glass. His hair was sticking up at all angles, the pockets of his flight jacket were hanging out, dirt and snow clung to his flight suit. He staggered, panting and reeking into the lobby, unable to see anything not directly ahead of him. He had little control of his tongue. Overwhelmed with embarrassment, slobbering, he attempted to account for himself with the cute English desk clerk on morning duty while trying to request a key to the room they had occupied the night before. He did not remember where he had left his bag.

With dripping disdain, she retrieved a key. Malik groped his way down the hall, examining each room number at close range until he found the right one. He staggered into the dark room and collapsed face down on the cot, certain he was close to death. The world spun and shrank. His mind saw horrors.

He awoke in utter darkness with no remembrance of where he was, alarmed to see tiny demons, or imps, flying up from the sides of the cot, swarming around him. Had he awakened in hell? Had eternity begun? Rolling over, he turned over the cot and fell onto the floor, now dimly aware he was in the VOQ room. He crawled lizard-like in the darkness in several directions for some time, running into walls, hearing the wheezing of sleeping bodies. The air in the room smelled so strongly of alcohol and bad breath that the atmosphere may have been combustible. With increasingly sick desperation, he groped his way until his hand and cheek felt cold tile. He heaved himself forward and found the toilet. Embracing it with both arms, he began throwing up. Again, and again, his guts erupted until he fell unconscious, rolled away from the commode onto the cold tile floor with one hand still touching the violated toilet bowl.

He awoke at dawn to somebody nudging him aside to access the toilet. He was alive but mentally catatonic.

With no memory of how he got there, he found himself with the others at Base Ops. The other pilots decided Malik was to be the leader of a five-ship—to make the formation symmetrical. The Deuce would lead with two F-4s on each wing.

Malik got airborne; the F-4s rejoined on his wings below a 4,000-foot ceiling then they penetrated the weather in formation. The flight of five broke out in sunlight at altitude with the English Channel passing beneath them as a dark return on the radar scope.

Though Malik flew the aircraft, he said nothing on the radio, nor did he respond to Regel on the interphone. Malik smelled of puke.

The controller cleared the flight out of altitude. Malik began descent with two F-4s hanging on each wing. He drove down through the weather, glancing indifferently at his wingmen and the ice forming on the wings. Regel, who was handling the radios requested a vector from approach control that would take the flight down the centerline of Runway 04 at Hahn at 300 knots in the weather—this was unheard of. At 1,000 feet over the end of the runway, the F-4s on the left-wing peeled off successively, turning to downwind for a radar approach to landing, with the field just above approach minimums. Malik was third to land.

Once clear of the runway, Malik pulled the aircraft onto the 496th ramp and held the brakes as the chocks were installed and the crew chief gave the cut signal. With the ladder on the canopy rail, Malik collected his things, climbed out of the cockpit, and retrieved his bag from the missile bay. He staggered to the equipment room, stowed his flight gear, then wandered into the parking lot to his MG. In the two days they spent together, Malik did not look at Regel nor did he speak to him except to initiate and respond to checklists in the cockpit.

* * *

The next day, Malik showed up to fly a single ship down to Torrejon Air Base, Spain. He arrived at 0600 to find the entire squadron assembled. Though it was a cold Monday with snow on the ground, Malik's flight suit was drenched with sweat; and sweat streamed down his blanched face. His unfocused eyes were guided only by turning his head. No one spoke to him.

When the squadron commander saw Malik, he raised holy hell. Was no one going to keep Malik from flying in his condition? Did he alone see that Malik was delirious and had a raging fever?

Someone drove Malik to the hospital. He was admitted and remained there, bedridden on IVs for a week.

CHAPTER 23
The Hula Girl

For John Malik, winter in the Hünsruck Mountains was endless miles of dark fir trees contrasting with drifts of snow dimly visible under 35,000 feet of overcast and swirling ice fog. It seemed winter would never end for him. He longed for the desert; he longed to be warm.

Malik returned to flight duty as the squadron was preparing to deploy to Wheelis AB, Libya. There in North Africa, they would fire live missiles over the Mediterranean and conduct training unrestricted by weather. Some of the married pilots volunteered to remain in Germany and sit alert. Not Malik. He wanted to be warm.

The pilots had been talking for months of the deployment. They said the sun always shone at Wheelis. There everyone lounged around in shorts sipping tall drinks beside the pool, getting rays.

Malik had read several history texts on the Roman presence in North Africa in the period after their destruction of Carthage. The Romans built several cities on the Libyan coast that had remained intact; they were rarely visited because of their remote location.

As the lowest ranking of the pilots, Malik did not get to fly an airplane to Wheelis. He had to ride as a passenger with the support-people on a C-124 Globemaster that would carry maintenance stores along with missiles, a spare deuce engine, and equipment in the belly.

When he arrived at the base the morning of the deployment, the 496th ramp was a hive of activity. Crews were loading the C-124. Flights of F-102s were starting, taxiing, and taking off into the overcast in a steady stream.

When the time came, Malik walked up the ramp of the Globemaster with his gear and luggage, found a seat, and strapped in. Once airborne with the seatbelt sign off, Malik climbed up the stairs to the cockpit. They were in solid weather at 16,000 feet and indicating 170 knots. The aircraft commander got up from the left seat and invited Malik to fly. From that point Malik hand-flew the aircraft for almost six hours before the captain roused himself from his bunk and resumed command as the coast of North Africa came into view.

The base sat on the coast. A long stretch of sandy beach framed the sparkling blue-green Mediterranean from which a balmy breeze blew gently inland. Gazing across this vista from the ramp, Malik's soul seemed at peace. Inland the desert was postcard-beautiful in cloudless 78-degree weather.

Malik was billeted with a major from the squadron whom he did not know. Malik called him "sir" until he discovered his name. He was so kind to Malik. How was it that Malik did not know his name?

* * *

The squadron pilots flew local missions. Most of them fired live missiles that had aged-out. This mission exercised the aircraft systems and expended obsolete munitions. Malik did not get to live fire.

Since there was no air traffic control to speak of there were no rules once beyond the airport control zone. Most days, Malik checked out an F model and beat up the coast at low altitude searching for the Roman cities Leptis Magna and Sabratha. And he found them, about 100 miles apart. They were built on the beach, abandoned since the time of the Romans. He flew many hours in low, tight circles over these ruins. There was no sign of life for many miles around Leptis Magna, a bleak derelict city locked in the embrace of desert. Several-storied buildings, temples, and a coliseum were remarkably well-preserved, stretching inland along cobbled streets from the sea for a half mile.

One afternoon he took a taxi into Tripoli and wandered through the souks, or marketplaces, assaulted by sights and smells utterly foreign to him. The wares displayed in the open-air markets included the heads of donkeys and shanks of flesh speckled with dried blood and covered with flies. There were vegetables, fruits, and mounds of spices under canopies shading a labyrinth of narrow alleyways. Middle Eastern music blared from competing radios along the narrow dark passages. Displayed in front of shops were fabrics, knives, carpets, bronze objects, and many household utensils constricting the walking space.

If he was uncomfortable in Germany, he was an alien here. He sensed a smoldering animosity against Americans among the locals. The new regime under Colonel Muammar Gaddafi seemed committed to ousting them from Wheelis.

On a final flight, Phil Murphy and John Malik flew a TF-102 on a nape-of-the-earth dead reckoning navigation mission 200 miles into the Sahara. Maintaining about 100 feet and holding 400 knots they navigated by time and heading but had few recognizable landmarks on a featureless map. One hundred miles south of the coast, they crossed over a deep pit in the earth. They pulled up and circled to see people living in caves excavated into the walls of the pit.

At about 200 miles, they came low and fast over the crest of a high dune and watched a herd of camels scatter under the wings. Malik pulled up and circled what was likely a Berber encampment. The occupants of the camp stood watching them. And he wondered what they must have thought of this strange apparition that thundered out of utter stillness. Had they ever seen a fighter plane? Did they know what it was?

Malik turned north for the coast and climbed. This intimate view of the northern Sahara was his final flight in Libya. The squadron soon packed up and returned to the gloom of Germany.

* * *

Winter transitioned to a glorious spring. John spent balmy evenings with Alice sitting at outdoor tables at restaurants on the Mosel River. They enjoyed Bernkastel, a picturesque village amid vineyards on both slopes of the valley.

John didn't frequent the Stag Bar, but he went often enough to eventually get to know the American women he'd seen there. Alice, a schoolteacher, was particularly easy to talk to. They became good friends. Other than Christine, there had been no one else he could talk to candidly. Though he did not really like the local white wine, drinking it lightened his mood, and loosened his tongue. Yes, he thought he could tell Alice anything. Well, just about anything. He could never tell her, or anyone else, that he had killed his brother. The vision of that day never left him. He dreamed of it, seeing his brother's corpse rising from the spring.

He found the passage in a text by Augustine that spoke of the hollow place within every human. Malik wanted to believe he could fill that empty ache with something, with total involvement in meaningful activity. What he was doing, flying airplanes to defend his country was meaningful. But if Augustine was right, only God could actually fill that void. All other pursuits would eventually fade to desolation.

There was a story the Greeks told of a man named Tantalus who had perpetrated a monstrous act against the gods. They had cursed him to endlessly die of thirst and hunger, unable to reach the fruit just above his head, or to bend down to drink the spring-water at his feet. Perhaps God had consigned John Malik to a life of unfulfilled longing, a fitting punishment for his heinous crime.

Alice and John often went to the Mosel River on Friday and Saturday evenings to watch the sunset from an outdoor restaurant surrounded by lights strung in the trees amid vibrant lawns and beds of flowers. They listened to the sound of wooden oars working in the oarlocks of rowboats and the squealing of children. Each time the sun's disk touched the hills, they agreed to say nothing until it sank out of sight and the night came.

Sometimes they traveled as far as Bavaria and the Black Forest, even into Switzerland and Austria—that is, when he could take a few days off, and Alice got a sub to take her classes. Most of their dates were just the two of them. John never attended social events with the squadron until the infamous South Sea Gala.

* * *

Lieutenant Colonel Slavin decreed a squadron party. It was to be a South Sea extravaganza. For the event, he ordered all the pilots to grow mustaches. Malik complied and soon had a bushy, but trimmed-to-regs, cookie duster. Alice wasn't sure she liked it. It took away his boyish look, she said. He almost looked sinister.

Malik assumed the planning for the South Sea bash surely would not involve him, given his disposition. But he was wrong. He found he was to be a hula girl along with one other unlikely squadron pilot. The organizers booked a large facility, arranged the catering, engaged a band, laid in vast amounts of booze, and drafted squadron support personnel to do the table set-up and decorations work. When John drove by the facility, anxiety flooded his mind. This event would surely be the ultimate humiliation of his life.

The night arrived. Neither John nor his fellow hula girl knew exactly what was expected of them. They were told to show up backstage just before their performance.

The audience was fed, moderately inebriated, and in a riotous mood when John rose from his table struggling to swallow. Panic stricken, he glanced at Alice who forced a smile. He took a deep breath and proceeded through the door to backstage. Jerry, his costar, was there along with the commander's wife, who had their costumes.

Mortified, Malik stripped to his skivvies, put on a grass skirt, and donned a pair of combat boots. He left them untied with the tongues protruding as instructed. He was topless but for two coconut halves strapped to his chest as a bra. On his shoulder-length wig, he wore a wreath of flowers.

The commander's wife gave these instructions: Enter the stage when the band begins a particular South Sea tune. Do your best imitation of a hula dance. When the tune is over, bow and exit the stage.

Jerry and John regarded each other with grave misgivings. John felt light-headed. Then they heard the band start their song. Jerry walked out rather confidently, John thought. But John, in a crouch, snuck out behind him and hid behind the bass drum. Resigned to his fate, he got up, and threaded his way through the band equipment, and swayed. He tripped on the laces of his boots and fell against Jerry, clutching his grass skirt to keep from falling, tearing the skirt nearly off of Jerry.

Jerry jerked most of his skirt out of John's grip, but his underwear was still showing. They were both inept, out of synch with each other, their hips bumping, feigning interest in each other's coconuts. They got into a brief scuffle and stumbled into the band. The drummer, unscripted, reached out and cracked John on the head with a drumstick. He told John to get away from his drums.

The hula girls finally found their stride. When the music ended, they stepped forward and bowed with a flourish, then raised their arms showing hairy chests and underarms, staring up into the lights as though acknowledging the acclaim of the mob in the upper tiers of the Roman colosseum. John took his wreath of flowers and flung it into the audience to wild cheers and a standing ovation from the dazzled audience.

Backstage, John dressed and came back to his table where everyone was wildly enthusiastic about his performance. The eight people at his table shouted above the band that they could not believe that was him up there. What struck them, apparently, was the utter incongruity of who they thought John Malik was and his self-effacement on stage. It would seem they did not know how to accommodate this different impression of him.

As the evening wound down, the commander called forward the players in the evening's performance. When John's name was called, there was a standing ovation. He accepted his certificate of appreciation appended with a set of lips on the bottom with the acronym S.W.A.K., "sealed with a kiss."

CHAPTER 24
A Dangerous Watershed

John had been at Hahn for a year when word came down that F-4Es would replace the F-102s in the air defense mission. This new F-4 model had an internal Gatling gun. This was a real gunfighter, and its radar was far superior to the F-102's. The excited squadron pilots would rotate state-side for training in the F-4E and return to the unit. But this transition was only for Vietnam veterans. Malik would be reassigned for combat duty to Vietnam when the 496th became operational with the F-4. But that would be another year, and another winter.

Malik began negotiations with the assignments people at Lackland AFB via a landline. The initial word was that he would get a Forward Air Controller, or FAC assignment in a light aircraft, spotting targets for fighters. No! He wanted a fighter. By some stroke of providence, the assignments people got him into the pipeline for an F-100 slot.

While the squadron pilots rotated state-side for training, Malik assumed assignments as a first lieutenant usually held by a major. He became a flight commander of temporary duty guard pilots from stateside units; he also became a squadron test pilot. Any significant modifications to an aircraft that might affect aerodynamics, including engine change, required rigorous flight testing around the flight envelope to ensure the aircraft was combat ready.

On a test flight, Malik would climb to the service ceiling of 50,000 feet and accelerate supersonic to the red line on the Machmeter. At that altitude, the pneumatic system pressurized the cockpit to a maximum of 25,000 feet, the human ceiling. For that reason, pilots were forbidden to exceed 50,000 feet without a pressure suit.

He discovered on climb-out in max thrust in a clean F-102 that it was a rocket without drop tanks; a different airplane—very impressive. He made 50,000 feet in a matter of minutes and drove through the Mach to the redline. Each time he did this, holding supersonic, he recited the poem "High Flight." But no transformation of his mind or spirit occurred. He was dead inside.

Christine's monthly letters continued to arrive on time, at the first of the month. Of late, the letters had dwelled on his mother's failing health. Her uterine cancer had metastasized. She would reach stage four soon.

Having read this news, he stared out the window into the forest and decided on a course of action. He would write to his mother while there was time. If he confessed what he had done, he might give her the chance to forgive him. That might change her spiritual destiny. He summoned the courage and wrote his confession.

Mom,

I am sorry for your heartache in life and my part in your desolation. Do I have to tell you I had no choice in being born to you? But I have brought you a great loss. I am responsible for Ian's death. He drowned in a cave. I convinced him to go into it though he didn't want to. I am so sorry. I hope my confession may give you some peace in knowing the truth of what happened.

I remember times of joy in our house when we used to sing together, and hope filled our lives. If I never communicate with you again, know that I am sorry beyond words for my actions and pine for the love we once had.

Please forgive me. Do it for your sake, if not mine.

* * *

By late October 1968, the days and nights were shrouded once again under the gloom of overcast skies and rain. Reporting for duty one morning, John was called to the squadron commander's office. Colonel Slavin told him to call Christine Charis. He handed John a slip of paper with a phone number. He could place the call at government expense.

John went down the hall to an open office and sat down at a desk. He placed the call. He could hear it ringing.

"Hello," came Christine's sweet voice.

His heart raced with anticipation to savor every syllable of the words she would utter. "Christine, this is John. What's the matter?"

"It's your mother, John. She has only days to live. I think you'd better come home." Christine sounded sleepy, her voice sultry, silken, angelic.

"Are you in Springfield?" John wanted to go see his mother, but he desperately wanted Christine to be there when he got home.

"No, I'm at Baylor, but I'm going home. She's going to pass any day now."

"I'll get an emergency leave. I'll try to be home in three days. You'll be there?"

"That's the plan. Our families have too much history to ignore this passing. I'm concerned about her soul, Johnny. Come while she's still coherent. Your being there and your confession may be a factor."

"My confession?" John stopped breathing. What did Christine know? Had she read his letter to his mother, or learned the substance of it?

"It's what I've always wanted you to do. Why haven't you done it? I am so upset with you. I have been for so long. You drive me crazy. And I want to beat you!" Her voice was angry, frustrated, her words rapid and emphatic. "I asked you once if you thought I was a fool. Ian didn't drown in the James River, did he? You never confessed, even to me, your soulmate. It happened in a cave, didn't it, Johnny? And it was your fault, wasn't it?"

John said nothing.

"Look, Johnny, it doesn't matter if she forgives you or not. She may be too far gone into the darkness. But you have to do the right thing. That's what God requires of us. Your Uncle Sean will be at your house by the time you get there. Call the old number, and he'll pick you up at the airport."

"I'm on my way." There was a long pause. "I miss you so much," he said.

There was silence on the other end. "Oh, Johnny. What can I say? What I have said to you stands. But you know why it won't work. If only you'd open your eyes. I am so weary of waiting for you …. I'll see you in three days. Please be safe. Be well, my dear one." She was crying as she hung up.

* * *

The Ozark Airlines DC-9 landed at Springfield twenty hours after John had departed Frankfurt on a Lufthansa flight to Newark. With layovers and bad connections through Chicago's O'Hare and St. Louis, he arrived exhausted and jet-lagged in Springfield. His Uncle Sean greeted him at the arrival gate.

His uncle was not the stereotypical professor. He wore a navy blazer, blue button-down shirt, and khaki trousers over his athletic build. He could pass more easily for an Ivy League grad student than a full professor. He was another of the Riley line that carried the genius gene. And there was also a second cousin of John's, Leonidas Riley, who was a phenomenon.

"John," he said, extending his hand. "How was your flight?"

"Brutal." John accepted the extended hand. "Good of you to pick me up, Professor Riley."

"Just Sean. You look beat."

"I haven't slept in thirty hours." John yawned and stretched. "Tell me what's going on." John hefted his suitcase off the conveyor belt at the luggage claim.

"I'm sorry to say she passed this morning, about 4 a.m."

"Were you there?" John stared blankly ahead toward the parking lot.

Sean stopped and waited for John to turn toward him. "Yes. I was beside her in a chair at the house. I woke up just as she sat up with a terrified expression and screamed. She collapsed with a look of horror frozen on her face. I wish I hadn't seen that."

John did not reply but took a deep breath that seemed to serve as the finale of a former life that had become a bad dream. He turned to stare at the parking lot.

Sean directed him toward the street exit. "I'm sorry, John." The sincerity in Sean's voice was enough to make a tough man feel like crying. "Christine told me you wanted to talk to her before the end."

"Yeah …. I don't know what I expected to come of it."

Sean unlocked the trunk for John's baggage, then the passenger door.

John slid in the car and waited for Sean to get situated in the driver's seat. "I've rarely talked to you, Sean. I often wanted to call you and see if you had some insight into why my mother was so bitter." He watched Sean's expression. "Why did she hate me so much? And what did Rutger have against me? They never loved me. I've got to know why."

"You refer to Rutger. Not your dad. I guess you figured out you weren't Rutger's son." Sean glanced at John as he maneuvered through the round-about at the airport entry.

"Mom told me the day I brought Ian's body home that I was a bastard. I felt so … rootless. Like I didn't belong anywhere. How could a mother not love her own child? Why could she not love me?"

Sean focused on the road ahead, chewing his lip. "John, only a few people knew you weren't Rutger's son. You were the child of a liaison my sister had with a titled British fighter pilot named Allister Higham. He came to Penn just after the Battle of Britain; it was some intelligence thing. He fought in that battle; he shot down a half-dozen German fighters over the Channel. Anyway, Claire was married to Rutger, but they weren't getting along. They were estranged and living apart." He glanced at John and continued.

"I don't know if you knew this, but Rutger was a foster child. He had terrible security issues that he couldn't overcome. Allister was the polar opposite of Rutger. Allister was brilliant, handsome, charming, and rich. No woman could resist him … and your mother was so good-looking back then. Anyway, when Allister discovered Claire was married, he dropped her. But he left her pregnant with you. I'm sure he never knew that.

"The RAF recalled him to England. That's the last I heard of him. He was a good friend of mine. I introduced him to Claire. If I hadn't, you wouldn't be sitting here with me." Sean focused on making a light and stopped talking.

"Tell me about him. I need to know. You're the only person that knows about him." John stared intently at Sean, watching his expression.

"Well, like I said, he was a remarkable man." He looked at John. "And you look just like him, your intellectual capacity … well, that comes from the Rileys, but your mannerisms, even down to the sound of your voice, it's pure Allister Higham."

"Is he alive? Does he know about me? Where does he live?"

"I wish I could tell you more, John. But I don't know anymore. I never heard from him after he left. I suspect he was killed in his Spitfire fighting the Germans. I think he would have written me if he had survived the war. His family was landed gentry, by the way. Quite wealthy."

John stared out the windshield, clenching his teeth, his stomach churning as he watched the passing stores and streets he once knew so well. He followed the A&W Drive-In as it passed by on the right. Reality had moved on and stranded his memories.

"So, what happened after my father left for England?"

"I guess you need to know this to get some closure, but I don't think it will make you feel any better. After Allister left, Rutger and your mom got back together, and they made a go of it for a time, more or less. But when Rutger looked at you, as you were growing up, he continually saw Claire's betrayal. He and Claire became the bitterest people I have ever known. Ian was all they had together."

"And I killed him," John said softly.

If Sean heard what John said he did not respond. He stared intently ahead and finally added, "I always felt so sorry for your situation, John."

They had turned north off Sunshine onto Barnes Street when Sean reached into a pocket of his sports coat and extracted a sealed letter. "I hesitate to give this to you. I can only imagine what it says. Claire asked me to be sure you got it. I hope it's a comfort. But knowing her, I'm afraid the pen was dipped in poison. I urge you to prepare yourself and be in a good place before you read it."

He handed the letter to John and turned into the driveway of the house. John stuck the envelope in the pocket of his sports coat. He stared at Christine's home, his heart racing at the prospect of seeing her. He licked his lips, feeling again the disquiet that surrounded sights and sounds of her. Should he go over? There were several cars in the drive. No, he would wait for her.

Sean and John got out, and John carried his bag into the house, taking it into his old bedroom. He was awash with nostalgia, assaulted by smells and sights that churned his gut with conflicting emotions of remorse, of melancholy, and of rising passion in anticipation of seeing Christine.

He plopped down on the bed and stared out the window toward Christine's bedroom. From the hallway, Sean called, "Take a nap, and we'll go get something to eat in a few hours. The funeral is tomorrow at the Good Spring Church in Niangua."

"Thank you, sir. Do you know if Christine is home next door?"

"I think she is. She'll be at the service tomorrow. We'll take separate cars if that's okay with you. I need to visit some of the relatives in the country after the funeral."

* * *

John sat midway in a wooden pew right of the aisle in the Good Spring Church, 25 miles northeast of Springfield near the small settlement of Niangua, Missouri. The 100-year-old church creaked and groaned, causing John to look up with concern into the exposed rafters. John had driven his mother's car, arriving early, hoping to see Christine. There were a few people there. Some may have been Claire's distant relatives, but John didn't know any of them. He had no family left besides his Uncle Sean. And Rutger had no family. He had been an orphan.

More people arrived. John figured these were academic types from the college. Then Sean arrived, driving his rental car. He visited and shook hands with everyone. It didn't seem appropriate for John to do this.

As he watched the casket and his mother's profile, he felt the dread passing. He breathed deeply, exhaled, and repeated. If the ancient Hebrews were right, her spirit might hover in the corpse's presence for three days. Perhaps she saw him now, here to see her off. Maybe she was knocking on heaven's door, but John doubted that. As he remembered the Scripture, God's forgiveness of sin was contingent upon one's forgiveness of others. Unremitting bitterness is the passport to eternal torment. There seemed little hope she had opened her eyes in glory. But maybe he was wrong. He hoped so.

John pulled the envelope from his blazer pocket, slid his finger beneath the sealed flap, and extracted the letter. He sucked air through his teeth, dreading the words that would forecast his mother's destiny. These were the last words of the one who gave him life, who at the moment she penned them was standing on the threshold of life's greatest mystery. She had written in an unsteady hand,

> *I have read your confession. I do not forgive you.*
>
> *Yes, I am rational and recognize you had no choice in being born out of my sin. But you are the reincarnation of Sir Allister Higham, everything I ever wanted but was not worthy of. I was the woman scorned.*
>
> *He turned his back on me and left me disgraced. He damned me to a life with the bitterest, most insecure human imaginable, Rutger Malik. You are Allister's mirror image. I never found out what happened to him, but I hope he died in his damned Spitfire.*
>
> *To quote Shakespeare's Mercutio, you, my hateful paramour, have made worm's meat of me. I am unredeemed.*
>
> *I will see you in hell.*

The letter dropped from John's hand. He sat staring at the floor. He had done what Christine insisted he do. But to what effect? He wanted to believe that at some level, his mother had once loved him as her son. But she had not. He had lived his formative life unloved, a burden to his mother.

Could he bear the tension to be soon sitting beside Christine, wanting to envelop her, while processing what he had just read? His mother had declared him a thing of no worth. It was she, above all others, who should have loved him without condition and given him a sense of worth that only unconditional love can impart.

John turned every few minutes to look back at the entry door, uncertain whether he could contain the colliding emotions. The door creaked open. He turned to see Christine's father and mother enter. Behind them came Christine and walking beside her was a handsome blond-haired young man gripping Christine's hand.

John's mouth was open. What he saw pierced him through the heart and emptied him of life force. He stared at her, at her hand gripped tightly in his, at him, back to her. She glanced at John with an uncertain expression as she sat down on the opposite side of the aisle beside the young man. She barely glanced his way as the service began.

John sat for several minutes, unable to get a full breath, fidgeting, his vision narrowing, his mouth dry. As the preacher began his insipid comments, John stood up abruptly, made his way into the aisle, and stalked out of the church, taking no care to buffer the closing of the door as it slammed shut behind him.

He strode to his mother's Audi, yanked the door open, slammed it shut, started the engine, and tore out of the parking lot with gravel pinging off the side of the church and the windows. Driving as a man possessed, he careened around curves, passing on the right and left of traffic. Pulling up into the driveway of the house on Barnes Street, he stormed into the house, stuffed his clothes into his bag, and called a taxi.

At the Ozark Airlines ticket counter, he presented his military travel voucher and got a boarding pass on the next flight eastbound out of Springfield.

CHAPTER 25
Death Wish

From that time, it no longer mattered to John whether he lived or died. Distant, distracted, indifferent, he engaged with no one in the squadron. And no one tried to talk to him. Perhaps they thought he was grieving over the loss of his mother, so they gave him space. In his mailbox, he found official orders assigning him to Luke AFB, Arizona, to train in the F-100. He was going to war, and soon.

As the senior pilots rotated state-side for transition training in the F-4E, John continued to sit alert and engage in training flights. Stateside Guard units sent pilots on temporary duty to fill the vacant slots. John's briefings and debriefings were uninspired, perfunctory. And B. B. Regel, who had not yet rotated state-side for training, continued steadfastly in his unexplained hatred for John Malik. But John didn't care anymore. He didn't care about anything.

On a relatively clear day, Malik had completed routine intercepts butting heads with his flight leader. They broke off, returning to base separately. As Malik turned back toward the Hahn TACAN, Regel's flight crossed above him. Malik saw Regel rolling in to attack him. Regel had the advantage of altitude and airspeed.

Malik watched him closing to his six. Regel had closed to firing range when Malik turned into him with full power. Regel yo-yoed and stayed behind Malik, whose only option to shake Regel required a violent maneuver. He pulled the stick aft to the stop and bottomed the left rudder. The aircraft pitched up 90 degrees as it spun one full rotation about the vertical axis. The aircraft slowed dramatically in seconds. Only a violent maneuver in the opposite direction by Regel kept him from moving ahead of Malik. Regel took a big chance. During the rotation, he could not see Malik.

When they came out of their opposite rotations, Regel and Malik were out of airspeed. They entered into a vertical rolling scissors at full power, stagnated behind the power curve, canopy-to-canopy in a spiral with a high rate of sink, plummeting toward the forest 20,000 feet below. They plunged through 15,000 feet, then 10,000 feet grunting against high Gs and struggling to breathe, trying to hold their heads up against the sustained Gs, willing this to be over.

There were only two outcomes. Either Regel or Malik would roll out of the spiral and lose the fight, or they would both explode in a single fireball in the forest below in just over a minute.

Regel was playing chicken with the wrong man. Within 30 seconds of impact, passing 5,000 feet, Regel rolled level, Malik rolled into his six and recorded a kill.

That evening Malik went by the Stag Bar for his obligatory weekly beer. He was sitting on a stool at the bar when Regel strode in, heading straight toward him. Malik turned just as Regel hit him in the mouth with the back of his fist. Malik flew backward off the stool onto the floor. He tasted blood and wiggled his front teeth with his tongue. Everyone in the bar gasped, horrified.

As Malik struggled to get up, Regel hissed, "You are a cold-blooded bastard!" And he spat on Malik. Malik got to his feet, set the bar stool upright, laid a five on the counter, and left the Stag Bar for the last time.

* * *

A month passed. Dark overcast with rain and periodic snow flurries had returned to cover the Hünsruck Mountains with a blanket of gloom and fog. Malik had sold his MG; he had packed up his stuff and finished out-processing. He would catch the morning bus to Frankfurt.

John stood looking through a leaded glass window of a castle's great hall-turned-restaurant. He stared at the lights of a small German village below. Swirling ice fog blurred and sometimes obscured the town. He peered to the left and could see part of the drawbridge that spanned a 300-foot chasm separating the escarpment, which the citadel occupied, and the plateau that stood above the valley.

Sixty-foot-high walls of stone enclosed the keep and other structures of the ninth-century fortress still maintained in pristine condition by the descendants of the baron who once ruled the region. Now, revenues from a small restaurant sustained the cost of upkeep.

"Is it clearing any?"

Alice's question awakened John from his musings. Spending time with Alice was his only comfort since the funeral.

"It's getting worse. But we'll be all right. The road seems pretty clear." He walked back to their table near the fireplace as the waitress arrived with coffee and strudel. He admired the impressive collection of medieval weapons and armor adorning the walls. Faded tapestries hung from either side of the 10-foot-wide fireplace in which logs blazed.

The fire warmed and mesmerized them. John visualized the same fireplace warming bold knights and gentle ladies in centuries long gone. He fancied himself a modern-day knight. He rode a supersonic fighter; his lance and mace were missiles and rockets. He jousted with the knights of other NATO countries on their various mounts, training to face the Russians and East Germans.

But unlike his colleagues, John Malik had never conformed to the fighter pilot mold. He had been coping for a time, but he couldn't do it anymore. He was adrift far from shore. The anchor that had held him to life, Christine, had held another man's hand at his mother's funeral. She was lost to him, and he to the world.

"Not much business tonight," he said, feeling nostalgia, homesickness, and sorrow seeing Alice for the last time. She was his last mooring.

"How did you find this romantic place?" Alice ran her fingers along John's hand, from wrist to fingertips. Picking up her coffee cup, she sipped quietly and leaned in.

"I used to explore on the weekends before I met you. I've found castles tourists haven't discovered." John savored a bite of strudel as he glanced around at the medieval furnishings.

Alice set her coffee down. "John, I've never met anyone like you. You're so different from anybody else I know."

He glanced at her aware his eyes were lightless. "Socrates said the unexamined life is not worth living. But I've discovered that self-analysis leads to hopelessness if you don't have a faith." John used his fork to push strudel around his plate.

"What does that mean?" She asked this with urgency, as though she had only minutes left to discover who this was.

"It means I've seen behind the curtain and beheld the wizard of Oz. He is us, and he knows nothing. There are no absolute truths the human mind can establish. I wonder how people carry on. Am I the only one who knows he's standing before an unscalable wall?"

"John, in my experience, faith is where the absolutes come from. I know you don't have that, but I wish you weren't so sad all the time. Well, maybe it's not so much that you're sad as you're so withdrawn. Are you even aware of the people around you?" Alice placed her hand over John's hand for just a moment.

"Believe me, I'm not feeling sorry for myself when I say this, but I'm not worth worrying about. And I don't have anything to spare for anyone else." John laid his fork down and gave up trying to spear the lasts sliver of apple on his plate.

"You are worth worrying about." She reached up and turned his head toward her. "Look at me. It's a little late to be asking you this, but are you trying to kill yourself? That's what pilots in the squadron say."

"What? Who told you that?"

"Certain people. It's too late for it to matter now, I guess, but you scare the daylights out of the other pilots. Did you know that? They say you're too aggressive. One pilot said you haven't figured out it's a game. And that brings up B. B. Regel. What happened with that?"

John huffed and looked at her with narrow eyes. "Are you sure you want to hear the answer?"

She nodded. "Yes. Your pain is killing me. If I don't get closure, I'll always wonder if I could have helped you."

He smiled faintly and ironically. Looking at the flames in the fireplace he said, "I'm broken, Alice. I can't fix myself. All I've got is a memory, Christine."

"I'm so sorry, John. But I have to believe this thing with you and Christine will work out." They stared at the fire. "But look, you've got to talk about the Regel incident. Can you help me understand that and why people say you've got a death wish? I don't want you to die."

He turned to give her his full attention. "Okay, why not? Here it is. They say confession is good for the soul. So, here's the bloody truth nobody will ever know but you and me.

"I was running a 110-degree rocket beam attack on Regel—he was the target. The attack is a computer-steered collision course until reaching 1500 feet. At that point, you fire and break hard for the stern of the target. The rockets hit the target—can't miss. If you don't break at 1500 feet, you will hit the target. Regel said at the board he believed I was going to hit him. At a thousand knots closure it looks suicidal. Regel panicked. He pushed the stick forward against the stop and suffered a red-out. That's where you take negative Gs, and blood is pressurized into the brain, your vision goes red. You don't want to do that.

"When he regained consciousness, he was flamed out, spinning out of control. He ejected just before his aircraft hit the ground."

"What did the board say?"

"They ruled pilot-error. Regel's fault. He lost the airplane."

"But he said you tried to hit him."

John looked back at the fire. "The board didn't ask me if I tried to hit him." He turned to stare at her. "I passed just over his vertical fin. If he hadn't pushed over, we would both be dead." John shrugged. "Is that what you want to know? That I'm a suicidal monster?"

Her mouth hung open, staring at him with a look of revulsion twisting her features, tears swimming in her eyes.

Regel's career was over. His medical discharge included a diagnosis of multiple brain aneurysms and loss of vision in one eye.

The smell of burning wood and the yellow flames refocused John's meditations. He noted the irony of the tapestry beside the fireplace. A unicorn was lying within a circular fence amid a field of daisies, a medieval mythic depiction of the Christ incarnate, captured by a virgin.

One part of John felt compassion for Regel, the man who had been Malik's tormentor in many undisguised ways. Regel had hated Malik without a cause. But another part of Malik felt vindicated. Regel's hatred had been his undoing. Regel had destroyed himself.

Malik did not know himself well enough to recognize his own motivations. Was he a killer? He had pondered the same question as he peered into the crevice that opened into Lost Man's Cave where his brother had disappeared into the darkness.

The Regel incident had produced a chilling effect on the squadron in the last weeks of Malik's tour. No one messed with him. The pilots had given him a wide berth in the air and on the ground.

Emerging from deep in his own thoughts, he heard Alice saying, "This may be the last time I see you, John. I wish I could know how your life will turn out, whether you and Christine can be together. If that doesn't happen, I don't know what will become of you. I'm so afraid for you."

A long awkward silence followed. What could he say? He was an empty husk, damned. They finished their coffee.

"Are you afraid to go to Vietnam?" Alice leaned back in her chair.

John laughed, amused by his own self-loathing. "Afraid? Do you know where I'm supposed to be tonight? I'm supposed to be at a squadron going-away party in my honor. But I was afraid to go. Do you hear what I said? I was afraid!"

"No. Oh, John. What will they think? I would have gone with you."

"They'll all be at the restaurant, waiting for me, the guest of honor. They'll decide I'm not coming. Then they'll eat and go home. They'll think my car broke down, or I got delayed. They have a tradition. When everybody's finished eating, they make the guest of honor stand up on a table and give a going-away speech.

"I couldn't deal with the thought of it. I've been in a cold sweat for a month. So, I decided not to go. Let the chips fall where they may. Who cares? I won't see them again." He pushed back from the table and laid his napkin on his plate.

"Why didn't you tell me this? Are you that afraid of public speaking? It's normal to be a little anxious about it, but this sounds pathological. I didn't think you were afraid of anything."

In a lucid moment of self-discovery, John heard himself say, "It's about playing a role, Alice, trying to be who people expect you to be. But I can't act. I just want to be left alone."

The waitress arrived and cleared the dishes. They waited.

John looked intently at Alice. "I want to die, but I dare not. This *has* to be settled first." John hadn't intended to say that out loud. He forced a pathetic smile. "You don't know what I'm talking about, do you?"

"Oh, John." She held her head in her hands and cried. "I don't understand why you feel this way."

Through the speakers playing softly, he heard the song again, the singers speaking of those days they thought would never end, how they would sing and dance forever and a day.

PART VII:

SURVIVAL

CHAPTER 26

Pipeline to War

On a Monday afternoon in the first week of April 1969 John Malik finally got warm. Except for his hand-made German flight boots and socks, he was completely naked. He sat in an aluminum lawn chair beneath the left wing of a rented Cessna 172. His palms were up on the armrests, and his eyes were closed as he faced the sun hovering just above the western horizon. Volcanic cinder cones, saguaro cactus, sagebrush, and empty desert stretched west to Blythe, California 60 miles away. And 70 miles behind him were the western suburbs of Phoenix, Arizona.

His touchdown on the long-abandoned WWII emergency landing strip was uneventful. There was nothing here but the remnants of two 4,000-foot intersecting runways. Though sagebrush dotted one of them, he had plenty of clearance to land on the other. Malik had sat in the utter solitude facing the sun for two hours, his body warmed to the core, his mind at peace in the therapeutic sunlight. On the ground beside him were the wrappers from four Roy Rogers roast beef sandwiches and two empty Coke bottles. These artifacts accounted for his distended belly.

Not until first starlight, when coyotes began howling to one another, did he finally get up, dress, pack up the airplane, and take a last walk down the runway. He thought he might catch a late, late movie in town. He strapped into the Cessna, cranked the engine, and took off into the night heading for the lights of Phoenix and the Goodyear Airport.

* * *

Newly promoted Captain John Malik had arrived at Luke AFB before a training slot was open for him. He had three months with nothing to do. For the record, he was assigned some trivial admin duties—which he never performed. He mostly did nothing once he had read and committed to memory the F-100 flight crew operating manual and all other operations manuals. He saw every movie that came out—after first eating several Roy Rogers roast beef sandwiches before show time.

The local lore surrounding the Superstition Mountains and the legend of the Lost Dutchman's Mine interested him. He checked out in a Cessna 172 at the Goodyear airport and flew at low altitude into the wild and dangerous canyons of the Superstition Mountains.

Finally, class started. Luke AFB, Phoenix, Arizona was the home of 150 F-100s and a large contingent of West German F-104s. Like interceptor school, fighter-bomber training at Luke initially involved half academics and half simulator and flying. Flight missions focused on dropping bombs, firing the 20-millimeter cannons, aerial refueling, some dogfighting and instrument work.

The air-to-ground combat training was conducted at the vast gunnery range south of Luke near the Mexican border. He dropped inert iron and small practice bombs, learning to converge the ballistic variables that ensured the weapons hit the target. He pounded a column of bombed-out trucks and vehicles that snaked immobile through a mountain pass. And he strafed the hulks, learning well the hazards of pressing too low on a strafing run. It was quite possible to shoot yourself down with ricochets.

Malik also trained in the delivery of nuclear weapons. One mission involved a 300-mile low-level oil-burner route on the nape of the earth that took him north of the Grand Canyon, thence south near the New Mexico border, then west for the final run-in. As he approached the Initial Point, he accelerated to 500 knots. At the IP, he engaged afterburner, pressed the pickle button, and held heading. At the correct timing, an instrument commanded a pitch up to a 45-degree climb. He pressed and held the pickle button until the bomb released and began its five-mile flight to a 100-meter circle on the desert floor, the nuclear bullseye.

He pulled hard onto his back into a half-Cuban-eight, went full throttle and burner to accelerate in the opposite direction from the simulated detonation. Streaking over the desert floor he could achieve ten miles of separation from the blast, but it wouldn't be enough, if it were for real. The blast of the nukes he might carry would overtake him; radiation would pass through his aircraft and fry the pigment from his skin. One of his instructors had been a test subject for this scenario. It bleached his skin white.

* * *

During his training, Malik received an unexpected call from Alice who wanted to come to Phoenix and spend several months. She had come home to Louisville from Germany for the summer and drove on to Phoenix to see John.

John rented an airplane and flew her up to the Grand Canyon and elsewhere. He checked out camping equipment from the base, loaded the rented Cessna with gear, a cooler with food, and took off to the west on a Saturday afternoon, heading for the emergency strip he had discovered months before in the desert to the west.

They set up a tent and spread out a blanket. While Alice fixed dinner, John took off and climbed to a thousand feet where he shut down the engine by pulling the fuel mixture to cutoff. He then dead-sticked the airplane onto the runway. On the roll out, he pushed in the mixture control, the engine started, and he took off again. He did this repeatedly until Alice waved him in for dinner.

It was a magical night. They had a cozy fire going when the evening chill came. The sky grew immense, brilliant with stars. In the distance, coyotes yipped. Those distant voices were the only sound besides the sagebrush cracking in the fire. They lay out watching the stars late into the night, disturbed only by a herd of cattle that meandered across the runway in the darkness.

* * *

Alice and John had agreed early on that they were just friends. He knew Alice was okay with that, aware of the powerful hold Christine held over him. She seemed to admire his unique purity. But she pined for him for reasons neither of them fully understood. She said she felt like she was playing a part in a Shakespearian tragedy in which John Malik was the tragic hero. In her words, she was drawn to the siren's song that emanated from him without understanding why.

They agreed to write. John said goodbye, leaving her at the departure gate at the Sky Harbor Airport. He was on his way to Fairchild AFB, Washington to attend Global Survival School en route to Vietnam.

* * *

Since his mother's funeral, John had continued to receive letters from Christine. But she said nothing about the young man that sat beside her at the funeral. Nor did she mention John's rude exit from the funeral. Her tone was neutral, describing the bare facts of her academic progress.

She had taken five years to complete the BS in biochemistry and was about to enter a master's program that could take another two years before applying to Baylor Med school in Houston. She asked for continuing contact information as John transitioned from Luke to his new base in Vietnam.

Over and over, he read these letters, searching for the faintest hint of hidden meaning. The letter and envelope no longer had a scent. He could not visualize her at her desk typing these passionless missives. The letters seemed to be an obligation, nothing more. But that could not be true. He had to believe otherwise.

In his shirt pocket, he carried Christine's 12th-grade school picture. On the back she had written, "I will always love you, no matter what." This picture and her words were his light in the darkest of times.

And now he was going to war. He had a purpose; he was serving a noble cause, the defense of his country against the global threat of communism. And if it cost him his life, so be it. In what other way could his life ever have meaning?

CHAPTER 27

The Discipline of Survival

John reported for Global Survival School at Fairchild AFB in Washington state as snow began to fall in the mountains. He expected this to be a life-changing experience. The stories of those who had gone through this school persuaded him that he would be facing the extremity of pain, fear, and exhaustion. He expected to discover his physical and psychological limits, though there were certainly much tougher military programs.

The academic content exposed Malik to human savagery on a scale he did not want to know about. Interrogators described methods they used to gain intel from captured enemy soldiers and sympathizers. The enemy was even crueler. Slides of atrocities showed what the enemy might do to him, if he were captured. The instructors presented case studies illustrating that successful escape and evasion depended on mental toughness and physical conditioning.

John sat on the back row of an assembly of 500 men or more. Sensing someone looking at him, he glanced left down the row and saw a second lieutenant leaning forward, staring at him. The lieutenant nodded with a smile and waved. John nodded, clueless who this might be, and turned his attention back to the speaker.

A Protestant chaplain was speaking about the vital necessity of grounding one's faith before shipping out to war. "Some of you will not come home. Deal with the possibility now. Faith is fundamental to your physical survival, to your will to live, and for the peace that comes from knowing where you will open your eyes in death."

The chaplain described a case study. A WWII fighter pilot ran out of fuel and landed his P-51 on a snowpack in northern Alaska. When rescuers found him, they saw his tracks around the airplane, the butts of a dozen cigarettes, and a spray of blood across the snow. He had taken out his revolver and shot himself. Why?

The chaplain told stories of men shot down in the jungle who were too enervated to hold on to the jungle penetrator to be hoisted up into the rescue helicopter. They lacked the will to survive, a force that has to be greater than one's physical limitations. Only a strong will to survive, and a reason to live, will force one's body beyond its limits, he said.

"Some of you will surrender to death, rather than endure another day without hope. War is a bleak business that hemorrhages the life force of many. Establish your faith upon solid ground; do it now before you are in the crosshairs." The chaplain said a prayer for all of the men in the room, that they would all return to their families.

John leaned forward and looked left again. The lieutenant was still looking at him. Who was this guy and what did he want? When the commander dismissed the assembly, John searched for the lieutenant but didn't see him.

His thoughts now transitioned to the imminent horror of the concentration camp.

* * *

John peered out the windows of the blue USAF bus into cold darkness. The bus had stopped on the edge of a blasted landscape dominated by obsidian and mud. Exhaust and a cloud of condensation enveloped the vehicle. In the distance, a half-mile away, he could see flood lights illuminating bleak wooden structures and fences topped with concertina wire, a scene that inspired dread.

From what he had heard, this was a place of physical, mental, and moral testing that would forever change those who went through it. Some would discover they were not the men they wanted to be and thought they were. A few would be surprised they were better men than they thought.

The busload of men filed out to stand at attention on the edge of the muddy dirt road. They stood facing their destination, looking through the cold whipping mist and intermittent drizzle falling from a black overcast. A sergeant addressed them without a hint of deference for the predominant officer ranks among them—which included several full colonels. All these men were now prisoners, and they were to be treated as war criminals.

"American running dog lackeys. That is a no-man's-land." The sergeant pointed to the expanse, separating them from the concentration camp. "You are going to cross this on your bellies. There are pyrotechnic booby traps out there; they will detonate if you touch a tripwire. Two feet above you is concertina wire. Live 50-caliber machine gun fire will rake above the wire. If you raise up, you will be cut in half. You are here to experience the rigors of evasion and final capture." The sergeant paced as he continued his speech. His voice rose with the intensity of his message.

"Guards will roam the terrain. They may designate you as killed because of your incompetence on this course. If you are so identified, stand, and surrender. It will be worse for you.

"Remember, you are the enemy. Your captors hate you; they want to hurt you; they want to kill you. All they are looking for is a provocation. If you want to survive this experience, remember what you have learned, and do not provoke your own death."

The sergeant stopped pacing, the tone of his voice became calm, determined. "I now change my hats and speak for your country. We will tolerate no traitors. We will tolerate no weak-spined collaborators. You will conduct yourselves in a manner that reflects credit upon our nation. Prepare your minds.

"When the whistle blows, you are to assume a prone position and crawl toward the lights. There is no possibility you can escape this experience. Do you understand me? ... I say again, do you understand me?"

"Yes, Sergeant!" the men shouted in unison.

They stood at attention for five minutes, shivering in the wind and rain. A whistle blew. They spread out along a 100-yard expanse, got down on their bellies, and began wallowing through mud and over the sharp rock beneath concertina wire. The ear-splitting chatter of a machine gun began, and tracers buzzed over their heads.

After 30 minutes, bloodied, freezing, panting with exertion, John had drawn near a telephone pole with a single light illuminating a high fence of razor wire. Behind the fence were rough plywood buildings. He emerged from under the concertina wire 20 yards from the fence. Guards in North Vietnamese Army uniforms holding AK-47s approached and screamed at him to get to his feet.

Malik stood at attention as more and more of his colleagues joined him in a line. The guards harassed them, insulted them, evidently trying to provoke a physical reaction. But if he responded physically, he would have to repeat the course, because he would be declared dead.

A guard came through the wire gate with a stack of dusty burlap bags. He threw one to each man. The guards ordered them to place the bag over their heads. Touching the man in front, they marched lockstep into the camp and were processed.

They lined up in a corridor. The guards positioned them five feet apart. They faced left, breathing dust through the burlap bags. Malik heard plywood doors opening. A guard opened a door behind him and then shoved him backward into a cell. The guard commanded Malik to stand at attention, to be silent, to keep the bag on his head, and not to lean against the walls or to sleep.

The door slammed. Malik heard it lock. He pulled the bag off his head. His cell was a four-foot square of plywood. Ten-foot-high walls were open above to rafters. In the corner of his cell was a 2-gallon tin can, his toilet.

Sing-song music came through speakers, probably Vietnamese. Sometimes a silky-voiced Asian woman interrupted, describing the atrocities of the Yankee air pirates who were destroying the peace-loving people of Vietnam. Her propaganda was relentless. It seemed persuasive after a time.

Undetermined hours passed. There was no change in the light's intensity. How long had he been here? Was it day or night? He discovered that the guards crept along the passageway, jerking open doors, surprising the prisoners. There were screams, scuffling violence.

It was impossible to tell how many days had passed when, without warning, Malik's door flew open. The guard had caught him without the bag over his head and leaning against the wall. The guard's scream sprayed spittle into Malik's face. Malik lowered his eyes in terror and cowered before the guard.

The enemy slammed him against the wall. With his finger in Malik's face, he warned Malik that if he violated the rules again, he would march Malik out of the camp and shoot him dead.

At that moment, Malik learned something about himself that he would not do again. He had shown cowardice, and he despised himself for it. Never again would he let fear, pain, or imminent death reduce him to cowardice.

Sleep deprivation and the fear of being brutalized weighed on his mind. But having stood before physical threat his resolve was firm. He repeated to himself, "I will never cower before anyone again."

Malik had no basis for knowing how long he stood in the cubicle, but he estimated at least three days had passed when a guard again jerked open his door. Malik stood up the instant he suspected the guard was at the door. He pulled the bag over his face.

The guard grabbed him by his flight suit and pulled him into the corridor. He bound Malik's hands painfully behind his back, then guided him along the corridor to an interrogation room. The guard jerked the bag off Malik's head and shoved him into the room. An interrogator sat at a small table.

The inquisitor's words and demeanor were frightening, demoralizing, brutal. He laced questions with violent threats and insults, and increasingly so, for Malik's only reply to questions was with name, rank, and serial number. This continued for 20 minutes. Then the interrogator left. Malik stood to attention. He remained in this position until the man returned with a large bulky object in his hands. Another man was with him.

The interrogator threw the object at Malik; he instinctively caught it. Then the other man snapped a Polaroid photo of Malik holding an aerodynamic shape three feet long that resembled a bomb. It was stenciled with letters that identified it as a biological weapon. This photo would prove that Captain John Malik, USAF, had dropped this weapon from his airplane on the peaceful people of Vietnam, an international war crime.

The interrogator took the object from Malik and laid a document on the desk. It was a confession of his crimes against the people of Vietnam. Malik stared at the wall, unmoving, reciting his name, rank, and serial number in response to every question or statement.

"You *will* sign the document," the interrogator said. "You will *plead* for the chance to do it."

Malik persisted in his recitation.

The interrogator smiled and nodded to the guard and pointed. "To the black box. Leave him in it until he begs to sign his confession."

The guard jerked Malik toward the door. With the bag over his head, he was shuffled along a corridor toward the sounds of screaming.

Malik stood with his nose and his toes against a wall of rough-hewn slats, from what he could tell. He was ordered to raise one knee and place it on a sharp wooden ledge. He did this. A guard pushed him from behind and ordered him to raise his other knee, to bend over, and to enter the space before him. Two men pushed and stuffed him into the opening until his head hit the end, forcing him to bend his neck. Once fully inside, he was folded in the fetal position, confined on all sides by wooden slats.

His captors then pulled wooden levers to drive the walls of the box against his back and sides, squeezing him on all sides. When he exhaled, they cinched the levers until his lungs could not expand for a full breath. They closed the opening behind him and bolted it shut. Malik instantly felt the electrocution of panic. Around him, men were in elemental frenzy. Malik could not move any part of his body, even an inch.

To fend off insanity, he closed his eyes and focused on his fingertips. He could move his fingertips. So, he typed the alphabet. A hundred times, then a thousand times, he continued typing the alphabet letter by letter. Competing with imminent suffocation were the muscle cramps and spasms that migrated through his legs, back, and arms. But his focus did not waver despite the screams and pandemonium around him. The captors exacerbated the howling chorus of madness by hammering with bats and clubs against the boxes while screaming mad obscenities at the prisoners.

But John Malik did not utter a sound.

How long the ordeal lasted, he could not guess. But it finally ended. The door opened behind him, the walls expanded, and he struggled backward on command. Guards pulled him out and dropped him on the floor. His body was frozen in the fetal position by continuous muscle tetany.

With the bag still over his head, two of his captors dragged him by the arms outside the torture building and dumped him on the cold muddy ground where he writhed in breathtaking pain. Someone pulled the bag off his head. Two soldiers in U.S. fatigues dragged him to his feet and carried him out the gate, onto a bus, and into a seat.

***

Three days later, in the dark of 0400, Malik and a hundred other men reported to an assembly area where they separated into flights of seven, each group commanded by the senior ranking individual, one of whom was Captain John Malik. Among his charges was the second lieutenant who had tried to get John's attention in the briefing hall.

"Do I know you?" John asked, as they stood shivering in a cold wind, awaiting buses.

"No, sir, I don't think so. I was in the class behind you at Luke. I hear we may both go to Phan Rang."

"And you are … William Bjorn," he said, reading the name patch on the lieutenant's flight suit. He turned to look to the north where the dim sky looked heavy with snow.

Clouds had covered the distant mountains the evening before. Now, city lights glowed against a low overcast.

"The weather forecast last night called for heavy snow in the mountains. Do you think they might delay or cancel our tour in the mountains?" Bjorn asked.

"No."

Bjorn groaned.

Like all the men, they were wearing a temporary-issue winter parka over a flight suit. Beneath that, they wore long johns and two or three pairs of socks. They each carried a 60-pound backpack containing a mummy sleeping bag, a tarp, a pup tent, snowshoes, and enough of everything else needed to survive the coming ordeal—everything but food.

"I'm not used to cold weather." Bjorn shifted his pack to get relief on his shoulders. He shuffled his feet and wrung his gloved hands.

They boarded their bus. John worked his way to the back, followed by Bjorn, who asked for permission to sit beside him. John nodded, hoping he wouldn't have to engage in small talk with this garrulous surfer-boy, which is what John judged the blond-haired Californian to be. He figured Bjorn didn't have to be an airhead, he had chosen that demeanor.

And Bjorn wanted to talk. His knee was bouncing. He glanced toward Malik, who finally turned toward him. "What is it, Lieutenant?"

"Sir, I don't understand why we have to do this. I've heard people die on this trek. We're headed for the jungle, so why do we have to go into a winter survival situation?"

"They haven't told me why. But you should be able to figure it out."

"I can't. It makes no sense to me."

"What we're supposed to learn has nothing to do with where we learn it. We're supposed to reach what we think is our physical limit. What happens then? That's the question." He leaned his head against the window and closed his eyes.

Bjorn moaned. "Oh, I don't want to do this."

"Look, Bjorn, like it or not, if you get shot down, you need to know what you're capable of. Save your strength; you'll need it." Malik shifted his body away from Bjorn and drifted off.

They were soon beyond villages and farms on a winding two-lane road climbing through a forest. After two hours, they reached the snow line. When Malik awoke, feathery snowflakes were drifting down out of the black sky. The scene was magical in the headlights. The driver downshifted and selected high speed on the windshield wipers that began slapping the snow from the windshield.

The bus turned off the paved highway onto a gravel road and continued climbing at a steeper grade. Wheels slipped traction, and the engine and transmission whined, muffled by the surrounding snow-covered forest. A Currier and Ives winter-wooded panorama unfolded outside the windows. Malik turned to watch an elevation marker pass slowly by the window: 8,000 feet.

Bjorn hugged himself, rocking fore and aft, his knees bouncing. The heater fan was on high, but it didn't have much effect toward the back of the bus. At last, John saw their disembarkation point appearing through the windshield. Idling in a gravel turnout were the first two buses, lit by their headlights and the glow of dawn diffusing through the overcast. Malik's driver stopped and set the air brake with a hiss. They were several miles from the Canadian border in bitter cold and falling snow. Malik and his seatmate struggled into the aisle.

Malik's team rallied to their training instructor who would lead them to their first encampment, six hours away. After that, they would be on their own for five days, navigating using a map and compass to an unknown final destination many miles distant.

These were the rules: They were not to use any roads or trails they might cross. They were not to travel along ridgelines where the aggressor forces might spot them. And yes, they were being hunted. They had to reach a designated encampment each day before dark. There they were to retrieve a flag to certify they had followed the assigned route.

The routes the fifteen teams followed diverged, making it unlikely they would encounter another living soul during their trek. If they could catch and kill game, or find edible forage, they should do that. Otherwise, they would not eat for six days.

With the instructor and Captain Malik in the lead, his team struck off, trudging up-slope through the trees. The effects of the heavy pack and the thin atmosphere were immediately evident. The instructor stopped when a distant view appeared through the falling snow. Everyone dropped their packs and gathered around to examine the map. They watched the instructor sight mountain peaks and take bearings to locate their position on the contour map.

Malik turned to the instructor. "What do you do if you can't find a clear view?"

"You keep going, maintain your last bearing, sighting as far ahead as you can see, tree-to-tree if you have to. Keep going until you find an overview where you can see landmarks and plot your position."

"But what if it's snowing and you can't see far enough?" Malik asked.

The instructor raised his eyebrows and shrugged.

* * *

Toward the end of the first day's trek, the men donned their snowshoes in deepening snow. When they reached the encampment, they collapsed, unable to move for 10 minutes. When they had somewhat recovered, they foraged for burnable wood and spent an inordinate amount of time producing a small fire in a place hollowed out of the snow. The remaining hours of daylight were dedicated to listening to the instructor describe survival skills.

With pup tents set up and sleeping bags placed within, over a tarp, Malik began a night of unprecedented misery. With boots and parka stuffed inside the mummy sleeping bag, he had to wiggle inside and zip up the bag until only his nose was exposed to the subzero cold. It was a night of panic, fighting the terrors of claustrophobia within the straight jacket of the mummy bag. He had controlled his claustrophobia in the black box, but this was different, zipping open the bag to breathe and move his limbs lost heat he could not replace. The danger of freezing to death was very real. By dawn, Malik was exhausted, having alternated through the night between suffocating panic and bitter cold.

When everyone was packed up, they watched the instructor mark Malik's map with the location of the next night's encampment. The instructor gave Malik a sealed envelope with the coordinates of the ultimate destination. He should open it only in an emergency. And the instructor reminded them, if they did not complete this phase of their training, they would have to repeat the entire course, including the concentration camp.

With bellies growling for want of food, the men waved farewell to their instructor and struck off on a bearing into the trees. After a grueling day, they reached the second night's encampment. They had nothing to eat. Their snares produced no rabbits, and efforts to find anything edible were unsuccessful. The night was a repeat of the first.

The days passed slowly, one foot in front of the other, trudging under heavy packs, enduring gnawing hunger and relentless cold. Malik continuously took sightings, laid out a heading, and plodded ahead of his silent band, too weary to speak, and fearing the numbing effect of falling temperatures as the day wore on. He did not share his concern, but he believed these were dangerous conditions that exceeded the program's safety margins.

They were nearing total exhaustion when they reached the encampment on the fifth night. Malik endured yet another night of claustrophobic distress swaddled in his mummy bag.

On the morning of the sixth day, Malik's team awoke under heavy snowfall. They had to dig their way out of their tents, now past hunger pangs and fatigued beyond their experience. They moved out at a sloth-like pace. The dominant sound was snow crunching beneath their snowshoes.

Malik was on an uncertain bearing. Unknown to the others, Malik had lost his orientation in the snow flurries. There were no aiming points visible.

Their halting progress was reduced to a dozen steps followed by heaving efforts to restore their oxygen debt. Then another dozen steps, inch-worming on an uncertain bearing. Upon every stop Malik looked back to see if their tracks were in a straight line. He was seeing stars, his mind a fog. With every breath, the frigid air stabbed his chest like a knife, certain he was incurring irreparable damage to his lungs. All the years of his life and all the days he had remaining vanished from his imagination. Only the intensity of the moment occupied his mind.

Known only to Malik, they had been lost for the last two hours. He was responsible for the navigation; he had the maps and expensive compass; it was his job to get them home. And now panic pounded on his consciousness; they were going to freeze to death unless he could find their way soon. Even if he found an overlook with enough visibility, he was uncertain whether his mind could plot a map solution, his brain was so addled.

Conditions were now a whiteout. Snow pellets stung his face as he struggled to lift one foot then another. The men behind did not speak. Their heads were down, mindlessly following Malik's fast-disappearing tracks in the snow.

There was no provision for navigating in such extreme conditions. Should he stop and set up camp and wait for someone to find them? But they could freeze to death before that happened. Better to keep moving. The snowfall might abate; he might find an overlook and plot a heading for the final destination.

He lifted his head and saw far enough ahead to discover he had entered a dense thicket of 20-foot fir trees. The interval was so tight between the trees he could not get through them. He turned ponderously. Trees were all around him. They were trapped. His feet burned as though being stabbed with hot pins; his face had no feeling; he did not believe he had enough energy to lift his foot one more time. His men had entered the thicket and jammed up behind him.

Seeing their circumstance, they fell headlong into the snow, one after the other. And Malik gave up, fell over, and surrendered to death by freezing. This was a better fate than any he had conceived. He had no reason to live, nor did he want to.

He had no conception of how long he lay in the snow, drifting beyond all sensation. The snow had drifted over his face; he had surrendered to the cold. He would go to sleep now and die.

But something stirred his consciousness. Someone was staring at him. He blinked his eyes and move his head sufficient to clear the snow. William Bjorn, lying two feet away, was staring at him with a haunted, pleading expression. From some dim recess of his mind, Malik knew it mattered that Bjorn and the other men live. And their survival was why he had to live. He was responsible for them.

With a strength he did not know he had, he pulled first one arm, then the other, from the shoulder straps of his pack. He struggled to get to his feet, entangled in the webbing of his snowshoes. Tottering upright, he bellowed through his numbed features at the men. "Get on your feet! You've had your rest. We're getting out of here. Get up! That's an order."

Panting and stumbling with the strain, Malik pulled several men to their feet, kicking others, shouting in their faces. "Hot coffee … sandwiches … not far …."

They dumped most of the contents of their packs and turned to backtrack several hundred yards downslope before reversing course into larger trees. Then, through the stinging flurries, John saw someone in the distance for just an instant. A man dressed in a white snowsuit, waving his arms.

He pointed. "You … see … him?" he stuttered to Bjorn who was just behind him.

Bjorn squinted into flurries, moving his head. He shook his head no.

"He … wants … go that way." Malik changed direction and plodded on.

Thirty minutes later, they came upon a logging trail marked with evidence of recent vehicle traffic. They removed their snowshoes, recovered their breath, and stumbled off along the easy trail. An hour later in darkening gloom, they came upon their destination. Idling buses sat in a turnout. There were steaming pots of coffee and a small mountain of sandwiches laid out on tables amid roaring fires in oil drums.

* * *

When he got back to Fairchild, Malik soaked for an hour in a hot tub, then dressed and went to a nearby steak house where he ate three full-course meals in succession. He had lost 15 pounds in the mountains.

Back in his quarters, soaking in another steaming tub of hot water, he jerked open his eyes from a vision. He had seen snakes.

CHAPTER 28

Snake School

Malik departed the Seattle-Tacoma airport on a flight to Honolulu, en route to Clark AB, Philippines. Between dozing, watching movies, and studying the endless miles of whitecaps far below, he rehearsed again a decision he had reached: he would never let himself be captured alive by the enemy. If he could not avoid capture, he would force the enemy to kill him.

Three hours out of Honolulu, Malik had the same impression again that someone was looking at him. He turned and looked back down the aisle and saw Bill Bjorn on the opposite side of the aisle three rows back. Bjorn was smiling at him. This guy was like a bad penny.

Malik grimaced, gave him a sarcastic smile, and opened a magazine. Bjorn was heading for Clark also; and he even had orders for Malik's squadron at Phan Rang.

At Clark AB Malik was to undergo yet another ordeal to test his limits and his capacity to survive, this time in the jungle. Clark was the home of the notorious Jungle Survival Training, better known as Snake School.

* * *

Breathing the humid air at Clark, 15 degrees north of the equator, was easier and the temperature milder than Malik had expected. Verdant lawns and Banyan trees spread across the base that was bounded by unbroken jungle to the west. He was going out there to see if he could survive.

Ten students, including John Malik and Bill Bjorn, assembled on the grass outside of the classroom. The enlisted instructor stood before a pit with a wire covering over the top. He invited the class to look into the hole. They huddled around to see an angry writhing 10-foot king cobra that was recently captured on the base. The sergeant's topic today was snakes; he had everybody's attention.

"All of you have the potential of bailing out into the jungle. If you do, you need to know what can kill you, especially snakes. There are lots of snakes in Vietnam. More than 30 of the species are venomous. Part of your training out here is to develop an awareness of your surroundings and to avoid snakebite.

"The King Cobra is very dangerous because of the volume of poison it injects in a single bite. Snakes that may not look dangerous to you may be dangerous. You probably won't be able to identify any species other than the aroused cobra, so, avoid all snakes. Assume they are poisonous."

Malik raised his hand. "At Global Survival School we heard about the 'two-step,' a snake so deadly it'll kill you in two steps. What is it, and is that true?"

The sergeant nodded. "That is what the Vietnamese call *cham quap*. A captured Vietcong unit document claimed more of their fighters died from the bite of this snake, and from malaria, than from American airpower. I'm convinced this snake is the many-banded krait. But it's not as deadly as a Taipan or black mamba, for instance. You may have several hours to live, untreated, if you're bitten by the many-banded krait. So, not that big a deal, eh?"

Malik and the other students exchanged glances. The instructor was in his element. He loved the jungle. He loved snakes.

***

When the academic training was complete, Malik and his classmates, one-by-one, were lowered on a jungle penetrator from a hovering helicopter into a trackless region of jungle. It was so remote their base camp was inaccessible by any means but helicopter.

Malik and his class received practical training on how to survive and how to avoid capture. They rigged sleeping hammocks well off the ground between trees with lines far enough from the trees to avoid one of the chief night predators in the Philippines jungle, giant rats that could eat your lips off while you slept.

The class learned jungle-craft, including how to get water from vines. They learned to identify things edible and poisonous, and what could kill them. They were never to use personal hygiene products that had any aroma, including soap and shaving cream.

Because they sweated buckets and were not acclimated to the jungle, they produced an odor not natural to the jungle. The aggressors who would be hunting them would be able to smell them.

The evening of the second day the instructor gathered the students around a stone-lined fire pit for another lecture before dinner. Stacked beside the circle of stones were limbs and twigs that were periodically fed into the fire. Everyone was waiting on Bjorn who was off some distance in the bush. Malik, as the ranking officer, stood up and called him. His lackadaisical attitude was wearing thin with Malik. Bjorn kept saying he didn't like it out here.

When Bjorn finally blundered into the clearing, he made his way to a rotting log just outside the group circle, plotted down, and laid his right arm back onto the log.

Malik jumped to his feet. "Bjorn! Look at me! Do not move!"

Bjorn jerked his head toward Malik with an alarmed expression. At that instant, a glistening golden liquid trickled down his right cheek. He looked wide-eyed toward Malik who was striding rapidly toward him with a three-foot limb raised over his head.

Malik smashed the limb down onto a large cobra three feet from Bjorn that was rearing back to strike. The cobra writhed under the blow, coiling, twisting, striking. Malik pinned his head with the limb and grabbed it just behind its head, squeezing hard. He lifted it up and smashed its head into a tree as the body whipped and wrapped around Malik's arm.

Bjorn was in a petrified stupor. He raised his hand to his face.

"Stop! Don't touch that, it's poison," the instructor yelled as he moved toward him.

Everyone else had backed up.

"Hold still," the instructor said, as he wiped the poison off Bjorn's face with a rag and dropped it in the fire.

Malik threw the twisting remains of the cobra into the fire.

The instructor smiled broadly. "That's a spitting cobra, Lieutenant. They're very accurate with that spitting business up to five feet. If you hadn't turned your head, he would have hit you in the eyes and likely blinded you. And, it was about to hammer you. You could have been blind and dead.

"Wow, isn't this fun! What a good time I'm having. You guys are such fun. Everything I could tell you about snakes and other dangerous things out here you'll forget. But I doubt any of you will forget this."

Bjorn was speechless, his mouth hung open, and the color was gone from his face. He huddled near the fire, checking all around himself. The others returned to the firepit to watch the instructor pull the cobra out of the fire and skin it, whistling a happy tune. He then skewered it and propped it over the fire while he prepared the rest of the evening's meal. Rice packed in bamboo sections roasted in the coals, grubs, and other delicacies from the jungle's bounty were sizzling on skewers.

* * *

Malik and the others had the standard gear combat pilots carried in their survival vests. On base they had practiced repelling from trees using nylon tapes and a friction device each carried in their vest. If a pilot bailed over the jungle, his chute would likely foul in the trees—if he was not skewered by limbs.

The class had two escape and evasion exercises. The human aggressors were the as-yet-unseen Negritos, pygmy aboriginals, who survived in the region in a stone-age jungle culture by hunting and foraging. They were motivated to capture Malik and his classmates because each student carried two chits, pieces of paper each worth a 10-pound bag of rice. When caught, the student was to surrender a chit to his captor.

After several days of jungle-craft, Malik was awakened in his hammock by a soft voice at first light. "Run. Run for your life," the instructor whispered to him.

Malik rolled out of his hammock and took off along an animal trail to get as far as he could from the encampment from whence his pursuers would come. Dense cover was the only hope of evasion. He found such a cover and burrowed into a thick clump of ferns, convinced no one could see him there; he waited.

Thirty minutes passed. Malik moved only to flick off ants and other insects that tested his flesh as a food source. A faint patter of bare feet came along an animal trail near his location. The feet stopped a few yards from Malik. Long seconds of silence. Then he saw the ferns parting. A fearsome-looking Negrito used the blunt end of a five-foot-long spear to spread the foliage, exposing Malik. The man wore only a loincloth. Barefooted, he stood between three- and four-foot-tall. He held out his hand. Malik dug out one of his chits and handed it to him. The man turned and disappeared without a sound.

Back in the camp, the instructors reviewed with the students what they had learned. The Negritoes found every one of them. The instructor asked such questions as, "What could you have done differently? Do any of you want to spend the rest of your lives in the Hanoi Hilton? What are you willing to do to avoid capture?"

The afternoon exercise began. How could Malik avoid capture this time?

In his flight from the encampment on the second exercise, Malik came across a spot he reasoned might be one place they could not find him, nor could they smell him. A four-foot-high pile of rotting vegetation lay on the slope of a ravine. He crawled beneath the decay, burrowing well into it, and lay still.

What he had not considered was that it was alive with stinging ants and centipedes and other insects that converged upon him immediately. In a matter of minutes, his flesh teemed with crawling things, biting, injecting him with poison, eating his flesh, sucking fluids from his body. His body was on fire; he throbbed with fever and chills. Yet he lay still, typing the alphabet with his fingertips and only flicking away ants attempting to enter his nostrils and ears.

A Negrito approached. He stopped near Malik and stood still for a long minute, listening, smelling, aware Malik had come this way. Soon he padded on. The minutes passed. His agony rose in intensity. Finally, a whistle sounded in the distance, and Malik exploded from his hide. He stripped off his flight suit, shook it out, and clawed his skin bloody, slapping and rubbing his skin to rake off the insects and ants hanging onto his skin by their mandibles.

When he reached the encampment, he was barely conscious. He remembered the instructor administering something, a salve, an ointment, maybe a hypodermic shot. Malik handed his instructor the other chit—apparently, a unique achievement.

Malik's reward for evading capture was 24 hours on IVs in the infirmary. The doctor said the scars would probably fade, eventually.

PART VIII:

ON THE DARKLING PLAIN

CHAPTER 29
To War

The World Airways Boeing 727 mounted up majestically from Clark's Runway 02R. John studied the rising terrain from a right window seat aft of the wing as the aircraft turned west, ascending the slope of the volcanic Mt. Pinatubo, 15 miles west of Clark. Interlaced between the drainage scars radiating from its summit was dense jungle. Maybe that's where he had been.

The aircraft was still climbing as the western coastline passed beneath. Malik then settled back to watch the play of sunlight glittering off the featureless South China Sea. It would be unbroken by landforms for 1,000 miles until raising the coast of Vietnam.

His life would change now. He was prepared to give his life for his country, but he was having doubts about the cause, persuaded the U.S. had a tiger by the tail. This war would not end well.

He also now had the distinct impression that he would not be going home again, whatever that meant—for he had no home. And what he had of Christine was only a picture and her long-ago claim of undying love. He could imagine no scenario in which a life with her was possible. It had been nearly two years since he had seen her, and she was with someone else at his mother's funeral.

A striking young flight attendant was passing out drinks and snacks to the troops as she made her way down the aisle behind a galley cart. There was something about her eyes. They were like Christine's. He stared at her until she reached his row. She looked up at him, smiled, and handed him a Coke. Their eyes locked on to each other. She glanced away only momentarily when she had to scoop some ice or grab a can from the cart. As she moved on, she glanced back several times.

Thirty minutes later, John made his way into the aisle, heading back toward the galley. The young woman stood beside a cart, digging out drinks and snacks for several soldiers who were giving her their complete attention. She seemed unfazed by the attention until John approached. She turned and stared into his eyes. It was as though they both were adrift on a raft at sea, suddenly seeing a distant island.

Many seconds passed. Her bottom lip quivered; her eyes glistened with tears. She walked the five feet separating them, wrapped her arms around John and kissed him hard, tears rolling down her cheeks, oblivious to the bystanders.

Whatever pierced her heart when she looked at him was not vocalized. Did she believe she was looking at a handsome young man about to die? Entwined with her clear passion, was the expression of overwhelming sorrow in those moments as time stood still. Several flight attendants and soldiers, embarrassed or interested in this strange encounter, watched or turned away to give them space.

She whispered, "My name is Kim. If you have no one else to think of, remember me when you're scared and lonely. I'll come to you in your dreams if I can. Please live." She backed up, shuddering, biting her lip. "How I wish you were mine."

She wiped her eyes, then reached into the galley cart and handed him another Coke and a cup of ice. "If I could, I would give you everything I am," she said.

He brushed his tears away, nodded, and turned to walk back down the aisle.

There were 180 soldiers aboard. As John glanced back at Kim, he surveyed the faces of soldiers, masks of grim resignation. Some were thumbing through a magazine or reading a novel. No one was smiling; there was no light of anticipation, no conversations, no banter. Some gripped the armrests.

Until that moment, John did not understand how deeply he needed human contact and affirmation. He took deep breaths as he settled into his seat, now encouraged that he could do what was before him. Kim's affirmation had lifted his head.

Out the right window, he saw a far-off coastline. He pulled a map from the seatback pocket and determined their position was 50 miles south and abeam of Phan Rang AB, Vietnam. That would put them about 200 miles out of Saigon. He turned around several times to see if he could see Kim.

Ten minutes later, the captain reduced thrust to idle at the top of descent, 120 miles out of Saigon. The flight attendants began their briefings. Kim moved past, reaching over to squeeze John's hand.

Now he could see white beaches. Villages and jungle passed beneath, and then they were over the teeming suburbs of Saigon. The aircraft slowed, the slats and flaps extended, the gear came down, and the command came over the PA for the flight attendants to be seated. Beneath the flight path were the approach lights and the end of the runway. The aircraft touched down, reversed thrust, slowed, and taxied clear of the runway. The page had turned. A new chapter was beginning.

Parked on the tarmac, Malik made his way into the aisle and dragged his carry-on out of the overhead. When Kim opened the L1 door, a hot blast of humid air, perfumed with combusted jet fuel, swept into the fuselage and rocked Malik back on his heels. The exhaust of a multitude of jet engines shimmered the atmosphere with suffocating heat.

Out the windows, he could see a mile-long conga line of aircraft snaking toward the takeoff position on the right runway. Beyond, on the left runway, an uninterrupted parade of landing aircraft touched down with curls of smoke from their wheels, their engines spooling up in reverse. Each cleared the runway even as another aircraft behind them was crossing the approach lights on short final.

It was organized chaos on a massive scale with one aim: Stop the communists. It was vital that no more dominoes fall.

Kim stood by the L1 door, wishing everyone well. As John passed, she squeezed his arm. Their hungry eyes lingered on each other as he stepped out the door onto the airstairs.

Two steps down, his abs tightened, and he leaned forward with a twinge in his chest. His heart skipped beats, reacting to a spike of fear—the momentary irrational belief a mortar or rocket round was inbound and about to detonate on his position. He noted no one else seemed to sense the threat. The fear passed.

The atmosphere was like a sauna. Waiting on the airstairs, sweat was beading Malik's forehead. Glancing into the distance he could see the base perimeter and the tangle of concertina wire that marked the margin of the no-man's-land, the minefield. Ahead of him on the stairs, a silent column of men continued shuffling down to a dread destiny for many of them.

Malik boarded one of several waiting buses and turned to see Kim at the top of the airstairs watching him. She blew him a kiss. The bus doors closed in his face, and the bus moved off, making its way through a jam of rushing vehicles and baggage carts.

His bus pulled up at an open hanger where he and others got out to stand in a long line before alphabetically designated tables. He boarded another bus that stopped beside a C-130 with the aft ramp lying open. With his duffel bag over his shoulder, he walked up the ramp and sat down in a sling seat against the fuselage wall and buckled in for the 200-mile ride to Phan Rang.

The flight operated at low altitude, where the afternoon thermals produced continuous turbulence that slammed Malik's kidneys and made his stomach queasy. The cavernous cargo bay was hot, uncomfortable, and noisy. Several of the troops vomited into barf bags. But the flight was soon over. The flaps and gear came down, and they touched down at his new home for the next year of his life, Phan Rang AB called "Happy Valley."

He caught a shuttle to the 612th tactical fighter squadron hootch. It was a long single-story structure with a central common area or bar. At his room number, he knocked and entered to find it cool inside, thanks to a humming window air-conditioner built into the wall. His roommate was not in. Malik dumped his gear beside the empty bunk and laid down. He loathed Vietnam, Phan Rang AB, his quarters, the heat and humidity, and, without doubt, the food.

* * *

There were briefings and orientation at the squadron building on the flight line. Weeks of indoctrination passed, and he settled into the routine. His mantra was engaged: He was involved in meaningful activity, as unpleasant as it was.

His obsession with Christine and his metaphysical musings receded from his consciousness as he entered into the rarified atmosphere of combat. Resigned to his lot, he soon learned to endure the heat and humidity, the smells, and the sinister vista of the jungle that seemed to beckon to him from beyond the perimeter fence.

Two weeks after Malik arrived, five homebound pilots boarded a C-123 at Phan Rang for the 30-mile flight up to Cam Rahn Bay. Under lowering weather, the pilot attempted to stay visual beneath the ceiling and hit the mountain defining the east side of the pass north to Cam Rahn Bay. All aboard were killed. Their remains were unreachable because the terrain was impenetrable. A helicopter crew reported sighting a tiger near what they could see of wreckage.

Malik flew his first 20 missions on the wing of experienced pilots. He consistently hit the targets. Pilots he knew were shot down; a firebase he had supported was overrun; a convoy was annihilated in the vicinity. Mounting American losses were appalling, including almost two hundred F-100s destroyed in combat so far. His vision of war from afar and its brutal reality up close were profoundly different.

Three weeks after his arrival, on a Friday evening after dinner at the O' Club, Malik was watching the nightly TV news in the barracks bar. A seasoned captain, whose name Malik did not yet know, slammed a beer bottle down on the bar and got in the face of a young second lieutenant.

"Look newby," he said, and he could be heard over everyone in the bar, "you don't know what you're talking about. Where are you getting this crap about the war being over by Christmas? This friggin' war is never going to end."

"But, sir, just look at the Killed-By-Air numbers. If the enemy's losing that many, the north is being depopulated of a whole generation of young men. They can't keep it up." The lieutenant's voice was full of sincerity and American pride. "The tide has to turn," he said.

"You idiot," the captain said, smirking and shaking his head. "The numbers aren't real. Don't you get it? They can't be real. Every commander has to compete for body count. That's what this is all about. Numbers. The commanders don't care if the numbers are real. It's how they get promoted."

* * *

Malik's combat prowess continued to be recognized. A Forward Air Controller recommended him for a Distinguished Flying Cross for heroism for an action in Laos. He had taken out a cluster of 23 mm antiaircraft guns while taking heavy fire. The Air Force approved the medal.

He was upgraded to flight lead. Soon after, orders came down, designating him an instructor. One of his duties now was to check out new pilots and certify them combat-ready in-theater.

CHAPTER 30

A Message from Charlie

John's roommate, Carl Anders, was in a deep depression. Even before he fell into lethargy, he seldom spoke to John. And now he wouldn't even look at John. He was chronically irritated with him for having the light on until all hours, but their differences were deeper. Carl was embittered against John, and John did not know why.

One night, John got up around 2 a.m. to use the latrine. He glanced into the bar where he saw the glow of a cigarette in the dark. Carl was sitting alone, chain-smoking. In front of him was an ashtray overflowing with butts.

"Carl? What's wrong?" John asked softly, peering around the corner at his dark form.

Carl glanced up, contempt written across his face. "You knew about Lila, didn't you? You knew she was cheating on me even before we got married. Didn't you? Were you sleeping with her?"

"No! My God, no! Why would you ask me that?" John stood in his unlaced combat boots, clad only in his skivvies and a T-shirt, backlit by the night light from the latrine.

"Something you said at Luke. Like you knew what she was."

"I was just giving you an opinion about marrying her. She had just divorced a pilot. I was urging you to be careful; that's all. I'm sorry if I offended you."

Carl tamped another cigarette from a pack and lit it off a smoldering butt. He turned away, staring at the wall, his face a mask of bitterness in the glow of his cigarette. Seconds passed. He said nothing. John turned away and said over his shoulder, "I'm sorry, Carl, for whatever is going on."

That was last week. Tonight, Carl lay on his bunk with his back to John. The nightly tumult from the bar had died out. John glanced up from a novel he was reading as his digital clock clicked, rotating new digits that showed 1 a.m. At that instant, he jerked his head up toward a ripping noise streaking over the roof of the hootch. The ripping sound terminated in a bone-jarring detonation that rocked the structure of the plywood building, bringing down a rain of plaster dust from the ceiling.

John leaped off of his bunk and screamed at Carl, "Get up! Incoming!"

Scrambling, shouting men filled the hallway. Doors slammed, and in the distance came the faint initial wail of an air-raid siren rising in intensity to ear-piercing decibels. Malik jabbed his feet into his flight boots, pulled on a shirt, slid Christine's picture into his shirt pocket, and slammed open the door to the hall with Carl staggering out of deep sleep after him.

"The next correction will be through the roof," someone hollered.

A dozen men were bottle-necked at the double doors of the main exit, all pushing and shouting as everyone tried to get through the door at the same time. In other settings, it would have been a comic scene. "Stop fooling around, you idiots!" Malik practically screamed to be heard above the din.

Ripping sounds continued overhead, and the flash of detonations lit up the doorframe. From a mile away came the roar of the alert fighters running up on the runway. As their engines reached max rpm, the boom of an afterburner ricocheted between the buildings followed in six seconds by a second boom that merged with the sound and the fury of perimeter guns of all calibers firing toward the west and spraying the no-man's-land minefield on the western perimeter of the base. As tracers reached out into the darkness to the west an explosion occurred at the fence.

Once through the door, Malik pivoted toward Charlie's Mountain. Rising from the darkness of the jungle slope, the red arc of a rocket rose in a parabolic path, climbing high before it slanted downward. Malik followed its path to expected impact near a sister squadron barracks and support buildings a hundred yards away. And that's where it hit.

Everyone had scrambled toward the squadron bomb shelter. Then the gaggle of skivvy-clad pilots stopped in their tracks, all trying to avoid being the first to enter the darkness of the bunker.

Someone shouted, "Get in there. What's the problem?"

Everybody knew what the problem was. Cobras. They had begun appearing on the base.

A nearby explosion started the stampede again, and the first man groped down into the darkness, clearing filaments of cobwebs with his waving arms, urged on by those less likely to be snake-bit.

Near the rear of the crowd inside the bunker with his hand on someone's shoulder, Malik shuffled his boots along the crunching gravel, hoping to drive from underfoot any coiled poisonous snakes. He shouldered his way into an eerie forest of silent, weaving, nearly naked bodies. It was like a scene from a zombie movie. The space reeked of mildew, limestone dust, and the body odor of stressed men who would not break a sweat on a combat mission under fire but were deathly afraid of snakes.

Skin-against-skin, Malik found a place where people stopped pushing him. A buzz of stressed voices continued just above a whisper; the men were scared for various reasons, including the fact that a direct hit on the tin roof would pierce it like tissue paper.

Malek raised his hand and touched his shirt pocket, feeling his heartbeat and the contours of her picture. He tasted the burn of bitter bile in the back of his throat and felt the throb of a migraine competing for his attention.

From overhead came the blare of the alert aircraft in afterburner, climbing to the perch with their speed brakes extended, trying to burn out as much fuel from the drop tanks as possible. The drop tanks, with fuel, were not stressed to withstand delivery speeds of 450 and 500 knots, the only defined parameters for which the bombsight was calibrated. But the flight would surely attack before their tanks went dry, before the Vietcong could vacate their firing positions on the mountain ... in theory.

But the truth was, as everybody knew, the enemy was already gone. In the past, when the VC attacked the base with rockets, they used time-delay devices to fire the rockets. These devices had been discovered on the slopes of Charlie's Mountain. They could be far away before the responding firestorm rained down on the launch sites, triangulated by the army's forward observation posts directing artillery batteries.

Thirty seconds passed, then a minute with no incoming. Though it would be some time before the all-clear siren sounded, someone ventured out to look toward Charlie's Mountain. Its dark silhouette blocked the western horizon several miles beyond the perimeter defenses.

"Hey, you gotta see this," the voice came from outside. Men piled out to see the lights of the alert fighters in orbit over the base. They were maneuvering for an attack.

"There they go," someone called, as Blade Lead rolled in off the perch for his attack. Lead leveled off and drove southwest toward the black terrain of the mountain. Then he released. Four cans of napalm tumbled off in succession. Lead's impacts laid down a fire that splashed across a quarter mile of the mountain slope, lighting up the west like the sunrise. The wingman delivered an identical swath up-slope from Lead.

Perimeter artillery resumed dropping rounds on Charlie's Mountain, and automatic weapons raked the minefield under floodlights. The gunfire soon ceased, and base army troops began a street-by-street sweep looking for infiltrators.

Malik's flight commander, nicknamed Buddha, called for everyone's attention. "Listen up." Everyone crowded around the entrance to the bomb shelter. "We wait for the all-clear. Hang out right here. Anybody snake-bit?"

After the responding banter, someone called, "Hey Major, why can't we get weapons?"

Someone else added, "And some flashlights."

"The base commander doesn't trust you hooligans. You get drunk and start shooting in the middle of the night, and we've got a big problem. That's why we can't have weapons in the hootch. Anyway, you see what happened here?"

He continued. "Our barmaid didn't show up tonight. Do you think that's unusual? I do." He let the idea of the barmaid's involvement in the attack sink in. "Did you hear the explosion on the wire? That was probably a sapper getting blown away. Other infiltrators might have made it through. We, gentlemen, and the aircraft on the flight line, are the prime targets of the enemy.

"One sapper with a satchel charge could kill all of us in the bunker. They know this base like the palm of their hand. They work among us every day. I'm telling you this, so you'll be aware."

The pilots all stood staring into the dark, hovering near the entrance to the bunker. After 10 minutes, the all-clear sounded and they began wandering back into the barracks.

Someone demanded that the bar be opened, and everyone else agreed loudly. Someone pumped up the kegs, and the suds flowed.

CHAPTER 31
Unclean

When not otherwise assigned, Malik spent duty time at the Wing Intel shop as the squadron intelligence officer, where he reviewed general intel and wing-specific bomb damage assessment. He did this by examining before- and after-reconnaissance photos of targets hit by the wing's aircraft as well as after-action reports of forward air controllers and flight crews. To his dismay, he found instances where the reported bomb damage assessment by the forward air controllers and the actual evidence did not seem to agree. Nobody seemed to care when he brought this to the attention of the professional staff.

Leaving the shop one afternoon, he elected to walk to the hootch, five blocks away. He passed the ballpark, rows of barracks, then through an area of storage containers where he came upon a young puppy in obvious distress. The pup was overheated and panting for water. She lifted her pleading eyes. John couldn't resist her. He picked her up and carried her with him to the hootch.

He watered and fed her, took her into the shower with him, and shampooed and dried her. She became an instant source of joy. Every night she sat on somebody's lap, enjoying herself, but when everybody went to bed, she would scratch on John's door. She always slept with him in his bunk. She was a balm for John's soul.

It wasn't long before she began acting oddly. John watched her stand in front of her water bowl, coughing or choking, unable to drink. The squadron maintenance officer, who lived with the pilots, stuck his finger down her throat, thinking the pup was choking on something. "Hey, I wouldn't do that," John cautioned him.

Within days the pup was feverish and aggressive, still unable to drink or eat. The squadron flight surgeon heard about this and came to look at the puppy. He warned everybody not to touch or even get close to her. The security police came and put the dog in a cage and dispatched her on a priority flight to Saigon. From there, she was expressed to a medical lab somewhere.

In the meantime, the flight surgeon gathered a list of the names of everyone who had any contact with the animal. When the lab called him with the results, he assembled the squadron and confirmed his suspicions, the puppy was rabid. The entire squadron, 30 pilots, and assorted support officers could be infected with rabies. If not treated with a vaccine within six days of infection, they were unlikely to survive. Rabies is almost always fatal once neurological symptoms appear, and the end comes with violent convulsions. A victim can only be strapped down until he dies, raving mad.

The flight surgeon delivered this news with enthusiasm, as though his boring life had gotten interesting. He said he was going to document this event and write a paper for a medical journal. He would be famous.

Malik and all the other residents of the 612th barracks, known by their squadron callsign "Tide," began a month-long series of injections in the stomach. All received treatment in time. No one in the squadron manifested the deadly symptoms. However, the sister squadrons now had a reason for jeering at the Tides. They were now considered pariahs. The episode even eclipsed in luridness the discovery of a nest of cobras in a nearby storage container.

* * *

It was Saturday night. The pilots drifted into the bar after dinner at the O Club. By 2200, almost everyone but Malik was in the bar, drinking, telling war stories, playing cards, or watching TV. Malik was lying on his bunk reading. Carl was in a deep sleep as usual.

Suddenly all the entry doors of the hooch slammed open at the same instant. Malik stuck his head into the hallway. A hush fell over the Tides as strange figures appeared out of the night.

Dozens of men, clad only in their skivvies, combat boots, and gas masks, came through each of the doorways carrying sticks of incense and picket signs with such epithets as "Unclean," "Down with the Tides," "Clean up the neighborhood," and other messages alluding to the notorious status of the Tides.

The Yellow Jackets, a sister squadron, led the assault. In Malik's opinion, the Tides richly deserved what they were about to receive.

Yellow Jackets streamed in chanting some unintelligible limerick, and behind them came Mopeds buzzing up and down the halls. Next came a gas-powered lawnmower at full throttle and ensembles of the galvanized tub- and bucket-beaters. A blue haze of exhaust filled the hallways. Deafening noise included the sounds of crashing glass and shouts. The wrath of Tide's neighbors, three sister-squadrons, was to fall in retribution for the many Saturday night depredations of the Tides upon their neighbors' bars.

Malik locked his door and propped a chair against the handle. He stuffed earplugs into his ears.

"I hate living with these animals."

Carl slept through it all.

CHAPTER 32
Engine Fire Light

Malik had a premonition about the northern mountain ridge they crossed during every northern departure from Phan Rang. He imagined what he would do if he were the enemy; he would climb one of the 150-foot-high trees. Sitting in the branches, he would wait for an F-100 to pass overhead and fire rifle rounds into the belly, hitting the engine or the fuel tanks.

On a standard departure off Runway 04 one afternoon, Buddha reported a blinking fire light just after crossing the ridge. His wingman advised him of trailing smoke. Buddha cleaned his wings by blowing off his bombs and drop tanks and continued to climb.

Three minutes after the fire light had begun to blink, Buddha reported it went steady; that meant that both fire loops had burned through. His aft fuselage was a blowtorch. And yet Buddha would not eject and would not answer radio calls to do so. His wingman stood well off, expecting him to explode. Buddha reached a top of descent altitude for Pleiku, a short runway 175 miles north-northwest of Phan Rang. He transmitted, "I'm going to make Pleiku."

Again, his wingman called, "No, you won't. You're going to blow up. Eject, Buddha!"

From an idle descent into Pleiku Buddha turned final way too fast despite his wingman's warning. He came over the approach end so fast he had to spike the aircraft onto the runway to make contact. He deployed the drag chute; it immediately separated. His wingman watched in horror as Buddha's aircraft cartwheeled off the end of the runway into the jungle in a stream of fire.

* * *

John had already attended eight memorial services at the base chapel. Today he attended yet another, this time for Buddha. How he wanted to believe the chaplain; he wanted to believe that death had no sting for Buddha. At the end of the service, John walked out the door in time to see a flight of four F-100s approaching silently over the southern base perimeter. They came low and fast.

Over the chapel, Number Three abruptly pulled up out of the formation into a vertical climb and engaged afterburner. A mighty boom merged with the thunderclap of four engines at full power. The sonic energy slammed into Malik and nearly knocked him off his feet. He could not contain his emotion. Watching Number Three rolling to the zenith, Malik and the others screamed, punched their fists to the sky, shouting, "Go, Buddha!"

CHAPTER 33

The Doppelgänger

Several days after Buddha's memorial, there came a soft rap on John's door in the early afternoon. He looked up from his desk. "Come."

The door opened, and a young second lieutenant stepped in and came to attention. "At ease, Lieutenant." John smiled.

"Sir, I am to introduce myself to you. I just checked in. The company clerk told me you are to be my instructor."

"Sit down." John motioned toward his bunk. "What can I do for you?"

"Uh, I don't know, sir. I was told to introduce myself," he repeated. He struggled to get onto the high bunk.

"Okay. Check the schedule, and you'll see when we fly. We'll do our briefings in the squadron building on the flight line. Meanwhile, read all the manuals and write out your questions. We'll cover everything you need to know." John paused, staring at the young man.

"Is something wrong, sir?"

"Where are you from?"

"Arkansas, sir."

John nodded, his eyes narrowly focused on the young man's face. "You look just like my brother. If he had lived." His voice trailed off as he studied the young lieutenant.

The young man cleared his throat.

"What's your name?" Malik stood now and leaned against his desk.

The young man jumped off the bunk and stood to attention. "Ronald Sauer, sir."

"I don't suppose you play the guitar, do you, Ronald Sauer?"

"Yes, sir. I do. How did you know that?" A smile tugged at the corners of his mouth. "I brought my guitar. Do you think the guys would like me to play sometime?"

"I'm sure they would." Sauer's resemblance to Ian and his musical ability defied John's comprehension. This could be Ian. John shook his head as though trying to rejoin the moment. "Uh, sorry if I'm staring. It's just that you … you're so like my brother. My brother drowned. It's been twelve years now. The summer of 1958. He would be your age."

"I'm sorry, sir."

John took a deep breath. "Well, I appreciate your coming by. We'll get together soon. How about dinner at the O Club tonight?"

"I'd like that, sir. It will be an honor to fly with you. I heard about you at Luke."

John nodded and stood to his full height. Ronald stiffened. John smiled. "You don't have to do that. We're pretty relaxed here. I'll see you at the Club at six?"

"I'll be there, sir." He appeared about to salute then reconsidered. He turned to leave.

"Do you have a nickname, Ronald Sauer?" Malik liked this kid.

Sauer turned back. "I just go by Ron, sir."

* * *

One month later, John was listening from his room to the music down the hall in the bar. Ron Sauer had become the most popular man in the squadron. He often played his guitar with his harmonica hung around his neck on a wire frame. Between harmonica runs, he sang poignantly, his soul-stirring melodies and lyrics entranced his audience. He could sound just like Bob Dylan or John Fogerty from Credence Clearwater Revival. Wild applause erupted as he played his last song of the night.

When the music stopped, John got up and walked down the hall to the bar. He didn't like to drink, and small talk stressed him and anyone who engaged him. But tonight, he felt anxious about Ron and felt the need to check on him.

John took a seat on the well-worn couch in the bar and watched Ron being feted by the other pilots. No one had ever bound the squadron together like this young man. Ian had made people feel good about themselves. Ron could do that too. He was everybody's best friend, a fine moral young man, an Eagle Scout.

John watched him at the bar. He had never seen Ron drink. He always refused but not tonight. Beers kept sliding in front of him. He clearly did not want to drink but he was being cajoled mercilessly. After three or more empty bottles had collected in front of him, teetering on the barstool, he swooped around to acknowledge his admirers and saw John Malik staring at him.

Like John, Ron did not fit the classic fighter pilot persona. This episode of binge drinking was out of character for the man Malik had come to know over the past four weeks.

Someone had loaded the tape player. Through the speakers came an early release of a new song, "American Pie." Malik heard snippets of the lyrics.

Ron slipped off the stool, staggered over, and plopped down beside John. "I've gotta say this to somebody," he said, squirming into the couch, his head wobbling, his glassy unfocused eyes looking for John. "You're the only one I can tell … I don't know why that is, do you, sir?"

John shrugged. This drunken sot was not the Ron that Malik knew. The Ron he knew would not presume to sit down without asking. Nor would he have broached personal information without an invitation.

"It's my wife. She's a really, *really* good person." Ron smacked his lips and rocked his head side to side. "Yes, sir. She would cut off her arm for me. But, just between us"—he leaned forward with a grin—"she's awful, I mean *awful* ugly." He belched a vapor that would wilt a flower. John turned away and coughed.

Unfazed, Ron continued, "I can't believe a woman can be *sooo* ugly! She's got these terrible teeth." He curled his fingers from a balled fist and brought his hand up to his mouth. "You don't want to make her laugh, she's a hillbilly girl.

"You know, I had to marry her, do the right thing. What a bod. That she's got. Turns out she lost the baby, she says. But I don't think she was pregnant. What do you think of that? You're the great Captain Malik you must know what I should do."

Ron had his right index finger in the neck of an empty beer bottle, swinging it. Then he set the bottle on the coffee table and twisted his hands. He wiped the sweat off his forehead with his T-shirt. His eyes wandered. He convulsed several times like he would throw up. John slid further away.

Then Ron said, "I am going to divorce her. I'm a rotten person, and I don't deserve to live, do I?" He studied John's face, then lowered his head and seemed about to cry. With no conversational transition, he got up and staggered away toward the bar.

Two rumbling window air conditioners embedded high in the thin walls of the squadron bar churned the smells of stale beer, the jungle, and the third world. They were drowned out by "American Pie" and a chaos of voices.

"Sauer," John shouted. Ron turned and nearly fell.

John pointed to his watch. "We've got alert. Remember? You need to get some sleep."

Ron stood as though in a trance, staring past John. He came to attention and saluted. John did not respond. Ron turned away and rejoined the others.

For an instant, in a lull in the din, John heard several lines of the lyrics. Something about a widowed bride and then ... "the music died."

The following day, Ron Sauer would be obliterated at Prey ToTueng.

CHAPTER 34
The Day the Music Died

John Malik led Ron Sauer through violent thunderstorms en route to a target in Cambodia where thousands of men were in a mortal struggle; he saw Ron Sauer blown away. Though hit himself, Malik survived and went head-to-head in a gunfight with an antiaircraft gun, which he silenced. In the final act of his performance, he climbed to altitude, ran out of fuel 45 miles from Bien Hoa and dead-sticked his F-100 onto Bien Hoa's Runway 09R. He engaged the barrier at high speed and came to a stop one hundred feet from the end of the overrun.

Oblivious to the screaming sirens racing toward him, he stared at the glow of Saigon's northeastern suburbs. His mind was in another time, another place. Perhaps he was in shock.

As he saw it, his brother Ian had died for the second time, and John had killed him, again. He knew it would happen, but he did not do what was necessary to prevent it. He should never have certified Ronald Sauer combat ready. And now divine judgment was imminent; he would surely face a trial far greater than what he had just survived in the skies over Cambodia.

He closed his eyes, searching for that memory, the kiss on the swing, Christine's body against his. "I will always love you," she said.

Someone was pounding on the left side of his canopy. He turned. A man stood on a ladder, yelling, "Sir, unlock the canopy, or I'll have to blow it!"

* * *

Maintenance towed his airplane into a hanger blazing with lights. Malik watched a dozen maintenance people swarming over the airplane, inspecting, testing, pulling panels open. They reinstalled the pylons and drop tanks, slightly dented. The maintenance chief signed off the aircraft as airworthy.

For the several hours this required, Malik paced impatiently. When the rescue team found him sitting catatonic in the cockpit, they called the flight surgeon. But Malik waved off the queries of the doctor who had come to check him out.

Maintenance filled his main tanks; he climbed aboard, started the engine, and got airborne at 2100 hours, climbing out into a velvet night. There was only the sound of his breathing in his headset, the hiss of the slipstream, the purr of the engine. At level-off, he leaned his head back and peered into a vast field of stars, so brilliant in this latitude. Alone above sullen earth, he drew as near to God at that moment as he had ever been except once when he was supersonic at 50,000 over Germany. This was a passing encounter. And yet it sustained him in some way.

Ahead he saw the lights of Phan Rang. He executed a jet penetration from altitude, touched down without incident, and taxied to the ramp. Lieutenant Colonel Bernside, his squadron commander, and the chief of Intel, along with several other officers, were waiting for him at the squadron building. They debriefed Malik for an hour, recording every detail. When finished, Bernside drove Malik to the O Club, where the night staff had a hot pizza waiting for him. Bernside handed the pizza to Malik and drove him to the hootch. Neither spoke a word.

Malik walked into the barracks and checked the mission roster. His next flight paired him with William Bjorn for an o' dark thirty frag mission in 26 hours. He sat alone in the bar and ate the pizza. Somehow, he had to get in touch with Ron's wife. What would he say to her?

* * *

The battle at Prey ToTueng continued. Malik slept through day two and into the night of the third day. He occasionally stirred as flight after flight of F-100s departed into the darkness.

Carl slept through the grumbling of the air conditioner, the thunderclap of afterburners, and the now-subdued nightly gathering in the bar. Everyone was remembering the fair-haired Ron Sauer who had gone west. Were they blaming John Malik?

In and out of sleep, Malik's memory wandered again to Christine Charis as the 10-year girl at the fence, calling to him, her arms through the wire reaching out to him. She idolized him from that age. She was a beautiful girl, the makings of a striking woman. He visualized her when she was 16, remembering how his heart ached at the sight of her. He was in graduate school, searching for answers to the questions of origins and purpose, which she had resolved. All things were divinely initiated, she told him. He had examined every possible philosophical and scientific alternative and had reached the same conclusion. But it made no difference in his life.

She continued to write one obligatory letter each month. Her tone remained neutral. She reported events in her life, how her family fared, news about Socrates—getting gray around the muzzle—and updates on Rachel Hixson. Christine would finish her masters in biochemistry in June. She was feeling confident about her application at Baylor Medical School in Houston. She was going to do the three-year program if she got accepted.

As always, she typed her letters and closed with "love," and signed it. The letters were single-page notes that one might write to a distant acquaintance as an obligation. He now had eight such letters in his desk drawer marking his time in Vietnam. He had read them countless times, looking for the faintest evidence of continuing affection for him. Had she not said, "Come home to me, Johnny. I will love you forever"? Did she not mean it, or was it figurative, something soon forgotten?

Several times on day two of the battle raging at Prey ToTueng, Malik struggled to lift his legs over the edge of the bunk, to get up and go to the O Club to eat before the dining hall closed for lunch and then dinner. But he missed both meals. He slept on, replaying in mental twilight the bright flash that incinerated Ron Sauer.

Night fell again. Malik awoke, soaked with sweat. He glanced at the clock, just past midnight, the beginning of day three of the battle at Prey ToTueng. He turned off the alarm as it sounded.

His bunk stood three feet off the floor with shelves and storage built below. This arrangement required some physical effort to get to the floor. He swung his legs over the edge, dropped to the linoleum, and rummaged in a drawer for a clean flight suit. In his flip-flops, he plodded to the latrine for another shower.

* * *

Captain Malik stared at the wall, sipping coffee, waiting for his intel and weather briefers. Beside him, at the briefing table in the squadron building, sat his sleepy-looking wingman, First Lieutenant William Bjorn. Bjorn had not shaved. He smelled faintly of alcohol.

John knew little about Bjorn. He had been through Global Survival School and Snake School with him, but he had few dealings with him at Phan Rang. He lived at the far end of the hootch, so their paths did not cross often. John had never flown a mission with him nor given him a check ride. The only additional impressions Malik had of Bjorn were forming as they sat under the harsh fluorescent lights of the briefing room at 0200 hours. The room was silent except for the hum of the window air conditioner.

Bjorn deferred to Malik, not just because of his rank but out of respect. Almost all the squadron pilots deferred to John Malik. Bjorn's adulation puzzled Malik. As he glanced at Bjorn, Malik figured women would find him appealing, but not for his intellect nor his surfer vocabulary.

From experience, Malik understood the relational dynamics between a flight lead and his wingman. They bet their lives on each other; on first flights, the wingman was typically tense, the leader vigilant.

Malik did not speak; he only stared at the wall. Bjorn did not seem to know what to do with himself as he watched 10 minutes tick by on the wall clock. The briefers were running late.

Finally, in a flurry, a young first lieutenant intelligence officer hurried in and introduced himself with an apology for being tardy. He was sweating, his voice shaky. Like many other people, he was apparently intimidated by John Malik. The lieutenant explained his delay: he had late-breaking target information.

"Captain, your target is Prey ToTueng." He placed some reconnaissance photos on the table. "Before your first mission, here." He pointed at a photo. "At last light today." He presented a second photo. "And then this infrared shot taken one hour ago." He showed a grainy third photo.

"The friendly perimeter has been sterilized to a half-mile. It's being maintained by gunships. The friendlies are secure for now, but they're in bad shape. At 1800 hours, they reported 30 dead, 50 wounded, leaving 170 effectives. An airdrop has resupplied them. They desperately need medevac, but we can't do it with U.S. assets. It's a political issue. The road to Phnom Penh has to be cleared for the Cambodian Army to reach them. And the North Vietnamese are not withdrawing despite their massive losses."

"What are our losses?" Malik asked.

The briefing officer swallowed, glanced down at his folder, and said, "Uh, we've lost three F-100s in the target area in the last 24 hours. All three KIA. These are the names." He turned his briefing folder so Malik and Bjorn could read the names. Malik winced and turned away.

The briefer cleared his throat then continued. "Your wingman, Lieutenant Sauer, makes four. A fifth aircraft from the 50th went down west of the target." He pointed to a name on a fax sheet. "We think allied Cambodians picked him up. And a Navy A-4 pilot ejected over the Tonlé Sap." The briefer used a pointer to show on a wall map this large lake and river system in western Cambodia. "His leader saw him eject over the lake with a good chute. But he has not been recovered." The briefing officer, took a breath, bit his lower lip, and added, "Crocodiles may have gotten him."

They were silent as each processed this information. The briefer waited for Captain Malik to speak.

"Okay, what's our target?" Malik's eyes moved over the photos. He looked up and focused intensely on the briefer.

"It's a suspected NVA truck park, a convoy that has apparently just arrived. It either made it down the Trail undetected, or it came up from the Gulf of Thailand. The NVA has been shipping massive supplies to the coast of southern Cambodia and then moving them north along the western border of South Vietnam. It's blatant, and everyone knows this is happening.

"These trucks were just detected by an RF-101 recon aircraft as infrared signatures in the trees a mile north of Prey ToTueng. They are no doubt carrying munitions and fuel. This is your target.

"Your load, Captain Malik, is Mk 82s with point two-five delay fusing. Two carries unfinned napalm. Your controller will be Nail Six. Here are the numbers. Do you have questions for me?"

Malik and Bjorn both shook their heads.

"I'll be here to debrief you when you get back. Good hunting."

The intel briefer left, and the weather briefer walked in and spread out weather maps. He summarized teletyped forecasts advising Malik to expect a broken ceiling of 10,000 feet over the target.

Malik wrote down the pressure altitude in the target area since this would determine bomb release altitude. He asked if they could make it to the target VMC, in visual meteorological conditions. The briefer shrugged. This uncertainty increased Malik's blood pressure; he could feel it as a throbbing in his temples.

CHAPTER 35
Dangerous Rejoin

Takeoff was uneventful until reaching the three-mile ridge. Malik looked back in the darkness for Bjorn's rotating beacon and flashing nav lights. There he was, closing with what appeared to be dangerously high overtake and cutoff angle. Malik kept watching, incredulous, as imminent collision became obvious. Bjorn was going to hit him! Malik pulled up steeply an instant before Bjorn swept just below him with more than 100 knots of closure. Enraged, Malik watched as Bjorn swung far to the north, slowing, drifting back toward Malik.

Was the fool drunk? Some pilots flew missions drunk from time to time. No one ever said anything about it. If Bjorn wasn't drunk maybe he had vertigo. Whatever the problem, he could not judge closure in the dark.

On departure control frequency Malik broke protocol and transmitted, "Bjorn, stay away from me. Do not rejoin. Acknowledge."

There was a double click on frequency. Malik watched Bjorn drift back into trail.

Getting his breath and emotions under control, Malik studied the blackness ahead. He could see no visible electrical storms. Even a few stars appeared through the high clouds. And the light from a late-rising moon glinted in the corridors between towers of cumulus. It appeared they could make it westbound clear of the weather. But if they did encounter weather, Malik was not going to let that idiot fly on his wing.

There were few F-100 pilots who were comfortable in night combat operations in the aircraft. The Hun was a day fighter. Night operations were rare, except for "Combat Sky Spots." Malik had flown these on targets northwest of Pleiku and into Laos. These single-ship missions dropped delay-fused slick bombs, scheduled for around an 0300 release over known or suspected underground bunkers, tunnel systems, and truck parks. From altitude, the single ship steered precisely, altering heading by one or two degrees as directed by a controller who might ask for plus 2 knots on airspeed. Approaching release, the controller announced, "Standby ... standby ... mark-mark," and the pilot salvoed, releasing all bombs at the same time.

Somewhere, 20,000 feet below, unsuspecting troops holed up in burrows and warrens under the jungle floor never woke up. Out of utter silence, an ear-splitting concussion was followed by a compression wave that collapsed their underground works and buried them alive.

Malik tried to hate these people, to polarize their cause as evil and his as good. For a while, he had avoided his qualms by disengaging and sometimes telling himself the enemy intended to destroy the American way of life. But the argument, relative to the VC, wore thin. Most of these people were democratic-minded, intent on freedom from oppression. But the intentions of the North Vietnamese Army were focused on the subjugation of the south, as Malik saw it.

He thought about Ben Perry, the only avowed Christian in the squadron other than Ron Sauer. Returning from a Sky Spot Ben was killed one night when he penetrated for an approach at Phan Rang from altitude and hit the jungle 10 miles short of the runway. The consensus was that he misread his altimeter by 10,000 feet. Night flying combat ops were inherently dangerous for F-100 drivers.

* * *

Malik and Bjorn drove silently westbound. There was no radio traffic on Moonbeam, the night en route controller's frequency. Malik weaved his way through canyons of cumulus wreathed in the moonlight with Bjorn in trail. The tops of high electrical storms flashed over the horizon. He kept tabs on Bjorn, watching him meander around astern.

The check-in with Nail Six occurred 40 miles out from the target. Malik listed the flight's munitions. Nail Six, almost sleepy in tone, said, "Okay, Tide, copy your load. Flash your beacon."

John switched on his rotating beacon.

"I've got you. Beacon off. I've been on this target for fourteen hours in the last two days. This should be a milk run. But they're going to light up the sky. You can expect it. These guys do not sleep."

Malik double-clicked his transmitter in acknowledgment.

"FYI, my fuel is running low. I've got about 15 minutes. I think we can get it done in that time." Before he could release his mic button, he yawned. "As to the friendlies," he continued, "I haven't heard a peep out of them for hours.

"I want you to hit a truck park in the trees north of the friendlies. I've seen a few lights, but it's the infra-red that found them. I want single deliveries. We'll try to blanket the area. Any problem with that?"

"Negative. We'll give you singles.

Given the environment, that seemed reasonable to Malik. Nail Six wanted to probe the mechanized concentration, hoping for secondary explosions from munitions and fuel. Malik's take was that the flight had little fear from ground fire, given the delivery mode and being invisible in the darkness.

"Tide, arm your weapons. Set singles," Malik transmitted.

Bjorn replied with two clicks on his transmitter.

They set and armed their weapons panels and began descent to initial attack altitude, accelerating to 450 knots. Ahead they saw a string of magnesium flares ignite, drifting down on parachutes, dropped from an orbiting C-130.

The Tide flight turned in a wide arc around the target at 10,000 feet. They watched Nail Six launch a brilliant white phosphorous marker that ignited on the ground. A shower of tracers reached toward the sound of the Nail Six's engine.

Cool as ever, Nail Six transmitted, "Okay, Lead, hit fifty meters north of the mark."

Malik doubled clicked and rolled in off the perch. "Lead's in from Texas," he said.

Adjusting power, he rolled into a 120-degree bank pulling the nose 30 degrees below the horizon, on instruments, turning in to parallel the line of flares on his left. He played the bank and Gs to sweep the nose toward the target, modulating the throttle, to achieve an exact 30-degree dive angle. Then, with wings level, he adjusted pitch slightly up/down to bring the bomb reticle onto a point in the darkness that he estimated to be 50 meters north of the bright-burning marker.

With the reticle holding steady on Malik's intended impact point, he reduced thrust to maintain 450 knots. The altimeter unspooled down to 3,300 feet. At that exact instant, he pressed and momentarily held the pickle button on top of the stick, holding the sight picture until he felt the thump of the explosive ejectors blow the bomb off the right outboard pylon. Then he pulled back hard on the stick. Once the nose started up, he pushed the left rudder pedal to begin a turning climb as the nose continued to rise to 30 degrees above the horizon. He topped out on his back at 12,000 feet and looked out the top of the canopy, watching for his impact.

A flash of yellow light spread beneath the trees trailing a visible compression wave that radiated ahead of secondary explosions that lit up the jungle from beneath.

"Wow! Good hit, Lead. Two, hit one hundred meters north of Lead's impact."

Bjorn double-clicked and rolled in. As Bjorn released, AAA tracers flashed around his aircraft, missing him by a good margin. Bjorn's napalm splashed across the target setting off more secondaries. They had found the center of a munitions stockpile. Trucks burned, munitions erupted, and a fuel dump exploded.

One after the other, Malik and Bjorn dropped with successive corrections. On his fourth delivery, Malik pulled off without making his drop. The sight picture wasn't right. That left him with one bomb remaining.

He watched as Bjorn rolled in for his final delivery. Expecting to see the impact, Malik saw nothing but tracers. Then he saw Bjorn's afterburner plume. The fool was in burner, a perfect target for the gunners. He was climbing, and tracers were showering him.

Bjorn transmitted, "I've been hit! I'm losing fuel."

* * *

Bjorn's reported fuel-remaining was below that required to make Phan Rang. His unsteady voice made it clear he desperately did not want to bail out into the dark unknown. He convinced Malik his situation was critical and infected Malik with panic. With this uncharacteristic loss of discipline, Malik's judgment was momentarily impaired.

Malik transmitted, "Nail, what's the closest 8,000-foot strip of concrete?"

"That's Phnom Penh, two-six-zero degrees for seventy miles."

What Malik did not process was that Bien Hoa, a sister base which he now knew well, was only 85 miles southeast. He should have remembered this. But if Bjorn had to eject right away, the low terrain west of Prey ToTueng was the best choice because the Cambodians held it.

Bjorn was convinced he had only minutes left before flameout. He reported his airplane was sluggish with a heavy right wing. Malik made a snap decision. He told Bjorn to blow everything off his wings and climb west as high as he could. Malik would join on him.

Meanwhile, Malik rolled in and dropped his last bomb. Pulling out on instruments, he engaged afterburner once his nose came above the horizon and turned west to begin pursuit of Bjorn, who was climbing on a heading for Phnom Penh. The turn west in burner eliminated all other options. They would either make it to Phnom Penh, or they would both have to eject.

But Nail had no immediate information on Phnom Penh—since it was unthinkable that American fighters would ever land there. The delay was a complicating factor. The nightly news was continuously anticipating a siege of the city by the Khmer Rouge and the NVA. After searching his flight bag, Nail confessed he had no information on the status of the field. He was calling 7th for any information.

Malik carried no maps nor approach plates for Phnom Penh either.

Even as the Tide flight committed on a westerly heading, they heard what they did not want to hear: 7th Air Force HQ in Saigon advised Nail who relayed to Malik that Phnom Penh was closed, unlit, and had no navaids. The commercial/military field had no airport beacon, no approach lights, no runway lights, and no air traffic control.

Malik was in full burner on Bjorn's tail when he got this news. It was too late to change his mind. Neither of them could reach the Vietnam border now.

Bjorn was reporting his fuel and passing altitudes holding 300 knots in the climb. To complicate matters, the weather to the west of the target was building to broken stratus with tops well above Tide's capability. Malik's only possibility of finding Bjorn was to see his lights and rotating beacon ahead and rejoin from astern—a challenging procedure even in daylight.

Malik could see nothing ahead except dark against the dark of towering cumulus. He streaked through them on instruments, sheeted in the rain, holding high overtake with the vertical speed pegged at 6,000 feet/minute.

This pursuit was at high cost. Malik's fuel had dropped well below bingo as the afterburner, at three times normal burn-rate, emptied the main tanks. He could almost see the fuel gages moving. He had joined his fate to Bjorn's.

Nail's last transmission advised the flight that 7th Air Force HQ had been apprised of the situation. Nail wished Tide good luck and added one vital piece of information: the runway was aligned northeast-southwest in the western suburbs of the city. He apologized that he had nothing else to offer. His transmission faded, and Malik and Bjorn were on their own, running out of fuel with no assurance they would ever sleep in a bed again.

CHAPTER 36
Phnom Penh

It was intuition alone that prompted Malik to advise Bjorn to reduce his throttle to idle and begin descent. Bjorn was calling his altitude and airspeed. Malik was 200 knots faster than Bjorn, streaking in and out of the weather. Bjorn suddenly appeared in the middle of Malik's windscreen.

He screamed, pushed the stick forward into high negative G, extended speed brakes as he jerked the throttle to idle. His helmet cracked off the top of the canopy, and every loose item in the cockpit flew upward, including dirt and debris. His head was spinning.

Malik's eyeballs were ticking like a slot machine and wouldn't focus. When he could make sense of the instruments, he discovered he was past the vertical, on his back, out of control. He was trained to recover from "unusual attitudes" in the simulator. But what the simulator cannot duplicate is vertigo, nausea, and G load.

He forced his eyes to hold steady on the attitude indicator, the central gyro instrument that allowed him to roll his wings level and pull the nose up to the horizon against high G loads. He stopped his vertical descent and leveled off, now concerned that Bjorn was descending on top of him. Choking down vomit he started looking for Bjorn again.

Bjorn was at idle, holding 300 knots, still calling his passing altitude. Malik pulled up, searching for him, and suddenly saw him glowing in the clouds, in and out of the weather with moonlight breaking through. Malik was in a cold sweat, nauseous, holding a death-grip on the stick and throttle. Closing on Bjorn from below and behind was a tremendously scary maneuver in the dark. Malik told Bjorn to push up his power. He couldn't stay behind him at idle power.

Malik stabilized behind Bjorn and slowly closed on him. He approached under Bjorn's left wing with his refueling probe-light on, scanning for evidence of battle damage. He saw none. Bjorn still had his left fuel drop-tank and bomb pylons. They should have been blown off. Malik moved to under the belly. There were the typical streaks of hydraulic fluid but no holes that he could see, and no streaming fuel leaks.

He then moved to beneath Bjorn's right wing and was puzzled by what was directly in front of his canopy. At first, he didn't process what he was seeing. It was a can of napalm wobbling by a single forward lug, about to come off and smash through Malik's canopy.

Malik pushed over, extended speed brakes, and lost control of his aircraft again. And again, he recovered.

He saw Bjorn breaking out of the weather and rejoined well off his right wing. The napalm on the right inboard was wallowing on the forward lug.

Malik took the lead as they continued to descend. They broke out beneath a broken ceiling to behold the vast sprawl of Phnom Penh's western suburbs. Malik turned back toward the Mekong River, glittering in intermittent moonlight, and descended to 1,000 feet. He gave Bjorn the lead, moved away from him, and told him to blow his wings clean over the river.

Bjorn could not land with the armed weapon on his wing. The shock of touchdown might drive it onto the runway, and it would probably detonate. This was all based on the assumption they could find the airport. And it was looking like they would both have to bail out and hope the Khmer Rouge did not capture them.

Repeatedly Bjorn tried to blow the wings clean with the emergency jettison button, but nothing happened. He checked the circuit breakers. That wasn't the problem.

* * *

Malik took the lead and turned from over the river toward the northwest suburbs holding 200 knots at 1,000 feet, hoping he could find an unlit runway. Only divine intervention could explain how he saw a dark patch amid neighborhood lights. He turned toward it. Descending below 500 feet, he crossed the patch of darkness with Bjorn behind him. It was a runway.

Malik maneuvered to align his heading with the runway-reciprocal and climbed to 1,000 feet. Estimating five miles out, he executed a teardrop turn back toward the runway. He told Bjorn to orbit and wait until he landed. If Malik could not land, Bjorn should eject.

Malik held the runway heading, descending to 200 feet with no ranging information but intuition. He lowered the gear and the flaps, maintaining 170 knots. The greatest danger was hitting power lines and towers. Unless he was directly lined up on the runway, the landing would be very dangerous.

His landing lights swept over houses and streets and then the dark expanse of an empty field. He saw concrete to the right and turned steeply at 200 feet, then immediately reversed. His wingtip just cleared a fence. He was still not aligned when his left main gear contacted the runway, slamming down the right gear. The aircraft bounced into the air, about to cartwheel. But with full cross-controls and a shot of power, he contacted the runway again using hard differential braking that resulted in a harrowing slalom. He bottomed the brakes and deployed the drag chute, expecting his tires to separate from the rims under the sideload. But they held.

The airplane rolled out toward the east end of the runway with smoking wheels. Malik turned off at the first taxiway and released his drag chute into the grass. Now idling on the parallel taxiway, he faced the approach end of Runway 05 with his lights pointing down the runway.

"Do you have my lights?" he transmitted.

"Affirmative."

"Okay, I'm sitting just to the left of the runway. Guide on my lights …. Listen to me, if the nape comes off on touchdown, go burner and eject. You got that?"

A double click. Malik watched Bjorn's landing lights approaching. Bjorn's main gear barked on the runway while Malik held his breath. It was a smooth touchdown. The can of napalm held.

Bjorn rolled past Malik to the turnoff where he released his drag chute. The can of napalm was swaying on the right inboard station as Bjorn pulled into position beside Malik, his engine still running.

They nodded to each other, opened their canopies, and shut down. Both of them slid over the canopy rails and dropped 10 feet to the ground and ran to each other. They embraced, weeping hot tears, laughing, and screaming, hysterically bouncing each other up and down, calling each other derogatory names. Who had ever done what they just did?

* * *

Anxiety displaced hysteria. They may have escaped the frying pan only to land in the fire. The Khmer Rouge were out there somewhere. They were violent, heartless, and brutal beyond measure. Malik and Bjorn paced and searched the darkness in all directions. Nothing stirred, no hum of traffic on the roads beyond the perimeter, not even a dog barked. Malik checked his watch, 0415. A light breeze came from the east bearing a potpourri of smells, exotic and unpleasant, unfamiliar food, garbage, exhaust fumes.

Bjorn kept close, uneasy, turning, and looking. He took out his .38, opened the cylinder, and confirmed it was fully loaded. Malik did the same, counting 30 additional rounds in his vest.

"Let's agree on what we do if bad guys show up," he said. "If they're hostile, they'll point their weapons at us and either shoot us or try to capture us. I won't let them capture me, not these crazy Khmer Rouge bastards. I'll tell you what I'll do. If they're coming at me, I'll take some of them out before they kill me."

"Let's play it by ear," Bjorn croaked.

"If you don't know what you will do, you're as good as dead or captured. Decide now. I know what I'll do."

Bjorn paced and peered into the dark. Malik watched him.

"Look, it's likely the friendlies hold the field, and they'll help us out. Don't worry yet."

Malik did a walk-around inspection of his airplane. It had taken a beating on landing, and he worried about the landing gear. The overheated brakes were glowing. Bjorn and Malik walked back up the taxiway and bundled up their drag chutes.

They did a walk-around on Bjorn's airplane but saw no evidence of battle damage. Malik grilled him about his fuel readings. Did the gauge decrease slowly, freeze, or just drop? Bjorn didn't remember much. They sat down under Malik's airplane.

The diffused city lights shown against the broken clouds scudding west. Moonlight flickered through.

They had been sitting beneath Malik's airplane for 30 minutes when they heard boots and the distinctive clanking of military equipment of troops. They jumped to their feet and unsnapped the tie-downs on their pistols.

Fifteen soldiers appeared. They wore pith helmets and gray or green uniforms, all holding AK-47s. They stopped 10 yards away, holding their weapons up at an angle, not pointed at Malik and Bjorn. A good sign.

A staring contest followed. Minutes passed, and no one moved. They heard the whine of an engine, a Jeep. It stopped behind the aircraft. An officer jumped out and walked toward Malik, examining the aircraft with a sideward glance.

* * *

The officer was a lieutenant colonel in the Cambodian Air Force, not Khmer Rouge, not NVA, an ally. Malik took a deep breath and looked at Bjorn whose expression of alarm faded.

After shaking hands with Malik and Bjorn, he ordered the troops to start pushing the aircraft. In perfect English, he explained to Malik that they had shut down their engines on the civilian side of the airfield where foreign journalists would be present when the field opened. The aircraft had to be moved across the field to the military side and hidden in hangers before dawn. He assured Malik the airport was secure for the moment, that he had talked with 7th Air Force and cleared this action, and that the two American pilots would receive every courtesy and protection.

It would not be easy to move the aircraft. The Cambodians had no start cartridges for the F-100, no equipment for an air start, nor a tractor and tow bars to move the fighters.

The troops, therefore, would have to hand-push the aircraft, bracing against any surface where they could get a purchase—mainly the landing gear. It was exhausting work. Malik steered from the cockpit with only brake pressure to align the nose gear.

Next was Bjorn's airplane. The wobbling can of napalm alarmed everyone but there was no equipment available to download it. They had no choice but to move the airplane with it hanging by the single lug. To move Bjorn's airplane, someone found a rope that the troops tied to the nose gear strut. The Jeep towed the aircraft down the runway with a jerking motion, then along a taxiway past rows of derelict MiG 15s and 17s to an empty hanger on the military side of the field, a distance of about one mile.

Bjorn and Malik were soaked in sweat watching the doors of the hanger close as the eastern sky glowed with approaching dawn.

* * *

Malik advised the colonel that if they could get the can of napalm off the airplane, he could have it. The colonel nodded. He'd figure out something.

A staff officer drove Malik and Bjorn into the city, past checkpoints and sandbagged gun positions, to a hotel where they were ushered into a room by plainclothes officers.

Though they laid down on the beds, they were so wired they could not rest. There came a knock on the door. An officer entered, followed by a small man with a measuring tape and a tablet. This man measured them for civilian clothes. The assassination of U.S. Air Force pilots would have been a high priority for the Khmer Rouge.

In less than one hour, the tailor returned with clothes, shirts, and trousers. Security escorted Bjorn and Malik downstairs for the breakfast buffet. The sun was bearing down when they left the hotel. The humidity was insufferable.

They were driven to a military office building and directed into the office of the Cambodian Air Force Chief of Staff. They exchanged salutes. The chief explained that an American C-47 with maintenance people would arrive by afternoon to check out the aircraft and, if possible, configure them for starting.

In the meantime, the commander spread out a map before Malik and Bjorn and briefed them on the situation at Prey ToTueng. The beleaguered Cambodian troops still held their position. He confirmed the initial estimate of 5,000 NVA surrounding the village. Their destruction would delay and perhaps prevent an attack on Phnom Penh.

Intel estimated enemy losses at Prey ToTueng at 2,000 dead on the perimeter of the friendlies. The friendlies, still pinned down in the school yard, had been resupplied with airdrops at first light. The ground was blasted to a desert around them. Beyond their perimeter, nothing lived for a half-mile.

Malik asked about the downed F-100 pilot, the one shot down the day before. Yes, the Cambodians had picked him up unhurt. He would probably return on the C-47, according to the commander.

Though exhausted, Malik and Bjorn listened attentively to the chief who had one aim: To make a case for Malik to persuade the Americans to provide him with A-37s to prosecute the war against the Communists. The A-37, in his opinion, could turn the tide. Malik promised to relay his request.

The commander asked how they wanted to pass the time. Though dazzled with fatigue, Malik suggested the museum. He knew it was famous for its artifacts from Angkor Wat, the 12th century "Temple City" north of the Tonle Sap. The commander made some calls.

The military closed the museum and evacuated it, leaving only guards and a young lady who spoke broken English. She was Bjorn's and Malik's guide through the museum.

* * *

After another meal, Malik and Bjorn were driven to the airport where they donned their crusty flight suits and met with the maintenance people from Phan Rang who had just arrived. The Cambodians had 55-gallon drums of unfiltered jet fuel but no means of getting it into the F-100s. Then someone found a hand pump. It was inserted into the drums, and Malik began hand-cranking fuel into his drop tanks until he could crank no more. Others took over.

The drops held 335 gallons each. He pumped only as much as he thought he needed to make it to Phan Rang. He had some fuel remaining in the main tanks to start the engine.

Then came the answer to the burning question of why they had ended up at Phnom Penh, the condition of Bjorn's aircraft. Both men's faces turned red, Bjorn's with embarrassment, and Malik's with anger. There was no detectable battle damage. The fuel indicator system was defective. And the release circuits to the pylons were shorted. An apparent drop in fuel, coupled with the unusual aerodynamics of the swaying can of napalm, provided the illusion of battle damage—a reasonable assumption. There would likely be no board of inquiry. It would take time for Malik to cool off. This was a hell of a lot of ado for nothing.

Bjorn would stay behind until his aircraft could be jury-rigged with fuel indicators and the short in the explosive ejectors system could be corrected. It would take several hours before Bjorn could get airborne.

But Malik was ready to go. Maintenance installed a start cartridge in his aircraft and pulled it out of the hanger. Malik strapped in and started. Assured that fuel was transferring from the drop tanks, he called ground control for a clearance. He taxied out and took off to the east, climbing as high as practical before beginning an idle descent into Phan Rang.

* * *

Malik was the reluctant center of attention at Phan Rang when he landed. There were people from 7th Air Force gathered with the commanders of the 35th Tactical Fighter Wing. They asked him many questions. He repeated all the details of the mission and relayed the Cambodians' request for A-37s.

He had initially offered an observation that a multitude of dzus fasteners had popped out on the exterior panels of his aircraft. Somehow this morphed into a story that the Cambodians had been taking the aircraft apart for undetermined reasons. Malik was confronted with this story and provided his explanation. The runway at Phnom Penh was rough. He believed the fasteners were shaken loose on his hair-raising contact with the runway. That seemed to satisfy everyone.

Finally, he got to the hooch, took a shower, and slept like the dead.

CHAPTER 37
Into Cambodia, Again

A week passed since his last mission at Prey ToTueng. The battlefield cooled and the enemy withdrew, having suffered high losses. Malik flew several frag missions against the Ho Chi Minh Trail and had cycled back onto alert as Blade 5 with a napalm load.

He had assumed the callsign at 1200 hours as flight lead. Soon after reporting ready, his flight scrambled against an ephemeral target across Cambodia on the Gulf of Thailand.

The target was near the limit of their combat radius, 425 miles one-way. They had no loiter time. If they were to make it home, they could make only one pass followed by an immediate climb to optimum altitude. Malik contacted the forward air controller 50 miles east of the target.

"Blade, your target is a bunch of kids digging clams on the beach. I'm estimating forty of them. I'm sure they'll take cover in the trees as soon as I mark them. We'll hit them in the trees."

"What do you mean, kids?" Malik replied. "I'll tell you right now I will not burn a bunch of kids."

The FAC went off frequency and returned. "Let me rephrase, Blade. I confirmed the target with the Cambodian ground commander. These are not 'kids' but bona fide enemy troops. Black pajamas. They're foraging for a larger force, according to the locals. This is a good target, Blade."

Malik turned his head toward his wingman and saw him nod. "You need to be careful with your wording," Malik chided the FAC. "We'll hit the target. Go ahead with your briefing."

The FAC clearly resented the criticism. His briefing was curt. "I understand your limitations, so I want a single pass, line abreast will do. Ripple all eight cans parallel to the beach—you'll see what I want when you get here."

"Roger, Blade Five copies. Break. Two, arm your weapons."

Overhead at 5,000 feet, Malik watched the marking rocket streak toward the beach. A plume of white smoke rose in the still air. From downwind, Malik and his wingman turned to base and then final in formation, descending to 400 feet above the trees, leaving a half-mile run-in. At 450 knots, Malik counted down for his wingman who was holding two-ship widths off his right-wing. "Five, four, three, two, one, release!"

They pressed their pickle buttons and held them. In rapid succession, the weapons rippled off their wings—thump, thump, thump, thump. A wall of flames hundreds of feet high rolled along the line of trees. There could have been no survivors.

The FAC gave the flight 40 killed by air. Malik pulled off the target and began climbing for Phan Rang. Before handoff, the FAC asked for Lead's name and unit. That was not a common request, and Malik felt a cold chill run down his spine.

* * *

Two days later, appended to the duty roster in the squadron building, was a note for Captain Malik to report to the squadron commander, Lieutenant Colonel Bernside. Malik felt faint.

He was hyperventilating as he walked down the hall toward the commander's office. Bernside was 6' 4," a former football player and decathlon Olympian from the Air Force Academy. He was an incomparable pilot, former Thunderbird Lead, and on a fast track to general's stars. His hard discipline was the standard he imposed upon his men. But beyond all his virtues and heroic stature, Bernside had a lethal temper. The pilots of the 612th TAC Fighter Squadron feared the VC, the NVA, and most of all, Colonel Bernside.

John stopped at the doorway and knocked on the door frame.

Bernside sat at his desk, head down, doing paperwork. "Come."

John walked in, came to attention before the desk, and saluted. "Captain Malik, reporting as ordered, sir." He held his salute.

Bernside's neutral expression turned grim as he stared up at Malik, jaw set, eyes narrowing. He raised his right hand with impeccable form to return Malik's salute. Malik dropped his salute and remained at rigid attention, staring at the wall behind Bernside.

"Captain, I have here a message sent via 7th to our wing commander, who has forwarded it to me for action. It appears you have insulted the highest-ranking FAC in the Air Force. A brigadier. What he was doing controlling your strike two days ago on the far side of Cambodia, I can't imagine, and it doesn't matter. He demands you be censured. What did you say to him?"

John swallowed with some difficulty and addressed the wall in front of him, "Sir, as I checked in, he reported that my target was kids digging clams on the beach. I replied that I would not drop napalm on children, or words to that effect, sir. He went off frequency to confirm they were bona fides and came back to advise me it was a legitimate target. I suggested, sir, that he be more judicious. His words put me in a position of knowingly killing children. Those were not my exact words, sir, but that's the essential point I was trying to make."

"Well, the general demands a written apology for addressing him in the manner you did. He wants your record annotated, citing a refusal to hit a target, and insulting a general officer. I want you to write an apology and have it on my desk tomorrow. I will not, however, annotate your record. Do you have anything else to say?"

"No, sir."

Bernside studied Malik for long seconds. "You don't march to the same drummer as the rest of us, do you?"

Malik didn't have time to think of a response. "I ... I don't know, sir."

"Well, I do. Someone like you doesn't belong in a fighter squadron." The colonel stood and leaned across the desk toward Malik. "Yes, my pilots are rowdy and crass, not like you. But they're coping with this terrible business. I'd rather have them than a squadron full of guys like you. You make my men uncomfortable. You know that, don't you?"

Malik continued to stand at attention, staring at the wall. He did not answer; he truly had no answer.

"You were up to replace Buddha as flight commander, but I passed on you. The men don't relate to you. Most have never talked to you. Astonishing. They consider you 'unapproachable'. And this business at Phnom Penh; what a fiasco. You could have lost two aircraft, not to mention the international implications if you hadn't pulled it off. Seventh wants to give you a medal, but I think you ought to stand before a review board for bad judgment.

"I don't know where your head is, Malik. I've never met anyone like you. Whatever you are, you are not a leader of men. Unless something changes, you won't even make major. You're too ... withdrawn. You may be the best natural pilot anyone has ever seen, but that's all you've got going for you. I'm in dread every time you get airborne, worrying about what you'll do next. And I'm tired of hearing your name." The colonel leaned even closer to Malik and spoke in a low voice. "Be very careful, Captain. I'm looking for an excuse to get rid of you."

John did not answer.

"Have that letter of apology on my desk in the morning. Dismissed."

CHAPTER 38

How the Mighty Has Fallen

A disturbing pattern that developed in Malik's attitude toward the end of his tour in Germany was resurfacing. He was losing heart and belief in what he was doing. And he feared his reputation would erode. The onset of this fear occurred a week after his meeting with Colonel Bernside. Malik dreamed of Christine, of an escape from what was overtaking him. A dam was about to break.

Malik was on a mission inside Laos against NVA troops. He was flying the well-loved airplane named "Thunder Chicken." His load was four large bombs, each one a 750-pound canister containing hundreds of bomblets. They had to be dropped at a precise altitude with 30 or 45 degrees of dive angle at 450 or 500 knots in order to arm. Upon activation, the canisters opened like a clamshell and spread hardball-sized bomblets over a wide impact area.

One variety exploded on impact. Another type scattered the bomblets. As they hit the ground, each bomblet fired fine threads of tripwires in multiple directions. Once armed, the bomblets waited for someone to trip the wires that triggered a grenade-blast. The weapon had the effect of immobilizing large numbers of troops.

Malik seemed to have suddenly lost his judgment. As Lead, he rolled in on the target to salvo all four bombs. But his airspeed was way too slow—a grave mistake. Once committed in the dive, the FAC reported intensive anti-aircraft fire coming up at Malik. Distracted by the tracers, Malik passed release altitude.

Without releasing the weapons, he pulled out of the dive with such force it pegged the G-meter above 9 Gs. With 3,000 pounds of munitions on the wings, the wing spar could have snapped under nearly 30,000 pounds of additional instantaneous weight. But the aircraft held together, and he struggled back to altitude in afterburner. The next delivery, again, was too slow on the roll in. He had no choice but to release the bombs. They failed to arm. In the pull-out, he over-G'd the aircraft again.

Clearing the target area, his eyes started burning. Hydraulic fluid fumes were pouring into the cockpit. He selected 100% oxygen under pressure, depressurized the aircraft, and turned toward the base, expecting imminent hydraulic failure that would require ejection. He prepared the cockpit but did not advise his wingman nor the controller of any problem.

The aircraft held together. As he began the descent into Phan Rang, Malik considered the consequences of what he had done. He reached up and pressed the reset button on the pegged G meter. Now, no one would know of the overstress on the airframe.

After landing, he alluded to possible overstress but only wrote up the hydraulic fumes in the maintenance log. He lied and thereby put other pilots who would fly this airplane in jeopardy. Malik had become a person without honor. But what else could he do? If he reported what he had done, it might cost him his career.

Four days later, a pilot of the 612th was on short final in Thunder Chicken when the engine seized—or that's what Malik heard. Too low to eject, the pilot stayed with the aircraft hoping to make the overrun. Short of the runway, the tail hook, in the retracted position, contacted the stanchions of the run-in lights a hundred yards from the overrun. The arresting forces ripped the aircraft apart. Only the cockpit survived intact and slid up onto the overrun. The pilot opened the canopy and stepped over the rail. He was standing beside the remains of Thunder Chicken when the rescue vehicles arrived searching for the pilot. He had some difficulty convincing them he was the pilot.

There was no doubt in Malik's mind that he had caused the loss of this aircraft and the near loss of a pilot. The forces on the engine likely warped the shaft or the bearing mounts. This incident was the first dramatic evidence of his deteriorating capability, judgment, and character.

He had been an exceptional pilot in his F-l00 class at Luke AFB. On one eval flight, Malik rolled in on a strafing mission and fired an astonishing 87 out of 100, 20-mm rounds through the acoustic bullseye on the firing range—some kind of record. But now, mission after mission, he was a disappointment to the FAC, to his wingman, and himself.

Diverted in Cambodia to destroy a line of dugout canoes hauling munitions to insurgents along a Mekong tributary, Malik rolled in for strafe almost a hundred knots slow. He emptied his guns, missing the targets by a hundred yards.

Mission after mission, it was the same. Pilots watched him, clustered in groups, going silent as he walked by. They were talking about him. He couldn't sleep, or he overslept. Bad dreams inhabited his fitful sleep.

With each passing day, Malik withdrew further into himself, avoiding everyone. He couldn't look anyone in the eye, and no one would talk to him.

When he was alone in the latrine, he studied his sallow face in the mirror. Deep lines were forming, bags appeared under his eyes, his cheeks were sagging, his eyes were lifeless, his hair stood out at all angles or matted close to his head, and his scalp flaked no matter what he used for the problem.

Seeing his reflection in a mirror or in the glass of a window was a trigger that shattered his ability to function. He despised himself. Unshakable fatigue sapped his energy. He only wanted to sleep, to escape, to die, to cease to exist.

Then the unthinkable occurred; he found his name on the duty roster for an 0630 briefing with Lieutenant Colonel Bernside on his wing for a check ride. Why?

Malik awoke out of a death-like sleep. He had slept through his alarm and was already late for the 0630 briefing. Unable to hitch a ride, he ran the mile to the squadron operations building on the flight line, arriving out of breath and soaking wet with sweat. Bernside sat in a flight briefing room with an intelligence officer, waiting for him. Bernside was drumming his fingers when Malik walked in with his head down, apologizing. He was unshaven, he smelled, and it was obvious he had just gotten out of bed.

"This is it, Malik. You've busted your check ride. You are no longer a check pilot. And I'm downgrading you to wingman for the rest of your tour. Your Air Force career is over. If I could get rid of you today, I would. But I can't."

Bernside's face was a mask of disdain. "Malik, I think it's as simple as this: you just don't care about anybody. The chickens have come home to roost. You can't even hit the targets anymore. So, what are you good for?" He shrugged. "Maybe you can't help it, Malik. But maybe you can. You need to find another line of work. This is your last fighter assignment."

He stared at Malik. Malik stared at the floor. "God is your only hope now. The mission will go. I'm Lead. Questions?"

Malik did not respond. He stared at the floor.

He did a sorry job of bombing on the mission. In the debrief room, after the mission, Bernside glared at Malik, shook his head, and walked out on him without a word. Malik sat in the briefing room, staring at the floor.

CHAPTER 39
The Smell of Alienation

John sat on his bunk in the darkness, his back against the wall, his eyes closed, knocking his head against the wall. He breathed the alienation adrift on the smells of this far-away place. The vision of his remains moldering to the elements on Charlie's Mountain was what he saw when he closed his eyes.

The air-conditioner in the thin walls labored at the maximum setting to strip the humidity from the air that cycled into the room. But the unit did not eliminate the fetid stink of mildew and decaying vegetation wafting in from the surrounding jungle, nor the kaleidoscope of aromas carried by the hot salty breeze off the South China Sea. In its nightly cycle, the ocean's breath flowed inland across the nearby seaward village bearing the smoke of charcoal fires, the lingering aromas of meals, incense, garbage, and engine exhaust fumes.

The smells triggered despair. He had exhausted every means of achieving redemption. Should he endure unremitting divine retribution that would end in death anyway? Or end it all himself?

He had moments of nostalgia. On a summer evening, he sat on the porch swing with his mother. Her arm was around him. She kissed his head. She loved him once. And then there was Christine.

Fumbling just above his head John switched on a reading light mounted on the wall and opened his eyes to gaze again upon the face of the most beautiful girl in the world. She was smiling at him from the frayed school picture, a golden-haired twelfth grader with green eyes. He supplied from memory the flakes of amber and iridescent yellow in her irises.

John smiled at her, knowing she had posed for him, forming that crooked little grin the instant the photographer snapped the shot. In a long-ago memory, before he had seen her for what she would become, he heard her calling to him, her arms through the wire fence between their houses.

"Come home to me, Johnny. Please come home to me."

No one ever loved him like she did … once upon a time.

"Come home to me," she pleaded again. "I love you, Johnny! How can I live without you?"

But John would not go home again. She was a child of the light. He was not. She would never be his. Even if that were possible, she could not fix him. There was only one way out. If God would not take his life, he would do it himself. He had reached the end of the tether.

Some noble gesture would present itself. Within several seconds it would happen. He saw it as a movie. He would delay pull-out on a bomb run and be blown away by shrapnel from his own weapons. Or he would attack an anti-aircraft gun site, head-to-head, all four cannons blazing. His fighter would hit the position in a searing explosion, his right index finger frozen on the trigger. Others would live because of his actions. At the ending of his life, perhaps, he might achieve some nobility. One life, given for others. A partial repayment for an unfulfilled life.

Except for the noble aspect of this melodramatic vision, he would have likened himself to Minifer Cheevy, the poet's child of scorn. It was he who cursed his fate and wished he'd never been born.

The window air conditioner across the room shuddered, threatening to stall, and blasted a cloud of Freon-tainted fog across the ever-inert Carl Anders. John looked over to see if he moved at the sound of the frost breaking free from the air conditioner coils. He didn't stir. He remained catatonic, a condition that had not relented for more than a month. He was worse off than John, in some ways; and yet he was still combat effective, as Malik was not.

Carl lay unmoving in the fetal position, face to the wall. The only evidence he was alive was the fact that he periodically arose from his bunk with vacant eyes and dressed, arrived at the flight line, briefed a mission, and flew a combat mission. Returning, he debriefed, ate at the O Club, and returned to his bunk to lie curled up in the same position with his face to the wall.

Carl had married his hot Las Vegas wife a month before deployment. She had emptied his substantial bank accounts and liquidated all his assets to cover her expenses and to pay for an attorney who sent divorce papers for him to sign, leaving him penniless. John witnessed his signature on the documents. That was the last time Carl spoke to John outside of a mission briefing.

Anyone with a brain could have seen this divorce coming. Lila's physical endowments had blinded Carl. She was every boy's dream and every man's nightmare. As witless as John was about women, he could read Lila's agenda.

Carl's back was to John. His posture spoke for all who had turned their faces from John Malik in recent weeks, evidence of dishonor, imminent judgment, an approaching coup de grâce. He believed he bore the mark of Cain, cursed by God, forced to wander as an alien in the world. He was supposed to have been his brother's keeper, but he had killed him. That's how he saw it. And now the foaming cup of God's wrath had topped the rim.

John stared at his unmoving roommate for a minute before the red digits of his clock diverted his eyes. They morphed to 3:30 a.m. He could sleep, now that his way forward was clear. Whatever awaited him could not be worse than the life he now endured. Or could it? He hoped his eyes would never open. Or, if they did, that they would witness nothingness in some place far from God, his relentless tormentor.

*　*　*

The next morning John discovered his name was not listed on the duty roster for the day. What did this mean? But then, what did it matter; except that if he didn't fly, he couldn't kill himself. And he was determined to do that.

He checked his mail slot and found a typed letter with no return address. The postmark was from Waco, Texas. He hurried to his room, crawled up onto his bunk and tore it open. It was a letter from Justine, Christine's best friend and roommate at Baylor University where Christine was in her seventh and final year. He read,

> *John,*
>
> *You must know who I am. I am writing because something is happening to Christine. You need to know this. And I have a deep feeling that you are the only one who can do something about it. Christine is fading. I don't know how else to describe what is happening to her. She cries continually. She won't eat. She can't sleep. She is wasting away.*
>
> *She has chosen not to tell you how she feels, but I will. Her life is bound to yours. I have never seen or heard of anything like this. She did not tell you what happened at your mother's funeral, but I will. The man who brought her into the church was in love with her, insisted on driving her to the funeral from Waco, and grabbed her hand as they entered the church so you would conclude they had a relationship. He was intensely jealous of you.*
>
> *Let me assure you, Christine has never had a heart for anyone but you. I'm not telling you this to comfort you. I don't care how you feel, frankly. I am furious with you.*

Her commitment to God surpasses all other considerations in her life. She has prayed for hours beyond counting that you would find your way so you two could be together. But now she senses you have entered a dark and dangerous place. She is afraid for you. I am telling you, John Malik, if you do not bend your knee to God and get right with Him, you will kill my friend. I believe she will literally die.

She does not know I am writing to you. But I am out of ideas. My impression of you is that you are willful, prideful, self-centered, and so inward-oriented that you cannot empathize with anyone else.

You have one way forward: Be magnanimous. Do something for someone else. Godly love is defined by what you do; it is an act of the will. It has nothing to do with feelings or emotion. You must know this since you're a New Testament Greek scholar (aren't you?). (Not that it has done you any good.)

So, do something for someone who needs you. Look for the chance to do it. And whatever you do, do it quickly if you love Christine and care for your own soul.

Justine

CHAPTER 40
Firebase Six

Three days later, Carl Anders was leading Tide 13 flight with John Malik as wingman. The flight reached cruise altitude heading northwest out of Phan Rang on a frag mission against an interdiction point on the Ho Chi Minh Trail, just inside Laos. Anders later recalled that they were over the Central Highlands 60 miles south of Pleiku when Hillsboro contacted him with an urgent divert to a tactical emergency. A company of Marines at Firebase Six on top of a mountain, 30 miles northwest of Anders's location, had come under overwhelming assault by a NVA regiment.

Anders and Malik had helped prep this landing zone a week earlier, dropping 500- and 750-pound slick bombs with fuse extenders to blast a clearing on the mountain top. Heavy lift helicopters then inserted the Marines and artillery pieces into the LZ. On this prep mission, an armed bomb had come off Malik's aircraft short of the target. The errant bomb blasted a clearing in the trees two miles south of the LZ. The best guess was pilot error, considering the pilot.

Unknown to anyone, the Marines had been inserted into a hornet's nest. A vast network of underground enemy facilities neared completion in the vicinity. It included a hospital, dining halls, troop quarters, and a weapons depot. New NVA units were arriving daily.

The enemy did not respond initially to the LZ insertion. They watched and waited until the leading edge of an extensive monsoon weather system reached the Highlands. They knew American fighters and gunships could not operate under a low weather ceiling. When the weather rolled in, the NVA attacked Firebase Six in force.

Tide 13 arrived overhead, in and out of the weather. They followed three other sets of fighters on the target that were greatly hampered by the lowering ceiling, all taking heavy ground fire including 37 mm. The lowering weather forced the flights to revert to shallow angle deliveries to stay under the ceiling. Anders rippled his high-drag bombs in a single 15-degree pass. He held overhead in and out of the weather to watch Malik's deliveries.

The FAC orbited mostly in the weather on instruments, unable to witness most deliveries. He relayed the Marine's request for ordnance on the red smoke at their northern wire. Malik acknowledged.

Anders saw Malik descend beneath the ragged ceiling. His delivery parameters would have been undefined and unpredictable. Through the intermittent holes in the clouds, Anders observed Malik's aircraft just above the trees being pummeled with ground fire. He saw puffs of smoke and debris flying off the aircraft.

Then, in a sudden sheet of flame, Malik's airplane smashed through treetops on the ridgeline. The airplane careened westbound out over the valley. Anders dove beneath the weather in time to see Malik's aircraft explode. But in an instant, before it hit the trees, he saw a parachute open.

Anders continued to circle at dangerously low altitude, looking for Malik's chute. It had disappeared into the trees. He transmitted on guard, hoping Malik would reply on his hand-held radio. But he didn't. The emergency beeper continued to sound. Malik was the last fighter to engage at Firebase Six.

During the debrief, when asked his opinion on Malik's status, Anders ventured that Malik was dead. If Malik ejected at delivery speed of 450 or 500 knots, he could have suffered severe injury with a near immediate chute opening. And if he were alive, he would have shut off the beeper to prevent the enemy triangulation on his position. He must be dead.

Flight crews passing overhead to other targets continued to report the beeper for more than an hour after the shoot-down, and then it went silent. The enemy found Malik's body. That was the consensus.

* * *

The cry of birds and the howling of monkeys awakened Malik from his concussion with the atmosphere, the result of a high-speed bailout. He grew aware of excruciating pain throughout his body. Blinking his eyes open, he recoiled at the sight of the jungle floor, swaying 70 feet below him.

A creaking sound thrummed through the taut risers that swung him like a puppet below a shredded parachute canopy fouled in the branches above. His chute was ripping.

Human voices, the sound of limbs snapping, and the thwacking of machetes came up from below. Fumbling up the right riser, Malik found the plug that activated the emergency beeper on his chute deployment. He reinserted it and shut off the silent warbling radio signal transmitting on guard frequency. Below, an NVA soldier crept through the ferns with an AK-47 at the ready, searching for him. Malik took a half breath and closed his eyes, afraid to look into the muzzle flash and feel mortal pain.

Seconds passed. He opened his eyes. The soldier moved on. Unaccountably, he had missed seeing Malik hanging in the trees just above him. From a zipper pocket of his survival vest, Malik extracted buckles and a hundred feet of flat nylon tape. With trembling fingers, he buckled the mechanism to the risers and to his chest harness. After three deep breaths, he opened the guards, placed his thumbs in the loops of steel cable on each riser, and jerked hard. His chest harness separated from the parachute risers, and he fell six inches onto the tape. He lifted the tape. It fed through the friction device, and he buzzed down to the ground.

He spun around, listening, watching, then stowed his helmet and parachute harness under vegetation and struck off into the undergrowth like a rabbit running from a fox. After 10 minutes of hard plunging, he burrowed into a clump of growth beside an animal trail, pulled the green around him like a cloak, and checked his watch. He had been hanging in the trees for an hour and a half.

Then pain displaced his fear. His joints, his groin, and his armpits ached as though someone had beaten him with a baseball bat. The flight crew operating manual stated that bailout over 400 knots could rip one's arms and legs off through flailing. He ejected 50 knots above this speed and survived intact. The shock of low altitude chute opening at that speed was like being hit by a semi. He should not have survived.

* * *

Grunting and straining to move his arms, he pulled out one of the two radios he carried, switched it on, and heard a reassuring hiss. Cupping his hand over his mouth, he transmitted, "Mayday, Mayday, Mayday. This is Tide One Four." After 10 minutes of repeating this call, he got an answer from a flight passing above the overcast.

"Mayday on guard, Red Devil Five, go ahead."

"This is Tide One Four. I'm down west of Firebase Six. Relay for Search and Rescue."

"Roger, Tide. Standby ... John Malik?"

"Affirmative."

"I just heard you were dead."

Malik winced and did not reply. A minute passed.

"Tide, Hillsboro says Search and Rescue aircraft were overhead your position but could not raise you. They pulled off for weather. What's your ceiling?"

John struggled to see through the canopy. "I'd say the clouds are on the deck now, but I can't tell."

"Well, it's thick. The top is about 20,000 feet. Standby ... Tide, SAR advises you to move west, as far and as fast as you can. The Marines on the firebase are bracing for overrun. You've got to put distance between you and them. Go ahead."

"I copy, Red Devil. When can they get me out?"

"They'll have to tell you that. I say again, their instructions are to move west to improve chances of pickup. They will attempt contact at 1500." The transmission faded.

Malik turned down the volume on the radio and stowed it. Four hours to go. Heaving to breathe the near 100% humidity, he shivered for a few minutes, aware the temperature was dropping. He could not get comfortable; he squirmed and moaned trying to cope with the pain. He focused on his surroundings to distract himself.

There were countless voices around him. Centipedes undulated around his boots, beetles crept over dead leaves beside him, a ball of swarming insects formed a few feet away, mosquitos buzzed past his ears. He was alarmed to hear the snap of rotting limbs trodden by a sizeable creature not far away. Whatever it was, it was moving away from him.

Moving west was not a safe option at the moment. In his thicket, well hidden, Malik huddled into the fetal position, vigilant for snakes, focused on brushing away stinging things that sought a way into his flight suit; they had quickly identified him as prey. He checked his revolver; loaded. He cut vegetation to improve his blind and endured the tedium of the passing hours. He pulled out his KA-BAR knife and the small whetstone from its sheath and began honing a razor edge on the blade. Then the rain began.

***

The rain fell in a pelting drizzle accompanied by drums of distant thunder and flashes of lightning illuminating the base of thickening nimbostratus clouds marching overhead. From the dark gray mass, cold rivulets followed a circuitous path through the triple canopy into his burrow, soaking his Nomex flight suit, now a sodden blanket.

Against the background of the rain came the throb of a recip engine. Malik turned up the volume on his primary radio, held it to his ear, and checked the time. It was 1500 hours.

"Tide One Four, this is Sandy Three on guard."

"Tide One Four, go ahead, Sandy."

"John, we can't get to you in this weather. We will get you out. What's your position relative to the firebase?"

"Based on the last known, I'd say I'm about two miles west. But I can't be sure."

"We'll be able to find your general position. But here's the thing, you need to put maximum distance between you and the American position. From what we're hearing, the enemy force is huge and continuing to concentrate around the firebase."

"How do you know this?"

"Hillsboro has had intermittent contact with the Marines on the firebase. All their scouts are dead, but their last reports estimate a force five times larger than their own. The Marines won't survive, and they know it. Some have been taking turns relaying short messages to their families and sweethearts via Hillsboro."

Malik cut in impatiently. "I say again, when can you get *me* out?"

"It'll be several days at least. This is a large system, and it's stalled out. The weather has shut down Search and Rescue operations, and most fighter wings are grounded, except for some Trail missions. Standby … I just now got a recall. I'm supposed to divert to Phu Cat. It's down to minimums. I'll check in with you tomorrow at 1600 if all goes well. I'm sorry, John. Move west, survive, get away from the firebase. It's a death trap. We'll get you out."

"I copy, Sandy. Tide One Four, out." Malik clicked off the radio and hung his head. A hard rain was now falling.

* * *

Malik pulled out his compass. He checked for an aiming point through the steaming rain to fix a course to the west. He should crawl out of his burrow and start moving, since the enemy would be looking for him, monitoring his transmissions, attempting to triangulate his position. But maybe they would ignore him for the present since their immediate objective was to destroy the Americans to his east. The enemy had surely heard his name, had heard that he was two miles west. He should move. But he didn't.

The time spent in idle misery passed slowly. Rather than feel sorry for himself, he directed his thoughts to the plight of his countrymen. Sandy said they had taken turns sending farewell messages to family and sweethearts. Malik had been impatient about his situation and had cut Sandy off. He was ashamed of himself for that, wishing he had responded differently. While it was possible Malik could survive, there was no hope for the Marines on Firebase Six.

With his eyes closed, he visualized them. They were hunkered down in foxholes and cringing behind logs. Mud soaked, suffering the rain, reeking of fear, they did not notice their hunger nor realize their exhaustion as they watched the trees, wide-eyed. Amid a continuous din of gunfire, the surviving Americans heard the clank of military equipment and the voices of the enemy massing around them in the trees. Beside them, friends stared sightless into the sky; their bodies dismembered, disemboweled, smelling of blood and guts.

For these Marines, there was no tomorrow, only the intensity of now. They waited moment by moment for the impact of a rifle round that would liberate their spirit. Bullets zipped over and around them like buzzing bees, thudding into the logs and mud. The American perimeter would be shrinking under the withering fire, leaving only the dead in the outer defensive positions. Those who were hit could not be reached, the wounded could not be helped. A soldier bleeding out was calling for his mother.

The lives of these doomed men had worth because people loved them. But what conferred worth upon John Malik? He had only the memory of Christine, beyond his reach. He regarded himself as deservedly unloved. Why would he want to survive? To do what? To endure on a darkling plain awaiting an inevitable and ignominious death?

He would go toward the firebase. There might be something he could do. If he could save even one life at the cost of his own, that act might bring some nobility to his life in the end. Maybe he could pass this life with a measure of righteousness. Had he not foreseen this very scenario? And then might Dickens's words be true of him, "It is a far, far better thing that I do than I have ever done; it is a far, far better rest that I go to than I have ever known."

He had no plan. He had no idea what he might be able to do. He only knew that he had no other reasonable choice; he would head east to almost certain death.

* * *

An hour had passed, and he had not moved. He heard a faint squelch on the radio. He held it against his ear and turned the volume up.

"Tide One Four, this is Yellowjacket Three. Do you copy?"

"Tide One Four. Go ahead."

A different voice came on the radio. "John, my name is Eric. I'm a reporter for *Stars and Stripes*. I'm riding along on a Trail mission in the back seat of an F model. I understand you are down west of Firebase Six. You are big news. Everybody wants to know how you're doing. Are you going west?"

"No, I'm going toward the firebase. There may be something I can do."

"John, I want to follow your progress. I will beg another ride tomorrow on a Trail mission passing this area. I want to talk to you then, okay?"

"Okay. I've got to move. Gotta go."

CHAPTER 41
Annihilation

When the rain abated, Malik struggled out of his shelter and struck out along an animal trail, moving east, according to his compass. An hour passed when he heard voices overtaking him from behind. He moved into a dense tangle and crawled under some fronds. Through gray-green drizzle, he saw patches of khaki and pith helmets bobbing along the trail.

An entire company of NVA troops approached and went by, unaware he was lying 10 feet from them, clutching his .38, barely breathing. The soldiers carried heavy loads of munitions, mortars, and machine guns, heading toward Firebase Six.

When they had passed, Malik got to his feet warily and struck out behind them. He soon lost them in the mist. Alone with the rain and its monotonous pelting of the canopy, he stopped to mop the water and sweat from his eyes and hair with a handkerchief. At any minute, he could come upon the enemy and be shot dead.

Near dark, he reached the base of the ridge upon which Firebase Six sat. He slumped down against a tree to rest. From the pit of his stomach came an icy fear. He turned his head slowly to look down at a patch of bark hacked away from the tree beside him. He saw another mark on another tree. And inches from his hand was a wire stretching from the tree against which he rested to an adjacent tree. It was a tripwire for a Claymore mine.

The NVA had mined the perimeter of the firebase, leaving no way out for the defenders.

Why had he stopped at this tree, one foot short of being a mass of hamburger? He crept away from the slope, burrowed into a thicket of bamboo, and suffered through hours of darkening rain, wishing himself out of existence.

* * *

He awoke to popping sounds coming from the firebase, the ignition of flares. Brilliant lights flashed against the base of the low clouds. The white-hot glare of magnesium flares floating on tiny parachutes produced flickering shadows that darted in a macabre dance through the trees.

And then a barrage of rockets, mortar rounds, and automatic weapons fire erupted through the stillness of the jungle night. Malik gazed in awe and dread through the bamboo at the pyrotechnics wreaking carnage upon his countrymen.

Five minutes after the assault began, the sound of running boots came fast along the trail. A squad of NVA peeled off from a larger unit, stopped, and took up ambush positions just in front of him—to his horror. He saw them crouching behind the trees, staring up the slope. They were not twenty feet from him.

The bombardment continued for thirty minutes and stopped in ringing silence. The flares burned out. Slowly the dim figures of the NVA troops reappeared behind the trees; they were expecting imminent action.

Out of the silence, crashing sounds came from above, American soldiers stumbling headlong down the hillside, fighting through the trees and vines. He wanted to yell, "Claymores! Go back!" Too late. All along the noose line, there were explosions and cries. The Americans who were not killed were captured. Throughout the night intermittent fusillades from the mountain top ensured the Americans would get no respite.

* * *

The bamboo was hard and unyielding against Malik's bones. He ached when he awoke in the late afternoon amid the swaying poles of polished green and yellow that had held him upright through the night and into the day. Above, he saw a patch of gray sky from which an incessant drizzle fell. He closed his eyes in resignation and dreamed of a cozy dry bed and of reaching out to touch Christine beside him.

With a start, he looked down at his feet for a cobra undulating through the dead sheathing of the clacking stalks. It was coming for him, intending to crawl up the leg of his flight suit!

The fear took his breath. But the snake wasn't there. He would either dominate his fear, or it would kill him.

The radio hissed. He pulled it out and pressed to transmit. "This is Tide One Four," he whispered.

"John, this is Eric, with *Stars and Stripes*. I talked to you yesterday afternoon. Tell me everything you have done since I talked to you last."

John softly described what he had done and seen in the last 24 hours.

"John, you are big news. People are praying for you. Tomorrow night Walter Cronkite may run my story—that is, your story. I'm so excited. I'm camping out at Phan Rang and will get every flight going northwest that I can. The wing commander will work with me on this and schedule some F models so I can follow your story. There's wide public concern about what's happening with you and with the Marines on the firebase. Local TV stations have interviewed your professors, your flight instructors, and other people who have known you. You are suddenly big news, John. Please don't get yourself killed."

The signal faded. John worked his way back toward the slope of the mountain. The rain and the gloom continued into the late afternoon. On the ridge, weapons fire continued sporadically.

* * *

From a bamboo thicket, Malik watched NVA soldiers huddled beneath their ponchos tied in the trees over their heads. They dodged the meandering smoke of their fires as they cooked their evening meal. The aromas watered John's mouth and cramped his stomach.

Through the droplets of water on his watch crystal, he checked the time, 1630. The sky was dark as twilight. A short distance away, he counted 18 GIs gagged and trussed up to low-hanging branches. They struggled from time-to-time against the pain of their bonds and against muscle cramping, unable to get comfortable. He breathed for them, as they tried to get enough air to satisfy themselves.

After their meal, at dusk, the NVA troops climbed into their hammocks. The camp was still again, except for the moans of the GIs who hung by their restraints.

At 2200 hours, the enemy camp stirred once more. The troops lit wet fires with gasoline sending smoke up into the trees to join a gauzy stratum a hundred feet above. The haze reflected the light of gas lanterns and flashlights glinting among the trees.

The enemy soldiers drove the Americans into a group, strung them together with ropes around their necks, and moved them out amid a column of hundreds of troops.

Malik wiggled out of his hiding place and fell in behind the last of them, guided by their lights. He followed them up the trail until they stopped and then moved passed a checkpoint held by three soldiers manning a heavy machine gun. Approaching the position, Malik crept off the trail, lay down on his stomach, and crawled around the gun, feeling ahead for a wire. And he found one.

He touched the taut silver thread and recoiled as if it was red hot, balling his fist. He crawled his way along it, then went around the tree to which the mine was attached and continued, finding no more. Once around the gun position, he moved back to the trail, stood up, and moved ahead.

The trail was grassy, muffling the sound of his running feet. He ran hundreds of yards until he sensed something else ahead. He froze at the sound of cracking twigs and the smell of a cigarette. Moving in slow motion to a low crouch, he again crept off the trail into the trees, and crawled, reaching out for tripwires.

Cigarette smoke grew stronger; the sound of cracking twigs grew louder until he moved to within six feet of a soft ripping sound and saw the form of a tall soldier urinating onto the leaf of an elephant ear plant—only one soldier.

With the plan forming in his head even as he did it, he pulled the knife from its ankle sheath and crept up behind the soldier. He watched himself clamp his left hand over the man's mouth and slice the blade across his throat, sawing until it hit bone.

The soldier ceased to writhe in his arms. Malik lay the body down and threw up. He sat with his hand over his eyes, smelling blood and puke and sweat, and heaved again.

When his gut was empty, Malik got to his feet and stripped the corpse. It was a struggle, but he pulled the trousers on, unbuttoned, over his flight suit, got his arms into the jacket, and put on the pith helmet. The soldier he had killed was only a boy, maybe fourteen years old, but tall for his age. The child's cold stare was unforgiving. "I'm sorry," Malik said.

As he turned away, fear seemed to leave him. Without that debilitating baggage, the tasks before him became academic. He took off up the trail carrying the boy's AK-47 in one hand and holding the helmet on with the other. There were no more checkpoints.

At the top of the ridge, the column of troops he was following had merged into a large force that had set up camp all across the ridgeline, a half-mile from the firebase perimeter. The enemy was preparing for another attack, evidence that at least some Americans still held the base. He crept through the shadows, trying to find the captive Marines.

A mortar attack began, then silence, then a human wave assault surged into heavy fire coming from the remaining firebase defenders. Beneath flares, tracers streaked in all directions like roman candles, there was a chaos of weapons fire, explosions, and men howling. The nightmarish scene burned into Malik's memory. With eyes open or closed, he could see nothing but this, and demons dancing in the flames, howling with glee as the dying breathed their last. Then whistles blew, and the firing stopped abruptly.

The NVA pulled back. Silence lasted for 30 minutes. From his hiding place, Malik saw five Marines being brought forward. He crept ahead, trying to keep them in sight. He passed several enemy troops who paid him no attention as he passed them.

On the edge of the clearing, he focused on the firebase defenses. The enemy tied the first prisoner to a tree in clear view of the base defenders, but beyond the range for an accurate shot. A pop and a flare lit up the scene. It drifted down on its parachute illuminating an enemy soldier with a shiny scar on his left cheek. This man turned to the bound Marine. With an ax in his hand and a hideous grin on his face, he raised the ax and struck three violent blows, chopping off the Marine's right arm at the shoulder.

Malik held his hands over his ears to silence the screams and slumped to the ground. In the next half hour, Scarface mutilated three other GIs in various ways within earshot of the firebase survivors.

Then he doused the last American in gasoline and ignited him.

The burning Marine ran toward the wire of the firebase screaming, "Kill me!"

Tracers reached out for him from the base until they connected on his flaming form. The rounds pounded into the man's chest, jerking him left and right until he stopped flopping, fell into a smoldering heap, and melted. Malik breathed through his mouth to avoid the sickening smell of his burning flesh.

And that was the end. The enemy overwhelmed the defenders of Firebase Six. Malik watched the flashlights and lanterns of the NVA moving among the foxholes and firing positions; he saw the blinking of their muzzles and as they fired point-blank into the heads of the wounded. All the Americans were killed except for those Malik had been following.

And the weather continued overcast.

CHAPTER 42

A Desperate Act

The glow of dawn penetrated the overcast, exposing yard-by-yard a scene of violent wreckage strewn through the trees and out across the Landing Zone. Mangled and burned bodies lay before Malik. The smell of blood, burned flesh, and cordite stirred on first light's breeze. The indifference of the enemy framed the horror of the scene. Their animated conversations and laughter around their breakfast fires gave no evidence of their humanity. Foragers worked across the LZ, collecting boots and personal effects from the gaping corpses; the enemy soldiers had armloads of ammunition, weapons, and food stores. They shouted to one another over their finds.

Malik stole away into the trees. Not one of the enemy soldiers glanced up at the quixotic form that passed by their outlying gatherings. Before his eyes, he saw a continuous loop—tracers, flashes of explosions, screams.

He descended some distance down the slope, crossed the trail into the trees, and found a hiding place of rotting palm fronds and limbs. Would this nightmare ever end? Would he live to see a blue sky again in happier times? Drizzle continued to fall from the low ragged clouds.

An hour passed. In the distance, a whistle blew, followed by the sound of many voices. The enemy was assembling for withdrawal from the site. They left the dead Americans as they lay, to rot, and to be devoured. The inexorable feast of the ravenous jungle would leave only rags and bones and finally corroded dog tags.

The enemy troops were coming down the trail. With dread Malik surveyed the mass of decaying vegetation immediately beside the trail. He pulled his flight suit and the soldier's tunic tight around him, raised his collar, and laid the AK-47 beneath some ferns. On his belly, he crawled beneath the decomposition being worked by countless stinging insects in a replay of his experience in the Philippines jungle. He steeled his mind against what he knew was coming.

Dirt and debris drifted down upon him. He lay still, guarding his ears and nostrils. Within minutes the stinging things had found his skin and began feeding, injecting him with poison.

His body and mind warred against each other as the tramping feet moved by. Unit after unit passed until he saw GI-issue jungle boots stumbling among a squad of guards, the tail end unit. When the sound of their passage receded, he scrambled out of his hide in a frenzy of pain.

He slapped, rubbed, and scratched his body, raking ants from his clothes and crushing those crawling beneath his clothes. He ran in a contorted gait down the trail in pursuit of the prisoner detail, without any thought for what he might do when he overtook them.

There they were, at the bottom of the ridge. They followed the left fork of a well-trodden trail hidden from the air by an overarching canopy. He checked the compass. They were moving west by south, making good time. He stopped several times, burning with fever, to listen for anyone behind him. The pursuit continued for half an hour.

Then the detail stopped. Malik drew near enough to see Scarface, the leader, amusing himself by slamming his rifle butt into the ribs or back of one Marine, then another, screaming in their faces and spitting on them. Some of the Marines were wounded, several were crippled in their legs; their faces were streaked with blood and drool and mud.

The detail moved on then stopped again after a short distance. Malik was now within 50 yards of the detail, lying on his belly beneath a tangle of vines, burning with poison.

He counted 13 Marines huddled in a degraded mass, a single rope around their raw and chafed necks connected them all. Their arms were bound tightly behind them at the elbows, placing stress on the shoulders. Their captors, five NVA soldiers and their leader, Scarface, sat on a log, smoking, in casual conversation. Scarface clearly intimidated the others.

Malik looked down to study individual insects working around him. He mashed them under his gloves and flicked them away. His body smelled, an acrid blend of sweat, fear, the stink of the dead soldier, and dried blood. Overhead a bird called, and another answered nearby. Monkeys hooted, drawing attention to the intruders who had interrupted their morning forage. Through the gray-green canopy above, a sudden shower pelted the leaves and fronds around him.

Surveying this world, Malik remembered the play-time of his memory with Ian in Rutger's '46 Dodge. In a favorite scenario from a Tarzan movie, they had crashed their plane into the jungle. Awakening, they peered out the windscreen, imagining what adventures awaited them. What was missing from their childhood adventures were the stinging things, the unbreathable humidity, the heat, the countless discomforts, and the threat of imminent death that made the reality barely endurable.

* * *

Down the trail, beyond the prisoner detail, heavy rain fell through the canopy in a curling mist. There was a clear edge to the rainfall, like a curtain just yards beyond the men who were at such odds with one another.

Far above the weather, the faint drone of jet engines increased in intensity and faded; fighters heading northwest against targets in

Laos, no doubt. There was a hiss on the radio, but he dared not answer it.

He no longer cared about how things were going in the world beyond this green hell. A normal life there seemed unimaginable after all he had experienced. He was too damaged. Far better to give up his pointless life for others who mattered.

And yet he wavered, waiting for some overpowering impulse to crawl out of his hiding place, stand up, and walk into the midst of the enemy and kill them all, or be killed. As he wrestled with the plan, he realized it was one thing to assent to a deed and another thing to stand up and do it.

In that moment of indecision, one of the Marines, in sore distress, squirmed, and moaned. The man's arms were dislocating from his shoulders. He struggled to his feet, tethered to the others, twisting and turning, struggling to cry out against a rope gag that bound his jaws open.

Scarface spat on the ground and got up with a bored expression. He raised the butt of his rifle and slammed it hard into the Marine's head. While the blow did not knock him off his feet, the Marine staggered and convulsed like an animal that had received a killing blow. Then he fell and flopped onto the ground, bucking and jerking. Scarface then placed his rifle muzzle against the Marine's head and fired, turning his face away with clear distaste at the spray of blood.

Malik jumped to his feet, gritting his teeth and growling. He clicked off the safety on the AK-47, fought his way out of the underbrush, breathing in quick short pants with a fire in his soul. At a fast pace, he strode in righteous rage along the trail with his eyes on Scarface. There was a round in the weapon's chamber, set to full-automatic, awaiting the trigger pull. Scarface turned to look at Malik striding toward him. He lowered his head and squinted, apparently trying to comprehend who this was.

Malik came upon him so quickly he did not have time to react. With extreme prejudice, Malik rotated the AK-47 with all his might and slammed the stock of the weapon into the enemy's face. The blow lifted Scarface off his feet; his jaw dislocated from his skull, his teeth flew out, his face was an instant mask of blood. He fell in a heap.

The entire detail shrunk back, the Marines and the enemy alike appeared stunned, unable to determine who or what Malik was. He leveled the AK-47 into the face of a second NVA soldier and fired. He killed a third man with a short burst. The fourth man had his mouth open, just starting to react. His small body shuddered under the impact of multiple rounds into his chest.

The fifth soldier was on his feet. He had rotated his weapon up and flicked the safety off. His finger tightened against the trigger; there was an explosion; Malik felt a fiery wind sear his left cheek with a tattoo of burning cordite. The enemy's finger kept pressing the trigger. His weapon had jammed.

Aiming, Malik squeezed his trigger as he saw a look of pleading in the man's eyes. The rounds blasted a cloud of blood and brain matter out the back of the enemy's head.

Malik lowered the weapon and stood for long seconds and stared, uncomprehending, at the bodies. He dropped the weapon. Aware of movement in the spreading pool of blood at his feet, he glared down at Scarface and recoiled at the sight of evil personified. Intense hatred twisted his ruined face as he struggled to pull his weapon to himself. Malik pulled the knife from the scabbard in his boot, took two steps toward him, dropped his entire weight on his right knee into the middle of the man's chest while raising the knife over his head in both hands. With all the hatred he ever experienced concentrated in a single moment, he drove the blade to the hilt through the enemy's throat. A fountain of blood shot up.

Malik stood up, knocked the pith helmet off his own head, ripped the enemy uniform tunic off, and slit the legs of the trousers, and tore them off. He dropped his knife and backed up a dozen steps in shock, rubbing his forehead with bloody fingers, and looked up through the canopy. Shafts of rain penetrated in places. He moved under one and shook his head under the shower. Through the canopy he saw a patch of gray sky.

Somewhere a long way away, and a long time ago, he lay on a blanket with Christine beside him, her head in the hollow of his shoulder. In the distance were mountains of summer cumulus. On a cool breeze came the fragrant scent of the forest and pastures reporting of recent rain. Birds sang, and he heard the tinkle of cattle bells in the vale below them. He looked at Christine, stirred by her form entwined with his. She whispered, "I pray God will give you peace."

Malik felt his face contort with grief and sorrow; his mouth was open in a wordless cry. He placed a bloody hand across his eyes and shuddered. Tears streamed down his face, convulsing with remorse and other emotions he could not disentangle.

Minutes passed. The intensity of the joyful memory and the horror of the moment receded. He lowered his hand and saw the Marines. Their faces were stone, their eyes wide as saucers as they stared at him through their masks of grime. They appeared to be in shock.

Clarity returned. Malik studied them with powerful empathy, a stronger emotion than he had ever felt. He retrieved his knife and began cutting them loose from their bonds.

One burly Marine lifted his fallen comrade in a fireman's carry. Malik consulted his compass and pointed southeast. They plunged into the jungle like a flight of startled geese.

CHAPTER 43
A Band of Brothers

For two hours, they fought their way through the undergrowth without stopping. Malik believed it was only a matter of a few hours before the enemy would be on their trail. They collapsed from exhaustion. They got up again and fought onward until long shadows turned to black of night. They burrowed into a thicket and settled in, huddled against each other with the body of the fallen man in their midst.

Malik could see but a few feet. No one had spoken a word since his sudden appearance out of the jungle. An hour passed before anyone could find words. At first, they began to whisper. Then they couldn't shut up. Tom Bellingham crawled over to Malik and took strong hold of his shoulders, pulling him within six inches, staring into Malik's eyes.

He blubbered, "When that bastard shot Pete, I screamed in my mind to God. If I had been loose, I would have torn the bastard's head off. But you came like some avenging angel."

The others voiced agreement and nodded.

"I'm telling you, John, you came like a mighty angel. God sent you. I know that's true …. I can't describe what I feel. I've never felt like this before." Tom spoke with the energy of the possessed.

He wiped his eyes and repeated, "I've never felt like this before. I cried out to God, and He answered me! Do you understand what I'm saying? God answered *me*! I don't have the words …." He seemed to address all of them. "You know, I think I've had one of those catharsis things. It's like my soul has been healed. I am alive like I've never been before. Everything makes sense to me now."

He grabbed Malik again, "I love you, man. I would follow you to the ends of the earth, even into hell. I would do anything for you. You saved our lives. Why did you do it?" He hugged Malik and kissed his neck and cheeks. "I love you, man."

They all worked their way over to Malik and took turns hugging him, telling him they loved him. They could not say it enough times.

Malik was nodding off when Ben O'Conner said to him, "John, when I saw you come over us in your airplane burning like that, and you crashed through the treetops, I was sure you were dead. But you were a flaming angel sent from God. He shot you down to save us. Nobody is going to tell me different."

Their manic chatter continued for hours. Every time Malik stirred to consciousness they were talking. Something extraordinary had overcome them, but they had not yet defined what it was. John dropped out of consciousness into dreamless sleep, undisturbed by biting things, drifting off with the vague awareness that his fever had passed, he had no pain, and he was at peace.

A radio hiss awakened him. He checked his watch. It was 0330. He turned up the volume.

"Tide One Four, go ahead."

"John! God Almighty, it's you, John! This is Carl. I'm heading back from a Sky Spot. I'm so glad to hear your voice. I saw a picture of you on Walter Cronkite this evening; he was interviewing this beautiful blond girl, Christine. I cried like a baby when I saw those interviews. The whole squadron, the whole country is praying for you, John. Tell me what you're doing."

John gave him a summary. There were a dozen Marines with him. He had killed their captors. They were fleeing southeast.

"Listen, John. I can never say how sorry I am for the way I've treated you. Will you forgive me? Everybody I talk to is praying for you. And these are guys who don't pray! None of us knew how much we admired you. We love you, John. You are a legend. Stay alive. Forgive me. You're the best man I've ever known."

Carl's transmission faded. John turned the volume down and convulsed in tears. When he recovered his composure, he looked up to see his band of brothers watching him, hovering within several feet of him.

"The world is following our progress," he said. "I think God is for us. Who, then, can be against us?"

* * *

John awoke at first light with an unprecedented sense of wellbeing. He was rested, breathing easy in the crisp morning air. He groped into his survival vest, pulled out his primary radio, and turned up the volume until he heard the hiss. "Mayday, this is Tide One Four and the U.S. Marines calling any station."

A flight of fighters passing overhead responded. "Tide One Four, good to hear your voice. Go ahead."

"Request relay for Search and Rescue. There are thirteen of us heading southeast from Firebase Six."

"I'll relay, Tide. God speed, John Malik."

When they were all awake, they got up and started fighting their way southeast. When the Marines talked, they spoke of nothing else than the strange transformation that had come over them.

They came to a consensus: God had delivered them. He had sent John Malik to do it. There was no turning back for them. They would be a band of brothers for the rest of their lives. They agreed to adopt John as an honorary Marine, leader of the twelve. Back in the world, they would eat steak and lobster and strawberry shortcake together often.

Malik was uncomfortable with their God-language, but he was no longer resistant to their conclusions. He pondered the repeated episodes of his survival against the odds. There was only one explanation. God's hand had been upon him his whole life, and he had been born for this time.

But the band's newfound perspective seemed in conflict with their lack of progress against the dense green. The way ahead was into ever-denser undergrowth. They were being impeded by increasingly boggy ground. They grew anxious about their ability to distance themselves from the enemy.

They made no more than a half-mile by nightfall on the second day. John was not confident they were heading southeast; the jungle was too dense to see far enough to track a straight heading. And they were growing weaker.

The jungle floor had given way to swampy conditions. Malik thought of Bilbo and his friends lost in Mirkwood Forest in Tolkien's *Hobbit*. The band of brothers was lost and growing discouraged. And the weather continued overcast.

* * *

From a deep and dreamless sleep, Malik blinked in the growing light of dawn on the third day. Through openings in the canopy, the overcast appeared ragged with patches of blue. The brothers were huddled together like a community of chimpanzees. He smiled, now convinced they were not going to die in this swamp.

In the growing light Malik turned his head and leaned forward, staring at what lay just yards from them: an opening in the trees. He struggled up and made his way into a clearing to find they had blundered upon a landing zone created by a single 500-pound slick bomb with a three-foot fuse extender. The bomb that had formed this clearing came off John's own aircraft two weeks ago during the prep of Firebase Six; he was convinced that was the case. Since maintenance had found no electrical anomaly in his weapon system that could not explain how the bomb had come off Malik's airplane, the conclusion was that he had released it. Colonel Bernside agreed with that assessment and so annotated Malik's records. But now, the reason was apparent. The electrical anomaly that blew the armed bomb off his wing was Providential.

A Search and Rescue chopper could get to them in this clearing. If they had passed 50 yards further west, they would never have seen the opening. God had slowed their pace to arrive on the morning of the third day at this precise location, just as the overcast was dissipating. That was Malik's conviction.

* * *

Large patches of blue appeared overhead. At 1000 hours, Malik worked his way out into the middle of the clearing through the splintered stumps and log-fall. Looking up, he was finally at peace, remembering Christine's prayer for him. How could he deny the obvious any longer? He had perversely misinterpreted the mark of Cain that he believed he bore. The mark was not to identify him as a murderer and stigmatize him in society, it was to protect him from death at anyone's hand. No one could have killed him before this day. Perhaps he could not have died by any means before this day had dawned.

Looking into the sky, he spoke the words of the prodigal son who had come to himself in the far country. He was welcomed home, and a new world opened before him. He now knew the truth, and he was free.

With great affection, he looked at the twelve standing in the tree line, laughing and crying. They were hysterical, and it was wonderful. Then he pulled out the radio from his vest, turned it on, and transmitted. "Tide One Four and the U.S. Marines on guard. Any station."

There was an instant response. There were relays to Hillsboro, who was even then controlling an airborne flight of Sandys from

Bien Hoa. They had launched to look for Malik and the others. Now Search and Rescue knew where Malik and the Marines were. They were in what was being called the "Glory Hole," two miles south of Firebase Six.

* * *

John stood in the clearing, looking up. His mind raced across wonderful possibilities that had opened before him. The riddle had been solved: he knew why he was alive. His life would matter now.

As he stood in the clearing, alternately crying and laughing, he remembered something. When he left the hootch in a panic to catch the shuttle van to the flight line for his ill-fated final flight, he had reached into his mail slot and found a single letter. He thought it was from Rachel Hixson since it was handwritten so he only glanced at it and stuffed it into a lower flight suit zipper pocket. He had forgotten about it until just then.

He reached down, unzipped the pocket, and pulled the crumpled letter out to survey exquisite penmanship that now seemed familiar. He turned it over. No return address. He tore it open and read.

The letter was from Christine. In a few lines, she informed him that she woke up from a dream that became a conscious vision. In her vision, she saw John standing in a clearing in the jungle surrounded by light. She knew he had been reconciled to God, that her prayers had been answered, and that he was at peace.

"I know everything has changed by the time you read this. We will live. I cannot be mistaken about this. I am so excited I can barely control myself. Come home to me, Johnny."

John wept, blinking away tears to read the final words. He fell to his knees with his hands raised to the sky. The twelve watched him, themselves brought to tears yet again for reasons they did not understand, only knowing that something wonderful was happening.

For John Malik, the burden of a lifetime of trauma fell away in an instant. The sun was dazzling. The air was fresh and bracing, washed clean by days of rain. And he was alive forevermore.

Only then did he raise his left hand to touch a bloody graze along his temple where the enemy's bullet had passed. He had missed eternity by a quarter of an inch.

John picked his way back to the tree line to join the others, beaming, weeping, hugging them one by one, kissing their cheeks. He yelled at them, "You guys didn't tell me I was shot!"

O'Conner replied, "Ah, the devil can't kill you, John Malik." And they all laughed hysterically.

From the south came the deep-throated purr of powerful engines at low altitude, coming fast. The men jumped to their feet and ran, stumbling, into the clearing.

The heavily armed A-1Es, like the cavalry, bore down to save the day, their props singing salvation that morphed into the approaching roar of four 2700 HP engines.

In his mind's eye, John rose above the jungle to look down on the four-ship formation of A-1s streaking over the treetops. The aircraft maneuvered from fingertip formation to trail, one behind the other. They throttled up to full power. John heard the drumbeat and the relentless lyrics,

When Johnny comes marching home again,
Hurrah! Hurrah!

We'll give him a mighty welcome then
Hurrah! Hurrah!

The men will cheer, and the boys will shout
The ladies, they will all turn out
And we'll all feel gay when Johnny comes marching home.

The leader of the Sandys thundered over the treetops at full power. He pulled up in a majestic arc overhead, followed by three others. John's chest was vibrating with the power of the engines that drowned out the cheers of the band of brothers.

The A-1s, turned in a tight radius,

A shield of power about them. The band breathed easy at last.

In the wake of the Sandys came the whump, whump, whump of the Jolly Green helicopter.

It appeared, it slowed, its nose rose, it crossed the tree line, it dropped into the clearing.

At that moment, John Malik loosened his constraints on the Sea of Faith,

It flowed back with a mighty rush to the full and round earth's shores,

Where it now lay like the folds of a bright girdle furled, as it once had.

And now came a brilliant light that illuminated the darkling plain

When John Malik lifted his eyes, he could see forever.

EPILOGUE

Near Niangua, Missouri
Twenty years later

The old timbers and wooden floors of the Good Spring Church creaked and lent the smell of age to the small sanctuary that sat out in the country near Niangua, 30 miles east of Springfield. Late afternoon shafts of golden sunlight slanted through the flawed panes of clear glass in the windows, illuminating drifting columns of dust. It seemed late in the day for a funeral. But the failing light was a metaphor for Christine Malik.

Out the windows, she could see the still-green autumn oaks, the brown of a dirt road, and, beyond that, the faded white of lichen-covered marble and weathered sandstone monuments standing askew in an old graveyard. And there was a mound of red dirt, a freshly dug grave.

Beside Christine sat her two beautiful children in the second pew of the little church. They gazed at the casket in which her beloved lay, his hands folded on his chest. His profile handsome, peaceful, now lifeless.

John wanted to be buried beside his brother Ian in the old cemetery in the trees across the dirt road. That's where Christine brought him.

It was quiet in the church, except for the creaking timbers and the occasional shifting of people in the pews. His Uncle Sean was there. All twelve of the band of brothers sat in the pews, along with their families. Their debt to John Malik could only be paid forward, and they had always aspired to do that. Many others were there, prominent people and common people whose lives John Malik had touched.

* * *

Two hundred miles northwest, Medal flight Lead received clearance from the Kansas City Center high altitude sector controller to begin descent 40 miles north of the Springfield VOR. The flight of four F-4s held tight fingertip formation as they reduced power and started down.

The flight was handed off to the low altitude sector controller and leveled at 10,000 feet.

"Kansas City, we'd like to cancel our instrument flight plan and continue visual. We'll call you for a return clearance in about fifteen minutes. The flight will split, and Medal Three will get separate clearance," the flight leader transmitted on the UHF frequency.

"That's approved, Medal. I understand you want clearance for an unrestricted climb for a single aircraft east of Springfield?"

"Affirmative. To above 50,000 feet."

"That should be approved, Medal. Have Three squawk two-three-zero-four commencing climb. I see no conflict."

"Roger," Medal Lead replied. He then asked his back-seater over the interphone, "How far to the initial point?"

"Twenty-eight miles, sir. I've got a good inertial update."

The flight leader glanced over at Three on his right wing, whose helmeted gaze was fixed upon Lead. On a discrete frequency, he asked, "You ready, Three?"

"Yes, sir. I'm honored."

"I wish I was doing it."

Three nodded.

Medal Lead reached down and changed his transponder squawk to 1200. He thought about it for a second, then switched the transponder off. Kansas City, seeing this, queried him.

"Must be inop. I'll recycle," he said to the controller.

The controller obviously got the point, knowing that the flight intended to exceed the speed limit below 10,000 feet and wouldn't be clocked with the transponder off. The controller likely strained to see the flight's raw return and clear any slow movers in its path.

Turning to the final heading at the initial point, Lead glanced left and right at his wingmen, raised his left fist and pushed it forward, then reached down and advanced the throttles. The flight accelerated in the descent, faster and faster, and the wingmen tucked in tight, bobbing in the evening thermals.

The back-seater read off the data to the aircraft commander. "You're now locked on heading; eighteen miles to go. Sir, we're at five hundred knots! Fifteen miles. We're ahead ten seconds."

Lead retarded the throttles, slowing until back on schedule, then re-advanced power to hold 500 knots. The flight was 200 knots above their maximum legal speed limit below 10,000 feet. The back-seater was evidently not comfortable with this.

Green forest and farmyards streaked under the nose, almost too fast to identify anything on the ground at close range. "Let me tell you a story," Lead said to the guy in his back seat. "On a dark and stormy night over Cambodia, this man we are honoring saved my life for the third time. He didn't even think about it on any of those occasions. He put his life at risk for me. Without him, my bones would probably be bleaching somewhere in the Cambodian jungle. I don't think he ever had a clue what happened to me that night. But what he did changed my life. I'm alive and a better man for having known him."

The back-seater made no reply. The speed with which the trees and roads passed beneath the aircraft was incongruous with the aircraft commander's slow and deliberate statements.

Seconds to go; now 300 feet over the trees. Colonel William Bjorn looked over at Three. "On my mark .... Five, four, three, two, one. Go!"

***

The people who were paying their last respects to the great John Malik sat on folding chairs or stood near the grave as a military honor guard fired volleys over the trees with machine-like precision. The bugler's mournful sound of taps echoed through the darkening forest. The Marine sergeant checked his watch again. His detail folded the flag covering the casket. He stepped before Christine, saluted her in slow motion, knelt before her with head bent down, and extended the folded flag to her. "From a grateful nation," he said.

Her tears dripped onto the flag. She clutched it, stroking the Medal of Honor pinned in the field of stars. This Medal and their beloved children were all she had left of him in this life. She had waited for him in life; now, he would wait for her in eternity.

It was quiet in the graveyard, except for the whip-o-wills calling in the darkening gloom. The night was coming on fast, and the sun was sinking, but the people continued to sit or stand, contemplating the casket and their own mortality.

"Is it over?" someone whispered. Then someone else pointed toward the west where the swollen red sun was just touching the horizon. Christine stood, tears welling, knowing what was coming.

Smoke came from the disk of the sun, and specks appeared on its face. Everyone strained to see. The specks were growing larger and larger, coming impossibly fast.

"Oh my ...!" someone cried, as the sky suddenly filled with four black F-4 fighters, silent forms just above the trees streaking ahead of the sound of their engines.

An instant before they swept overhead, the number Three aircraft wobbled, then snapped to the vertical as a tidal wave of sonic energy exploded over the graveyard.

In the wake of the single fighter receding above them, there was a throbbing, pulsing, deafening blare from its tailpipes that vibrated the ground. Long plumes of flame, strobed with bars of light, ejected from the afterburners as the Phantom rolled and rolled and rolled until it disappeared straight overhead into a deep blue heaven.

Its sound died away, and the mournful whip-o-wills resumed their calls.

Christine Charis Malik looked to the west. Through her tears, she watched the sun sink below the horizon as her Johnny went marching home.

THE END.

ACKNOWLEDGEMENTS

Isaac Newton once wrote, "If I have seen farther, it is by standing on the shoulders of giants." While he applied this to scientific advancement, we can agree that what we know of life and our circumstances has come from knowledge shared with us by those who have gone before. The writing of a novel enlivens the truths of the human condition. Hopefully even the actions of fictional characters can teach us much about how to live.

Among those to whom I am indebted for the finalization of this journey (*On a Darkling Plain*) are friends, critics, cheerleaders, and writing professionals who have altered the final text for the better. I am grateful to my friends Lavelle (who has sadly passed to glory) and Sally Jo Pitts. They steered me to writers' conferences and encouraged my writing. Most importantly, they gave me the use of the cabin in the woods on the lake, my fortress of solitude where this story was written.

I think of friends who read my clumsy first efforts, people like Judge Bill Cooper, Steven and Marilyn Kelley, Charlie and Susie Mabius (who often fed me and made sure I was taking care of myself). And I must acknowledge the radical improvement of the story arc, the writing style, and the timeline of the story that Sarah De Mey (a professional editor) imparted to the text. If the result is good, I give her a great deal of credit. Likewise, I sing the praises of Désirée Schroeder, a wonderfully deft editor and gentle critic who has burnished John Malik's story to its present luster. And there is the masterful artwork of Rolando Ugolini, whose cover art says so much and upon whom the success of this novel depends to a large degree.

Thanks also to best-selling author Rachel Hauch who provided a key plot point that made the story work.

I am thankful to Alice Braasch who dreamed with me again our days in Germany and Arizona. And one time there was a love who was my unstinting cheerleader, without whose belief in me this book would not have been written. She and I traveled the planet from the poles to the equatorial jungles, romancing the stone …. Once the best time I ever had.

But ultimately, I defer credit to the one to whom this story is dedicated. On one sunny morning (February 10, 1978 to be exact) I awoke, still blind on the Darkling Plain. Before noon that day I could testify to the truth of this text: "Those who sat in darkness have seen a great light; and upon those living in the land of the shadow of death, a light has dawned" (Matt. 4:15–16). Like John Malik, from that day I could see forever.

ABOUT THE AUTHOR

Larry D. Bruce was born in Marshfield, Missouri and grew up in Miami, Florida. After six years of undergraduate and graduate school, he joined the Air Force during the Vietnam conflict. His first assignment was to Germany as an F-102 air defense pilot where he sat 5-minute alert anticipating World War III. He then transitioned to the F-100 and was assigned to a fighter wing at Phan Rang AB, Vietnam. There he flew 185 combat missions. During his tour he earned a Silver Star, three Distinguished Flying Crosses (for heroism and extraordinary achievement), eight Air Medals, and a number of other decorations. His final Air Force assignment was as a T-38 instructor training new pilots.

Bruce's airline career involved the development of flight training programs for pilots (notably International Flight Training) for American Airlines at the DFW Flight Academy. At the same time, he flew full time as an international DC-10 captain, check captain, and manager for World Airways in global operations—sometimes circling the earth in a single series of flight legs. He retired from both companies.

His educational background includes a BA *magna cum laude* from the Western Carolina University, graduate study in philosophy as a Woodrow Wilson Fellow at the University of Kansas, an MDiv from Southwestern Baptist Theological Seminary, and a PhD in Biblical Backgrounds and Archaeology also from Southwestern; the six-year doctoral program involved excavation field training in Israel under eminent Israeli archaeologist Amihai Mazar. Bruce studied archaeometric techniques (scientific study of artifacts) for one year at Baylor University under the head of the chemistry department and conducted a neutron activation study of artifacts under a grant using the Texas A&M nuclear reactor.

Presently, he is an independent researcher specializing in the archaeological evidence for the origins of ancient Israel in the land of Canaan. He has served as an adjunct professor of biblical and archaeological studies at two colleges in northwest Florida where he currently lives.

Captain L. D. Bruce, Phan Rang AB, Vietnam. December 1970.

Made in the USA
Columbia, SC
08 January 2023